SANDRA MARTON

wrote her first novel while she was still in elementary school. Her doting parents told her she'd be a writer someday and Sandra believed them. In high school and college, she wrote dark poetry nobody but her boyfriend understood, though looking back, she suspects he was just being kind. As a wife and mother, she wrote murky short stories in what little spare time she could manage, but not even her boyfriend-turned-husband could pretend to understand those. Sandra tried her hand at other things, among them teaching and serving on the board of education in her hometown, but the dream of becoming a writer was always in her heart.

At last Sandra realized she wanted to write books about what all women hope to find: love with that one special man, love that's rich with fire and passion, love that lasts forever. She wrote a novel, her very first, and sold it to Harlequin Presents®. Since then, she's written more than seventy books, all of them featuring sexy, gorgeous, larger-than-life heroes. A four-time RITA® Award finalist, she has also received eight *RT Book Reviews* awards for Best Harlequin Presents of the Year and has been honored with an *RT Book Reviews* Career Achievement Award for Series Romance. Sandra lives with her very own sexy, gorgeous, larger-than-life hero in a sun-filled house on a quiet country lane in the northeastern United States.

Sandra loves to hear from her readers. You can contact her through her Web site, www.sandramarton.com, or at P.O. Box 295, Storrs, CT 06268.

SANDRA MARTON

Mistress of the Sheikh

The One-Night Wife

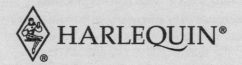

HARLEQUIN®

TORONTO • NEW YORK • LONDON
AMSTERDAM • PARIS • SYDNEY • HAMBURG
STOCKHOLM • ATHENS • TOKYO • MILAN • MADRID
PRAGUE • WARSAW • BUDAPEST • AUCKLAND

Recycling programs
for this product may
not exist in your area.

ISBN-13: 978-0-373-68805-0

MISTRESS OF THE SHEIKH & THE ONE-NIGHT WIFE

Copyright © 2010 by Harlequin Books S.A.

The publisher acknowledges the copyright holder of the individual works as follows:

MISTRESS OF THE SHEIKH
Copyright © 2000 by Sandra Myles

THE ONE-NIGHT WIFE
Copyright © 2004 by Sandra Myles

This edition published by arrangement with Harlequin Books S.A.

For questions and comments about the quality of this book please contact us at Customer_eCare@Harlequin.ca.

® and TM are trademarks of the publisher. Trademarks indicated with ® are registered in the United States Patent and Trademark Office, the Canadian Trade Marks Office and in other countries.

www.eHarlequin.com

Printed in U.S.A.

CONTENTS

MISTRESS OF THE SHEIKH

CHAPTER ONE

SHEIKH NICHOLAS AL RASHID, Lion of the Desert, Lord of the Realm and Sublime Heir to the Imperial Throne of Quidar, stepped out of his tent and onto the burning sands, holding a woman in his arms.

The sheikh was dressed in a gold-trimmed white burnoose; his silver-gray eyes stared straight ahead, blazing with savage passion. The woman, her arms looped around his neck, gazed up at him, her face alight with an unspoken plea.

What's the matter, Nick? she'd been saying.

There's a camera pointed straight at us, Nick had answered. That's what's the matter.

But nobody seeing this cover on Gossip magazine would believe anything so simple, Nick thought grimly.

His eyes dropped to the banner beneath the picture. If words could damn a man, these surely did.

Sheikh Nicholas al Rashid, the caption said, in letters that looked ten feet tall, carrying off his latest conquest, the beautiful Deanna Burgess. Oh, to be abducted by this gorgeous, magnificent desert savage...

"Son of a bitch," Nick muttered.

The little man standing on the opposite side of the sparely furnished, elegant room nodded. "Yes, my lord."

"No-good, lying, cheating, sneaky bastards!"

"Absolutely," the little man said, nodding again.

Nick looked up, his eyes narrowed.

"Calling me a 'desert savage,' as if I were some kind of beast. Is that what they think I am? An uncultured, vicious animal?"

"No, sire." The little man clasped his hands together. "Surely not."

"No one calls me that and gets away with it."

But someone had, once. Nick frowned. A woman or, more accurately, a girl. The memory surfaced, wavering like a mirage from the hot sand.

Nothing but a savage, she'd said....

The image faded, and Nick frowned. "That photo was taken at the festival. It was Id al Baranda, Quidar's national holiday, for God's sake!" He stepped out from behind his massive beechwood desk and paced to the wall of windows that gave way onto one of New York City's paved canyons. "That's why I was wearing a robe, because it is the custom."

Abdul bobbed his head in agreement.

"And the tent," Nick said through his teeth. "The damned tent belonged to the caterer."

"I know, my lord."

"It was where the food was set up, dammit!"

"Yes, sire."

Nick stalked back to his desk and snatched up the magazine. "Look at this. Just look at it!"

Abdul took a cautious step forward, rose up on the balls of his feet and peered at the photo. "Lord Rashid?"

"They've taken the ocean out of the picture. It looks as if the tent was pitched in the middle of the desert!"

"Yes, my lord. I see."

Nick dragged his hand through his hair. "Miss Burgess cut her foot." His voice tightened. "That was why I was carrying her."

"Lord Rashid." Abdul licked his lips. "There is no need to explain."

"I was carrying her into the tent, not out. So I could treat the—" Nick stopped in midsentence and drew a ragged breath deep into his lungs. "I will not let this anger me."

"I am so glad, my lord."

"I will not!"

"Excellent, sire."

"There's no point to it." Nick put the magazine on his desk, tucked his hands into the pockets of his trousers and threw his secretary a chilling smile. "Isn't that right, Abdul?"

The little man nodded. "Absolutely."

"If these idiots wish to poke their noses into my life, so be it."

"Yes, my lord."

"If people wish to read such drivel, let them."

Abdul nodded. "Exactly."

"After all, what does it matter to me if I am called an uncultured savage?" Nick's smile tightened until his face resembled a mask. "Never mind my law degree or my expertise in finance."

"Lord Rashid," Abdul said carefully, "sire—"

"Never mind that I represent an ancient and honorable and highly cultured people."

"Excellency, please. You're getting yourself upset. And, as you just said, there is no point in—"

"The fool who wrote this should be drawn and quartered."

Abdul nodded, his head bobbing up and down like a balloon on a string. "Yes, my lord."

"Better still, staked out, naked, in the heat of the desert sun, smeared with honey so as to draw the full attention of the fire ants."

Abdul bowed low as he backed toward the door. "I shall see to it at once."

"Abdul." Nick took a deep breath.

"My lord?"

"You are to do nothing."

"Nothing? But, Excellency—"

"Trust me," the sheikh said with a faint smile. "The part of me that is American warns me that my fellow countrymen are probably squeamish about drawing and quartering."

"In that case, I shall ask for a retraction."

"You are not to call the magazine at all."

"No?"

"No. It would serve no purpose except to bring further unwanted attention to myself, and to Quidar."

Abdul inclined his head. "As you command, Lord Rashid."

Nick reached out, turned the copy of Gossip toward him, handling it as gingerly as he would a poisonous spider.

"Phone the florist. Have him send six dozen red roses to Miss Burgess."

"Yes, sire."

"I want the flowers delivered immediately."

"Of course."

"Along with a card. Say…" Nick frowned. "Say that she has my apologies that we made the cover of a national magazine."

"Oh, I'm sure Miss Burgess is most unhappy to find her photo on that cover," Abdul said smoothly, so smoothly that Nick looked at him. The little man flushed. "It is most unfortunate that either of you should have been placed in such a position, my lord. I am glad you are taking this so calmly."

"I am calm, aren't I?" Nick said. "Very calm. I have counted twice to ten, once in Quidaran and once in English, and—and…" His gaze fell to the cover again. "Very calm," he murmured, and then he grabbed the magazine from the desk and flung it against the wall. "Lying sons of camel traders," he roared, and kicked the thing across the room the second it slid to the floor. "Oh, what I'd like to do to the bastards who invade my life and print such lies."

"Excellency." Abdul's voice was barely a whisper. "Excellency, it is all my fault."

The sheikh gave a harsh laugh. "Did you point a camera at me, Abdul?"

"No. No, of course—"

"Did you sell the photo to the highest bidder?" Nick swung around, his eyes hot. "Did you write a caption that makes it sound as if I'm a bad reincarnation of Rudolph Valentino?"

Abdul gave a nervous laugh. "Certainly not."

"For all I know, it wasn't even a reporter. It could have been someone I think of as a friend." Nick shoved both hands through his black-as-midnight hair. "If I ever get my hands on one of the scum-sucking dung beetles who grow fat by invading the privacy of others—"

Abdul dropped to his knees on the silk carpet and knotted his hands imploringly beneath his chin. "It is my fault, nevertheless. I should not have permitted your eyes to see such an abomination. I should have hidden it from you."

"Get up," Nick said sharply.

"I should never have let you see it. Never!"

"Abdul," Nick said more gently, "stand up."

"Oh, my lord…"

Nick sighed, bent down and lifted the little man to his feet.

"You did the right thing. I needed to see this piece of filth before the party tonight. Someone is sure to spring it on me just to see my reaction."

"No one would have the courage, sire."

"Trust me, Abdul. Someone will." A smile softened Nick's hard mouth. "My sweet little sister, if no one else. We both know how she loves to tease."

Abdul smiled, too. "Ah. Yes, yes, she does."

"So, it's a good thing you showed me the cover. I'd much rather be prepared."

"That was my belief, sire. But perhaps I erred. Perhaps I should not—"

"What would you have done instead, hmm?" Nick grinned. "Bought up all the copies from all the newsstands in Manhattan?"

Abdul nodded vigorously. "Precisely. I should have purchased all the copies, burned them—"

"Abdul." Nick put his arm around the man's shoulders and walked him toward the door. "You took the proper action. And I am grateful."

"You are?"

"Just imagine the headlines if I'd had this temper tantrum in public." Nick lifted his hand and wrote an imaginary sentence in the air. "Savage Sheikh Shows Savage Side," he said dramatically.

The little man gave him a thin smile.

"Now imagine what would happen if somebody manages to get a picture of me slicing into the cake at the party tonight."

"The caterer will surely do the slicing, sire."

Nick sighed. "Yes, I'm sure he will. The point is, anything is possible. Can you just see what the sleaze sheets would do with a picture of me with a knife in my hand?"

"In the old days," Abdul said sternly, "you could have had their heads!"

The sheikh smiled. "These are not those days," he said gently. "We are in the twenty-first century, remember?"

"You still have that power, Lord Rashid."

"It is not a power I shall ever exercise, Abdul."

"So you have said, Excellency." The man paused at the door to Nick's office. "But your father can tell you that the power to spare a man his life, or take it from him, is the best way of assuring that all who deal with you will do so with honor and respect."

A quick, satisfying picture flashed through Nick's mind.

He imagined all the media people, and especially all the so-called friends who'd ever made money by selling him out, crowded into the long-unused dungeon beneath the palace back home, every last one of them pleading for mercy as the royal executioner sharpened his ax.

"It's a sweet thought," he admitted after a minute. "But that is no longer our way."

"Perhaps it should be," Abdul said, and sighed. "At any rate, my lord, there will be no unwanted guests lying in wait for you this evening."

"No?"

"No. Only those with invitations will be admitted by your bodyguards. And I sent out the invitations myself."

Nick nodded. "Two hundred and fifty of my nearest and dearest friends," he said, and smiled wryly. "That's fine."

His secretary nodded. "Will that be all, Lord Rashid?"

"Yes, Abdul. Thank you."

"You are welcome, sire."

Nick watched as the old man bowed low and backed out of the room. Don't, he wanted to tell him. You're old enough to be my grandfather, but he knew what Abdul's reply would be.

"It is the custom," he would say.

And he was right.

Nick sighed, walked to his desk and sat down in the ornately carved chair behind it.

Everything was "the custom". The way he was addressed. The way Quidarans, and even many Americans, bowed in his presence. He didn't mind it so much from his countrymen; it made him uncomfortable, all that head-bobbing and curtseying, but he understood it. It was a sign of respect.

It was, he supposed, such a sign for some Americans, too.

But for others, he sensed, it was an acknowledgment that they saw him as a different species. Something exotic. An

Arab, who dressed in flowing robes. A primitive creature, who lived in a tent.

An uncultured savage, who took his women when, where and how he wanted them.

He rose to his feet and walked across the room to the windows, his mouth set in a grim line, his eyes steely.

He had worn desert robes perhaps half a dozen times in his life, and then only to please his father. He'd slept in a tent more times than that, but only because he loved the sigh of the night wind and the sight of the stars against the blackness of a sky that can only be found in the vastness of the desert.

As for women... Custom permitted him to take any that pleased him to his bed. But he'd never taken a woman who hadn't wanted to be taken. Never forced one into his bed or held one captive in a harem.

A smile tilted across Nick's mouth.

Humility was a virtue, much lauded by his father's people, and he was properly modest about most things, but why lie to himself about women? For that matter, why would he need a harem?

The truth was that women had always been there. They tumbled into his bed without any effort at all on his part, even in his university days at Yale when his real identity hadn't been known to what seemed like half the civilized world.

They'd even been there in the years before that.

Nick's smile grew.

He thought back to that summer he'd spent in L.A. with his late mother. She was an actress; it had seemed as if half the women who lived in Beverly Hills were actresses, starting with the stunning brunette next door, who'd at first taken him for the pool boy—and taken him, too, for rides far wilder than any he'd ever experienced on the backs of his father's purebred Arabians.

There'd always been women.

Nick's smile dimmed.

It was true, though, that some of the ones who were drawn to him now were interested more in what they might gain from being seen with him than anything else.

He knew that there were women who wanted to bask in the spotlight so mercilessly trained on him, that there were others who thought a night in his arms might lead to a lifetime at his side. There were even women who hoped to enter his private world so they could sell their stories to the scandal sheets.

His eyes went flat and cold.

Only a foolish man would involve himself with such women, and he was not a—

The phone rang. Nick snatched it from the desk.

"Yes?"

"If you're going to be here in time to shower and shave and change into a tux," his half sister's voice said with teasing petulance, "you'd better get a move on, Your Gorgeousness."

Nick smiled and hitched a hip onto the edge of the desk.

"Watch what you say to me, little sister. Otherwise, I'll have your head on the chopping block. Abdul says it's an ideal punishment for those who don't show me the proper respect."

"The only thing that's going to be cut tonight is my birthday cake. It's not every day a girl turns twenty-five."

"You forget. It's my birthday, too."

"Oh, I know, I know. Isn't it lovely, sharing a father and a birthday? But you're not as excited as I am."

Nick laughed. "That's because I'm over the hill. After all, I'm thirty-four."

"Seriously, Nick, you will be here on time, won't you?"

"Absolutely."

"Not early, though." Dawn laughed softly. "Otherwise, you'll expect me to change what I'm wearing."

Nick's brows lifted. "Will I?"

"Uh-huh."

"Meaning what you have on is too short, too low, too tight—"

"This is the twenty-first century, Your Handsomeness."

"Not when you're on Quidaran turf, it isn't. And stop calling me stuff like that."

"A," Dawn said, ticking her answers off on her fingers, "this isn't Quidaran turf. It's a penthouse on Fifth Avenue."

"It's Quidaran turf," Nick said. Dawn smiled; she could hear the laughter in his voice. "The moment I step on it anyway. What's B?"

"B, if Gossip can call you 'Your Handsomeness', so can I." She giggled. "Have you seen the article yet?"

"I've seen the cover," Nick said tersely. "That was enough."

"Well, the article says that you and Deanna—"

"Never mind that. You just make sure you're decently dressed."

"I am decently dressed, for New York."

Nick sighed. "Behave yourself, or I'll have you sent home."

"Me? Behave myself?" Dawn snorted and switched the portable phone to her other ear as she strolled through her brother's massive living room and out the glass doors to the terrace. "I'm not the one dating Miss Hunter."

"Hunter? But Deanna's name is—"

"Hunter of a titled husband. Hunter of the spotlight. Hunter of wealth and glamour—"

"She's not like that," Nick said quickly.

"Why isn't she?"

"Dawn. I am not going to discuss this with you."

"You don't have to. I know the reason. You have this silly idea that because Deanna has her own money and an old family name, she's—what's the right word—trustworthy."

Nick sighed. "Sweetheart," he said gently, "I appreciate your concern. But—"

"But you want me to mind my own business."

"Something like that, yes."

His sister rolled her eyes at the blond woman who stood with her back against the terrace wall. "Men can be clueless," she hissed.

Amanda Benning did her best to smile. "Have you told him yet?"

"No. No, not—"

"Dawn?" Nick's voice came through the phone. "Who are you talking to?"

Dawn made a face at Amanda. "One of the caterer's assistants," she said briskly. "She wanted to know where to put the cold hors d'oeuvres. And speaking of knowing, aren't you curious about what I got you for your birthday?"

"Sure. But if you told me, it wouldn't be a surprise. And birthday presents are supposed to be surprises."

"Ah. Well, I already know what my gift is."

"You do?"

"Uh-huh." Dawn grinned. "That shiny new Jaguar in the garage downstairs."

Nick groaned. "There's no keeping anything from you."

"Nope, there isn't. Now, you want to take a stab at what I'm giving you?"

"Well, there was that time you gave me a doll," Nick said dryly, "the one you wanted for yourself."

"I was seven!" Dawn grinned at Amanda. "Definitely clueless," she whispered.

"What?"

"I said, you're clueless, Nicky. About how to decorate this mansion of yours."

"It's not a mansion. It's an apartment. And I told you, I don't have time for such things. That's why I bought the place furnished."

"Furnished?" Dawn made a face at Amanda, who smiled.

"How somebody could take a ten-million-dollar penthouse and make it look like a high-priced bordello is beyond me."

"If you have any idea what a bordello looks like, high-priced or low, I'll definitely send you home," Nick said, trying to sound affronted but not succeeding.

"You don't, either, dearest brother, or you'd never have the time or energy to bed all the females the tabloids link you with."

"Dawn—"

"I know, I know. You're not going to discuss such things with me." Dawn plucked a bit of lint from her skirt. "You know, Nicky, I'm not the baby you think I am."

"Maybe not. But it won't hurt if you let me go on living with an illusion."

His sister laughed. "When you see what I've bought you, that illusion will be shattered forever."

"We'll see about that." Nick's voice hummed with amusement.

Dawn grinned, covered the mouthpiece of the phone and looked at Amanda. "My brother doesn't believe you're going to shatter his illusions."

Amanda thumbed a strand of pale golden hair behind her ear. "Well, I'll just have to prove him wrong," she said, and told herself it was just plain ridiculous for an intelligent, well-educated, twenty-five-year-old woman to stand there with her knees knocking together at the prospect of being the birthday gift for a sheikh.

CHAPTER TWO

AMANDA swallowed nervously as Dawn put down the phone.

"Well," Dawn said, "that's that." She smiled. "I've laid the groundwork."

"Uh-huh." Amanda smiled, too, although her lips felt as if they were sticking to her teeth. "For disaster."

"Don't be silly. Oh, Nicky will probably balk when he realizes I've asked you to redo the penthouse. He'll growl a little, threaten murder and mayhem..." Dawn's brows lifted when she saw the expression on Amanda's face. "I'm joking!"

"Yeah, well, I'm not so sure about that." Amanda clasped her arms and shivered despite the heat of the midsummer afternoon. "I've gone toe-to-toe with your brother before, remember?"

Dawn made a face. "That was completely different. You were, what, nineteen?"

"Eighteen."

"Well."

"Well, what?"

"Well, that's my point," Dawn said impatiently. "You didn't go toe-to-toe with him. He had the advantage from the start. You were just a kid."

"I was your college roommate." Amanda caught her bottom

lip between her teeth. "Otherwise known as The American Female With No Morals."

Dawn grinned. "Did he really call you that?"

"It may sound funny now, but if you'd been there—"

"I know how you must have felt," Dawn said, her smile fading. "After he hauled me out of the Dean's office, I thought he was going to have me shipped home and locked in the women's quarters for the rest of my life."

"If your brother remembers me from that night—"

"If he does, I'll tell him he's wrong. Oh, stop worrying. He won't remember. It was the middle of the night. You didn't have a drop of makeup on, your hair was long then and probably hanging in your face. Look, if it all goes bad and Nicky gets angry at anybody for this, it'll be me."

"I know. But still…"

Still, Amanda thought uneasily, she'd never forgotten her first, her only, meeting with Nicholas al Rashid.

Dawn had talked about him. And Amanda had read about him. The tabloids loved the sheikh: his incredible looks, his money, his power…his women.

Back then, Amanda didn't usually read that kind of thing. Her literary aspirations were just that. Literary. She'd been an English major, writing and reading poetry nobody but other English majors understood, although she'd been starting to think about changing her major to architectural design.

Whichever, the tabloids were too smarmy to catch her interest. And yet she found herself reaching for those awful newspapers at the supermarket checkout whenever she saw a photo of Dawn's brother on the front page.

Well, why wouldn't she? The man was obviously full of himself. It was like driving past an automobile accident; you didn't want to look but you just couldn't keep from doing it.

Dawn thought he was wonderful. "Nicky's a sweetheart," she always said. "I can't wait until you meet him."

And, without warning, Amanda did.

It was the week before finals of their freshman year. Dawn was going to a frat party. She'd tried to convince Amanda to go, too, but Amanda had an exam in Renaissance design the next morning so she begged off, stayed in the dorm room they shared while Dawn partied.

Unfortunately, Dawn had one beer too many. She ended up sneaking into the bell tower at two in the morning along with half a dozen of the frat brothers, and they'd all decided it would be cool to play the carillon.

The campus police didn't agree. They brought Dawn and the boys down, hustled them into the security office and phoned their respective families.

Amanda was blissfully unaware of any of it. She'd crawled into bed, pulled the blanket over her head and fallen into exhausted sleep just past midnight.

A few hours later, she awoke to the pounding of a fist on the door of her dorm room. She sprang up in bed, heart pounding as hard as the fist, switched on the bedside lamp and pushed the hair out of her eyes.

"Who's there?"

"Open this door," a male voice demanded.

Visions conjured up from every horror movie she'd ever seen raced through her head. Her eyes flashed to the door, and her heartbeat went from fast to supersonic. She hadn't locked it, not with Dawn out—

"Open the door!"

Amanda scrambled from the bed, prayed her quaking knees would hold up long enough for her to fly across the room and throw the bolt—

The door burst open.

A thin, high shriek burst from her throat. A man dressed in jeans and a white T-shirt stood in the doorway, filling the space with his size, his rage, his very presence.

"I am Nicholas al Rashid," he roared. "Where is my sister?"

It took a few seconds for the name to register. This broad-shouldered man in jeans, this guy with the silver eyes and the stubbled jaw, was Dawn's brother?

She started to smile. He wasn't a mad killer after all...but he might as well have been.

The sheikh strode across the room, grabbed her by the front of her oversize D is For Design T-shirt and hauled her toward him. "I asked you a question, woman," Nicholas al Rashid said. "Where is my sister?"

To this day, it bothered Amanda that fear had nearly paralyzed her. She'd only been able to cower and stammer instead of bunching up her fist and slugging the bastard. A good right to the midsection was exactly what the tyrannical fool deserved.

But she was just eighteen, a girl who'd grown up in the sheltered world of exclusive boarding schools and summer camps. And the man standing over her was big, furious and terrifying.

So she'd swallowed a couple of times, trying to work up enough saliva so she could talk, and then she'd said that she didn't know where Dawn was.

Obviously, that wasn't the answer the sheikh wanted.

"You don't know," he said, his voice mocking hers. His hand tightened on her shirt and he hauled her even closer, close enough so she was nose to chest with him. "You don't know?"

"Dawn is—she's out."

"She's out," he repeated with that same cold sarcasm that was meant, she knew, to reduce her to something with about as much size and power as a mouse.

It got to her then. That he'd broken into her room. That he was on her turf, not his. That he was behaving as if this little piece of America was, instead, his own desert kingdom.

"Yes," she'd answered, lifting her chin as best she could, considering that his fist was wrapped in her shirt, forcing herself to meet his narrowed, silver eyes. "Yes, she's out, and even if I knew where she was, I wouldn't tell you, you—you two-bit dictator!"

She knew instantly she'd made a mistake. His face paled; a muscle knotted in his jaw and his mouth twisted in a way that made her blood run cold.

"What did you call me?" His voice was soft with the promise of malice.

"A two-bit dictator," she said again, and waited for the world to end. When, instead, a thin smile curved his mouth, she went from angry to furious. "Does that amuse you, Mr. Rashid?"

"You will address me as Lord Rashid." His smile tilted, so she could see the cruelty behind it. "And what amuses me is the realization that if we were in my country, I would have your tongue cut out for such insolence."

A drop of sweat beaded on Amanda's forehead. She had no doubt that he meant it but by then, she was beyond worrying about saying, or doing, the right thing. Never, not in all her life, had she despised anyone as she despised Nicholas al Rashid.

"This isn't your country. It's America. And I am an American citizen."

"And you are a typical American female. You have no morals."

"Oh, and you'd certainly know all about American females and morals, wouldn't you?"

His eyes narrowed. "I take it that's supposed to have some deep meaning."

"Just let go of me," Amanda said, grunting as she twisted against the hand still clutching her shirt. "Dammit, let go!"

He did. His fist opened, so quickly and unexpectedly that she stumbled backward. She stood staring at the man who'd invaded her room, her breasts heaving under the thin cotton shirt.

For the first time, he looked at her. Really looked at her. She could almost feel the touch of those silver eyes as they swept her from head to toe. He took in her sleep-tousled hair, her cotton shirt, the long length of her naked legs…

Amanda felt her face, then her body, start to burn under that arrogant scrutiny. She wanted to cover herself, put her arms over her breasts, but she sensed that to do so would give him even more of an advantage than he already had.

"Get out of my room," she said, her voice trembling.

Instead, his eyes moved over her again, this time with almost agonizing slowness. "Just look at you," he said very softly.

The words were coated with derision—derision, and something else. Amanda could hear it in his voice. She could read it in the way his eyes darkened. There was more to the message than the disparagement of American women and their morality. Despite her lack of experience, she knew that what he'd left unspoken was a statement of want and desire, raw and primitive and male.

It was three in the morning. She was alone in her room with a man twice her size, a man who wore his anger like a second skin…

A man more beautiful, and overwhelmingly masculine, than any she'd ever imagined or known in her entire life.

To her horror, she'd felt her body begin to quicken. A slow heat coiled low in her belly; her breasts lifted and her nipples began to harden so that she almost gasped at the feel of them thrusting against the thin cotton of her T-shirt.

He saw it, too.

His eyes went to her breasts, lingered, then lifted to her face. Amanda felt her heart leap into her throat as he took a step forward.

"Sire."

He moved toward her, his eyes never leaving hers. The heat in her belly swept into her blood.

"Sire!"

Amanda blinked. A little man in a shiny black suit had come into the room. He scuttled toward the sheikh, laid his hand on the sheikh's muscled forearm.

"My lord, I have located your sister."

The sheikh turned to the man. "Where is she?"

The little man looked at his hand, lying against the sheikh's tanned skin, and snatched it back. "Forgive me, sire. I did not mean to touch—"

"I asked you a question."

Abdul dropped to his knees and lowered his head until his brow almost touched the floor. "She awaits your will, Lord Rashid, in the office of the Dean of Students."

That had done it. The sight of the old man, kneeling in obeisance to a surly tyrant, the thought of Dawn, awaiting the bully's will...

Amanda's vision cleared.

"Get out," she'd said fiercely, "before I have you thrown out. You're nothing but a—a savage. And I pity Dawn, or any woman, who has anything to do with you."

The sheikh's mouth had twisted, the hard, handsome face taking on the look of a predator about to claim its prey.

"Sire," the little man had whispered, and without another word, Nicholas al Rashid had spun on his heel and walked out of the room.

Amanda had never seen him again.

He'd taken Dawn out of school, enrolled her in a small women's college. But the two of them had remained friends through Amanda's change of careers, through her marriage and divorce.

Over the years, her encounter with the sheikh had faded from her memory.

Almost.

There were still times she awoke in the night with the feel of his eyes on her, the scent of him in her nostrils—

"Mandy," Dawn said, "your face is like an open book."

Amanda jerked her head up. Dawn grinned.

"You're still mortified, thinking about how Nicky stormed into our room all those years ago, when he was trying to find me."

Amanda cleared her throat. "Yes. Yes, I am. And you know, the more I think about this, the more convinced I am it's not going to work."

"What's not going to work? I told you, he won't remember you. And even if he does—"

"Dawn," Amanda said, reaching for the purse she'd dropped on one of the glass-topped tables on the enormous terrace, "I appreciate what you've tried to do for me. Honestly, I do. But—"

"But you don't need this job."

"Of course I need it. But—"

"You don't," Dawn said, striking a pose, "because you're going to make your name in New York by waving a magic wand. 'Hocus-pocus, I now pronounce me the decorator of the decade.'"

"Come on, Dawn," Amanda said with a little smile.

"Not that it matters, because you've found a way to pay your rent without working."

Amanda laughed.

"Well, what, then? Have you changed your mind about taking money from your mother?"

"Taking it from my stepfather, you mean." Amanda grimaced. "I don't want Jonas Baron's money. It comes with too many strings attached."

"Taking alimony from that ex of yours, then."

"Even more strings," Amanda said, and sighed. This was not a good idea. She could feel it in her bones—but only an idiot would walk away from an opportunity like this. "Okay," she said before she could talk herself out of it again, "I'll try."

"Good girl." Dawn looped her arm through Amanda's. The women walked slowly from the terrace into the living room. "Mandy, you know this makes sense. Doing the interior design for Sheikh Nicholas al Rashid's Fifth Avenue penthouse will splash your name everywhere it counts."

"Still, even if your brother agrees—"

"He has to. You're my birthday gift to him, remember?"

"Won't he care that he'll be my first client?"

"Your first New York client."

"Well, yeah. But I didn't really work when I lived in Dallas. You know how Paul felt about my having a career."

"Once I tell Nick you designed for Jonas Baron, and for Tyler and Caitlin Kincaid, he'll be sold."

Amanda came to a dead stop. "Are you nuts? Me, decorate my stepfather's house? Jonas would probably shoot anybody who tried to move a chair!"

"You did your mother's sitting room, didn't you?"

"Sure. But that was different. It was one room—"

"The room's in the Baron house, right?"

"Dawn, come on. That's hardly—"

"Well, what about the Kincaids?"

"All I did was rip out some of the froufrou, replace it with pieces Tyler had in his house in Atlanta and suggest a couple of new things. That's hardly the same as redoing a fourteen-room penthouse."

Dawn slapped her hands on her hips. "For heaven's sake, Mandy, will you let me handle this? What do you want me to say? 'Nick, this is Amanda. Remember her? The last time you met, you chewed her out for being a bad influence on me. Now she's going to spend a big chunk of your money doing something you really don't want done, and by the way, you're her very first real client.'"

Amanda couldn't help it. She laughed. "I guess it doesn't sound like much of a recommendation."

"No, it doesn't. And I thought we both just agreed you need this job."

"You're right," Amanda said glumly, "I do."

"Darned right, you do. At least redo the suite Nicky lets me use whenever I'm in town. Did you ever see such awful kitsch?" Dawn gave Amanda a quick hug when she smiled. "That's better. Just let me do the talking, okay?"

"Okay."

Dawn quickened her pace as they started up the wide staircase that led to the second floor. "We'll have to hurry. You put on that slinky red dress, fix your hair, spritz on some perfume and get ready to convince my brother he'd be crazy to turn up his regal nose at the chance to have this place done by the one, the only, the incredible Amanda Benning."

"You ever think about going into PR?"

"You can put me on the payroll after the first time your name shows up in the—oh, damn! We never finished our tour. You haven't seen Nick's suite."

"That's all right." Amanda patted the pocket of her silk trousers. "I'll transfer my camera into my evening bag."

"No, don't do that." Dawn shuddered dramatically as she opened the door to her rooms. "If Nick sees you taking pictures, he'll figure you for a media spy and…" She grinned and sliced her hand across her throat. "How's this? You shower first, get dressed, then grab a quick look. His rooms are at the other end of the hall."

"I don't think that's a good idea," Amanda said quickly. "What if the sheikh comes in while I'm poking around?"

"He won't. Nicky promised he'd be on time, but he's always late. He hates stuff like this. You know, public appearances, being the center of attention. The longer he can delay his entrance, the better he likes it."

Amanda thought about the walking ego who'd shoved his way into her room, unasked and unannounced.

"I'll bet," she said, and softened the words with a smile. "But I'd still feel more comfortable if you were with me."

"I promise I'll join you just as soon as I turn myself into the gorgeous, desirable creature we both know I am. Okay?"

Amanda hesitated, told herself she was being an idiot, then nodded. "Okay."

"Good." Dawn kicked off her shoes. "In that case, the shower's all yours."

Twenty minutes later, Amanda paused outside the door to the sheikh's rooms.

If anybody took her pulse right now, they'd probably enter the result in the record books. She could feel it galloping like a runaway horse, but why wouldn't it?

It wasn't every day she sneaked into a man's bedroom to take pictures and make notes. Into the bedroom of a man who demanded people address him as "Lord". A man to whom other men bowed.

Instinct told her to turn tail and run. Necessity told her to stop being a coward. She was wasting time, and there really wasn't much to waste. Ten minutes, if Dawn was wrong and the sheikh showed up promptly.

She ran a nervous hand through the short, pale gold hair that framed her face, took the tiny digital camera from her evening purse and tapped at the door.

"Sheikh Rashid?"

There was no answer. The only sounds that carried through the vastness of the penthouse were snatches of baroque music from the quartet setting up in the library far below.

Amanda straightened her shoulders, opened the door and stepped inside the room.

It was clearly a man's domain. Dawn had said her brother hadn't changed any of the furnishings in the penthouse and Amanda could believe that—everywhere but here. This one room bore a stamp that she instantly knew was the sheikh's.

She didn't know why she would think it. Asked to describe a room Nicholas al Rashid would design for himself, she'd have come up with mahogany furniture. Dark crimson walls. Velvet drapes.

These walls were pale blue silk. The furniture was satin-finished rosewood, and the tall windows had been left unadorned to frame the view of Central Park. The carpet was Persian, she was sure, and old enough to date back to a century when that had been the name of the country in which it had been made.

A sleek portable computer sat open on a low table.

The room spoke of simplicity and elegance. It spoke, too, of a time older than memory that flowed into a time yet to come.

Amanda began taking photos. The room. The bed. The open windows and the view beyond. She worked quickly while images of the sheikh flashed through her mind. She could see him in this room, tall and leanly muscled, stiff with regal arrogance. He belonged here.

Then she saw the oil painting on the wall. She hesitated, then walked toward it, eyes lifted to the canvas.

The room was a sham. All the sophistication, the urbanity…a lie, all of it. This was the real man, the one she'd met that night, and never mind the jeans and T-shirt he'd worn then, and the nonsense about his half-American ancestry.

The painting was of Nicholas al Rashid dressed in desert robes of white trimmed with gold, seated on the back of a white horse that looked as wild as he did. One hand held the reins; the other lay on the pommel of the elaborate saddle.

And his eyes, those silver eyes, seemed to be staring straight at her.

Amanda took a step back.

She was wrong to have come here, wrong to have let Dawn convince her she could take this job, even if the sheikh permitted it.

Wrong, wrong, wrong—

"What in hell do you think you're doing in my bedroom?"

The tiny camera fell from Amanda's hand. She swung around, heart racing, and saw the Lion of the Desert, the Heir to the Imperial Throne of Quidar, standing in the doorway, just as he'd been doing that night in her dormitory room.

No jeans and T-shirt this time.

He wore a dark gray suit, a white-on-white shirt and a dark red tie. He was dressed the same as half the men in Manhattan—but it was easy to imagine him in his flowing robes and headdress, with the endless expanse of the desert behind him instead of the marble hall.

Maybe it had something to do with the way he stood, legs apart, hands planted on his hips, as if he owned the world. Maybe it was the look on his hard, handsome face that said he was emperor of the universe and she was nothing but an insignificant subject....

Get a grip, Amanda.

The man had caught her off guard that night, but it wouldn't happen again. She wasn't eighteen anymore, and she'd learned how to deal with hard men who thought they owned the world, men like her father, her stepfather, her ex-husband.

Whatever else they owned, they didn't own her.

"Well? Are you deaf, woman? I asked you a question."

Amanda bent down, retrieved her camera and tucked it into her beaded evening purse.

"I heard you," she said politely. "It's just that you startled me, Sheikh Rashid." She took a breath, then held out her hand. "I'm Amanda Benning."

"And?" he said, pointedly ignoring her outstretched hand.

"Didn't your sister tell you about me?"

"No."

No? Oh. Dawn? Dawn, where are you?

Amanda smiled politely. "Well, she, um, she invited me here tonight."

"And that gives you the right to sneak into my bedroom?"

"I did not sneak," she said, trying to hold the smile. "I was merely…" Merely what? Dawn was supposed to handle all this. It was her surprise.

"Yes?"

"I was, um, I was…" She hesitated. "I think it's better if Dawn explains it."

A chilly smile angled across his mouth. "I'd much rather hear your explanation, Ms. Benning."

"Look, this is silly. I told you, your sister and I are friends. Why not simply ask her to—"

"My sister is young and impressionable. It would never occur to her that you'd use your so-called friendship for your own purposes."

"I beg your pardon?"

The sheikh took a step forward. "Who sent you here?"

"Who sent me?" Amanda's eyes narrowed. Nearly eight years had gone by, and he was as arrogant and overbearing as ever. Well, she wasn't the naive child she'd been the last time they'd dealt with each other, and she wasn't frightened of bullies. "No one sent me," she said as she started past him. "And there's not enough money in the world to convince me to—"

His hand closed on her wrist with just enough pressure to make her gasp.

"Give me the camera."

She looked up at him. His eyes glittered like molten silver. She felt a lump of fear lodge just behind her breastbone, but she'd sooner have choked on the fear than let him know he'd been able to put it there.

"Let go of me," she said quietly.

His grasp on her wrist tightened; he tugged her forward.

Amanda stumbled on her high heels and threw out a hand to stop herself. Her palm flattened against his chest.

It was like touching a wall of steel. The cover photo from Gossip sprang into her head. Savage, the caption had called him, just as she had, that night.

"Or what?" His words were soft; his smile glittered. "You are in my home, Ms. Benning. To all intents and purposes, that means you stand on Quidaran soil. My word is law here."

"That's not true."

"It is true if I say it is."

Amanda stared at him in disbelief. "Mr. Rashid—"

"You will address me as Lord Rashid," he said, and she saw the sudden memory spark to life in his eyes. "We've met before."

"No," Amanda said, too quickly. "No, we haven't."

"We have. Something about you is familiar."

"I have that kind of face. You know. Familiar."

Nick frowned. She didn't. The pale hair. The eyes that weren't brown or green but something more like gold. The elegant cheekbones, the full, almost pouty lower lip...

"Let go of my wrist, Sheikh Rashid."

"When you give me your camera."

"Forget it! It's my cam— Hey. Hey, you can't..."

He could, though Nick had to admit, it wasn't easy. The woman was twisting like a wildcat, trying to break free and keep him from opening her purse at the same time, but he hung on to her with one hand while he dug out her camera with the other.

She was still complaining, her voice rising as he thumbed from image to image. What he saw made him crazy. Photos of his home. The terrace. The living room. The library. The bathrooms, for God's sake.

And his bedroom.

She had done more than invade his privacy. She had stolen it and would sell it to the highest bidder. He had no doubt of that.

He looked up from the digital camera, his eyes cold as they assessed her.

She was a thief, but she was beautiful even in a city filled with beautiful women. She seemed so familiar...but if they'd met before, surely he'd remember. What man would forget such a face? Such fire in those eyes. Such promised sweetness in that lush mouth.

And yet, for all of that, she was a liar.

Nick looked down at the little camera in his hand.

Beautiful, and duplicitous.

She played dangerous games, this woman. Games that took her into a man's bedroom and left her vulnerable to whatever punishment he might devise.

He lifted his head slowly, and his eyes met hers.

"Who paid you to take these pictures?"

"I can't tell you."

"Well, that's progress. At least you admit you're doing this for money."

"I am. But it isn't what you—"

"You came here in search of information. A story. Photos. Whatever you could find that was salable." A muscle flexed in his jaw. "Do you know what the punishment in my country is for those who steal?"

"Steal?" Amanda gave an incredulous laugh. "I did not—"

"Theft is bad enough," he said coldly. "Don't compound it by lying."

His eyes were flat with rage. Amanda's heart thumped. Dealing with her father, her stepfather, even her ex, was nothing compared to dealing with a man who ruled a kingdom. She wasn't one of his subjects, but she had the feeling this wasn't exactly the time to point that out.

If Nick finds out, Dawn had said, *he'll be angry at me.*

But Dawn was among the missing, the sheikh was blocking

the doorway, and clearly, discretion was not the better part of valor.

"All right." Amanda stood straighter, even though her heart was still trying to fight its way out of her chest. "I'll tell you the truth."

"An excellent decision, Ms. Benning."

She licked her lips. "I'm—I'm your surprise."

Nick frowned. "I beg your pardon?"

"My services. They're your gift. What Dawn talked about, on the phone."

His gift? Nick's brows lifted. His little sister had a strange sense of humor, but how far would she go for a joke? It could be that Amanda Benning was willing to tell one gigantic whopper as a cover story.

"Indeed," he purred.

Amanda didn't like the tone in his voice.

"I'll have you know that I'm much sought after." Oh, Amanda, what a lie. "And expensive." Well, why not? She would be, one day.

"Yes," Nick said softly. "That, at least, must be the truth."

And then, before she could take a breath, Nick reached for the blonde with the golden eyes and the endless legs, pulled her into his arms, and crushed her mouth under his.

CHAPTER THREE

IF THERE was one thing Nick understood, it was the art of diplomacy.

He was the heir to the throne of an ancient kingdom. He represented his people, his flag, his heritage. And he never forgot that.

It was his responsibility to behave in a way that gave the least offense to anyone, even when he was saying or doing something others might not like. He understood that obligation and accepted it.

But when the spotlight was off and Nick could be himself, the truth was that he often had trouble being diplomatic. There were instances when diplomacy was about as useful as offering condolences to a corpse. Sometimes, being polite could distract from the truth and confuse things.

He wanted no confusion in Amanda Benning's mind when it came to him. She was sophisticated and beautiful, a woman who lived by her wits as well as her more obvious charms, but he was on to her game.

And he wanted to be sure she knew it.

That was the reason he'd taken her in his arms. He was very clear about the purpose, even as he gathered her close against him, bent her back over his arm and kissed her.

He'd caught her by surprise. He'd intended that. She gasped, which gave him the chance to slip his tongue between her lips. Then she began to fight him.

Good.

She'd planned everything so carefully. The tiny camera that he should never have noticed. The sexy dress. The soft scent of her perfume. The strappy black silk shoes with the high, take-me heels…

Seduction first, conveniently made simple by his foolish sister, whose penchant for silly jokes had finally gotten out of hand. And then, having bedded the Lion of the Desert, the Benning woman would sell her photographs and a breathless first-person account of what it was like to sleep with him.

Nick caught Amanda's wrist as she struggled to shove a hand between them. What a fool Dawn had been to hire a woman like this and bring her into their midst. But he'd have been a greater fool not to at least taste her.

He wouldn't take her to bed. He was too fastidious to take the leavings of other men, but he'd give her just enough of an encounter to remember. Kiss her with harsh demand. Cup her high, lush breasts with the easy certainty that spoke of royal possession.

When she responded, not out of desire but because that was her job, he'd shove her from him, let her watch him grind her camera under his heel. After that, he'd call for Abdul and direct him to hustle the lady straight out the door.

Then he'd go in search of his sister. Dawn needed to be reminded how dangerous it was to consort with scum. A few months in Quidar, under the watchful eye of their father, would work wonders.

That was Nick's plan anyway.

The kiss, the reality of it, changed everything.

Amanda had stopped struggling. That was good. She'd been paid to accept his kisses, welcome his hands as they caressed her pliant body…except, he suddenly realized, she wasn't pliant.

She was rigid with what seemed to be fear.

Fear?

She'd cried out as his mouth covered hers. A nice touch, he'd thought coldly, that little intake of breath, that high, feminine cry. Righteous indignation didn't go with the dress or the heels, certainly not with the face or the body, but he could see where she might try it, just to heighten the tension and his arousal before her ultimate surrender.

There were games men and women played, and a woman like this would know them all. Either Amanda Benning was an excellent actress or he'd started the game before she was ready.

Was she the kind who wanted to direct the performance and the pace? Or was her imagination running wild? Innocent maiden. Savage sheikh. The story wasn't new. Nick had come across women who hungered for it and would accept nothing else, but he never obliged. It was a stereotype, a fantasy that offended him deeply, and he refused to play it out.

Sex between a man and a woman involved as much giving as taking or it brought neither of them pleasure.

But this was different.

He had neither wooed the Benning woman nor won her. She hadn't seduced him with a smile, a glance, a touch. She was here because his sister had decided it would be amusing to give her to him as a gift.

In other words, none of the usual rules applied.

The woman was his. He could do as he wanted with her. And if what she thought he wanted was some rough sex, he could oblige. He could play along until it was time to toss her out.

A little rough treatment, maybe even a scare, was exactly what Amanda Benning deserved. She was a creature of no morals, willing to offer her body for information she could sell to the highest bidder.

Oh, yes. A little scare would do Amanda Benning just fine.

She was struggling in earnest now, not just trying to drag her mouth from his but fighting him, shoving her fists against his chest, doing her best to free herself from his arms.

Nick laughed against her mouth, spun her around, pressed her back against the silk-covered wall. He caught her wrists, entwined his fingers with hers and flattened her hands against the wall on either side of her.

She tried to scream. He caught her bottom lip in his teeth, moved closer, brushed his body against her.

God, she was so warm. Heat seemed to radiate from her skin. And she was soft. Her breasts. Her belly. Her mouth. Her hot, luscious mouth. He could taste it now, not only the fear but what lay beyond it, the sweet taste of the woman herself.

His body hardened, became steel. There was a roaring in his ears. Nick wanted to carry her to the bed, strip her of her clothes, bury himself deep inside her. Need for her sang in his blood, raced through every muscle.

The part of his brain that still functioned told him he was insane. He was kissing a woman his sister had bought as a joke, a woman with a bag filled with professional tricks. She was pretending she didn't want him, and he was, what?

He was getting turned on.

It was just that she fitted his arms so well. That her hair felt so silken against his cheek. That she smelled sweet, the way he'd assumed she would taste. The way he wanted her to taste, he thought. The hell with it. She wanted to give a performance? All right. He would comply, but he was changing the rules.

He wasn't going to take her. He was going to seduce her.

"Amanda," he said softly.

Her lashes flew up. Her eyes met his.

"Don't fight me," he whispered, and kissed her. Gently.

Tenderly. His mouth moved against hers, over and over; his teeth nipped lightly at her bottom lip. And, gradually, her mouth began to soften. She made a little sound, a whimper, and her body melted against his.

Nick groaned at the stunning sweetness of her surrender. He wanted to let go of her wrists and slide his hands down her spine, stroke the satin that was her skin, cup her bottom and lift her up into the urgency of his erection. When her hands tugged at his, seeking freedom, pleasure rocketed through him. He understood what she wanted, that she sought the freedom to touch him, explore him. It was what he wanted, too. He'd forgotten everything except that he was on fire for the woman in his arms.

He touched the tip of his tongue to the seam of her lips as he let go of her wrists and took her face in his hands. His palms cupped her cheeks; he tilted her head back so that her golden hair feathered like silk over the tips of his fingers, so that he could slant his mouth hungrily over hers—

—so that her knee could catch him right where he lived and drive every last breath of air from his lungs.

A strangled gasp of agony burst from his lips. Nick doubled over and clutched his groin.

"Amanda?" he croaked, and got his chin up just in time to see her coming at him again.

"You no-good bastard!"

He was hurting. The pain was gut-deep, but he fought it, jumped out of her path, caught her as she flew by and flung her on the bed. She landed hard, rolled to her side, sat up and almost got her feet on the floor, but by then he'd recovered enough to come down on top of her.

She called him a name he'd only heard a couple of times in his life and pummeled him with her fists.

"Get off me!"

It was like wrestling with a wildcat. She was small and

slender but she moved fast, and it didn't help that it still felt as if his scrotum was seeking shelter halfway up his belly.

Nick took a blow on his chin, another in the corner of his eye. He grabbed for her hands, captured them and pinned them high over her head.

"You little bitch," he said, straddling her hips.

Amanda bucked like an unbroken mare, her hips arcing up, then down.

"Stop it." He leaned toward her, his eyes hot with anger. "Damn you, woman, did you hear what I said? Stop!"

She didn't. She bucked again, her body moving against his, her breasts heaving, her golden hair disheveled against the blue silk pillows. Her eyes were wild, the pupils huge and black and encircled by rims of gold. She was panting through parted lips; he could see the flash of her small white teeth, the pink of her tongue. Her excuse of a dress was ruined; one thin red silk strap hung off her shoulder, exposing the upper curve of a creamy breast. The skirt had ridden up her hips. He could see the strip of black lace that hid the feminine delta between her thighs.

And all at once, he felt fine. No more pain, just the realization that he was hard, swollen and aroused, separated from the woman beneath him by nothing but his trousers and that scrap of sexy lace.

The air in the room crackled with electricity.

He became still. She did, too. Her eyes met his, and for the first time, what he saw in them took his breath away.

"No," she whispered, but his mouth was already coming down on hers.

She held back; he could feel her tremble.

"Yes," he said softly, and kissed her again. "Amanda..."

She moaned. Her lashes fell to her cheeks and she opened her mouth to his. Her surrender was real. Her need was, too. He could feel it in the pliancy of her body, taste it in the silken heat of her kiss.

Nick let go of her hands and gathered her against him. She moaned again and dug her hands into his hair, clutching the dark curling strands with greedy fists.

Greedy. Yes, that was the way she felt. Greedy for his mouth, for his touch. For the feel of Nicholas al Rashid deep inside her.

It was crazy. She didn't know this man, and what little she did know, she didn't like. Moments ago, she'd been fighting him off....

Her breath caught as he rolled onto his side and took her with him. He stroked his hand down her spine, then up again. All the way up, so that his thumbs brushed lightly over her breasts.

"Tell me you want me," he said.

His voice was as soft as velvet, as rough as gravel. His breath whispered against her throat as he licked the flesh where her neck joined her shoulder, and she moaned.

"Tell me," he urged, and she did by seeking his mouth with hers.

Nick sat up, tore off his suit jacket and his tie. She heard the buttons on his shirt pop as he stripped it off. Then he came back down to her, cupped her breasts in his hands and took her mouth.

His skin was hot against hers. She made a little sound of need, nipped his bottom lip. "Yes," she said, "yes, oh, yes..."

His knee was between her thighs. She lifted herself to it, against it; his thumbs rolled across her silk-covered nipples and she was caught up on a wave of heat, up and up and up. She cried out his name, shut her eyes, tossed her head from side to side.

"Look at you," Nick whispered. "Just look at you."

And as quickly as that, it was all over.

Amanda froze. Disgust, horror, anguish...a dozen different emotions raced through her, brought back by those simple, unforgotten words. They took her back seven years to that dormitory room, to the terrifying intruder named Nicholas al Rashid who'd branded her as immoral even as he'd looked at her and wanted her.

Bile rose in her throat. "Get off me," she said.

The sheikh didn't hear her. Couldn't hear her. She looked up at him, hating what she saw, hating herself for being the cause. His silver eyes were blind with desire; the bones of his face were taut with it.

Nausea roiled in her belly. "Get—off!"

She struck out blindly, fists beating against his chest and shoulders. He blinked; his eyes opened slowly as if he were awakening from a dream.

"You—get—the—hell—off," she said, panting, and struck him again.

He caught her flailing hands, pinioned them. "It's too late to play that game."

His voice was low and rough; the hands that held her were hard and cruel. She told herself not to panic. This was Dawn's brother. He was arrogant, imperious and all-powerful...but he wasn't crazy.

"Taking a woman against her will isn't a game," she said, and tried to keep the fear from her voice.

"Against her will?"

His eyes moved over her and she flushed at the slow, deliberate scrutiny. She knew how she must look. Her dress torn. The hem of her skirt at her thighs. Her lips bare of everything but the imprint of his.

A thin smile started at the corner of his mouth. "When a woman all but begs a man to take her, it's hardly 'against her will'."

"I'd never beg a man for anything," she said coldly. "And if you don't let go and get off me, I'll scream. There must be a hundred people downstairs by now. Every one of them will hear me."

"You disappoint me." The bastard didn't just smile this time; he laughed. "You sneaked into my home—"

"I didn't sneak into anything. Your sister invited me."

"Did she tell you that once the party begins, no one will be permitted on this floor?"

Her heart thumped with fear. "They will, if they hear me screaming."

"My men would not permit it."

"The police don't need your permission."

"The police can't do anything to help you. This is Quidaran soil."

"It's a penthouse on Fifth Avenue," Amanda said, trying to free her hands, "not an embassy."

"We have no embassy in your country. By the time our governments finish debating the point, it will be too late."

"You're not frightening me."

It was a lie and they both knew it. She was terrified; Nick could see it in her eyes. Good. She'd deserved the lesson. She was immoral. She was a liar. A thief. She was for sale to any man who could afford her.

What did that make him, then, for still wanting her?

Nick let go of her hands, rolled off her and got to his feet. "Get out," he said softly.

She sat up, moved to the edge of the bed, her eyes wary. She shot a glance at the door and he knew she was measuring her chances of reaching it. It made him feel rotten but, dammit, she wasn't worth his pity. She wasn't worth anything except, perhaps, the price his foolish sister had paid for her.

"Go on," he said gruffly, and jerked his head toward the door. "Get out, before I change my mind."

She rose from the bed. Smoothed down her skirt with hands that shook. Bent and picked up her purse, grabbed the camera and put it inside.

She stumbled backward as Nick came around the bed toward her.

"No," she said sharply, but he ignored her, snatched the purse from her hands and opened the flap. "What are you doing?"

He looked up. He had to give her points for courage, he thought grudgingly. She'd lost one of her ridiculously high heels in their struggle. Her dress was a mess and her hair hung in her eyes.

Those unusual golden eyes.

He frowned, reached for a memory struggling to the surface of his mind....

"Give me my purse."

She lunged for the small beaded bag. He whipped it out of her reach. She went after it, lifting up on her toes and batting at it with her hands.

"Dammit, give me that!"

Nick took out the camera and tossed the purse at her feet. "It's all yours."

"I want my camera."

"I'm sure you do."

Grinding the camera to dust under his heel would have been satisfying, but the carpet was soft and he knew he might end up looking like an ass if the damned thing didn't break. Instead, he strolled into the bathroom.

"What are you...?"

Nick pressed a button on the camera, took out the tiny recording disk and dumped it into the toilet. He shut the lid, flushed, then dropped the camera on the marble floor. Now, he thought, now it would smash when he stepped on it.

It did.

Amanda Benning was scarlet with fury. "You—you bastard!"

"My parents would be upset to hear you call me that, Ms. Benning," he said politely. He walked past her, pleased that the toilet hadn't spit the disk back—it had been a definite possibility and it surely would have spoiled the drama of the moment.

A little more drama, and he'd send Amanda Benning packing.

He swung toward her and folded his arms over his chest. "Actually, addressing me in such a fashion could get you beheaded in my homeland."

Amanda planted her hands on her hips. "It could get you sued in mine."

He laughed. "You can't sue me. I'm—"

"Believe me, I know who you are, Mr. Rashid."

"Lord Rashid," Nick said quickly, and scowled.

What was he saying? He didn't care about his title. Everyone used it. It was the custom but occasionally someone forgot, and he never bothered correcting them. The only time he had was years ago. Dawn's roommate...

The girl with the golden eyes. Strange that he should have remembered her after so long a time. Stranger still that he should have done so tonight.

"...and ninety-eight cents."

He blinked, focused his eyes on Amanda Benning. She hadn't moved an inch. She was still standing in front of him, chin lifted, eyes flashing. He felt a momentary pity that she was what she was. A woman as beautiful, as fiery as this, would be a true gift, especially in a man's bed.

"Did you hear me, Lord Rashid?" Amanda folded her arms, tapped her foot. "You owe me 620.98. That includes the film."

One dark, arched brow lifted. It made him look even more insolent. She was boring him, she thought, and fought back a tremor of rage.

"I beg your pardon?"

"The camera." She marched past him, plucked her purse from the floor, dug inside it and pulled out a rumpled piece of paper. "The receipt. From Picture Perfect, on Madison Avenue."

She held it out. Nick looked at it but didn't touch it.

"An excellent place to buy electronic devices, or so I've been told."

"I want my money."

"What for?"

"I just told you. For the camera you destroyed."

"Ah. That."

"Yes. Yes, 'Ah, that.' You owe me six hundred and—"

Nick reached for the phone. "Abdul?" he said, never taking his eyes from her, "come to my rooms, please. Yes, now." He put the telephone down, leaned back against the wall and tucked his hands into his trouser pockets. "Your escort is on the way, Miss Benning. Abdul will escort you down to the curb where the trash is usually left."

Enough was enough. Amanda's composure dissolved in a burst of temper. She gave a shriek and flew at him, but Nick caught her shoulders, held her at arm's length.

"You rat," she said, her breath hitching. "You—you skunk! You horrible, hideous savage—"

"What did you call me?"

"You heard me. You're a skunk. A rat. A—"

"A savage." He swung her around, pinned her to the wall. The memory, so long repressed, burst free. "Damn you," he growled. "You're Dawn's roommate."

"Her immoral, American roommate," Amanda said, and showed her teeth. "How brilliant of you to have finally figured it out. But then, I never expected a baboon to have much of a brain."

The door swung open. Dawn al Rashid stepped into the room. She stared at her shirtless brother, her red-faced best friend, and swallowed hard.

"Isn't that nice?" she said carefully. "I see that you two have already met."

CHAPTER FOUR

AMANDA stared at Dawn. Dawn stared back.

"Dawn," Amanda said, "thank God you're here! Your brother—"

"Did you invite this woman into my home?" Nick's icy words overrode Amanda's. He took a step toward his sister and Dawn took a quick step back. "I want an answer."

"You'll get one if you give me a min—"

"Did you invite her?"

"Don't browbeat your sister," Amanda said furiously. "I already told you that she asked me to come here tonight."

"I will do whatever I please with my sister." Nick swung toward Amanda. His face was white with anger. "You take me for a fool at your own risk."

"Only a fool would imagine I'd lie my way into your home. I know it may come as a shock to you, Sheikh Rashid, but I don't give a flying fig about seeing how a despot lives."

"Amanda," Dawn muttered, "take it easy."

"Don't tell me to take it easy!" Amanda glared at the sheikh's sister. "And where have you been? Just go take a look at my brother's rooms and I'll meet you there, you said."

"I know. And I'm sorry. I tore my panty hose, and—"

"It's true, then. You not only invited this person into my home, you told her she was free to invade my private rooms."

"Nick," Dawn said, "you don't understand."

"No," the sheikh snapped, "I don't. That my own sister would think I would welcome into my presence the very woman who corrupted her—"

"How dare you say such things?" Amanda stepped in front of Nick. "I never corrupted anyone. I came here as a favor to your sister, to do a job I really didn't want to do because I already knew what you were like, that you were a horrible man with a swollen ego."

Her eyes flashed. This was pointless and she knew it. Her rage was almost palpable. She yearned to slap that insufferably smug look from Nicholas al Rashid's face, but he'd never let her get away with it. Instead, she moved around him.

"I'm out of here. Dawn, if your brother, the high-muck-a-muck of the universe, lets you use the phone, give me a call tomorrow. Otherwise—"

Nick's hand closed on her arm. "You will go nowhere," he growled, "until I have answers to my questions."

"Dammit," Amanda said, gritting her teeth and struggling against his grasp, "let go of me!"

"When I'm good and ready."

"You have no right—"

"Oh, for heaven's sake!" Nick and Amanda looked at Dawn. She was staring at the two of them as if she'd never seen them before. "What in hell is going on here?"

"Don't curse," Nick said sharply.

"Then don't treat me like an imbecile." Dawn slapped her hands on her hips and glared. "Yes, I invited Amanda here tonight."

"As my 'gift'," Nick said, his mouth twisting.

"That's right. I wanted to give you something special for your birthday."

"Did you really think I'd find it appealing to have you provide a woman for my entertainment?"

"Holy hell," Amanda snarled, "I was not provided for your

entertainment! And don't bother telling me not to curse, Your Dictatorship, because I don't have to take orders from you."

"I can't imagine what my sister was thinking when she made these arrangements."

"I'll tell you what your sister was thinking. She thought—"

Dawn slammed her fist against the top of the dresser. "Why not let me tell you what I was thinking?" she snapped.

"Stay out of this," Nick said.

"This is unbelievable. All this fuss because I decided your apartment looked like an ad for the No-Taste Furniture Company!" Her mouth thinned as she glared at Nick. "What a mistake I made, fixing you up with the services of an interior designer."

Nick blinked. "A what?"

"A designer. Someone trained to figure out how to turn this—this warehouse for overpriced, overdone, overvelveted garbage into a home."

"Oh, go on," Nick said with a tight smile, "don't hold back. Just tell me what you really think."

"You know it's the truth." Dawn waved her arms in the air. "This apartment looks more like a—a mortician's showroom than a home. So I called Amanda, who just happens to be one of the city's best-known designers. Isn't that right, Amanda?"

Amanda glanced at the sheikh. He was looking at her, and the expression on his face wasn't encouraging.

"And one of its most modest," Dawn added hurriedly. "She was booked up to her eyeballs. The mayor's mansion. The penthouse in that new building on the river. You know, the one that was written up in Citylights a couple of weeks ago."

"Dawn," Amanda said, and cleared her throat, "I don't think—"

"No. No, you certainly didn't. I didn't think it, either. Who'd imagine my brother would want to turn down such a gift from his favorite sister?"

"My only sister," Nick said dryly.

"The gift of a brilliant interior designer," Dawn said, ignoring the interruption, "who made room in her incredibly busy schedule solely as a favor to an old friend..." She paused dramatically. "And what have you done to her, Nicky?"

Color slashed Nick's high cheekbones. "What kind of question is that?"

"A logical one. Just look at her. Her dress is torn. Her hair's a mess. She's missing a shoe—"

"Excuse me," Amanda said. "There's no need to take inventory."

"And you, Nicky." Dawn huffed out a breath. "I had no idea my brother, the Lion of the Desert, was in the habit of conducting business with his shirt off."

Amanda shut her eyes, opened them and looked at the sheikh. The flush along his cheeks had gone from red to crimson.

"I have no need to explain myself to anyone," he said brusquely.

"And a good thing, too, because how you could possibly explain this—"

"But since you're my sister, I'll satisfy your curiosity. We fought over Ms. Benning's spy camera."

"My what?" Amanda laughed. "Honestly, Dawn. This brother of yours—"

Nick's eyes narrowed. "Be careful," he said softly, "before you push me too far."

"Well, you've already pushed me too far." Dawn marched to Amanda's side and took her hand. "We'll be in my room, Nicky, when you're ready to apologize."

The sheikh stiffened. The room went still. Even the distant sounds of the party—the strains of music, the buzz of conversation that had begun drifting up the stairs a little while before—seemed to stop.

Amanda sensed that a line had been crossed.

She looked at Dawn, who seemed perfectly calm—but the grip of her hand was almost crushing. The women's eyes met. Hang on, Dawn's seemed to say and we can get away with this.

Together, they started for the door. It was like walking away from a stick of dynamite with a lit fuse. One step. Two. Just another few to go—

"An admirable performance, little sister."

Dawn let out her breath. Amanda did, too. She hadn't even realized she'd been holding it. Both of them turned around.

"Nicky," Dawn said softly, "Nicky, if you'd just calm down—"

"Do as you suggested. Take Ms. Benning to your room." His eyes swept over Amanda. She fought back the urge to smooth down her skirt, grasp her torn strap, fix her hair. Instead, she lifted her chin and met his look without blinking. "Give her something to wear. Let her make herself respectable and then bring her downstairs."

"I am not a package to be brought downstairs or anywhere else, for that matter. Who do you think you are, giving orders to your sister about me? If you have something to say to me—"

"The matter is settled for the moment."

"The matter is settled permanently." She tore her hand from Dawn's tight grasp. "I wouldn't so much as pick out the wallpaper for your kitchen, let alone—"

"Get her out of here." Nick waved an imperious hand. He knew he sounded like an ass, but what else was there to do? Dawn's story had holes in it the size of the Grand Canyon. He was angry at her, angry at the Benning woman, but he was furious at himself for losing control in the bed that seemed to loom, stage center, a thousand times larger than life.

What in hell had he been thinking, to have almost made love to her?

He hadn't been thinking, he decided grimly. That was the problem. His brain had gone on holiday, thanks to Amanda Benning's clever machinations. A far more dangerous part of his anatomy had taken over.

But his thought processes were clear now. He wasn't about to let this situation deteriorate any further, nor was he about to permit Amanda to walk away before he was certain of what she'd been up to.

"Go on," he said to his sister. "Get her out of here and I'll deal with you both when the night ends."

"Deal with us?" Amanda's voice rose. "You'll deal with us?"

"Oh, he doesn't really mean—"

"Silence!"

The command roared through the room. Amanda caught her breath. She'd never heard a man speak to a woman that way. Her own father had been strict, her stepfather could be crude, and her ex had specialized in sarcasm, but this was different. Nicholas al Rashid's voice carried the ring of absolute authority. Shirtless and disheveled, there was still no mistaking the raw power that emanated from him.

She looked at Dawn and waited for her to respond, to stand up to her brother and tell him that she didn't have to take orders.

To her horror Dawn bowed her head. "Yes, my lord," she whispered.

Amanda stepped in front of her friend. "Now wait just a minute—"

"As for you," Nick barked, "you will speak only when spoken to."

"Listen here, you—you pathetic stand-in for a real human being—"

Nick grabbed her by the elbows and hoisted her to her toes. "Watch how you speak to me."

"Watch how you speak to me, Your Horribleness. You might have your sister bowing and scraping like a slave, but not me!"

"Mandy," Dawn pleaded, "stay out of this. Let me explain—"

"Yes," Nick said. He let go of Amanda and folded his arms. "Do that. Now that I think about it, why should I wait until later for an explanation? Explain to me why I found your so-called friend, your interior designer, taking photographs of my things with a spy camera."

"I told you, it wasn't a spy camera."

"It was designed to be concealed."

"It was designed to fit inside a pocket or a purse!"

Nick gave a cold smile. "Exactly."

"It was not a spy camera, and if you hadn't stomped it into pieces, I could prove it!"

"You will learn to speak when spoken to," he growled. "And if you cannot manage that, I'll lock you away until I've finished with my sister. Do you understand?"

Amanda's heart bounced into her throat. He would do it, too. She could see it in his eyes.

"You're despicable," she said in a choked whisper. "How I could ever have let you—"

Nick said something in a language she didn't understand. She shrieked as he picked her up, slung her over his shoulder and strode toward a large walk-in closet.

"Put me down. Damn you, put me—"

He yanked the door open, dumped her inside the closet. She dived for the door, but she was too late. It shut in her face, and then she heard a scraping sound against the wood. Amanda rattled the knob, pounded her fist against the door until she was panting, but it was useless.

The sheikh must have jammed a chair under the doorknob.

She was trapped.

All she could do was listen to the murmur of voices. The sheikh's angry, Dawn's apologetic. After a while, she couldn't hear anything, not even a whisper. She could imagine Dawn, cowed into submission, while her abominable brother stood over her, glowering. Glowering was what he seemed to do best.

"Bastard," Amanda said softly.

Tears welled in her eyes. Tears of anger.

"Oh, hell," she whispered. Who was she kidding? They were tears of shame. Her rage at the sheikh's accusations, at what he'd done to her camera, at how he'd treated her, was nothing compared to the rage she felt at herself.

How could she have kissed him? Because she had kissed him; she'd have done more than that if she hadn't mercifully come to her senses just before Dawn came into the room. She'd lost control of herself in Nicholas al Rashid's arms. Done things. Said things. Felt things…

Let go, her husband used to say. What's the matter with you? Why are you such a prude when it comes to sex?

Well, she hadn't been a prude tonight. She'd behaved as if she were exactly what the sheikh had accused her of being.

"Oh, hell," Amanda said again, and she leaned back, slid to the floor, wrapped her arms around her knees and settled in to wait until His Royal Highness, the Despot of Quidar, deigned to set her free.

It wasn't a very long wait. But when the door opened, it wasn't the despot who stood outside. It was Dawn.

Amanda scrambled to her feet. "What happened?"

"Nick is furious."

"Not half as furious as I am." She peered past Dawn. "Where is he? I haven't finished telling him what—"

"He took his stuff and went to one of the guest rooms to

change." Dawn glanced at the diamond watch on her wrist. "By now, he's probably downstairs."

"Yeah, well then, that's where I'm—"

"Mandy." Dawn caught Amanda's hand. "What happened before I got here?"

Color swept into Amanda's face. "Nothing happened," she said, and wrenched her hand free. She smoothed down her dress, tugged uselessly at the torn strap and wished she knew what had happened to her other shoe. "Your brother caught me in here and jumped to all the wrong conclusions."

"Uh-huh." Dawn managed a smile. "So he thought I'd arranged a gift for his, uh, for his pleasure?"

"He most certainly did. As if I'd ever—"

"I know. Sometimes it's not easy dealing with Nicky."

"That's because his head is as hard as a rock."

"Do us both a favor, okay? Don't say things like that to him. You can't call him names, not when he's angry. It isn't done."

"Maybe not in your country, but this is America." Amanda hobbled past Dawn, eyes on the carpet as she searched for her shoe. "Freedom of speech, remember? The Bill of Rights? The Constitution? Ah. There it is." She bent down, picked up her shoe and grimaced. "The heel is broken. Okay, okay, that's it. Tell your brother he owes me for the camera and now for a pair of shoes."

"One dress, too, from the looks of it." Dawn hesitated. "You guys must have really tussled over that camera."

Amanda was glad she had her back to Dawn. "Yes. Yes, we did."

"The thing is, I never figured you'd get caught alone in his bedroom. I was sure I'd get here before he came home."

"Well, you didn't." Amanda heard the sharpness in her own voice. She stopped, drew a breath and turned around. "Look, what happened isn't your fault. Anyway, now that your brother knows the truth—"

"Well, he's not sure he does."

"You mean he still thinks you arranged for me to—"

"No. No, not that." Dawn sat down on the edge of the bed, sighed and crossed her legs. "Mandy, try to see things from his perspective. I mean, you saw that awful photograph on the cover of Gossip. People try to get close to him all the time just so they can find out personal stuff about his life."

"I'd sooner get close to a python."

"I know how you feel. But Nick is sensitive about invasions of his privacy."

"Your brother is about as sensitive as a mule. And you know damn well that I wasn't invading anything."

"Of course. And he'll know it, too." Dawn blew out her breath. "Just as soon as the party is over."

"Yeah, well, you can explain it to him by yourself." Amanda slung her evening purse over her shoulder and limped to the door. "Because I am out of here."

"You can't."

"Oh, but I can." She looked back as she curled her hand around the knob. "I feel sorry for you, Dawn. You're trapped with His Arrogance, but I'm... Dammit! This—door—is—stuck!" Dawn said something so quietly that Amanda couldn't hear it. "What?" she said, and rattled the knob again.

"I said, the door isn't stuck. It's locked."

Amanda stood perfectly still. When she let go of the knob and looked around, her face was a study in disbelief. "From the outside?"

"Uh-huh." Dawn swung her foot back and forth. She seemed to be contemplating her black silk pump. "I guess some nutcase owned this penthouse before Nicky did. Lots of the doors have locks on the—"

"I don't care who owned it, dammit!"

"I'm just explaining..." Dawn licked her lips. "Nicky locked the door."

"Nicky locked..." Amanda clamped her lips together. Be

calm, she told herself, be very calm. "Let me understand this. Your brother locked this door the same way he locked me into the closet?"

Dawn peered intently at her shoes. "Right."

"And you let him do it?"

"I didn't let him do anything." Dawn looked up. "He just did it. He has the right." Amanda laughed. Dawn's face pinkened. "Mandy," she said, "I know this seems strange to you—"

"Strange? Strange, that a man I hardly know doesn't think twice about locking me up?" Amanda grabbed for her dangling shoulder strap. "That he feels free to try to rip my clothes off? To tumble me into his bed?"

A grin, a real one, curled across Dawn's mouth. "Oh, wow," she said softly. "So that wasn't true, huh? Nicky's little speech about losing his shirt when you were fighting over the camera."

"The truth," Amanda said stiffly, "is that your dear, devoted brother is a lunatic. And so are you, for letting him lock that door."

Dawn shot to her feet. "I didn't 'let' him. I told you that. Nobody 'lets' him, don't you see? My brother is the future ruler of our kingdom. His word is law."

"For you, maybe. And for anybody else who's willing to live in the Dark Ages."

"Now, you just wait a minute before you say—"

The door suddenly swung open. Amanda spun around and glared at the man she despised.

How calm and collected he looked. While she'd been cooling her heels behind locked doors, the Sheikh of the Universe had been readying himself for his party. His dark hair was still damp from the shower; his jaw was smooth. She could see a tiny cut in the shallow cleft in his chin.

Good, she thought grimly. Maybe he wasn't as calm as he looked. The son of a bitch had cut himself while he shaved. She only hoped she was the reason for his unsteady hand on the razor. From the way he'd looked at her before and from how he was looking at her now, it was pretty obvious that Nicholas al Rashid wasn't accustomed to having anyone, especially a woman, talk back to him.

Women probably told him lots of other things, though. That he was exciting. That he was gorgeous, especially in that tux and pleated white shirt. That he could make a woman forget everything, even the code she lived by, with one kiss....

Amanda drew herself up. Snakes could be handsome, too. That didn't make them any less repulsive.

"You have one hell of a nerve," she said, "locking us in this room."

Nick looked at his sister. "Dawn?"

"This is the United States of America in case you haven't—"

"Dawn, our guests are here."

Amanda strode toward him. "Are you deaf?" Her words were rimed with ice. "I'm talking to you."

Nick ignored her. "Thanks to this unpleasant incident, I am not at the door to greet them."

Dawn cast her eyes down. "It's my fault, Nicholas. I apologize."

"I've decided to forgive you."

A glowing smile lit Dawn's face. "Thank you, Nicky."

Amanda made a little sound of disgust. Nick decided to go on pretending she was invisible.

"But this is the last time. One more transgression and you return home."

"Oh, give me a break."

Dawn shot Amanda a horrified look. Nick merely tilted his head toward her. "Did you have something you wished to say, Ms. Benning?"

"How generous of you to notice."

"Is that a yes?"

Amanda limped toward him. "It is indeed."

Nick looked at his watch, then at her. "Say it, then. I'm in a hurry, thanks to you."

"And I'm out a camera, a dress and a pair of shoes, thanks to you." It wasn't easy to maintain your dignity with one shoe three inches higher than the other, but Amanda was determined to manage it. "I'm going to send you a bill for—" she paused, furiously adding the numbers in her head "—for nine hundred and eighty dollars."

"Really."

Damn him for that annoying little smirk! "Yes," she said with a smirk of her own, "really. That camera was expensive."

"Oh, I'm sure it was." He folded his arms and raked her with a glance, his gaze settling, at last, on her face. "I'm just surprised that your dress and shoes would be so costly, considering what little there was of both."

Actually, Nick thought, that was overstating it. A wisp of red. Two slender straps. A pair of high-heeled sandals that made her legs long and endless…

One sandal. The other was broken, now that he took a closer look. That was the reason she'd lurched toward him. Still, those legs were as long and endless as he'd remembered. As long and glorious as they'd felt, wrapped around him when he'd tumbled her down onto the bed.

The feel of her beneath him. The soft thrust of her breasts. The scent of her hair. The taste of her mouth…

Nick frowned.

Terrific. He'd found a conniving little schemer in his bedroom, and just remembering what she'd felt like in his arms was enough to send his hormones into a frenzy.

Disgusted, he walked past her and paused before the mirrored wall that faced his bed, supposedly to straighten his tie when what actually needed straightening was his libido.

What was the matter with him? All right. Amanda Benning was beautiful. She was as sexy as sin. So what?

All his women were beautiful and sexy, but he hadn't stumbled across any one of them hiding in his bedroom, snapping photos with a camera that would have made James Bond envious, then coming to life in his arms when she'd decided the situation was desperate enough to require a distraction.

This was a setup. Nick was positive of it. What else could it be? His little sister, complaining about the furnishings of his apartment? It didn't ring true. Dawn never noticed her surroundings unless it was the once-a-year encampment their father demanded of her, and she only noticed then because she hated the heat, the dust, the inconvenience of sleeping in a tent.

As for Amanda—if she was an interior designer, then the moon was made of green cheese. And, dammit, she brought out the worst in him.

First he'd mauled her. No point in pretending, not to himself. He'd come on to her with the subtlety of a freight train, and never mind all his rationalizations about playing her game, or teaching her a lesson, or whatever nonsense he'd used to justify wanting to kiss her.

Then he'd come to his senses, started to let her go, but ended up trying to seduce her instead. That didn't make sense, either. Why would he try to seduce a woman whose motives for being in his bedroom were, at the very least, questionable?

And then there was the icing on the cake. The way he'd talked to Dawn, as if he really were the tottering ghost of old Rudy Valentino. Just thinking about it was humiliating. Nicholas al Rashid, stepping straight out of an outdated Hollywood flick, complete with flaring nostrils, attitude, and macho enough to make a camel gag.

The only thing he'd left out was the shoe-polish hair.

Yeah, he thought, yeah, he'd made a fool of himself.

And for what? Because he'd found Amanda Benning in his bedroom? He'd destroyed her disk, broken her camera. Abdul would give him a report on her in a little while and then he'd put the fear of God in her.

Nick's mouth twitched. The fear of his lawyers, to be specific. One well-worded threat and she'd be out of his life for good.

The world was full of women, lots of them as beautiful as this one. There was nothing special about her. His mouth thinned. There hadn't been anything special about her seven years ago, either, when his panic over Dawn was all that had stood between him and insanity—

"…an itemized bill."

Nick scowled at his reflection, turned and looked at Amanda, who'd come up to stand behind him. "What?"

"I said, I'll send you an itemized bill if you don't believe that I paid almost three hundred dollars for the dress."

"There's no need for that. Abdul—my secretary—will write you a check before you leave tonight."

"Good old Abdul," Amanda said pleasantly. "Still crawling around on his hands and knees, is he?" Her chin lifted. "Tell him to get busy, then, because I'm going straight out the front door the instant I get down—"

"No."

"No? But you just said—"

"You're not leaving so quickly, Ms. Benning."

"On the contrary, Sheikh Rashid. As far as I'm concerned, I'm not leaving quickly enough."

"You will leave here after I'm done with you. Dawn?" Nick smiled. "People are asking for you."

"Oh. But you said—"

"I know what I said. I've changed my mind. I'd prefer not to have to try to explain your absence."

"What's the matter?" Amanda said nastily. "Are you afraid people might be put off if they knew you were in the habit of locking women in your bedroom?"

The sheikh smiled at his sister. "Just behave yourself."

"Just behave yourself," Amanda said in wicked imitation. "What does that mean? Is she supposed to walk two paces to the rear?"

"Go on." Nick kissed Dawn's cheek. "Go downstairs and tell our guests I've been momentarily detained."

Dawn hesitated. "What about Amanda?"

Nick's smile thinned. "I'll take care of her."

"Dawn?" Amanda said, but Dawn shook her head and hurried out of the room. Abdul seemed to materialize in the doorway.

"There you are, Abdul," Nick said.

"My lord."

"Has it arrived?"

"Yes, my lord."

Nick nodded. Abdul bent down, then straightened up with two elaborately wrapped boxes in his arms.

"On the bed, please."

The little man walked to the bed and put the boxes down. Then he bowed his body in half and backed out of the room.

"Those are for you."

Amanda looked at the things lying on the bed as if they might start ticking.

"A dress," Nick said lazily, "and a pair of shoes."

"Are you crazy?"

"I would be, if I let you slip away without confirming your reasons for being here." He jerked his head at the boxes. "I guessed at your sizes."

"I'm sure you're an expert," she said coldly.

"And," he said, ignoring the taunt, "I did my best to describe the style of your things to the concierge."

"How nice for the concierge." She folded her arms and lifted her chin. "But you should have told her to order them in her size."

"In his size," Nick said with a little smile, "but I doubt if they're quite to his taste."

"Maybe you didn't hear me before, Sheikh Rashid. I said I wanted a check to pay for my things, not replacements."

"And you shall have a check. But I've no intention of letting you go just yet, Ms. Benning. Dawn's things won't fit you. And I certainly won't permit you to insult my guests by moving among them while you look like something no self-respecting cat would drag home."

Amanda's brows rose. "If you honestly think I want to go to your party—"

"I'm not interested in what you think, honestly or otherwise. But I must attend my party, as must my sister. And, since I need to keep you here for another few hours, I have no choice but to subject my guests to your presence."

Heat swept into her face. "You are the most insulting man I've ever had the misfortune to meet."

"Ah, Ms. Benning. That breaks my heart." Nick pointed a commanding finger at the boxes. "Now, take those things into the dressing room. Change your dress and shoes. Fix your hair and do whatever is required to make yourself presentable. Then you will emerge, take my arm, stay at my side all evening, comport yourself with decorum and speak to no one unless I grant permission for you to do so."

"In your dreams!"

"If you do all that, and if your so-called interior design credentials check out, you will be free to leave. If not…"

"If not, what?" Amanda's jaw shot out. "Will you lock me in the dungeon?"

His smile was slow and heart-stopping in its male arrogance. "What a fine idea."

"You—you…"

Nick looked at his watch. "You have five minutes."

"You're a horrible man, Sheikh Rashid!"

"I'm waiting, Ms. Benning." He looked up, his cold silver eyes locked on hers. "Perhaps you require my assistance."

Amanda snatched the boxes from the bed and fled into the dressing room. Angry tears blinded her as she stripped off her dress and kicked her shoes into a corner. Then she opened the packages and took out what Nick had bought her.

The dress looked almost like the one he'd ruined, except it had surely cost ten times as much and seemed to have been fashioned of cobwebs instead of silk. The shoes were elegant wisps of satin and slid on her feet as if they'd been made for her.

Nick rapped sharply on the door. "One minute."

She looked at herself in the mirror. Her eyes were bright. Her cheeks were pink. With anger, she told herself. Of course with anger. And it was anger, too, that had sent her heart leaping into her throat.

She ran her fingers through her hair, bit her lips to color them. Then she threw back her head, unlocked the door and stepped into the bedroom.

Nick was leaning back against the wall, arms folded, feet crossed at the ankles. He gave her a long, appraising look, from the top of her head to her feet, then up again. "I take it the dress and shoes fit."

His tone was polite, but when his eyes met hers, they were shot with silver fire. She could feel the heat swirling in her blood.

"I despise you," she said in a voice that sounded far too breathless.

He uncoiled his body like a lazy cat and came toward her. "Liking me isn't a prerequisite for the night we're about to spend together."

"We aren't," she said quickly, even though she knew he was baiting her, that he was really just referring to the time she'd be with him at his party. "There's no way in hell I'd spend the night with—"

He bent and brushed his mouth over hers. That was all he did; the kiss was little more than a whisper of flesh to flesh, but the intake of her breath more than proved she was lying.

She knew it. He knew it. And she hated him for it.

"The Sheikh," she said, her eyes cool.

"I beg your pardon?"

"The Sheikh, starring Rudolph Valentino. It's an old movie. You'd love it. Be sure and rent the video sometime."

Nick laughed. "I can see we're going to have a delightful evening." He held out his arm. She tossed her head. "Take it," he said softly, "unless you'd rather I lift you into my arms and carry you."

Amanda took his arm. She could feel the hardness of his muscles, the taut power of his body through his clothing—but mostly, she could feel the race of her own heart as he led her out of his bedroom and to the wide staircase that led downstairs.

CHAPTER FIVE

AMANDA knew all about making an entrance.

Her father, a California businessman who owned a department store and had hopes of building it into a chain, had put his three beautiful little daughters in front of the cameras whenever he could. They'd promoted everything from baby clothes to barbecue grills.

"Lick your lips, girls," he'd say just before he'd walk them out. "And give 'em a big smile."

The small-town lawyer she'd married had turned into a publicity-hungry politico looking for national office before she'd had time to blink.

"Smile," he'd say, and he'd put his arm around her waist as if he really cared, just before walking her into a room filled with strangers.

Her stepfather, Jonas Baron, was the exception. Jonas owned almost half of Texas but he didn't much care about entrances or exits. He never sought public attention but he couldn't escape it, either.

Still, nothing could have prepared her for what it was like to make an entrance on the arm of the Lord of the Desert.

"Oh, hell," Nick said softly when they reached the top of the stairs.

Oh, hell, indeed, Amanda thought as she looked down.

A million faces looked back. And oh, the expressions on

those faces! All those eyes, shifting with curiosity from the sheikh to her...

She jerked to a stop. "Everyone is watching us," she hissed.

"Yeah." Nick cleared his throat. "I should have realized this might happen. It's because I'm late."

"Well, that's not my fault!"

"Of course it's your fault," he growled.

"I'm not going down there. Not with you."

Nick must have anticipated that she'd move away because his free hand shot out and covered hers as it lay on his arm. To the people watching, it would have looked like a courtly gesture, but the truth was that his hand felt like a shackle on hers.

"Don't be ridiculous. They've all seen us. As it is, tongues will wag. If you run off now, there'll be no stopping the stories."

"That's your problem, Lord Rashid, not mine."

He looked at her, his eyes narrowed and hard. "You're my sister's oldest friend." Slowly, he began descending the steps with Amanda locked to his side. "And you've come to pay her a visit."

"I'm the immoral creature who led her astray. Isn't that what you mean?"

"You haven't seen each other in ages, not since—when?"

She looked at him. His mouth was set in a polite smile.

"How charming," she said coolly. "You can speak without moving your lips."

"When did you and Dawn last see each other?"

"Two weeks ago, at lunch. Not exactly 'ages', is it?"

Nick's hand tightened over hers. "Just keep your story straight. You're Dawn's friend. You've kept in touch over the years. She heard you were in town and invited you to her birthday party."

They were halfway down the steps. Amanda looked at all

those upturned faces. The only thing lacking was a trumpet fanfare, she thought, and bit back a hysterical bark of laughter.

"Did you hear me, Ms. Benning?"

"I heard you, Lord Rashid. But I'm not visiting New York. I live here. I know you'd prefer to think I live in Casablanca and that I'm a spy."

"What I think, Ms. Benning, is that you watch too many old movies."

"What am I supposed to say if people ask why you and I came downstairs together?"

It was, Nick decided, an excellent question. "Tell them... tell them I hadn't seen you in a long time."

"Not long enough," Amanda said, smiling through her teeth.

"You and I were catching up on old times."

"Ah. Is that some quaint Quidaran idiom that means you were trying to jump my bones?"

Nick stopped so abruptly that she stumbled. He caught her, his arm looping tightly around her waist.

"Listen to me," he growled. "You are to behave yourself. You will smile pleasantly, say the proper thing at the proper moment. And if you don't—"

"Don't threaten me, Lord Rashid. I'll behave, but not because I'm afraid of you. It's because I've no desire for ugly publicity."

"Afraid it might ruin your image?" he said sarcastically.

"Being seen with you will be enough to do— What are they doing?"

The question was pointless. She could see, and hear, what all those people down there were doing. They were applauding.

"They're applauding," Amanda said, and looked at him.

Nick gave her a smile so phony she wondered if it made his mouth hurt.

"I know."

"Well, why are they—"

"The applause is for me."

She looked down again, into that sea of smiling faces, at the clapping hands. Then she looked at Nick. Definitely, that smile had to be painful.

"They're clapping for you?" she said incredulously.

"Must I repeat myself?" A muscle tightened in his cheek. "It is the custom."

"The custom?"

"Do you think you're capable of making a statement, Ms. Benning, instead of following each question with another? Yes. It is the custom to applaud the prince on his birthday."

"Well, it's dumb."

Nick laughed. Really laughed. "It is indeed."

"Then why do you permit it?"

He thought of a hundred different answers, starting with three thousand years of history and ending with the knowledge that had come to him only after more than a decade of trying to push his country into the twenty-first century—the simple realization that not even he could accomplish such a thing quickly.

He could tell Amanda Benning all of that, but why should he? She wouldn't understand. And the odds were excellent that if he did, she'd rush to sell that morsel of news to the highest bidder.

As it was, he was doing everything possible not to think about her trying to sell the sordid little tale of what had gone on in his bedroom. Surely his lawyers' threats would stop her. And if that didn't do the trick, he'd deny whatever she said. But would he be able to deny the memory of those moments to himself? The feel of her in his arms? The taste of her on his tongue?

Of course he would, he thought calmly.

"I permit the applause," he said, "because it is the custom."

"That's ridiculous."

"We have other customs you would probably call ridiculous, as well, including one that demands a woman's silence in my presence until I grant her permission to speak."

"Is that a threat?"

"It's a promise."

Amanda shook her head in disbelief. "I have no idea how Dawn tolerates you."

"And I have no idea how someone like you managed to insinuate yourself into my sister's life. Now, smile and behave yourself."

"You're a horrible man, Lord Rashid."

"Thank you for the compliment, Ms. Benning."

They reached the bottom of the steps. Nick smiled. So did Amanda. The crowd surged forward and swallowed them up.

An hour later, Nick was still leading Amanda from guest to guest.

If her ex could only see her now, she thought wryly.

Not wanting to be stage center was one of the first things they'd quarreled over, but that was where she'd been all evening. If there'd been a spotlight in the room, it would have been beamed at her head.

Nicholas al Rashid might be the Lord of the Realm, the Lion of the Desert, the Heir to the Imperial Throne and the Wizard of Oz, but not even he could control people's tongues. And those tongues were all wagging. Wagging, Amanda thought grimly, at top speed.

"My sister's friend," he said each time he introduced her. "Ms. Amanda Benning."

The answers hardly varied. "Oh," people said, "how... interesting."

She knew that what they really wanted to say was that if she was Dawn's friend, why had she made such a spectacular entrance on his arm, with no Dawn in sight? For that matter, where was Dawn now?

On the other side of the room, that was where. Dawn had smiled and waggled her fingers, but clearly, she was going to adhere to the rules and keep her distance.

As Nick was walking her toward another little knot of people, Amanda snagged a glass of wine from a waiter and took a sip.

Rules. The sheikh was full of rules. And, fool that he was, he seemed to think people abided by them.

"You see?" he'd said smugly, after he'd marched her around for a while. "No one's asking any questions. It wouldn't be polite."

Idiot, Amanda thought, and took another mouthful of wine.

Etiquette could keep people from saying what they were thinking, but nothing could stop the thoughts themselves or the buzz of speculation that followed them around the room.

Finally, she'd had her fill.

"I don't like this," she murmured. "Everyone is talking about me."

"You should have thought of that possibility before you sneaked into my bedroom. Keep moving, please, Ms. Benning."

"They think I'm your—your—"

"Probably." Nick's jaw knotted; his hand clasped her elbow more tightly as he steered her toward the terrace door. "That's why it's important to show no reaction to the whispers."

"There isn't anything to whisper about," Amanda said crossly. "Can't you tell them that?"

Nick laughed.

"I'm glad you find this so amusing." She yanked her arm

free of his hand as they stepped into the cool night air. "Can't you tell them—"

"Sire?"

Amanda looked over her shoulder. Abdul, looking more like a pretzel than a man, came hurrying toward them.

"Your slave approacheth," she said, "O Emperor of the World."

Nick ignored her as Abdul dropped to one knee. "What is it, Abdul?"

The old man lifted his head just enough to give her a meaningful look. Nick sighed, eased his secretary to his feet and led him a short distance away. He bent his head, listened, then nodded.

"Thank you, Abdul."

"My lord," Abdul said, and shuffled backward into the living room.

"He's too old to be doing that whenever he comes near you."

"I agree. But—"

"Don't tell me. It's the custom, right? And we wouldn't want to ignore the custom even if it means that poor little man has to keep banging his knees against the floor."

Nick's jaw shot forward. "Abdul was my father's secretary. He was my grandfather's apprentice clerk. This is the way he's always done things, the way he expects to do..." He stopped talking. Amanda was looking at him as if he were some alien species of life. "Never mind," he said coldly. "I'm not going to spend the evening in debate."

"Of course not, because you know you'd lose."

"What I know," Nick said even more coldly, "is that Abdul's just reminded me of some things that need my attention. You're on your own."

Amanda raised her hands and flexed her wrists. "Off with the handcuffs," she said brightly.

"You're to keep away from Dawn."

"Certainly, sire."

"You're not to bother anyone with personal questions."

"Darn," she cooed, batting her lashes. "And here I was, hoping to ask the governor what he wore to bed."

"Other than that, you're free to move among my guests unattended."

"Does that mean I passed the background check?"

"It means I'm too busy to go on playing baby-sitter, and that if you try to leave before I'm done with you, you'll be stopped by my security people."

"How gracious of you, Lord Rashid."

Nick flashed a grim smile. "What man would not wish to be gracious to you, Ms. Benning?" he answered, and strolled back into the brightly lit living room.

"Good riddance," Amanda muttered, watching him.

"Nicky!"

He was halfway across the room when Deanna Burgess launched herself into the sheikh's arms. Amanda's eyebrows lifted. It was a warm greeting, to say the least, but the look she shot over his shoulder was far from warm.

Obviously, Deanna Burgess knew Nick had made his entrance with her on his arm. Of course she knew, Amanda thought grimly. She drank some more wine. Two hundred and fifty absolute strangers had witnessed that entrance and the odds were excellent that most of them were still talking about it.

Oh, if only she could get that sort of publicity for Benning Designs.

Amanda lifted her glass to her mouth. It was empty. She tilted it up and let the last golden drops trickle onto her tongue. Time for another drink, she thought, and strolled into the living room.

There had to be a way to turn this disaster into something useful. Dawn's original plan certainly wasn't going to work now. No way would the sheikh agree to let Benning Designs decorate the penthouse.

Amanda smiled at the bartender, put down her empty glass and exchanged it for a full one.

Think, she told herself, think. What would Paul do? Her ex, with his toothpaste smile, had been unsurpassed at turning political liabilities into political bonuses.

She took a drink. Mmm. The wine was delicious. And cooling.

Jonas, then. Her stepfather was the sort of man who'd never let a difficult situation stop him. What would Jonas do?

"…old friend, or so he…"

The whispered buzz sounded as clearly as a bell in the seconds it took the chamber quartet to segue from Vivaldi to Mozart. The little knot of people that had produced it looked at her. Amanda looked back, lifted her glass. One man colored and lifted his, too.

The bastards were, indeed, talking about her.

She buried her frown in her glass.

If only they'd talk about Benning Designs instead of Amanda Benning, but there was no way that would happen. Not even Jonas Baron could turn this silk purse into a sow's ear. Or maybe it was the other way around. Even old Jonas would be helpless in this situation. The best he'd do would be to come up with some creaky saying.

Like, you had to roll with the punches. Like, those were the breaks. Like, when life hands you lemons…

"Make lemonade," Amanda said, and blinked.

"Sorry?"

She swung around, gave the bartender a big smile. "I said, could I have another glass of wine, please?"

Glass in hand, smiling brilliantly, she headed straight for the little group of whisperers.

"Hello," she said, and stuck out her hand. "I'm Amanda Benning. Of Benning Designs. I apologize for making His

Highness late for his own party, but I had him all excited." She smiled modestly and wondered if the woman to her left knew her mouth was hanging open. "He's so private, you know."

"Oh," the woman with the hanging jaw said, "we know!"

"He probably thought it would upset me if he told anyone what we'd really been doing upstairs."

Four mouths opened. Four heads leaned toward her. Amanda tried not to laugh.

"I'd just shown him some fabric swatches, and he—Nicky—well, he just loved them." She did laugh this time, but in a way that made it clear she was sharing a charming anecdote with her new acquaintances. "And then he wanted to see some paint chips, and before we knew it, the time had just flown by."

Silence. She knew what was happening. She hoped she did anyway. The little group of guests was processing what she'd said. Come on, she thought impatiently, come on! Surely one of you wants to be first—

"You mean," the man who'd had the decency to blush said, "you're the sheikh's interior decorator?"

"His interior designer." Amanda smiled so hard her lips ached. "And I can hardly wait to get started. I had to shift my calendar around to make room for the sheikh—"

"Really."

"Yes. Really." Amanda curled her free hand around the slender shoulder strap of her evening purse and hoped nobody could see her crossed fingers. "The vice president will be a bit put out, I know, but, well, when the Lion of the Desert makes a request—"

"The vice president? And the sheikh?" The woman with the drooping jaw was almost drooling as she leaned closer. "Isn't it funny? That you should mention interior decorating, I mean?"

"Design," Amanda said, and smiled politely.

"Oh. Of course. But what I meant is, we've been thinking of redoing our cottage in the Hamptons."

Amanda arched a brow. A cottage in the Hamptons. She knew what that meant. A dozen rooms, minimum. Or maybe fifty.

"Really," she said with what she hoped was the right mix of politeness and boredom. "How nice."

A waiter floated by with a tray of champagne. She grabbed his elbow, swapped her now empty glass for a flute of bubbly and took a drink. Her head felt light. Well, why wouldn't it? She hadn't eaten in hours.

"I wonder, Ms Benning…would you have time to fit us in?"

Thank you, God. Amanda frowned. "I don't know. My schedule—"

"We'd be grateful if you could just come out and take a look."

"Well, since you're friends of the sheikh—"

"Old friends," the woman said quickly.

"In that case…" Amanda opened her evening purse and whipped out a business card. "Why don't you phone me on Monday?"

"Oh, that would be wonderful."

Wonderful didn't quite do it. Incredible was more like it. She fought back the desire to pump her fist into the air, made a bit more small talk and moved on to the next group of guests.

Before long, her cards were almost all gone. Everybody seemed to want one now that they knew she was Amanda Benning, the sheikh's designer. It wasn't a lie. Not exactly. She'd have been his designer if Dawn's plan hadn't backfired.

"Ms. Benning," someone called.

Amanda smiled, relieved a waiter of another flute of champagne and started toward the voice. Whoa. The floor was tilting. She giggled softly. You'd think a zillion-billion-million-dollar penthouse wouldn't have warped—

"Amanda."

A pair of strong hands closed on her shoulders. She looked up as Nick stepped in front of her. Wow. His head was tilting, too.

"Are you enjoying yourself?"

How come he wasn't smiling? Amanda gave him a loopy grin. "How 'bout you, Nicky? Are you envoy—enboy—enjoying you'self?" she said, and hiccuped.

Nick marched her through the room, out the door and onto the terrace. It wasn't deserted as it had been before. He clutched her elbow, kept her tightly at his side as he walked her past little clusters of guests.

"Hello," he kept saying. "Having a good time?"

"Hello," Amanda sang happily. "Havin' a goo' time?"

Someone laughed. Nick laughed, too, but his laughter died once they turned the corner of the terrace. "Just what do you think you're doing?" he demanded in a furious whisper.

Amanda blinked owlishly. It was darker out here. She couldn't see Nick's face clearly, but she didn't have to. He was angry, angry that she'd finally been having fun.

"Half my guests are marching around, clutching your address and phone number."

She giggled. "Only half?" Champagne sloshed over the edge of her glass as she raised it to her lips. "Jus' let me finish this and I'll— Hey," she said indignantly as he snatched the flute from her hand. "Give me that."

"Who told you that you could hand out business cards?"

"Who told me? Nobody told me. I didn't ask. I wouldn't ask! People don't need permission to hand out business cards."

"They do when they're in my home."

"Tha's ridiculous."

"I won't have you bothering my guests."

"Oh, for goodness' sake, I wasn't bothering anybody." She laughed slyly. "Matter of fact, your guests are eager to meet me."

"I'll bet they are."

"Ever'body wants the sheikh's designer to do their house."

"You're not my designer," he said coldly. "And as soon as they realize that, your little scheme will collapse."

"A minor teshnic—technic—a minor inconvenience."

Nick's eyes narrowed. "And you're drunk."

"I'm not."

"You are."

"No, I'm not," she said, and hiccuped again.

"Have you eaten anything tonight?"

"No."

"Why not?"

Amanda lifted her chin. "I was too busy drinking wine."

Nick said something under his breath. She looked at him.

"Was that Quidaran again? Must have been. I couldn't understand it."

"Be glad you didn't," he said, his voice grim. "Let's go, Ms. Benning."

"Go where?"

"You need a pot of strong coffee and a plate of food."

The mention of food made her stomach lurch. "No. I'm not hungry."

"Coffee, then. And something for your head before it starts to ache."

"Why should it…?" She caught her breath. "Ow," she whispered, and put the back of her hand to her forehead. "My head hurts."

"Indeed." Nick pulled her into the circle of his arm and led her to the end of the terrace.

"Is that a door?"

"That's what it is. Let me punch in the code."

The door swung open. Amanda took a step and faltered. Nick lifted her into his arms, carried her inside, kicked the door shut and switched on the light. She threw her arm over her eyes. "Agh. That's so bright."

"I'll turn it down. Okay. Sit here. And don't move."

She sat. It didn't help. Her head spun. Or the room spun. Either way, she felt awful.

"Nick?"

"Here I am. Open your mouth."

She opened an eye instead. He was holding out a glass and four tablets.

"What's that?"

"I know you'd like to think it's poison, but it's only water and something that'll make your head feel better."

"How about my stomach?" she said in a whisper.

Nick grinned. "That, too. Go on. Take them."

She took the tablets and gave them a wary look. "Are they from Quidar?"

Nick didn't just grin, he laughed. "They're from a pharmacy in Bond Street. Come on. Swallow them down."

She did. He took the glass from her.

"Now, put your feet up." His voice sounded far away, but he was right there, beside her. She could feel his hands, lifting her. Shifting her so her head was propped on something. A bed? A pillow?

His lap.

"Where are we?" she mumbled, and opened one eye.

"My study," Nick said.

The room was small, with an interior door that she assumed led into the rest of the penthouse. It was cozy, she thought. Everything looked lived in: the threadbare old rug, the battered leather sofa and the equally battered desk.

"Dawn didn't show me this."

"No." His voice hummed with amusement. "She doesn't have the combination, so it wouldn't have been on the dollar tour. Shut your eyes and let the tablets do their job."

She did. For five minutes. For an hour. Time passed; she

had no idea how long she lay there. A hand stroked her forehead and she sighed and turned her face into it.

A knock sounded at the door.

Nick lifted her head gently from his lap. She lay back, eyes closed, heard a door open, heard him say, "Thank you," heard the door swing shut.

"Coffee," Nick said. "Freshly ground and brewed."

"It's wonderful to be king," Amanda murmured.

"Wonderful," he said dryly. "Can you sit up?"

She did. He held out an enormous mug, filled to the brim with liquid so black it looked like ink.

She took it, held it in both hands. "It's hot."

"Clever of you to figure that out."

"It's black."

"Clever again."

"I like cream and sugar in my coffee."

"Drink it," he said, "or I'll grab your nose and pour it into your mouth."

He looked as if he might do just that. Amanda drank, shuddered, and drank again. When the cup was empty, she gave it to him. He refilled it, looked at her, sighed and put it down on the desk. Then he took a chair, turned it backward, straddled it and sat.

"Better?"

"Yes." Amazingly, it was true. "What was in those tablets?"

Nick smiled. "You'll have to let me take you to London to find out."

The words were as teasing as his smile, but they made her breath catch.

"You're not being a tyrant," she said.

"It's late, and I'm tired. It takes too much energy to be a tyrant twenty-four hours a day." He folded his arms along the back of the chair, propped his chin on his wrists. "Abdul finished checking you out."

"Ah. Am I Mata Hari?"

"He says you live alone."

Amanda sighed, shut her eyes and laid her head back. "He's a genius."

"He says you're divorced."

She put her index finger to her mouth, licked it, then checked an imaginary scorecard in the air.

"Why?"

Amanda's eyes popped open. "Why what?"

"Why are you divorced?"

"That's none of your business."

"You made everything about you my business when you crept into my room and started taking photographs."

"God, are we back to that? I told you—"

"You were getting data so you could redo my apartment." He reached down, picked up her foot. Amanda tried to jerk it back.

"What are you doing?"

"Taking off your shoes." His hands were gentle though the tips of his fingers felt callused. Why would a sheikh who never did anything except order people around have callused fingers? she wondered dreamily, and closed her eyes as he began massaging her arch.

"Mmm."

"Mmm, indeed." Nick cleared his throat. What in hell was he doing? Well, he wasn't a complete idiot. He knew what he was doing; he was sitting in the one room in the overblown, overfurnished, overeverythinged penthouse that really belonged to him with a woman's foot in his lap. And he was thinking something insane. Something totally, completely crazy.

He let go of Amanda's foot, shoved back his chair and stood up.

"You didn't do the mayor's mansion."

Amanda opened her eyes. "No," she said wearily. "I didn't do that penthouse, either."

"Then why did you lie?"

"Dawn lied, not me. I'm a designer, but not the way she said."

"Meaning?"

"Meaning, I've never had a real client."

Abdul had said as much. "Not one?"

"Not unless you count my mother. And my stepbrother. But I'm a good designer. Damned good."

"Don't curse," Nick said mildly. "It isn't feminine."

"Is it feminine for a woman to curl around a man like a vine?"

"What?"

"Deanna Whosis. The woman in that magazine photo. I couldn't tell if she was trying to strangle you or say hello."

Nick grinned, hitched a hip onto the edge of the desk and folded his arms. "You're still tipsy, Ms. Benning."

"I'm cold sober." But if she was, why would she have asked him such a question? "She did it again tonight, too. She seems to think two objects can be in the same space at the same time."

"Jealous?" Nick said with a little smile.

"Why on earth would I be?"

"Maybe because it's a feminine trait."

"You haven't answered my question."

"You haven't really asked one."

"I did."

"You didn't. You asked me about vines and the laws of physics, but what you really want to know is if I'm involved with Deanna."

"I didn't ask you that."

"You didn't have to. And the answer is no, I'm not. Not anymore."

The answer surprised her. "But I saw—"

"I know what you saw. And I'm telling you, Deanna Burgess is history."

Amanda licked her lips. "As of when?" she said softly, and held her breath, waiting for the answer.

"As of the minute I kissed you tonight," Nick said, and as he did, he knew it was the truth.

Amanda stared at him. Then she got to her feet. "It's late," she said, because it was all she could think of to say. Had he really gotten rid of Deanna Burgess because of her? No. The idea was preposterous. It was crazy.

Mostly, it was incredibly exciting.

Nick rose, too. "Deanna is gone, Amanda. From my home and from my life."

"I don't—I don't know why you're telling me this."

"Yes, you do." He put his hand under her chin and tilted her face up. "And I know why you asked."

"I don't know what you're..." Her breath hitched. He was moving his thumb gently over her mouth, tracing its contours. "Nick?"

"I like the way you say my name."

He bent his head, his eyes locked to hers and followed the path his thumb had taken with his lips.

"Kiss me," he said in a rough whisper. "Kiss me the way you did before."

"No," she said, and thrust her hands into his hair, pulled his head down to hers and kissed him.

Moments later, centuries later, she shuddered and pulled back.

"I didn't come here for this."

"No." Nick bent his head, pressed his open mouth to the pulse racing in the hollow of her throat. "Neither did I."

"Nick." She put her hands on his chest to push him away. Instead, her fingers curled into the lapels of his tux. "I'm not a woman who sleeps around."

"That's fine. Because I'm not a man who believes in sharing."

"And I'm not looking for a relationship. My divorce wasn't pleasant. Neither was my marriage. It will be a long, long time before I get involved with another—"

Nick kissed her again, his mouth open and hot. She moaned, swayed, and his arms went around her.

"My life is planned," she whispered. "I was my father's devoted daughter, my mother's rock, my husband's puppet."

"I don't want any of that from you."

"What do you want, then?"

He took her face in his hands. "I want you to be my mistress."

CHAPTER SIX

IT WAS, she realized, a joke.

A bad joke, but a joke all the same. What else could it be?

A man she hardly knew, a man she'd done nothing but argue with, had just told her that he wanted her to be his mistress. He'd said it—no, he'd announced it—with certainty, as if it were an arrangement they'd discussed and agreed to.

A joke, absolutely. Or a sign of insanity…but was what the sheikh had said any more insane than what she'd been doing? Kissing him. Hanging on to him. Aching for him, this rude, self-important stranger…

This gorgeous, sexy, incredible man who'd held her gently when she felt ill.

Amanda's head whirled. She stepped back, tugged down her skirt, smoothed a shaking hand over her hair. Homey little gestures, all of them. Well, who knew?

Maybe they'd restore her equilibrium.

Or maybe she'd misunderstood him. That was possible. After all, just a little while ago, she'd felt as if a crazed tap dancer was loose inside her skull. Could a headache make you hear voices? Could it leave you suffering from delusions?

Was she crazy, or was he?

"Amanda?"

She looked up. Nick's face gave nothing away. He looked

like a man waiting for a train. Calm. Cool. Collected. Surely he wouldn't look like that if he was waiting for her to say yes.

Heat spiraled through her, from the pit of her belly into her breasts and her face. What in hell was she thinking? She wouldn't. In fact, she should have slapped his face at his words. The sheikh wanted a new sexual toy and he figured she'd be thrilled to discover she was it.

He wasn't only crazy; he was insulting. She told him so, succinctly, coldly, carefully. And the SOB just smiled.

"I should have kept count of the number of times you've called me crazy tonight."

"Yes, you should. It might tell you something about your behavior, Lord Rashid."

"It's a little late for formality."

"It's never too late for formality and it's certainly not too late for sanity. Did you really think I'd agree to your offer?"

"Actually," he said, his mouth twitching just a little, "I thought you might slug me."

"An excellent idea." She stepped back, her hands on her hips, a look of contempt on her face. "I suppose it's been your experience that women become delirious with joy when you offer them such a wonderful opportunity."

Nick tucked his hands into his pockets. "I don't know. I've never, ah, made the offer before."

"Uh-huh. I'll just bet. Nicholas al Rashid, Lion of the Desert, Heir to the Imperial Throne, Lord of the Realm... and Celibate of the Century." She lifted a hand, examined her fingernails with care before looking at him again and flashing a toothy smile. "You never asked a woman to be your mistress?"

"No." He leaned back against the edge of the desk, crossed his feet at the ankles. "Usually the relationship simply... develops."

"Ah. You usually show a bit more finesse." She smiled brightly. "How nice."

Clearly, her sarcasm didn't impress him. He shrugged, his expression unchanging.

"Our situation is different. It called for a bolder move." His eyes, silver as rain, met hers. "You want a commission." The quiet tone in his voice changed just a little, took on a husky edge. "I want you."

Say something, Amanda told herself. Tell him he's being offensive, that he can't go around saying things like this to women. But he wasn't saying it to "women," he was saying it to her. She was the one he wanted. And she, heaven help her, and she...

Stop it!

She stood up straighter, cocked her chin and flashed a cool smile. "I see. You get a night in the sack. I get a job."

"No."

"Don't 'no' me, Lord Rashid." Amanda's tone hardened. "That's what you said. I'll sleep with you, and you'll give me a job. Do you have any idea how incredibly insulting and sleazy that offer is?"

Nick sighed and shook his head. "You're never going to make a success of—what was it? Benning Designs?"

"You're wrong. I'll make a huge success of it and I'll do it without accepting your charming proposition," she said caustically, "because I'm good. Damn good."

"You won't succeed," he said calmly, "unless you learn to pay attention." He folded his arms, lowered his chin, looked at her as if she'd just flunked the final exam in her business administration course. "I didn't say I wanted to sleep with you. I said I wanted you to be my mistress."

"It's the same thing."

"Not at all." Nick smiled coolly. "Sleeping with you would mean an hour of pleasure. Taking you as my mistress means pleasure for as long as our desire for each other lasts."

Heat seeped into her blood again, warmed her flesh and turned her bones to jelly. How could he talk so calmly about such a thing? Odder still, how could she hear those calm words and feel as if he were touching her skin?

"Either way, I'm not going to do it. I'd never trade my body for your checkbook."

"And a lovely body it is," Nick said, and uncoiled from the edge of the desk.

Amanda took a quick step back. The warning was there, burning in his eyes. "Nick," she said, "wait a minute—"

Her shoulders hit the wall as he moved forward. And when he reached for her, her heart leaped like a rabbit.

"I'll fight you," she said in a breathless whisper. "Nick, I swear…"

His hands encircled her wrists. That was all. He didn't kiss her, didn't gather her to him. Just that, the feel of his fingers on the pulse points in her wrists, but it was enough to turn her body liquid with desire.

"A spectacular body," he said softly. "And a face more beautiful than any I've ever seen." Nick lowered his head. She lifted hers. Lightly, lightly, he brushed his mouth across her slightly parted lips. "But I'm not asking for either in trade."

"No?" Amanda cleared her throat. Her voice sounded small and choked. "Then—then what's this all about?"

His eyes fell to her lips, then returned to lock with hers. "It's about desire," he murmured, and he bent his head and nuzzled the hair back from her face, pressed his hot mouth against her throat.

Don't, she thought, oh, don't. Don't fight. Don't move. Don't respond to him at all. But she trembled and made a little sound she couldn't prevent, and she knew that her pulse leaped under the stroke of his fingers.

"We're both intelligent adults, Amanda."

"Exactly. That's why I expect you to understand that what you want is impossible."

He smiled. "Anything is possible when you really want it."

She gave a little laugh that sounded forced even to her own ears, but it was the best she could manage at the moment. "Do you think I'm stupid? Or is that the plan, Nick? You're going to convince me of how foolish I am unless I agree to sleep…" She took a breath. Why was she arguing with him? He wanted something. She didn't. That was that. "Let go of me," she said.

He did. It was what she'd wanted, but she felt chilled without his hands on her, and that was silly. The night was warm. So was the room. And yet, without Nick to hold her…

Amanda swallowed, turned her back and walked to the window. It was very late. The moon had gone down and a breeze sighed around the windows. It made the shrubs that lined the terrace tremble under its touch, just as she had trembled under Nick's.

"You're right," she said, her voice low. "We're both adults. I'm not going to be coy and pretend I don't know what happens when you touch me. But I don't intend to give in to it." She took a breath, slowly let it out. "What went on in your bedroom? That wasn't me. You probably won't believe it, but I've never…I mean, no one has ever—"

"Except for me."

He spoke from just behind her, so close that all she had to do was take a step back to be in his arms again.

"Yes." She felt his hand move lightly over her hair and she fought back the urge to shut her eyes and give herself up to the caress. "But it won't happen again."

"I regret what happened, too." His voice thickened and he cleared his throat. "I've never come on to a woman with so little tact. I know I should apologize, but—"

"Don't." She spun around, looked at him, her cheeks on fire, her eyes glittering. "You wanted honesty. Well, the truth is that we were both at fault."

"We wanted each other. There's no fault in that."

"I don't much care how you choose to explain it, Nick. It was wrong. And I'm not going to change my mind about sleeping with—"

She gasped as he pulled her to him. "I could take you to bed right now."

"You could." Her chin rose and her eyes locked with his. "You're much stronger than I am."

His eyes went flat and cold. "Do you think I'm the kind of man who takes a woman by force?"

She didn't. She couldn't imagine him forcing himself on a woman any more than she could imagine a woman walking away from his bed.

"No," she whispered. "You're right. You wouldn't do that."

He shifted his weight, slid his hands up her body, leaving a trail of heat in the wake of his palms.

"All I'd have to do is kiss you. Touch you. How long would it take before you'd be naked in my arms, begging me to finish what we began in my bedroom hours ago?"

"No," she said again, but her voice trembled, and she couldn't meet his eyes.

"Yes," he said. "But that's not what I want. I want more. Much more."

He dropped his hands to his sides, turned away and walked across the small room. He stood with his back to Amanda, his hands clenched in his pockets.

Earlier tonight, in his bedroom, he'd wanted nothing more than a quick, hard ride. The blonde with the golden eyes beneath him, her skin slick with heat, her head thrown back...

That would have been enough.

Later, watching her drift from group to group at the party, seeing her make the best of what he knew had to be a difficult situation, he'd smiled a little, decided it might be pleasant to spend not an hour but a night with Amanda Benning in his bed.

Deanna had caught him looking. She'd said something cutting that was meant to remind him that his loyalty was supposed to be to her, but all she'd done was make him face what he'd known, and not admitted, for weeks.

He'd had enough of Deanna.

She was beautiful, but she was proof of the old adage. Beauty was, after all, only skin-deep. And so he'd taken her aside, gently told her that they were finished, and after a scene that had been uglier than he'd expected, he'd come back into the living room, taken one look at Amanda and realized she was drunk.

"Shall I deal with the lady, Lord Rashid?" Abdul had whispered, and Nick had sighed and said no, he'd take care of it… but somewhere between the living room and his study, he'd realized that he was wrong.

One night with Amanda wouldn't be enough.

He was hungry for her, and she was hungry for him, and only a fool would have imagined they'd have enough of each other between sunset and sunrise.

No, Nick thought, watching her face, one night wouldn't be sufficient. He wanted time to learn all the textures and tastes of this woman's mouth. Of the secret places of her body. She was a feast that would keep a man busy for a month of nights.

He turned and looked at her. "Have you ever gambled, Amanda?"

The sudden shift in conversation made her blink. "Gambled?"

"Yes. Did you ever bet on something?"

"No. Well, yes. I went to Las Vegas once. With my sisters. Sam played the slots. Carin played poker. I watched a roulette wheel for a while." Her brow furrowed. "What's this have to do with anything?"

"Indulge me," Nick said with a smile. He sat on the edge of the desk. "Did you bet? On the wheel, I mean?"

"Eventually."

"And?"

"And," she said, her chin lifting, daring him to say anything judgmental, "after I'd lost a hundred bucks, I quit."

Nick lifted his brows. "Interesting."

"I couldn't see the sense in losing more money."

"Ah. And you figured why bother betting unless you had a better chance of winning."

"Something like that."

"Suppose somebody offered you the chance to make a bet where you controlled the odds."

Something had changed in his smile. It made her uncomfortable. This whole conversation made her uncomfortable. She knew it was ridiculous, but talking about his wanting to sleep with her made her less uneasy than talking about bets and stakes and odds.

"Well," she said, "that, um, that would be, um, interesting."

Not as interesting as the way he was looking at her. His gaze was intense, as if she were the only thing in the universe worthy of his attention. It was flattering. It was disturbing. It reminded her of something she'd almost forgotten.

Once, just after her mother had married Jonas and gone to live at Espada, she'd visited the ranch and gone horseback riding in the hills that surrounded it. She'd dismounted beside a clear-running stream, tied the reins to a tree branch, strolled maybe a hundred yards—and come almost face-to-face with a cougar.

The cat had looked at her. She'd looked at the cat. And when it finally hissed and melted into the trees, she'd known that she'd gotten away because it had chosen to let her go, not because she'd been brave enough to stare it down.

That was how she felt now. Her heart gave a little shiver. As if she'd gone for an innocent stroll and ended up face-to-face with a cougar.

Nick reached back, slid open a drawer in the desk, took something from it. A coin, she saw. A bright silver coin. He smiled, tossed it, caught it in his hand. "Heads or tails," he said. "What do you think?"

"I think it's time I went home. Good night, Nick. It's certainly been—"

"Scared?"

She sighed, rolled her eyes, folded her arms over her chest. "Heads."

"Heads it is." The coin spun through the air. Nick caught it, showed it to her. "Good guess. How about another try?"

"Oh, for heaven's… Heads."

He tossed the coin again, caught it, held out his hand. The silver piece lay, heads up, in his palm.

"Great," she said with an artificial smile.

"One last time." Nick tossed the coin. It spun like quicksilver before he caught it and closed his fingers around it. "What's it going to be this time? Heads or tails?"

"This is… Okay, I'll humor you. Tails. It has to be. I remember enough of my college stats course to know that the odds of it coming up heads again are…"

He opened his hand. She blinked.

"…One in six," she said, and frowned. "How'd you do that?"

He smiled, tossed the coin to her. She caught it, examined it, then looked at him.

"Heads on both sides," she said. "It's a phony."

"The gentleman who gave it to me preferred to refer to it as a device for assuring a positive outcome."

Nick grinned. She almost smiled back at him. He had, she thought, a wonderful smile…but then she thought of the cougar, of how she could never have matched either its strength or its cunning, and she felt more like running than smiling.

"If there's a point here," she said carefully, "I don't get it."

He rose to his feet, came slowly toward her, his smile gone. The room seemed to have reduced in size until there was barely space in it for the both of them. Foolishly, she held out the coin. Nick shook his head, took her hand, folded her fingers around it.

"Keep it," he said softly.

"I—I don't want it. I don't—"

"Amanda." He clasped her shoulders, slid his hands down her arms, twined his fingers with hers. "We're going to make a bet, you and I." A slow, sexy smile curled across his mouth. "A bet that will assure you of a positive outcome."

"Nick, I told you. I don't gamble. Just that one time..."

"You're going to give me a week of your life."

Her eyes widened. "A week of my—"

"One week." He kissed her, his mouth tender, soft against hers. "Just seven days."

"Nick, listen to me. You can't just—"

"When the week ends, I'll sign a contract with Benning Designs."

"Damn you!" Amanda jerked her hands free. "Haven't you heard a word I said? I won't sleep with you for a contract."

"No," he said softly, "I'm sure you won't."

"Great. We understand each other. Now, I'm going to open this door. And you're not going to stop me."

"I'll sign the contract whether you've slept with me or not."

"What?" She moved past him, dragged a hand through her hair. "What is this? Another quaint custom straight from the homeland? I wasn't born yesterday. Do you really think I believe life is like that coin of yours? Heads on both sides?" She frowned, opened her hand and looked at the quarter. "Where'd you get this anyway?"

Nick sighed. "It's a long, dull story."

"Amazing." She smiled brightly. "I just happen to be in the mood for a long, dull story."

"I was sixteen, and I stopped to watch a guy working a three-card-monte game in Greenwich Village. Each time he thought a mark—"

"A what?"

"A player." Nick grinned. "Or, more accurately, a loser. Whenever he thought a loser was going to leave, he'd take a coin from his pocket, show it and say, 'Call it. Double or nothing.' It never came up anything but heads."

"And the reason the Heir to the Imperial Throne was standing on a corner, betting against a street hustler, was…?"

"Well, it was fun."

"Fun," she said dryly.

"Yeah. I was at a private prep school."

"Of course," Amanda said politely.

"My tuition was paid, but my father was strict about my allowance. I wanted more money for something—I don't recall what. And my mother was in Europe, making a movie. Anyway, I was pretty good with cards. It was a weekend and I had nothing better to do—"

"So you went down to the village and got hustled." She narrowed her eyes at him. He had to have invented the story. The Lion of the Desert, a cardsharp? "And, what? The guy gave you the coin?"

He laughed softly. "I paid him twenty bucks for it. I figured it made a great souvenir."

"Uh-huh. He hustled you. And now you're trying to hustle me. Did you really think I'd fall for that?" Amanda tossed the coin on the desk. "The 'you give me a week and I'll give you a contract' routine?"

"Well, no." Nick put one hand on the wall beside her and slid the other around the back of her head. "Actually, I didn't."

"Ha," she said, and tried to pretend she didn't feel the drift of his fingers along the nape of her neck. "I knew there was a catch."

He gave her the kind of smile that made her heart try to wedge its way into her throat. "I meant what I said. You'll give me a week. If we become lovers, you get the contract. If we don't…" He took her hand and brought it to his mouth. "If we don't, you still get the contract." His eyes met hers, and what she saw in them made her feel dizzy. "But if you do give yourself to me," he said softly, "then you'll agree to be my mistress. To be available only to me, accessible only to me, for as long as it suits us both." A quick smile angled across his mouth. "Despite what you may think, I believe in equality of the sexes."

His words, the way he was looking at her, conjured up images more erotic than anything she'd ever experienced in a man's arm. Talk, that was all it was. Not even Nicholas al Rashid could really expect her to accept such a proposition.

"I mean every word," he said softly.

She tilted her head up, stared into his eyes and knew, with breathtaking certainty, that he did.

He turned her hand over, brought it to his mouth again, kissed the soft flesh at the base of her thumb. "Are you afraid to trust yourself?"

Amanda laughed. "Such modesty. Do you really think—"

He kissed her even though he knew it was a mistake. The last thing a wise man would do right now was give Amanda Benning graphic proof of how sure he was he'd win the bet.

But he'd underestimated her. She made a little sound as their mouths met, but that soft, sweet whisper of breath was the only sign she gave of the emotional storm he knew raged within her. It made what lay ahead all the more exciting.

"You're very sure of yourself, Lord Rashid."

"As are you, Ms. Benning." He smiled. "You'll be a worthy adversary."

"If I were to accept your proposition. But it's out of the question. It's so outlandish."

"Is it?"

She started to answer, caught herself just in time and wondered if this was really happening.

Yes. Yes, it was.

Twenty-five stories below, a siren wailed through the night. Music from the party drifted under the door. Life was going on all around them; people were doing the things people did on a warm evening in Manhattan...and she stood here, discussing whether or not she'd agree to become the mistress of a man she hardly knew.

It wouldn't happen. There wasn't even a remote possibility she'd let Nick seduce her. He was handsome. All right. He was gorgeous. He was rich and powerful and he ruled a desert kingdom.

But a man would need more than that to get her into his bed. She was a twenty-first-century American woman. She was educated and independent and she couldn't be lured into a man's arms like some trembling virgin.

What she could do was win the bet.

A week. That was all he'd asked. Seven days of what would basically be simple dating. And, at the end of those days, she'd walk away from Nicholas al Rashid with her virtue intact, a contract in her pocket. She'd give the man who thought he could buy everything a lesson in how to choke down a large helping of humble pie.

She had to admit the possibility was intriguing.

"Well?" Nick said.

Amanda looked at him. She could read nothing in his face, not even desire. Oh, yes. He'd be very good, playing cards.

"Tell me," she said softly, "have you ever wanted something you couldn't have?"

"You're doing it again. Answering a question with a question."

"You've asked me to allow you to try to seduce me." She smiled tightly. "I think that entitles me to ask as many questions as I like."

"Are you afraid I'll succeed?"

"Seduction requires a seducer and a seducee, Lord Rashid. You can't succeed unless I cooperate." This time, her smile was dazzling. "And I promise you, I'd never do that."

"Is that a yes?"

Her eyes met his. She could see something there now, glinting in the silver depths. What do you think you're doing, Amanda? a voice inside her whispered.

"There'd have to be rules," she said.

"Name them."

"No force."

"I'm not a man who believes in forcing himself on a woman."

"No tricks."

"Certainly not."

"And I don't want anybody to know that we've entered into this— this wager." She hesitated. "It would be difficult to explain."

"Done."

He held out his hand as if they were concluding a business deal. She looked at it, then at him. Amanda, the voice said desperately, Amanda...

She took a quick step back. "I'll—I'll think about it," she said, the words coming out in a rush.

Nick reached for her. "You already did."

And then his mouth was on hers, she was curling her arms tightly around his neck, and the wager was on.

CHAPTER SEVEN

AT FOUR forty-three in the morning, Nicholas al Rashid, Lion of the Desert, Lord of the Realm and Sublime Heir to the Imperial Throne of Quidar, gave up all attempts at sleep. He threw back the blankets, swung his legs to the floor, ran his fingers through his tousled hair and tried to decide exactly when he'd lost his mind.

A man had to be crazy to do the things he'd done tonight. He'd found a woman going through his things, accused her of spying, made passionate love to her, locked her in his closet and, in a final show of lunacy, fast-talked her into a wager so weird he still couldn't believe he'd come up with it.

"Hell," Nick muttered.

He rose, paced back and forth enough times to wear a path in the silk carpet, pulled on a pair of jeans and went quietly down the stairs.

Not quietly enough, though. He'd hardly entered the kitchen when a light came on in the hallway that led to Abdul's rooms. A moment later, the old man stood in the doorway, wearing a robe and blinking against the light.

"Excellency?"

It was, Nick thought with mild surprise, the first time he'd ever seen Abdul wearing anything but a black, somewhat shiny, suit.

"Yes, Abdul. It's me."

"Is something wrong, sire?"

"No, nothing. I just… Go on back to bed, Abdul."

"Did you want a sandwich?"

"Thank you, no."

"Some tea? Coffee? I shall wake the cook."

"No!" Nick took a breath and forced a smile to his lips. "I don't need the cook, Abdul. I just—I'm thirsty, that's all."

"Of course, sire." Abdul bustled into the kitchen. "What would you like? Mineral water? Spirits? Sherry? You're right, there's no need to wake the cook. I'll—"

"Abdul," Nick said pleasantly but firmly, "go back to bed."

"But, my lord—"

"Good night, Abdul."

The little man hesitated. Nick could see that he wanted to say something more, but custom prevented it. And a good thing, too, he thought grimly, because he had the feeling his secretary had developed as many doubts about his sanity as he had.

"Very well, Lord Rashid. If you change your mind—"

"I'll call you."

Abdul nodded, bowed and backed out of the room. Nick waited until the hall light went out. Then he opened the refrigerator, peered inside, found a bottle of the New England ale he'd developed a taste for back in his university days, and popped the cap. Bottle in hand, he walked through the darkened apartment and out onto the terrace.

The city lay silent below him.

At this hour on a Sunday morning, traffic was sparse, the sound of it muted. Central Park stretched ahead of him, its green darkness broken by the diamond glow of lamps that marked its paths.

Nick leaned against the low wall, tilted the bottle of ale to his lips, took a long drink and wished he were home. There'd been times before when he'd felt like this, when thoughts had whirled through his head and sleep had refused to come. The night before he'd left for Yale and a course of study that he knew would set him irrevocably on the path toward eventual leadership of his people. The night word had come of his mother's death in a plane crash. The night before he'd left for New York and the responsibilities that came with representing his country's financial affairs...

Nick took another drink.

Each time, he'd found peace by riding his Arabian stallion into the desert, alone under the night sky, the moon and the majestic light of the stars.

He sighed, turned his back to the city and swallowed another mouthful of ale. There was no desert to give him solace now. He was trapped in the whirlwind of his thoughts and the knowledge that nothing he'd done tonight made sense.

He wasn't a man who'd ever forced himself on a woman, yet he'd come close to doing that with Amanda Benning. Not that he'd have needed force. The way she'd melted against him. The way she'd returned his kisses, fitted her body to his...

Nick held the bottle of ale against his forehead, rolled it back and forth to cool his skin.

And that proposal he'd made her. Give me a week, he'd said. If I can seduce you, you'll agree to be my mistress.

Talk about acting like a second-rate Valentino, he thought, and groaned again. It was ludicrous. Besides, who knew if he'd even want her more than once? The lady might turn out to be a dud in bed instead of a smoldering ember just waiting to be fanned into an inferno.

"Dammit!"

Nick swung around and glared out over the quiet park. What was wrong with him? He was standing alone in the middle of the night, thinking about a woman he hardly knew, and doing one fine job of turning himself on.

Okay, so she'd probably be good in bed. Terrific, even. There really wasn't much doubt about that. Still, a man needed

more than sex from a mistress. Well, he did anyway. She had
to be interesting and have a sense of humor. She had to like
some of the things he liked. Riding, for instance. Walking in
the rain. Could she watch the film, When Harry Met Sally,
for the third or fourth time and still laugh over that scene in
the delicatessen?

Nick frowned. What was he thinking? So what if it turned
out Amanda didn't like those things? Deanna certainly didn't.
Rain made her hair frizzy, she said. Movies were boring the
second time around. And riding was best done in a limousine,
not on a horse.

The women who'd come before her had tastes different
from his, too.

All he'd ever asked of a woman was that she be attractive,
fun and, of course, good in bed. If Amanda had those quali-
fications, fine. He wanted to sleep with her, not live with her.
And she'd agreed.

He was making a mountain out of a molehill. It was a bet,
that was all it was. And he'd win it. He had no doubt about
that. They'd go to bed together and he'd take it from there.

The sky was lightening, changing from the black of night to
the pink of dawn. Somewhere in the leafy bowers of the park,
a bird chirped a sleepy homage to that first hint of day.

Nick yawned and stretched, then decided he felt much
better. Amazing what a little clear thinking could do. Okay,
then. In a while, he'd tell Abdul to call Amanda and inform
her that his car would pick her up at, say, seven this evening. That would get her here by seven-thirty for drinks and
dinner.

If they ever made it to dinner, he thought with a little smile.
As wagers went, this was the best he'd ever made. How come
he'd wasted half the night figuring that out?

He strolled back through the darkened penthouse, put the
empty bottle neatly on the kitchen counter, went up to his
bedroom, pulled off his jeans and threw himself across the

bed on his belly. He closed his eyes, yawned, punched his pillow into shape...

Twenty minutes later, he was still awake, lying on his back with his hands clasped under his head as he stared up at the ceiling. The distant whisper of the fax machine came as a relief.

Nick put on his jeans and went down to his study. The fax was long and still coming in. He plucked the first page from the basket, smiled as he read his father's warm greeting, but his smile changed to a frown as he read further.

His father, whose Arabian horses were world renowned, had reached agreement with an old American friend. He'd arranged to fly a stallion to the States in exchange for the friend's gift of a Thoroughbred mare. He hated to impose upon Nicholas on such short notice, etc. etc., but would he meet with the friend and work out the details in person?

Nick huffed out a breath. He would do it, of course. It would mean a day, perhaps two, spent out of the city, time during which he wouldn't be able to do what he had to do to win his wager with Amanda.

"Oh, for God's sake," Nick said, and tossed the fax on the table.

Enough was enough. The truth was, the bet was a bad one. A man didn't win a woman as if she were the stakes in a hand of poker. He didn't tempt her into his arms with a contract.

A smart man wouldn't want Amanda Benning at all. She was as prickly as a porcupine, as unpredictable as the weather. She was city heat; she was desert night. She was either the roommate who'd pointed his sister toward trouble seven years ago or the one who'd been wise enough to avoid it.

The one, the only, thing she absolutely was, was female.

So what?

He'd wearied of Deanna. That had to be the reason he'd been attracted to Amanda. Right?

"Right," Nick muttered.

Well, he could be attracted to another woman just as easily. He could have any woman he wanted. He could have his choice—blondes, brunettes and redheads in such profusion they'd cause a traffic jam, just lining up outside the door.

Nick went back upstairs, pulled on a white T-shirt and tucked it into his jeans. He put on sneakers, grabbed his wallet, his keys and his cell phone, went down the steps and into his private elevator. There was only one way to deal with this. He'd go to see Amanda, tell her the bet was off and put this whole foolish episode behind him.

He was in the elevator, halfway to the underground garage, when he realized he didn't have the slightest idea where she lived.

"Hell," he said wearily, punched the button for the penthouse and headed back the way he'd come. Was she in the phone book? he wondered as the door slid open…but he didn't have to bother checking. There, lying forlornly on a table, was one of those little business cards she'd been handing out like souvenirs.

Nick picked it up, lifted it to his nostrils. The card still bore a trace of her perfume. He shut his eyes, saw her as she'd gone from guest to guest, chin up, back straight, facing down the whispers and making the best of a difficult situation.

He frowned, looked at the address, then tucked the card into his pocket and rode the elevator down again. If the situation had been tough, it was her fault, not his. The only thing he cared about now was making sure she understood that he wasn't the least bit interested in following through on their bet.

Not in the slightest, he thought as his Ferrari shot like a missile into the quiet of the Sunday morning streets.

Amanda sat cross-legged in the center of her bed and watched the hands of the clock creep from 6:05 to 6:06.

Was the clock broken? She reached for it, held it to her

ear. Ticktock, it said, ticktock, which was what it had been saying since she'd checked it the first time, somewhere around four.

She frowned, set the clock down on the night table and wrapped her arms around her knees. The only thing that wasn't working was her common sense.

What on earth had she done?

"You said you'd sleep with Nicholas al Rashid," she muttered. "That's what you've done."

No. Her frown deepened as she unfolded her legs and got out of bed. No, she thought coldly, she most definitely had not done anything as simple as that.

What she'd done was agree to become Nick's newest sexual toy, assuming he managed to seduce her in the next seven days.

God, it was hot in here!

She padded to the window where an ancient air conditioner wheezed like the Boston terrier her mother had once owned. She put her hand to the vents and waggled her fingers. An anemic flow of cool air sighed over her skin.

"Great," she said. No wonder she couldn't sleep.

Amanda jerked her nightgown over her head, marched into the bathroom and stepped into the shower, gasping at the shock of the cold water. It was the only way to stay cool in this tiny oven of an apartment. The place was so hot that when she'd awakened at four, she'd been drenched in very unladylike sweat.

She lowered her head and let the water beat against the nape of her neck,

She'd been dreaming just before she awoke. A silly dream, something straight out of a silent movie. Nick had been dressed in a flowing white robe and riding a white horse. She'd been seated behind him, her arms tight around his waist, her cheek pressed to his back. And then the scene had shifted, and he'd been carrying her into a tent hung with royal-blue silk.

"Amanda," he'd said softly as he lowered her to her feet, and she'd sighed and lifted her mouth for his kiss….

Shower or no shower, she was hot again. But not from the dream. Certainly not from the dream. It was the apartment, she thought briskly. The stuffy, awful apartment.

Amanda turned off the water and blotted herself dry. She ran her fingers through her hair, tugged an oversized cotton T-shirt and cotton bikini panties over her still-damp skin and headed for the kitchen.

"Forget about sleep," she muttered.

Obviously, it wasn't a very good idea to drink lots of champagne before bedtime, especially if you spent the time between the wine and the attempt at sleep in the arms of a man who thought he could talk you into something he was certain you couldn't possibly refuse.

She filled the kettle with water, set it on the stove and turned on the burner.

Thought, Amanda?

"Let's be honest here," she said.

Nick had talked her into it. And— to stay with the honesty thing—he hadn't had to work all that hard to do it.

What a smooth character he was. Proposing a wager like that, making it sound so simple…

But, of course, it was.

Amanda sighed, walked to the window and gazed at the view. It wasn't exactly Central Park, but she could see a tree. All she had to do was stand on her toes, crook her neck, tilt her head and aim at a spot beyond the fire escape.

Nick wouldn't know what that was like. To have to contort yourself for a view. For anything. What Lord Rashid wanted, Lord Rashid got.

And Lord Rashid wanted her.

Well, he wasn't going to have her. And wouldn't that come as a huge surprise? All he'd get out of their wager was a handsomely furnished home. As for a woman to warm his bed—he'd always have plenty of those. A man like that would.

The kettle whistled. She turned off the stove, took a mug from the cupboard, dumped a tea bag into it and then filled it with water. She looked at the sugar bowl, turned away, then looked at it again.

"The hell with it," she said, and reached for the bowl.

Calories didn't count tonight. Comfort did, and if that meant two, well, three heaping spoonfuls of that bad-for-you, terrible-for-your-teeth and worse-for-your-waistline overprocessed white stuff, so be it.

"Ah," she said after her first sip.

The tea tasted wonderful. Funny how a hot liquid could make you feel cooler. She hadn't believed it until she'd spent a couple of weeks visiting her mother in Texas last year.

"Hot tea cools you off," Marta had insisted, and when Amanda finally tried it and agreed it was true, she'd hugged her and smiled. "You just come to me for advice, sweetie, and I'll always steer you right."

Amanda took another sip of tea as she walked through her postage-stamp living room, sank into a rocker she'd rescued from a sidewalk where it had awaited death in the jaws of a garbage truck, and watched the sun claw its way up the brick sides of the city.

What advice would her mother offer about Nick? That was easy. She knew exactly what Marta would say.

"Mandy, you have to telephone that man this minute and tell him you can't possibly agree to the wager. A lady does not bet her virtue."

Excellent advice it would be, too.

Not that she was afraid she'd lose the bet. Amanda took a drink of tea and leaned back in the rocker. A woman who didn't want to be seduced couldn't be seduced. It was just that the implications of the wager were—well, they were...

Sleazy? Immoral?

"Humiliating," she mumbled.

Yes, she would call Nick and tell him the wager was off. She'd reached that conclusion hours ago. How best to do it, though? That was the problem.

She'd thought about calling Dawn for suggestions, but then she'd have to tell her all the details, and what, exactly, was there to say?

Hi, sorry we didn't get the chance to spend any time together last night. Are you okay? And oh, by the way, I've agreed to become your brother's mistress if he can first lure me into his bed.

No way. Discussing this with Dawn wasn't even an option. Neither was discussing it with Marta. How could a daughter tell her mother she'd even considered a proposal like that?

Amanda drank some more tea.

She could call one of her sisters for help, but there wasn't much sense in that, either. Carin would just tell her, in that irritatingly proper tone of voice, that if a deal sounded too good to be true, it probably was. As for Samantha...she couldn't begin to imagine what Sam would say unless it was something outrageously facetious, maybe that the deal sounded like lots of fun if it weren't for all the bother involved.

"Fun," Amanda muttered, and drained the last sugary drops from the mug.

Okay, then. She'd just have to do the deed without consulting anybody but herself. Phone Nick, tell him she was sorry but she'd changed her mind. Not that she was afraid she'd lose their bet, but...

Amanda scowled. Why did she keep telling herself that? Certainly she wouldn't lose it.

Someday she'd tell her sisters the story. They'd laugh and laugh; the whole thing would be one big joke.

"He was a sheikh," she'd say, "and he said, 'Come wiz me to zee Casbah.'"

Except he hadn't. If only he had. If he'd played the scene

as if he'd stolen it from a bad movie, with a smoldering look and a twirl of his mustache...

She groaned and closed her eyes.

The truth was, Nick was gorgeous and sexy. He could have any woman he wanted, but he wanted her.

She had to admit it was thrilling. Maybe that was the reason she'd lost all perspective. Maybe it was why she'd let him fast-talk her into agreeing to a bet on her own morality.

Was that the doorbell? Amanda sat up straight. Who'd be at her door at this hour? This building had awful security, but still, did burglars really ring the bell and announce themselves?

The bell rang again. She rose to her feet and hurried to the door. "Who is it?"

"It's Nick."

Nick? Her heart thumped. She opened the peephole, peered out. It was Nick, and he didn't look happy.

"Nick." Her mouth felt as dry as cotton. "Nick, you should have called first. I—"

"I didn't want to wake you."

"You didn't want to wake me? What did you think leaning on my doorbell at—at what, six in the morning, would do?"

"It's seven-thirty, and if you want to have a discussion about the propriety of phoning first, I'd prefer having it in your apartment. Open the door, please, Amanda."

Open the door. Admit Nick into this tiny space. Into her space, where he'd seem twice as tall, twice as big, twice as commanding.

"Amanda." There was no "please" this time. She jumped as his fist thudded against the door. "Open up!"

She heard a lock click, a door creak open. Oh, God. Her neighbors were preparing themselves for a bit of street theater. New Yorkers might live on the same floor in an apartment building, collect their mail at lobby boxes ranged side by side and never so much as make eye contact, but she suspected none of them would pass up a little drama going on right in the hall.

Amanda rose on the balls of her bare feet, put her eye to the peephole and looked at Nick. "People are listening," she whispered.

"And watching," he said coldly. "Perhaps you'd like to sell tickets."

She stepped back, slipped the lock, the chain and the night bolt. The door swung open and he stepped inside.

"An excellent decision," he said, and shut the door behind him.

"What are you doing here, Nick?"

What was he doing there? Just for a second, he couldn't quite remember. Amanda was standing before him, bare-footed. She was wearing a loose T-shirt and nothing else. Nothing he could see anyway. Her hair was tousled, her face was scrubbed and shiny, and he couldn't imagine anything more urgent than finding out if she tasted as sweet and fresh as she looked.

But that wasn't why he'd come here, Nick reminded himself, and folded his arms. "I want to talk," he said.

"Good." She lifted her chin. "That's—that's really good. Because I—I..." She stopped, the words catching in her throat, and stared at him.

"What's the matter?"

"You're not wearing a tux."

"No." His smile was all teeth. "No, actually, I've been known to get through an entire day without feeling the need to put on a pair of pants with satin stripes down the legs."

"I didn't mean—it's just that you look—you remind me—"

"Of the night we first met." She was right, he thought, and gave her a long, measuring look, except she was older now, and the soft curves outlined beneath the cotton shirt were more lush. "Instant replay," he said, and flashed a smile that upped the temperature in the room another ten degrees.

Amanda stepped back. "I'm not dressed," she said, and blushed when she realized how stupid she sounded. "For company. If you'll just wait—"

"I've been awake half the night. I'll be damned if I'll wait any longer."

"Look, Nick, I want to talk, too. About that bet. Just let me put on some clothes."

"You're already wearing clothes." His voice turned husky as he took a step toward her. "What else would you call what you have on?"

Provocative, he thought, silently answering his own question, although how a T-shirt could be provocative was beyond him to comprehend. He liked his women in silk. In lace. In things that flowed and shimmered.

"Nick?"

"Yes." Somehow, he was standing a breath away from her. Somehow, his hands were on her hips. Somehow, he was bunching the cotton fabric in his hands, lifting it, sliding it up her skin and revealing the smallest pair of white cotton panties he'd ever seen.

"Nick." Her voice was barely a whisper. Her head was tilted back; her eyes were huge, luminous and locked with his. "Nick, the bet is—"

He bent his head, brushed his mouth over hers. She gave a delicate moan, and he cupped her breasts, felt the delicate weight and silken texture of them in his palms. He feathered his thumbs over the crests and Amanda moaned again, trembled against him and lifted herself to his hungry embrace.

He kissed her over and over, offered her the intimacy of his tongue, groaned when she touched it with her own, then sucked it into the heat of her mouth. He backed her against the wall; she gave a cry of protest as he took his lips from hers to peel off her shirt, then his.

Oh, the feel of her satin skin against his, when he took her back into his arms. The softness of her breasts against the hardness of his chest. He trembled, felt the air driven from his lungs.

"Amanda," he whispered, and she sighed and kissed him, breathed a soft "yes" against his lips as he lifted her off her feet and into his arms—

A buzz sounded from his pocket.

"Nick?"

His pocket buzzed again.

"Nick." Amanda tore her mouth from his. "Something's buzzing."

He lifted his head, his breathing harsh. She was right. His cell phone was making sounds like an angry wasp. He mouthed an oath, let her down to her feet, kept an arm firmly around her as he dug the phone from his jeans.

"What?" he snarled.

"Sire."

Nick's eyes narrowed. "Abdul. This had better be important."

"It is, my lord. There is a fax from your father. I thought you would wish to know of it."

The color was high in Amanda's cheeks. He could read her eyes, see her growing embarrassment. She looked up at him, shook her head and tried to step away. Nick bent quickly and kissed her, his mouth soft against hers until, at last, she kissed him back.

"Lord Rashid? There is a fax—"

"I already saw it, Abdul. Goodbye."

"Excellency, it is a second fax and arrived only moments ago. Your father asks if you would fly to this place called Texas—"

"He asked me that in the first fax. Dammit, Abdul—"

"He asks if you would fly there today. The stallion he sent

arrived much sooner than expected, and the animal has been hurt in transit."

Nick uttered a violent oath. The only place he wanted to be right now was in Amanda's bedroom, but he knew the importance of duty and obligation. Would the woman in his arms be as understanding?

"Call the pilot," he said gruffly. "Have him ready the plane. You are to pack me some clothes, Abdul. Meet me at the hangar in an hour with the things I'll need."

Abdul was still speaking when Nick hit the disconnect button, tossed the phone aside and tried to gather Amanda close to him again, but she was unyielding, moving only her arms, crossing them over her naked breasts in a classic feminine gesture that somehow went straight to his heart.

"It's good that you're leaving." Her voice was steady, but her face was pale. "You're not to come here again, Lord Rashid. I know I agreed to the terms of our wager, but—"

"The wager is off, Amanda. I came here to tell you that." Her golden eyes widened; he knew it wasn't what she'd expected him to say. He wanted to draw her close and kiss her until the color returned to her cheeks. Instead, he picked up her discarded shirt and wrapped it gently around her. "Here," he said softly. "You must be cold."

Cold? She was swimming in heat from his touch, from imagining what would have happened if Abdul hadn't called—but she knew better than to let him know that.

"Thank you," she said stiffly.

"I don't want you as my mistress because of a bet," Nick said, his eyes locked to hers. "I want you to be mine because you desire no other man but me. Because you find joy only in my arms."

Her heartbeat stumbled, but the look she gave him was sharp and clear.

"You amaze me," she said with a polite smile. "You're always so sure you'll get what you want."

"We'd be making love right now if that call hadn't interrupted us."

"I'm not going to argue with you."

"No." He smiled. "You won't, because there's nothing to argue about. You know that I'm right."

She took a step back. "I want you to leave. Right now."

"I don't think that's what you want at all."

He moved quickly, drew her into his arms and kissed her. She told herself his kisses meant nothing, that she wouldn't respond…but it was Nick who ended the kiss, not she.

"All right," she said stiffly, "you've proved your point. Yes, I—I've thought about what it would be like to—to…" She gave a shuddering breath. "But it would be wrong. I know that. And, unlike you, I don't always give in to my desires."

"Why would it be wrong?"

"Why?" Her laugh was forced and abrupt. "Well, because…because…dammit, I don't have to justify my decision to you!"

"You can't even justify it to yourself." Nick put his hand under her chin and tipped her head up until their eyes met. "I can't get out of this trip, Amanda. Do you understand?"

"I'm not a child," she said coldly. "Certainly I understand. You're going away on business and you'd like me to be waiting for you when you get back. Well, I'm sorry to disappoint you, Lord Rashid, but I won't be."

"You won't have to be, not if you go with me."

"What?"

"We'll only be gone a day or two." He bent his head, brushed his mouth over hers. "Come with me, Amanda."

"No!" She laughed again and tried to wrench free of his hands. "You must think I'm an idiot!"

"I think you're a woman with more courage than she gives herself credit for. And I think you want to say yes."

"Well, you think wrong. We've agreed our wager is—"

"Off. And it is." And what, exactly, was he doing? He never

mixed business with pleasure. Then again, this wasn't really a business trip. It was just a couple of days on a ranch in Texas. "Come with me," he urged, rushing the words together, knowing that his thinking was somehow flawed, that it would be dangerous to think too long or hard about what he was asking her to do. "We'll simply be a man and a woman, getting to know each other."

"I know you already. You're a man who can't take no for an answer. Besides, I can't just—just up and leave. I have a business to run."

"And I'm your client. Don't look so surprised, sweetheart. I said our wager was off. I didn't say I wanted to go on living in an apartment that looks like an expensive hotel suite." Nick linked his hands in the small of Amanda's back. "If you come with me, you can ask me all the questions you like. About my tastes. My preferences. You need to know them in order to decorate my home, don't you?"

"Yes." She chewed on her lip. "But…"

But what? He was making it sound as if going away with him was the most logical thing in the world, but it wasn't. She'd just trembled in his arms. His hands had been on her breasts, and oh, she'd wanted more. Much more. She'd wanted to touch him as he'd touched her. To lie naked in his arms, to feel the weight of him as he filled her—

"Amanda?"

His voice was low and rough. She didn't dare look at him because she knew what she'd see in his eyes.

"We'll talk. Only talk, if that's what you want." Nick raised her face to his. "Say you'll come with me."

She knew what her answer should be. But she gave him the answer they both wanted—with her kiss.

CHAPTER EIGHT

NICK wouldn't tell her where they were going.

"It's a surprise," he said, when she asked.

He knew it was crazy not to tell her, but what if he said they were flying to a ranch in Texas and she said she hated ranches and everything about them? What if she said she didn't like riding fast and hard across the open range? It might turn out she'd never seen a horse except maybe in Central Park and that would be all right just so long as she smiled and said yes, that would be wonderful, when he offered to teach her to ride.

"Hell," Nick muttered as he paced the length of Amanda's living room.

Maybe he really was crazy. He'd met this woman last night. Well, he'd met her years ago, but he'd never gotten to know her until last night, never held her in his arms until then. What did it matter if she liked horses or hated them? If she didn't want to sit behind him in the saddle, her arms wrapped around his waist, her breasts pressed to his back as they rode not across the green hills of north-central Texas but over the hot desert sands?

Crazy was the word, he thought grimly, and swung toward the closed bedroom door. All right. He'd knock on the door, tell her politely that he'd changed his mind. She was right. There was no reason for her to go with him. He'd phone when he got back and they'd have drinks, perhaps dinner....

The door opened just as he reached it. Amanda stood in the opening, holding a small carry-on bag. "I packed only what you said I'd need. Jeans. Shirts." She gave a little laugh. "I don't know why you're being so mysterious about this trip. I mean, it's hard to know what to take when you don't know the destination. What is it, Nick?"

Her face was flushed, her eyes bright. She was wearing jeans and a cotton shirt, she hadn't bothered putting any makeup on her face, and he wanted to tell her he'd never seen a more beautiful woman in his life.

"Whatever you've packed is fine," he said gruffly, and he took the carry-on from her, linked his fingers through hers and tried to figure out exactly what was happening to him.

His plane was a small, sleek jet.

Amanda had flown in private aircraft before. Two of her stepbrothers owned their own planes. Her stepfather did, too; in fact, Jonas had a small jet, similar to Nick's in size— but Jonas's plane didn't have a fierce lion painted on the fuselage.

Nobody bowed to Jonas, either, but half a dozen people bowed as Nick approached the jet, half-prostrating themselves even though he waved them all quickly to their feet.

The Lion of the Desert, Amanda thought. Goose bumps rose on her skin. Yesterday, the words had been nothing but a title. A silly one, at that. Now, for the first time, she looked at the stern profile of the man walking beside her and realized that he was, in fact, a prince.

She tore her hand from his and stumbled to a halt.

"Amanda?"

"Nick." She spoke quickly, breathlessly. Her heart was racing as if she'd run here from her apartment instead of riding in Nick's Ferrari. "I can't go with you. I can't—"

Nick clasped her shoulders and turned her to face him. "My people won't blink an eye if I lift you into my arms and carry you on board," he said softly. "You could scream and kick, but they'd ignore you. Kidnapping a woman and keeping her in his harem is still the prerogative of the prince of the realm."

He was smiling. He was teasing her; she knew that. Still, she could imagine it happening. Nick, scooping her up in his arms. Carrying her onto the plane. Taking her high into the clouds, stripping away her defenses as he stripped away her clothes because yes, she wanted him. Wanted him...

"I made you a promise, sweetheart. And I'll keep it. You'll be safe. I won't touch you unless you want me to."

He held out his hand. She hesitated.

Have you ever gambled, Amanda?

The question, and her answer, were laughable. What was losing a hundred dollars at the roulette wheel compared to what she stood to lose now? And, thinking it, she put her hand in his.

He led her into a luxurious compartment done in deep shades of blue and gold. A pair of comfortable upholstered chairs flanked a small sofa. Everywhere she looked she saw the embroidered image of the same fierce lion that was painted on the outside of the plane.

"The Lion of the Desert," she said softly.

To her surprise, Nick blushed. "I suppose it seems melodramatic to someone who's lived only in the United States, but it's the seal of Quidar. It's been the emblem of my people for three thousand years."

"It's not melodramatic at all." Amanda looked at him. "It must be wonderful, being part of something so ancient and honorable."

"Yes," he said after a few seconds, "it is. Not everyone understands that. In this age of computers and satellites—"

"Of small, swift jets," she said with a little smile.

"Yes. In these times, it would be easy to forget the old ways. But they're important. They're to be honored even when it's difficult..." He paused in midsentence and smiled back at her. "Forgive me. I don't normally make speeches so early in the day." He bent down, pressed a light kiss to her forehead. "I'll be back in a minute, sweetheart. I just want to talk with Tom."

Who was Tom? she wondered. More importantly, who was this man who spoke with such conviction of the past? This man who'd taken to calling her "sweetheart"? It was far too soon for him to address her that way. She could tell him that, but it would have seemed silly, even prissy, and what was there in a word, anyway? He'd probably called a hundred other women "sweetheart." Set a hundred other women's hearts to beating high and fast in their throats.

Taken them away with him, as he was taking her.

But she wasn't those other women. She wasn't going to let anything happen between them. This was just a trip. A chance for her to discuss business with Nick. Business, she reminded herself when he came back into the cabin, sat on the sofa and drew her down beside him.

"We'll be in the air in a few minutes."

"Good," she said, and cleared her throat. "Who's Tom?"

"The pilot." Nick laced his fingers through hers. "I'm usually up there in the cockpit. But today I decided I'd rather be back here, with you."

"Ah," she said with a little smile. "So the prince sits beside his pilot and makes him nervous, hmm?"

He grinned. "The prince sits beside his co-pilot and flies the plane himself."

"You know how to fly?"

Nick settled back, put his feet up on the low table before the sofa and nodded. "I learned when I was just a kid. Distances are so vast in Quidar…flying is the easiest way to get from place to place."

"My stepbrothers say the same thing."

"It's the logical thing to do, especially when you're expected to put in appearances."

"Expected?"

"Uh-huh. It was one of my earliest responsibilities back home. Standing in for my father."

Amanda tried to imagine a boy with silver eyes taking on the burden of representing an absolute monarch.

"Back home. You mean, in Quidar."

"Yes." He lifted her hand, brought it to his mouth and brushed his lips over her knuckles. "I've spent a lot of my life in the States. My mother kept a home in California even after she married my father. But Quidar has always been 'home'. What about you?"

"Don't…" Her breath hitched. "Nick, don't do that."

His brows rose. "Don't ask about your childhood?"

She made a sound she hoped would pass for a laugh. "Don't do—what you're doing. Kissing my hand. You said you wouldn't. You said—"

"You're right." He closed his fingers over hers, then put her hand in her lap and folded his arms. "Tell me about yourself. Where is home for you?"

Her hand tingled. She could almost feel the warmth of his mouth still on her skin.

"I don't really think of anyplace as 'home'," she said briskly. "I was born in Chicago, but my parents were divorced when I was ten." Why had she stopped him from holding her hand? There was nothing sexual in it.

"And?"

"And," she said, even more briskly, "my mother got a job in St. Louis, so we moved there. After a year or so, she sent us—my two sisters and me—to boarding school. We'd go to visit her some holidays and my father on others." Take my hand, Nick. It was silly telling you not to. I like the feel of your fingers entwined with mine. "So, when I think of 'home'," she said, stumbling a little on the words, "sometimes it's Chicago. Sometimes it's St. Louis. Sometimes it's Connecticut, where I went to school. And there are times it's Dallas, where I lived when I was married."

"What was he like? Your husband?"

"Like my father," she said, and laughed. "I didn't realize it, of course, when I married him, but he was. Self-centered, removed...I don't think he ever thought of anyone but himself." Her breath hitched. Nick had taken her hand again. He was playing with her fingers, examining them as if they were new and remarkable objects.

"Did you love him?"

She blinked. He'd lifted his head. He was looking at her now, not at her hand, and he was still smiling, but the smile was false. She could see the tautness in his face, the glint of ice in his silver eyes.

"I thought I did. I mean, I wouldn't have married him if I—"

"Do you still?"

"No. Actually, I don't think I ever really...Nick? You're hurting my hand."

Nick looked at their joined hands. "Sorry," he said quickly, "I just—I..." He frowned, wondered why it should matter if Amanda Benning still carried the torch for her ex, then answered the question by telling himself he wouldn't want to bed any woman if she was still thinking about another man. "Sorry," he said again, and let go of her hand. "So." His tone was brisk, his smile polite. "You left Dallas and moved east. That must have been quite a change."

Amanda smiled. "Not as big a change as it must have been for you, going from Quidar to New York."

"Well, I spent lots of time in the States, growing up. And I went to school here." His smile softened. "But you're right. New York is nothing like Quidar."

"What's it like? Your country?"

He hesitated. Did she really want to hear about the desert, about the jagged mountains to the north and the sapphire sea to the south? She looked as if she did and, slowly, he began telling her about his homeland, and the wild beauty of it.

"I'm boring you," he said after he'd been talking for a long time.

"Oh, no." She reached for his hand, curled her fingers around his. "You're not. It sounds magnificent. Where do you live when you're there? In the desert, or in the mountains?"

So he told her more, about Zamidar and the Ivory Palace set against the backdrop of the mountains, about the scented gardens that surrounded it, about long summer nights in the endless expanse of the desert.

He told her more than he'd ever told anyone about his homeland and, he suddenly realized, about himself. And when he fell silent and she looked at him, her golden eyes shining, her lips bowed in a smile, and said Quidar must be incredibly beautiful, he came close to saying yes, it was. Very beautiful, and he longed to show it to her.

At that moment, the phone beside him buzzed. He picked it up, listened to his pilot give him an update on their speed and the projected time of arrival. He let out his breath and knew he'd never been so grateful to hear such dry statistics. The interruption had come at just the right time. Who knew what he might have said, otherwise?

The path back to reality lay in the sheaf of papers he knew he'd find inside the leather briefcase on the table beside him.

Carefully, he let go of Amanda's hand, reached for the case and opened it. "Forgive me," he said politely. "But I have a lot of reading to do before we reach our destination."

She nodded. "You don't have to explain," she said, just as politely. "I understand."

She didn't. He could see that in the way she shifted away from him. He'd hurt her. Embarrassed her. Taking his hand was the first gesture she'd made toward him and he'd rejected it.

Nick frowned and stared at the papers in his lap as if he really gave a damn about what they said. He was the one who'd direct their relationship. He would make no move unless she made it clear that was what she wanted, but inevitably, the start—and the finish—of an affair was up to him. It had always been that way, would always be that way.

Nick stopped thinking. He reached out, put his arm around Amanda's shoulders and drew her close.

"Come here," he said a little gruffly. "Put your head on my shoulder and keep me company while I wade through this stuff."

"Really, Nick, it's all right. I don't want to distract you."

"It's too late to worry about that," he said with a little laugh. "Sorry. I just—I have some things on my mind, that's all."

"Second thoughts about this trip?" she said, her tone stiff.

"Yes," he said bluntly, "but not about you."

"I don't understand."

"No, I don't, either." She looked up at him, her eyes filled with questions, and he sighed. "My brain is in a fog. Thinking about you kept me awake most of the night."

"That makes it unanimous."

"Well, why don't you take a nap, sweetheart? It'll take a few hours for us to get to Texas."

Amanda lifted her eyebrows. "Is that whe-ah we're a'goin'?" she said in a lazy drawl. "To Tex-as?"

Nick groaned. "That's terrible," he said, and grinned at her.

Amanda grinned back. "It's the best I can do. I'm not a native Texan."

"Better watch that phony accent." He touched the tip of her nose with his finger. "Our host is known for having a temper."

She yawned and burrowed closer, inhaled the scent of him. "Must be a Texas tradition. He can't have more of a temper than my stepfather. Are we going to a ranch? Is that why you told me to pack jeans?"

"Clever woman." She was cuddled up to him like a kitten, all warm, soft and sweet-smelling. Nick turned his head, buried his nose in her silken hair. "Yes. We're going to a ranch."

"Oh, that's nice," she said, and gave another delicate yawn.

"It is?"

"Uh-huh. Maybe we'll get the chance to go riding. I like horses. And I love to ride."

"Do you?" Nick said, knowing he was grinning like an idiot. "Like to ride, I mean?"

"Mmm."

"I do, too. My father breeds Arabian horses. They're an ancient breed. Graceful, fast—"

"Mmm. I know something about Arabians."

He smiled. "Really?"

"Arabian horses," she said, and laughed. Her warm breath tickled his throat. "My stepfather has a weakness for them."

"Well, so does the owner of the ranch we're going to. My father shipped a stallion to him, but something must have gone wrong during the flight."

"Where is this ranch? What part of Texas?"

"It's near Austin. Do you know the area?"

"A little. I've spent some time there. My mother and stepfather live nearby."

Nick put the briefcase aside, leaned back and gathered Amanda closer. He didn't much care about reading through the papers Abdul had provided. Not right now. All he wanted to do was enjoy the feel of Amanda, nestled in his arms.

"Perhaps they're familiar with the ranch we're going to."

"What's it called?" She smiled. "The Bar Something, right?"

Nick grinned and kissed her temple. "Wrong. It's called Espada."

Her body, so soft and sweetly pliant seconds ago, became rigid in his embrace.

"Espada?" She sat straight up and stared at him. "We're going to Espada?"

"Yes. Do you know it?"

"Do I...?" Amanda barked a laugh, pulled free of his arms and shot to her feet. "Yes, I know it. For heaven's sake, Nick! Jonas Baron owns Espada."

"Right. He's the man we're going to see."

"Jonas is married to my mother."

It took a minute for the message to sink in. "You mean— you mean, he's your stepfather?"

Amanda chuffed out a breath. "That's exactly what I mean."

Nick couldn't believe it. How could something like this have happened? The irony was incredible. He'd never taken a woman with him on a business trip until today—and now, his business trip was taking Amanda straight into the bosom of her family.

No, he thought, and bit back a laugh. No, it was impossible.

He never got involved with the families of the women he dated. Oh, he met mothers and fathers from time to time. You couldn't live the life he did and not have that happen. New York seemed like a big city to outsiders but the truth was that the inner circle, made up of financiers and industrialists, politicians and public figures, was surprisingly small.

After a while, the Joneses knew the Smiths and the Smiths knew the Browns and the Browns, of course, knew the Joneses. The names and faces all took on an almost stultifying familiarity.

But that wasn't the same as spending a weekend—a weekend, for God's sake—with a woman's parents.

He'd always been scrupulously careful about that. He'd turned down simple invitations to spend days in the country or on Long Island if it meant Daddy or Mommy would be there, and it hadn't a thing to do with anything as simple as the propriety—or the impropriety—of sharing the bed of the daughter of the house.

It had to do with far more delicate matters.

Family weekends were complications. They were far too personal. They created expectations he never, ever intended to fulfill.

"Dammit, Nick, say something! Didn't you hear what I said?"

He looked at Amanda. She was standing in front of him, her hands on her hips.

"Yes," he said slowly, as he rose to his feet. "I heard you."

"Well, I can't go there. To Espada. You'll have to tell Tim—"

"Tom," he said as if it mattered.

"I don't care what the pilot's name is!" She could hear her voice rising and she took a deep breath, told herself to calm down. "Nick, I'm sorry, but you'll have to take me back to New York. Or—or have your pilot—have Tom—land at an airport, any airport. I can take a commercial flight back to—"

"Amanda." He took her hands. "Take it easy."

"Take it easy?" She snorted, looked at him as if he were out of his mind. "Do you know what they'll think if I show up with you? Do you have any idea what my mother will—what Jonas will… Oh, God!"

She swung away. Nick caught her, drew her to him and wrapped his arms tightly around her. She was stiff and unyielding, but he didn't care. If anything, that was all the more reason to hold her close.

"They'll think we didn't want to be apart," he said roughly.

"Nick—"

"They'll think we just met and yes it's crazy, but the thought of being away from each other, even for a couple of days, was impossible."

"Nick," she said again, but this time her voice was soft and her eyes were shining when she lifted her face to his.

"They'll think I'm the luckiest man in the world," he whispered, and then her arms were around his neck, her mouth was pressed to his, and nothing mattered to either of them but the joy and the wonder of the moment.

CHAPTER NINE

THE afternoon sun was high in the western sky as Marta Baron settled into her chair on the upper level of her waterfall deck, smiled politely at her guests and wondered what on earth she was supposed to say to the stranger who was her daughter's lover.

At least, she assumed Sheikh Nicholas al Rashid was Amanda's lover.

It hadn't been a very difficult assumption to make.

The expression on the sheikh's handsome face when he looked at Amanda, the way he kept his arm possessively around her waist, even the softness in his voice when he used her name, were all dead giveaways.

He might as well have been wearing a sign that read, This Woman Belongs To Me.

Amanda was harder to read.

There was a delicate pink flush to her cheeks, and she had a way of glancing at the sheikh as if they were alone on the planet, but Marta thought she'd noticed an angry snap in her daughter's eyes when the sheikh's arm had closed around her—a look he had studiously ignored as he drew her down beside him on the cushioned teak glider.

"...so I said, well, why would I want to buy a horse from a man who couldn't tell the front end of a jackass from the rear?" Jonas said, and Marta laughed politely, along with everybody else.

She'd always considered herself a sophisticated woman, even before she'd assumed her duties as the wife of Jonas Baron. She'd lived through the sexual revolution, looked the other way when her girls were in college and one or the other of them had brought a boy home for the weekend. Not that she'd put them in one room, but she'd known that closed doors hadn't kept them from sleeping—or not sleeping, she thought wryly—in the same bed.

Not Amanda, though.

Marta smiled at something the sheikh said, but her attention was focused on her middle daughter.

Amanda had never brought a boy home. She'd never brought a man home, either; surely that ex-husband of hers didn't qualify. He'd been a self-serving, emotionless phony. Marta had only figured out why Amanda married him after the marriage ended, when she realized her daughter had been looking for the father she'd never really had.

Marta lifted her glass of iced tea and took a delicate sip.

One thing was certain. No one could ever mistake Sheikh Nicholas al Rashid for a father figure. He was, to use the indelicate parlance of the day, a hunk.

And she had to stop thinking of him as Sheikh.

"Please," he'd said, lifting her hand to his lips, "call me Nick."

She looked at him, seated beside Amanda. He was watching Jonas, listening to him, but his concentration was on the woman at his side. There was no mistaking the deliberate brush of that hard-looking shoulder against hers, the flex of his hand along her hip.

If Nick and Amanda weren't yet lovers, they would be, and soon. This was a man who always got what he wanted, and he wanted Amanda. But would he know what to do with her once he had her?

No, Marta thought, he wouldn't.

Nick was like a much younger version of her own husband. He was strong, powerful and determined. He was also, she was certain, often unyielding and immovable. A successful monarch needed those traits to run his empire—Jonas to rule Espada, Nick to rule Quidar.

Men like that were difficult to deal with. They could break a woman's heart with terrifying ease. It didn't help that they also attracted women as readily as nectar attracted humming-birds. And because men were men, they'd always want the freshest little flower with the brightest petals.

Marta sighed.

She waged a constant battle against time's cruel ravages, but, paradoxically enough, time was her ally in matters of the heart. She'd come along late enough in Jonas's life so that she could be fairly certain she was the last woman he'd want to taste. It wasn't an especially sentimental view but it was a realistic, even reassuring one, because she loved her husband and would never willingly have given him up.

Amanda was enough like her so that she'd love the same way, once she found the man she really wanted. Marta could only hope Nick wasn't that man. He had the look about him of a man who would love one woman with heart-stopping intensity, but only on his terms.

For a woman like her daughter, that would not work.

Amanda, Marta thought, Amanda, sweetie, what are you doing?

"…have known it instantly, Mrs. Baron, even if we'd met accidentally."

Marta blinked. Nick was smiling at her, but she had no idea what he'd said.

"Sorry, Your Highness—"

"Nick, please."

"Nick." Marta smiled, too. "I'm afraid I missed that."

"I said, I'd have known you were Amanda's mother even if no one told me. You look enough alike to pass as sisters."

"And you must have a bit of Irish in your blood," Marta said, her smile broadening, "to be able to spout such blarney without laughing."

Nick grinned. "It's the truth, Mrs. Baron, though, actually, my mother always claimed she had an Irish grandfather."

"Please. Call me Marta. Yes, now that you mention it, I think I've read that your mother was American."

"She was, and proud of it, as I am proud of my American half. I've always felt very fortunate to be the product of two such extraordinary cultures."

"One foot in the past," Marta said, still smiling, "and one in the future. Which suits you best, I wonder?"

"Mother," Amanda said, but Nick only chuckled.

"Both have their advantages. So far, I've never found it necessary to choose one over the other."

"No. Why would you, when you can have the best of both worlds? Here you are, blue jeans and all—"

"It's difficult to handle horses in a suit," Nick said, and smiled.

Marta smiled, too. "You know what I mean, Nick. Any time you wish, you're free to turn into the ruler of your own kingdom, do as you will, come and go as you please, answering to no one."

"Mother, for heaven's sake—"

"No." Nick took his arm from around Amanda, lifted her hand to his mouth and kissed it. "No, your mother's quite right. Perhaps it's a simplification, but it's pretty much an accurate description of my life." He rose to his feet. "Marta? I noticed a garden behind the house. Would you be kind enough to walk me through it?"

"Of course." Marta rose, too. "Do you like flowers, Nick?"

"Yes," he said simply. "Especially those that are beautiful and have the strength to flourish in difficult climes."

Marta smiled and took his arm as they strolled down the steps, along the path and into the garden.

"There aren't many flowers that can manage that," she said after a few minutes.

"No, there aren't." Nick paused and turned toward her. "Let's not speak in metaphors, Marta. You don't like me, do you?"

"It isn't that I don't like you. It's…" Marta hesitated. "Look, I'm not old-fashioned. I'm not going to ask you what your intentions are with regard to my daughter."

"I'm glad to hear it." He spoke politely, but his words were edged with steel. "Because it's none of your business. Our relationship, Amanda's and mine, doesn't concern anyone but us."

"I know. Like it or not, my little girl is all grown up. But her welfare does concern me. I don't want to see her hurt."

Nick jammed his hands into the back pockets of his jeans. "And you think I do?"

"No, of course not. It's just… A man like you can hurt a woman unintentionally."

"A man like me," he said coldly. "Just what is that supposed to mean?"

"Oh, I'm not trying to insult you…" Marta gave a little laugh. "But I'm doing a fine job of it, aren't I?" She put her hand lightly on his arm. "Nick, you remind me of my husband in so many ways. All the things that make you successful can be difficult for a woman to deal with."

"Are you saying being successful is a drawback in a relationship?"

"On the contrary. It's a wonderful asset. But sometimes success can lead to a kind of selfishness." Marta clicked her tongue. "Just listen to me! I sound like one of those horrible newspaper advice columnists." She looped her arm through

Nick's and drew him forward. "Jonas would tell me I'm meddling."

"Well, he'd be right." Nick softened the words with a grin. "But I understand. You love your daughter. And I—I…" God, what was he saying? "I can promise you, Marta, I care about her, too."

"Good. And now, let me show you the vegetables I grow, way in the back garden. Tomatoes, actually. Hundred-dollar tomatoes, Jonas calls them." Marta smiled. "And, Nick? I'm very happy to have you here at Espada. Whatever happens, a woman should have at least one man in her life who looks at her the way you look at Amanda."

"Every man who sees her must look at her that way," Nick said, and cleared his throat.

"Well, let me put that another way, then. I've never seen a man look at her the way you do."

Nick stopped in his tracks. "Not even her husband?"

Marta shook her head. "Especially not her husband."

"He must have been an idiot."

Marta laughed. "What a perceptive man you are, Nicholas al Rashid!"

Nick spent most of the remaining afternoon at the stables with Jonas, the ranch foreman and the vet. By evening, he was satisfied that the Arabian stallion was suffering from nothing more serious than a minor sprain and a major case of nerves.

"Who could possibly blame him?" Nick had said when he'd come back up to the house. "He's gone from Quidar to Texas. That's a one-hundred-eighty-degree change in any life."

A one-hundred-eighty-degree change indeed, Amanda thought as she slipped into the emerald-green dress Marta had loaned her to wear for dinner.

Before last night, the only thing she'd known about Nick was that she didn't like him. She liked him now, though. More than was reasonable or logical…or safe.

Her mother had tried to tell her that when she'd brought her the dress and a matching pair of shoes.

"Good thing we're about the same size," Marta had said with a smile. "Not that you don't look charming in denim, but Jonas likes to dress for dinner. He'd never admit it, of course. He lays the blame on me."

Amanda sighed. "I just wish I hadn't listened to Nick when he told me to pack nothing but jeans."

"A good thing his valet didn't." Marta grinned. "That was a delightful story the sheikh told, about unpacking his bag and finding a dark suit tucked in with his riding boots."

"Mmm. That was probably the work of his secretary. That's what Nick calls him anyway, this funny little man who bows himself in and out of rooms."

Marta plucked a loose thread from the dress's hem. "Well, after all, sweetie, Nick is heir to the throne of Quidar."

Amanda held the dress up against herself and looked in the mirror. "It's perfect. Thanks, Mom."

"I gather you didn't even know you were coming to Espada."

"No. Nick didn't mention it. He just said we were flying somewhere."

"And you said you'd go with him."

Was that a gentle note of censure in her mother's voice? Color rose in Amanda's cheeks as the women's eyes met in the mirror.

"Yes. Yes, I did."

"And no wonder. He's a fascinating young man. Charming, intelligent, Incredibly good-looking. And, I would think, very accustomed to getting his own way." Marta smiled. "Actually, he reminds me of Jonas."

Amanda turned around. "Nothing's going on between us," she said flatly.

"Oh, I think you're wrong, sweetie. I think a lot is going on. You just aren't ready to admit it."

"Mom—"

"You don't owe me any explanations, darling. You're a grown woman. And I have every confidence in your ability to make your own decisions." Marta reached for her daughter's hands and clasped them tightly. "I just don't want to see you get hurt."

"Nick would never—"

"There are different ways of being hurt, Mandy. Loving a man who may not be able to love you back in quite the same way is perhaps the worst pain of all."

"I don't love Nick! I admit, I'm—I'm infatuated with him, but—"

Marta had smiled and put her finger over Amanda's lips. "Go on," she'd said gently, "make yourself beautiful for your young man."

Beautiful? Amanda thought as she finished dressing. She wondered if Nick would think so. There'd certainly been more stunning women at the party last night, and she'd never be an eye-catching knockout like Deanna Burgess.

But she wanted Nick to like what he saw tonight. Any woman would. That didn't mean she was in love with him...

And then she opened her door to Nick's polite knock and knew, without any hesitancy, that she was. Everything her mother had said was true.

"Hi."

"Hi yourself." Her heartbeat stuttered. Amanda took a breath, dredged up a smile. "You're right on time."

"Always."

He grinned, and she wondered frantically how it could have happened. She hadn't been looking to fall in love. And if she had, it wouldn't have been with the Lion of the Desert.

"My father drummed it into me."

"What?"

"The importance of being on time. Sort of the eleventh commandment. You know, 'Thou shalt never be late.'"

"Yes." She swallowed dryly, fought to hang on to whatever remained of her composure. How? How could she have fallen in love so quickly? "Well, it worked. You're certainly prompt."

His smile tilted. "And you," he said softly, "are incredibly beautiful."

His words, the velvet softness of them, even the way he was looking at her, ignited a slow-burning heat in her bones.

"Thank you. It's my mother's dress. I didn't—"

"I know. I should have anticipated that the Barons would expect us to dine with them." A muscle danced in his jaw. He moved toward her, his eyes a burnished silver. "But I didn't think of anything except you. Since last night I haven't been able to think of anything but you."

"Nick…"

Gently, he took her face in his hands, lifted it to his. He could feel her trembling with the same excitement that burned inside him.

"One kiss," he said softly, "just one, before we go downstairs."

"All right. Just—"

His mouth closed over hers. Amanda moaned, closed her eyes, lifted her hands and laid them against his chest. His heart was racing, but no faster than hers. She moved closer to him, closer still, and he swept his arms around her, gathered her against him so that she could feel his hunger.

"Nick," she said in a choked whisper, "oh, Nick…"

He took her hand from his chest, brought it down his body, cupped it over his arousal. He groaned, or maybe it was she who made that soft, yearning sound. It didn't matter. Her needs, and his, were the same.

"To hell with dinner," he whispered. "Amanda, I want to

touch you. To undress you. To bury myself inside you while you lift your arms to me and cry out my name."

"Oh, yes! It's what I want, too." She took a shaky breath, lifted her hand from the heat and hardness of him and leaned back in his arms. "But Jonas and Marta expect us to join them."

Nick bent his head, nipped gently at her throat. "I don't give a damn what they want."

Amanda gave a breathless laugh. "Nick, that's my mother downstairs."

He laughed, too, or made the attempt. "I'm sorry, sweetheart. Of course it is. Okay. Just give me a minute. Then we'll make our entrance, pretend we're interested in drinks and dinner and polite conversation for a couple of hours—"

"Only for a couple of hours."

He tugged her towards him and she went willingly, thrust her hands into his hair, dragged his mouth down to hers and kissed him.

Nick felt the kiss pierce his heart like an arrow.

A couple of hours, he'd said. Since when could a couple of hours seem like an eternity?

Drinks first, out on the deck, where they were joined by Tyler and Caitlin Kincaid. They lived nearby, Jonas said. He clapped Tyler on the back, gave him a proud smile and said Tyler was his son and Caitlin his stepdaughter.

Any other time, Nick would have found that intriguing. A son who didn't bear the old man's name. A stepdaughter, but obviously not of Marta's blood. Interesting, he thought—but then his curiosity faded.

His only interest was Amanda.

Still, he went through the motions. Made pleasant small talk. Murmured something about the excellence of the wine. Agreed that dinner was a masterpiece. He supposed it was.

Everybody said so. The thing was, he couldn't taste any of it.

Nothing had any flavor. How could it, when the only taste that mattered was Amanda's? That last kiss lingered on his mouth. The memory of it. The way she'd pulled his head down to hers, the way she'd initiated that all-consuming, hungry kiss...

Ah, hell. Nick shifted uneasily in his chair.

He was too old for this. Boys worried about their hormones making them look foolish, and he was far from being a boy. But just thinking about her...the heat of her in his arms; the sweet sounds she made when he kissed her; the way she fitted herself against him...

Hell, he thought again, and cleared his throat.

"...oil strike?"

He blinked, looked around the table blindly. Everyone was looking at him.

"Sorry," he said, and cleared his throat again. "Tyler? Did you say something?"

"I was just wondering about that oil strike in Quidar last year. Was it really the gusher our people said it was?"

"Oh. Oh, yeah. Absolutely. The field was huge, bigger than..."

Nick talked about oil. He talked about oil prices. And all the time part of his brain was doing such sensible things, another part was wondering what Amanda was thinking. She was seated beside him, and every now and then when he trusted himself to do it without pulling her into his arms, he looked at her. Her golden eyes were wide; her cheeks were flushed. And when he took her hand under the table, he could feel her tremble.

Was she aching, as he was, for these endless hours to pass so that she could come into his arms and ask him to take her? Because she had to ask. He'd told her that she had to ask, and he was a man of his word, would remain a man of his word, even if it killed him. It would, if he didn't have her. If he didn't make her his.

"Nick?"

And if any son of a bitch tried to take her from him, he'd—

"Nick?"

Nick frowned. They were on the deck again, just he and Tyler Kincaid, though he had only the haziest recollection of finishing dessert and agreeing it would be great to go outside for a breath of air.

"Yes." Nick inhaled deeply, then let out his breath. "Kincaid. Tyler. I…hell, I'm sorry. You must think I'm—"

"What I think," Tyler said with wry amusement, "is that if you and Amanda don't get behind a closed door pretty damn soon, the rest of us are going to be in for an extremely interesting night."

Nick swung toward him, eyes narrowed. "What's that supposed to mean, Kincaid?"

"It means that the temperature goes up a hundred degrees each time you look at each other," Tyler said carefully. "And that if you think you'd rather work it off by taking me on, you're welcome to try it."

The two men stared at each other and then Nick gave a choked laugh. "Sorry. Damn, I'm sorry. I just—"

"Yeah. I know the feeling." Tyler leaned back against the deck rail. "Amazing, isn't it? What falling in love with a woman can do to a perfectly normal, completely sensible male?"

"In…?" Nick shook his head. "You've got it wrong. I'm not—"

"Tyler?" Caitlin Kincaid smiled as she came toward them. "Tyler, darling, it's late. We really should be leaving. It was lovely meeting you, Nick."

"Yes." Nick took her hand and brought it to his lips. "I gave your husband my card. Give me a call the next time you're in New York."

Caitlin rose on her toes and kissed his cheek. "I think it's wonderful," she whispered.

Nick felt bewildered as she stepped back into the arc of her husband's arm. "What's wonderful?"

Tyler looked at Nick, started to say something, then thought better of it. "Well," he said, and held out his hand, "it's been a pleasure meeting you."

"Yeah," Nick said. "Uh, Tyler? You're definitely wrong. About what you said. I mean, I'm not—I'm certainly not—"

"Of course you're not," Tyler said solemnly.

Nick thought he heard Kincaid chuckle as he and his wife walked into the house. Not that it mattered. The laugh was on Tyler if he thought any rational man would ever confuse lust with love.

After a while, the lights in the house went off. He straightened up, looked at the lighted dial of his watch. How long had he been out here? Had Amanda gone to her room? Had he misread what he'd seen in her eyes all evening?

"Nick?"

He turned and saw her standing in the doorway, a beautiful shadow in the soft light of the moon. The sight of her almost stopped his heart, but then, desire—lust—could be a powerful thing. Any thinking man knew that.

"Nick," she said again, and Nicholas al Rashid, the Lion of the Desert, stopped thinking, went to the woman he wanted, the woman he'd always wanted since the beginning of time, took her in his arms and kissed her again and again until he could no longer tell where she left off and he began.

CHAPTER TEN

THE world was spinning out of control, the stars racing across the black Texas sky like a kaleidoscope gone mad.

"Tell me, sweetheart." Nick's voice was hoarse and urgent. "Tell me what you want."

Amanda looked up at this man who'd turned her life upside down, this dangerous, gorgeous, complex stranger, and framed his face with her hands. "You," she said softly. "I want—"

Nick's mouth closed hungrily over hers. His hands slipped down her spine, cupped her bottom, lifted her into his heat and hardness.

Desire sparkled in her blood. She moaned, caught his lip between her teeth, bit gently into the soft flesh and traced the tiny wound with the tip of her tongue. His arms tightened around her and he whispered something in a language she couldn't understand, but words didn't matter.

Not now.

Nick drew back, just enough so he could see Amanda's face in the pearlescent glow of the moon.

"You're so beautiful," he whispered, and kissed her again, heating her mouth with his, parting it with his, feasting on the taste of her, on the little sounds she made as she returned his kisses. She was trembling in his arms, straining against him, fitting her body to his until nothing but the whisper of their clothing separated them.

Nick knew he couldn't take much more of this sweet torment.

The moon slipped behind the surrounding hills. The silver-shot night swooped down, embraced them in a cloak of velvet darkness.

He drew Amanda closer, settled her in the inverted vee of his legs. His erection pressed against her belly and she sighed his name.

"Please," she whispered, "Nick, please…"

"Amanda." His voice was raw. "Sweetheart, come upstairs with me."

"Please," she said again, and kissed him, took his tongue into her mouth, and he was lost.

He bunched the silk of her skirt in his fists and pushed it up her thighs. She was wearing stockings and a small triangle of silk. His brain registered that much and, in some still-functioning part of it, he thought about how exciting it would be to see her now, see those long, elegant legs, that scrap of silk, but then she moved her hips and he forgot everything but the uncontrollable need to possess her.

"Amanda," he groaned, and he slipped his hand between her thighs and cupped her, felt the heat of her, and the dampness. He moved against her, moved again, and she moaned.

She slid her hands up his chest, shoved his jacket half off his shoulders, fumbled at his tie, at the buttons of his shirt, and put her hands on his skin. She felt her knees go weak. Oh, the feel of him! The hot male skin. The whorls of silky hair, the ridges of hard muscle.

Nick caught her hands, held them against the thudding beat of his heart.

"Amanda." He dragged air into his lungs, told himself to breathe, to think, to slow down. He'd waited all these years for this moment. He knew it now, knew that he'd lived with the memory of the woman in his arms since he'd first seen her. Now, at last, she would be his—but not like this.

She was as soft as the petals of a rosebud, as lovely as a dream. He wanted to pleasure her slowly, take her slowly, see her eyes turn blind with passion as he took her to the brink of ecstasy over and over again before they tumbled over the edge and fell through time, joined together for eternity.

Nick shuddered.

Unless she moved against him. Yes, like that. Unless she lifted herself to him like that. Just like that. Unless her delicate tongue searched for his. Unless she rubbed her hot, feminine core against his palm...

A cry broke from his throat. He drew her closer into his embrace, deeper into the inky silence of the moonless night, and pressed her back against the railing.

"Look at me," he whispered, and when her eyes met his, he ripped away the bit of silk between her thighs, found the tiny bud that bloomed there. Touched her. Stroked her. And kissed her, kissed her and drank in her cries as she came against his hand.

She sobbed his name, pulled down his zipper, found him, held him, stroked him, and then, oh then, she was a hot silken fist taking him deep inside her.

Nick strove for sanity. Wait for her, he told himself, dammit, wait.

Amanda trembled and arched like a bow in his arms, tore her mouth from his and sank her teeth into his shoulder. The sound, the feel, the heat of her surrender finished him. He stopped thinking, slid his hand around the nape of her neck, took her mouth with his and exploded deep within her satin walls.

For long moments, neither of them moved. Then Nick let out a breath, pulled down her skirt and gently kissed her lips. "Sweetheart," he whispered.

She shook her head, made a weak little sound and tried to turn her face from his, but he caught her chin, kissed her again and tasted the salt of her tears.

Nick cursed, damned himself for being such a selfish fool. He enfolded her even more closely in his arms, cupped her head and brought it to his shoulder.

"Forgive me, sweetheart," he murmured, rocking her gently in his embrace. "I know it was too quick. I meant to go slowly, to make it perfect."

Amanda lifted her head, silenced him with a kiss. "It was perfect."

"But you're crying."

She gave a soft little laugh. "I know. It's just..." It's just that my heart is full, she thought. Full with love, for the first time in her life. She smiled, put her hand to his cheek. "Those weren't sad tears," she whispered. "This was—what we just did—I've never..."

He felt his heart swell with joy. "Never?"

She shook her head. "Never."

He kissed her again until she was breathless with desire. Then he put his arm around her, led her into the sleeping house and took her, at last, to bed.

Amanda awoke to Nick's kisses just before dawn.

"Hello, sweetheart," he whispered.

Safe and warm in the curve of his arm, she smiled up at him. "Good morning."

He bent to her, kissed her mouth with lingering tenderness. "You slept in my arms all night."

"Mmm."

"I liked having you there."

"Mmm," she said again, and laced her fingers into his dark hair.

He smiled, nipped gently at her bottom lip. "You're not a morning conversationalist, huh?"

Amanda laughed softly. "I'm not a morning anything. I don't... " Her breath hitched. "Nick?"

"You see, sweetheart?" His voice roughened as he caressed

her breast, licked the nipple and watched it bead. "It isn't true that you're not a morning anything. You just need to find something that appeals to you."

She caught her breath, lifted herself to his mouth.

"Like this for instance. Or..." He shifted, moved farther down her warm flesh and gently parted her thighs. "Or this."

He loved the soft sound she made as he put his mouth against her, loved the sweet taste of her, like honey on his tongue. And the scent of her, of aroused woman, filled him with hot pleasure. How could he want her again? He'd had her endless times during the long, miraculous night.

But he would never have her enough, he thought suddenly, and he rose above her, looked down into her passion-flushed face and spoke her name.

Her lashes flew up. Her wide golden eyes looked into his as he entered her and he saw the blur of pleasure suffuse her face. He withdrew, slid into her again, drove deeper, saw her eyes darken and her lips form his name.

"Yes," he whispered, "yes," and he caught her hands, laced his fingers through hers and stretched her arms to the sides, still moving, still seeking not just that incredible moment when they would fly into the sun together but something more, something he'd never known.

"Nick," she moaned, just that, only that, but he could hear—he thought he could hear—everything a man could hope for, long for, in the way she said his name.

"Come with me," he said, "Amanda, love..."

She wrapped her legs around his hips, sobbed his name, and Nick stopped thinking, stopped wondering, and lost himself in the woman in his arms.

Afterward, they lay in a warm, contented tangle, her head on his chest, his arms holding her close.

He gave a dramatic groan. "I'm never going to be able to move again."

She laughed softly, propped her chin on her wrist and looked at him. "Be sure and explain that to the housekeeper when she finds your naked body in my bed."

"I'll just smile and tell her that I died and went to heaven."

"Uh-huh. My mother will probably love that explanation."

"Hell," Nick grumbled. She squealed as he rolled her onto her back, gently drew her hands above her head and manacled them with his. "Let me be sure I understand this, Ms. Benning. You expect me to get up, get dressed and beat it back to my room before the sun rises." He bent his head, kissed her mouth. "Is there no pity in your heart for a man who's given his all?"

Amanda gave a little hum of satisfaction. "But you haven't given your all," she said huskily, and shifted beneath him. "Or am I imagining things?"

"What?" Nick said with mock indignation. "You can't be referring to this."

"But I am."

And then, neither of them was laughing.

"Amanda," he whispered, "sweetheart."

He drew her into his arms and they made love again, slowly, exploring each other, tasting each other, coming at last to a climax no less transcendent for all the sweet, gentle steps that had led them to it.

Nick held Amanda close for long moments, savoring the slowing beat of her heart against his. How could he have thought he knew what sex was, when he'd lived without ever knowing this sense of completion in a woman's arms?

He'd been with many women, all of them beautiful, almost all of them skilled in bed. Amanda was beautiful, yes. And she was eager, even wild in his arms, but skill...?

He drew her more tightly into his embrace.

She wasn't skilled. There'd been moments during the night

when she'd caught her breath at some of the things he'd done. "Oh," she'd whispered once, "Nick, I never…"

Shall I stop? he'd said, even though stopping would have half killed him, but there was nothing he wouldn't do to please her. And she'd sighed and touched him and said no, please, no, don't ever stop.

Which, he thought, staring up at the ceiling, just about terrified him. Because he didn't want to stop. Not ever. Not just making love to her, although he suspected he could do that for the rest of his life without ever tiring of it.

The thing of it was, he didn't want to stop being with Amanda. Laughing with her. Talking with her. Even arguing with her. He didn't want any of that to stop.

And it scared the hell out of him.

What was happening here? He'd met this woman less than two days ago under what could only charitably be called suspicious circumstances. He didn't know very much about her. And now, he was thinking—he felt as if he might be—he had this idea that—

Nick slid his arm from beneath Amanda's shoulders and sat up.

"It's getting late," he said, and flashed a quick smile as he got out of bed, stepped into his trousers and pulled on his shirt. "The sun's coming up."

"Nick?" Amanda shifted against the pillow, rose on her elbows and looked at him. "What's the matter?"

"Nothing. Nothing's the matter. I just, uh, I dropped a cuff link."

He bent down, collected the rest of the clothing he'd practically torn off last night, then searched the carpet vigilantly for a cuff link that had gone astray. It was much easier to think he might have lost a cuff link than a far more vital part of himself, one he'd never given any woman—one he wasn't sure he could retrieve.

"Found it," he said, straightening up, holding out the link

and smiling again as he quickly made his way to the door. "I'll see you at breakfast. Okay?"

She nodded, then drew the blanket to her chin. She looked lost and puzzled, and he came within a breath of dropping his stuff, going back to her and taking her in his arms.

"Go on," she said, "before you turn into a pumpkin. Or whatever it is sheikhs turn into when the moon goes down and the sun comes up. Dammit, Nick, I can smell coffee. Someone's awake, and I don't want them to find you here."

Her voice had taken on strength. She looked neither lost or puzzled, just annoyed. Annoyed, because he wasn't getting out of her room fast enough? Because someone might find him with her?

Nick's mouth thinned. What if he told her he damned well wasn't going anywhere? That he belonged in her bed just as she belonged in his arms?

"Will you please leave?"

"Of course," he said politely, and shut the door after him.

Amanda stared at the closed door. She wanted to roll over on her belly, clutch her pillow and weep. Instead, she grabbed the pillows, first his, then hers, and hurled them at the door.

What a fool she'd been, thinking this had been anything more than sex to Nick. And what a fool she'd been, thinking she was in love with him. She was far too intelligent to fall for a man like Nicholas al Rashid. What woman would want a man who could never love anyone as much as he loved himself?

This, she thought grimly, this was what he'd been after, all along. To sleep with her and add another conquest to his list.

She hadn't been a fool, she'd been an idiot.

No wonder he'd called off their wager. He'd known she'd sleep with him. After all, he was irresistible. He thought so, anyway. But why saddle himself with keeping her, or having her, or whatever the hell you called the responsibility a man like that assumed when he took a mistress?

Look at how easily he'd rid himself of Deanna. No second thoughts. No hesitation.

Amanda sucked in her breath. "Stop it," she said.

She rose quickly, stepped over the little pile of silky clothing that lay on the carpet. She wouldn't think about how Nick had undressed her, how they'd barely closed the door before he'd been pulling off his clothes and hers, arousing her so fast, so completely, that they'd only just made it to the bed before he was inside her again.

Don't look, she told herself hotly, not at the clothes, not at the mirror...

Too late.

She'd already turned, sought out her reflection in the glass and found a stranger. A woman with tousled hair and a kiss-swollen mouth. With the marks of a man's possession on her body.

There, on her mouth. At the juncture of shoulder and throat. On her thighs.

Amanda trembled.

Nick hadn't hurt her, but he'd marked her. Marked her as his own. No man had ever done that. Well, there'd only been one other man. Her husband. And his idea of sex had been something done quickly, almost clinically. Like—like brushing your teeth. That was how she'd assumed it was supposed to be. A couple of kisses, a fast, slightly uncomfortable penetration.

How could she have known that making love could be wild one moment and tender the next? That nothing in the world could compare to what happened when you spun out of control in the arms of your lover, and he came apart in yours?

Tears blurred her vision. She swung away from the mirror and hurried into the bathroom.

What was done, was done. She didn't regret it. Why should

she? she thought, as she stepped into the shower. Actually, she owed Nick a debt of gratitude for the night they'd spent together. He'd taught her things about herself, about her capacity for passion and pleasure, she might never have known.

She turned off the water, reached for a towel and dried herself briskly.

This wasn't some Victorian melodrama. She wasn't a virgin whose innocence had been sullied. Neither was she a woman who could possibly fall in love with a man in, what, forty-eight hours? She'd only told herself that because facing the truth—that she'd wanted to sleep with a stranger—had been too difficult.

"Silly," she murmured, and looked into the mirror again and smiled at her self-confident, coolly-contained reflection.

She dressed quickly in a silk T-shirt and jeans and went down the stairs. Her mother was having coffee in the breakfast room.

"Good morning, darling," Marta said. "Did you sleep well?"

"Very well," Amanda replied. She could feel herself blushing and she went straight to the buffet and poured herself coffee. "Where's Jonas?"

Marta smiled. "Oh, he was up hours ago. He's outside somewhere, probably driving his men crazy." She took a sip of coffee. "Have you seen Nick?"

"No," Amanda said quickly. Too quickly. She saw her mother's eyebrows lift. "I mean, how could I have seen him? He's probably still sleeping."

"He isn't," Marta said slowly. "Sweetie, he had a phone call a few minutes ago. I don't know what it was about, but he said he had to leave for home right away."

"Ah." Amanda smiled brightly, as if the news that he hadn't even wanted to say goodbye to her was meaningless. "I see. Well, that's no problem. I'll call the airport and book myself a seat—"

Strong hands closed on her shoulders. She gasped as Nick swung her toward him. His eyes were dark, his expression grim.

"Is that what you think of me?" he said coldly. "That I'd leave you without a word?"

"Yes," she said. Her voice trembled, but her chin was raised in defiance. "That's exactly what I thought."

Nick's mouth twisted. He wrapped his fingers around her wrist and started for the door. "Excuse us, please, Marta." He spoke politely, but there was no mistaking that the words weren't a request, they were a command.

"Amanda?" her mother said.

"It's all right, Mother."

It wasn't. Did Nick think he had to add to her humiliation by dragging her after him like a parcel? Amanda wrenched free of his grasp as soon as they were in the hall.

"Just who in hell do you think you are?" she said in an angry whisper. "Strolling out of my bedroom without so much as a look. Making some pathetic excuse so you can fly back to New York. Grabbing me as if you owned me, right in front of my mother—"

"I'm not flying back to New York."

"Frankly, Lord Rashid, I don't give a damn where you're—"

"I'm flying to Quidar. My father's having political problems. Serious ones."

Amanda folded her arms. As excuses went, this was a good one but then, a man who was the son of an absolute monarch wouldn't be reduced to pleading absence because of a sick grandmother.

"It's the truth."

It probably was. Nick might not have much loyalty to the women who warmed his bed, but she had no doubt that he was loyal to his king and to his kingdom.

"I'm sorry to hear it," she said stiffly.

"I'll be gone a week. Or a month. I can't be certain."

"You don't have to explain yourself to me, Your Highness."

"Dammit," Nick growled, clasping her elbows and lifting her to her toes, "what's the matter with you?"

"Nothing's the matter with me."

"Don't lie to me, Amanda."

"Why not? I asked you that same question a little while ago. Remember? 'What's the matter?' I said, and you gave me the answer I just gave you."

"Yeah, well, I lied." His hands tightened on her. "You want an answer? All right. I'll give you one." He took a deep breath. "I was afraid."

"Of what?"

"Of…" He let go of her, ran his hands through his hair. Color striped his cheekbones. "I don't know." He hesitated. "Dammit, I was afraid of you."

"The Lion of the Desert? Afraid of me?" She laughed and took a step back. "Nice try, Your Loftiness, but—"

Nick pulled her into his arms. "This isn't a game! I'm trying to tell you what happened to me this morning. When I kissed you, when I knew it was time to leave you…" His throat constricted. "Amanda." He drew her close, cupped her face and looked into her eyes. "Come with me."

"Come with you?"

"Yes. I don't want to leave you. I can't leave you." He kissed her, then looked into her eyes again. "Come with me, sweetheart."

"No!" Marta Baron's voice rang out like the hour bell from a campanile. Amanda spun around and saw her mother, standing in the entrance to the breakfast room. "Amanda, darling, don't go. Please. I have this feeling…"

"Amanda," Nick said softly, "I want you with me."

What was the good of pretending? Amanda turned to the man she loved. "And I want to be with you."

An hour later, they were in the air, en route to an ancient kingdom where the word of the Lion of the Desert was law.

CHAPTER ELEVEN

NICK wasted no time once Amanda said she'd go with him.

They were in the air in record time. Shortly after takeoff, he took out his cell phone and made a flurry of calls. Then he sat back and took Amanda's hand.

"Abdul will meet us in Quidar."

"You've asked Abdul to fly to Quidar?"

"Yes, of course. He's familiar with the situation back home. He's worked with me for years, and before me—"

"I know. Your father, and your grandfather, too."

"Exactly." Nick brought her hand to his mouth and kissed it. "You don't like Abdul, do you?"

"I don't know him well enough not to like him. It's just…I get the feeling he doesn't like me." Amanda looked at their joined hands, then at Nick. "I doubt if he'll be very happy when he sees you've brought me with you."

"He's my secretary. He's not required to think about anything other than his duties. My private life isn't his concern."

"You don't really believe that," she said with a little laugh. "Everything about you is Abdul's concern."

"No, sweetheart, you're wrong. The duties of the secretary to the heir to the throne are very clear. It is—"

"—the custom," Amanda said, more sharply than she'd intended.

"Yes. Such things are very important in my country."

"Customs. Duties. And rules."

"Sweetheart, don't look like that."

"Like what?" she said, and even she could hear the petulance in her voice.

Nick put his arm around her. "You'll like Quidar." He smiled. "At least, I hope you will."

Amanda sighed and let herself lean into him. "How long is the flight?"

"Too long for us to try to make it in this plane. We'd have to stop for refueling at least twice, and I don't want to waste the time. We'll board a commercial jet in Dallas. And..." He glanced at his watch. "And twelve hours from now, we'll step down on the soil of my homeland."

The soil of his homeland. A place called Quidar. A country so remote, so ancient, that it had only opened its borders to outsiders under the rule of Nick's father...

Amanda sat up straight. "Nick. I just realized I don't have my passport."

He smiled and reached for her hand. "That's not a problem."

"But it is. They won't let me out of the country without—'

"You only need a passport to get back into the States. And, of course, to enter Quidar." He tugged gently on her hand and drew her close to his side. "You forget, sweetheart. You're traveling with me. I'll see to it you'll have no difficulty reentering your country." His smile tilted. "And I can guarantee you'll be allowed to enter mine."

"But..."

She hesitated, trying to find the right words. His explanation was simple. What wasn't simple was the sudden panic she felt at the thought of leaving everything familiar and going into the unknown with a man she hardly knew.

Without a passport, she'd be totally dependent on Nick. And

she knew what that kind of dependency could do to a woman after seeing the mistakes of her mother's two marriages and experiencing the problems of her own.

"I'd just feel better if I had my passport." She tried to soften the words with a smile. "It would seem strange to travel abroad without—"

The phone beside Nick buzzed. He picked it up.

"Yes?" he said brusquely, and then he frowned. "Please tell my father I'm on my way. No, no, I'm glad you called. Yes. I understand." He put the phone down slowly, his face troubled.

"Nick? What is it?"

A muscle knotted in his cheek, a sign she'd come to know meant he was worried.

"That was my father's physician. My father hasn't been well. And now this added stress…" He fell silent, then cleared his throat. "Well," he said briskly, "what were we talking about?"

Amanda twined her fingers through his. "You were explaining why I didn't need my passport."

"And you were explaining why you did."

"Well, I was wrong." She brought his hand to her face and pressed it to her cheek. "Ah, the joys of traveling with the Lion of the Desert," she said lightly.

Nick looked deep into her eyes. "I'm not the Lion of the Desert when I'm with you," he said, and he drew her into his arms and kissed her.

They changed planes in Dallas and settled into the first-class cabin of the commercial flight that would take them to Quidar.

The flight attendant who brought them champagne recognized Nick and dropped a quick curtsy. "Your Highness. How nice to have you with us again."

She turned brightly curious eyes on Amanda. Nick took her hand.

"Thank you," he said politely, and asked something inconsequential about the projected flight.

"Forgive me for not introducing you," he said softly when they were alone again.

"That's all right." It wasn't. Amanda knew how stiff her words must sound. "You're under no obligation to—"

"Sweetheart." Nick leaned close and brushed his lips over hers. "I'm only protecting you from reading about yourself in tomorrow's papers."

"Are you serious?"

"Deadly serious. I've no reason to distrust the attendant, but why take chances? There's a heavy market in celebrity gossip."

"Yes, but…" But you're not a celebrity, she'd almost said because she didn't think of him that way. He was a man to her, a man with whom she'd fallen in love, but to the rest of the world, he was the stuff of tabloid headlines. She sighed and rubbed her forehead against his sleeve. "It must be awful," she murmured. "Never having any privacy, never being able to let down your guard."

"That's the way it's been most of my life…until now." Nick put his hand under Amanda's chin and smiled into her eyes. "I've let down my guard with you, sweetheart."

"Have you?" she said softly.

He nodded. "I've told you more about myself than I've ever told anyone. And I've never taken anyone with me to Quidar."

Her heart leaped at what he'd said.

"No one?"

"No one," he said solemnly. "You're the first." He leaned closer. "The first woman I've ever—"

"Dom Pérignon or Taittinger, Your Highness?" the flight attendant asked cheerfully.

"It doesn't matter," Nick said, his eyes locked on Amanda's face. "What we drink doesn't matter at all."

They ate dinner, though Amanda was too wound up to do more than pick at hers. What would her first glimpse of Nick's homeland be like? What would his father think about her being with him? What would Nick tell him?

She stole a glance at Nick. He'd opened his omnipresent briefcase and read through some papers. Then he'd reached for the telephone and made several calls, sounding more purposeful, even imperial, with each conversation. He even looked different, his mouth and jaw seemingly set in sterner lines, as if he were changing from the man who'd made such passionate love to her into the man who was the heir to the throne of his country.

Her throat tightened.

"Nick?" she said as he hit the disconnect button.

He frowned, blinked, stared at her as if, just for a moment, he'd all but forgotten her presence.

"Yes," he said a little impatiently, and then he seemed to give himself a little shake. "Sorry, sweetheart." He put his arm around her, drew her close. "I wanted to take care of some things before we land."

"Have you told your father that you're bringing me with you?"

Nick hesitated. "Yes, I told him."

"And?"

"And what?"

"And what did he say?"

"He said he hoped you were even more beautiful than Scheherazade," Nick said lightly. "I assured him that you were."

"I don't understand."

"There's an ancient legend that says Scheherazade visited Zamidar and the Ivory Palace centuries ago."

Amanda gave him a puzzled smile. "The same Scheherazade who saved her neck by telling that sultan all those stories?"

"The very one." Nick smiled. "Unfortunately, she didn't tell any tall tales when she visited the monarch of Quidar."

She grinned. "Your grandpa, no doubt, a zillion times removed. Well, why didn't she? Tell him stories, I mean."

"There was no reason."

"Ah." Amanda tucked her head against Nick's shoulder. "Nice to know."

"Hmm?"

"That the monarch of Quidar didn't have the power to..." She sliced her hand across her neck and Nick laughed.

"Of course he did."

"He did?"

"Yes." He tipped her chin up and lightly folded his hand around her throat. "He still can," he said softly. "The rulers of my country have always held life-and-death power over those who cross into the kingdom."

"Oh." Her heart skipped a beat. "Does that include the heir to the throne?"

Nick smiled into her eyes, then brushed his mouth over hers. "I can do anything I want with you, once we reach Quidar."

His tone was light, his smile gentle. Still, even though she knew it was foolish, she couldn't help feeling a little uneasy.

"That sounds ominous," she said, and managed a smile in return.

Nick kissed her again. "Come on. Put your head on my shoulder. That's it. Now, love, shut your eyes and get some sleep."

She let him draw her head down, let him gently kiss her eyes closed.

He could do anything he wanted with her, he'd said. And what he wanted was to bring her to the Ivory Palace and call her his love.

* * *

They changed planes in Paris, going from the commercial jet to a smaller plane, similar to the one they'd flown to Espada. It, too, bore the emblem of Quidar on the fuselage.

Butterflies were beginning to swarm in Amanda's stomach.

"How much longer until we reach your country?" she asked.

"Just a few hours." Nick took her hand. "Nervous?"

"A little," she admitted.

Why wouldn't she be? She was flying to an unknown place to meet a king. The king was Nick's father, and yes, Nick was a prince—but the Nick she knew was only a man, and her lover.

So long as she kept sight of that, she'd be fine.

The final leg of their journey went quickly. Nick held her hand but spoke to her hardly at all. He seemed—what was the right word? Preoccupied. Even distant. But he would be, considering that all his energies would have to be centered on the problems that had brought him home.

The plane touched down, coasted to a seamless stop. Nick rose to his feet, held out his hand and she took it.

"Ready?" he said softly, and she nodded, even though her heart was pounding, and let him lead her to the exit door.

Blinking, she stepped out into bright sunlight.

All during the past few hours, she'd tried to envision what she'd find at the end of their long journey. She'd conjured up an endless strip of concrete spearing across a barren desert.

What she saw was a small, modern airport, graceful palm trees and, just ahead, the skyline of a small city etched in icy-white relief against a cerulean sky. A line of limousines stood waiting nearby, but she'd lived in New York long enough to have seen strings of big cars before.

The only really startling sight was at their feet, where a dozen men, all wearing desert robes, knelt in obeisance, their foreheads pressed to the concrete runway.

Amanda shot a glance at Nick. His face seemed frozen, as if an ancient, evil wizard had changed him into a stranger.

One of the men stirred. "My Lord Rashid," he said, "we bid you welcome."

"English?" Amanda whispered.

Nick drew her beside him. "English," he said softly, a touch of amusement edging his voice. "The Royal Council usually uses it when addressing me. It's their very polite way of reminding me that I am not truly of Quidar."

"I don't understand."

"You couldn't understand," he said wryly, "without roots that go back three thousand years."

He stepped forward, thanked the council members for the greeting and told them to rise. He didn't mention her or introduce her, but she felt the cold glances of the men, saw their stern expressions.

A shudder raced along her skin.

"You didn't introduce me," she said to Nick as their limousine and the others raced toward the city.

"I will, when the time is right."

"Won't those men wonder who I am?"

"They know you're with me, Amanda. That's sufficient."

The shudder came again but stronger this time.

"Nick?" She took a deep breath, let it out slowly. "Nick, I've been thinking. Maybe...maybe I shouldn't have come with you."

"Don't be ridiculous."

"I mean it. I want to go back."

"No."

"What do you mean, no? I'm telling you—"

"And I said, no."

Amanda swung toward Nick. He was staring straight ahead, arms folded, jaw set.

"Don't speak to me that way," she said carefully. "I don't like it."

Seconds passed. Then he turned toward her, muttered something under his breath and took her in his arms. "Sweetheart, forgive me. I have a lot on my mind. Of course you can leave if that's what you really want. I'm hoping it isn't. I want you here, with me."

"I want to be with you, too. It's just that...I think—"

Nick stopped her with a kiss. "Remember what I once told you? Stop thinking."

She knew he was teasing, but the throwaway remark still angered her. "Dammit," she said, pushing free of his arms, "that is such a miserably chauvinistic—"

"Okay. So I'm a chauvinist." Nick put his hand under her chin and gently turned her face away from him. "Chew me out later, but for now, wouldn't you like to take a look at the Ivory Palace?"

"No," she said tersely. "I'm not the least bit..."

Oh, but she was.

The Ivory Palace rose from the dusty white city of Zamidar like a fairy-tale castle. Ornate, brightly polished gates swung slowly open, admitting them to a cobblestone courtyard. Flowers bloomed everywhere, their colorful heads nodding gently in a light breeze. Beyond the palace, jagged mountain peaks soared toward the sky.

Their limousine stopped at the foot of a flight of marble steps. Amanda reached for Nick's hand as a servant opened the door, then all but fell to the ground as they stepped from the car. Nick didn't give any sign that he'd noticed. He didn't seem to notice the servants who lined the steps as they mounted them, either, even though each one bowed to him.

It was, Amanda thought dazedly, like being passed from link to link along a human chain that led, at last, into the vast entry hall of the palace itself, where Abdul, shiny black suit and all, waited to greet them.

Until that moment, she hadn't realized how good it would be to see a familiar face.

"Abdul," she said, holding out her hand, "how nice to—"

"My lord," the old man said, and bowed. "Welcome home."

"Thank you, Abdul. Is my father here?"

"Your father has been called away from the palace. He says to tell you he is happy you have returned and that he will dine with you this evening. I trust you had a pleasant journey."

"Pleasant but tiring." Nick gathered Amanda close to his side. "Ms. Benning and I will want to rest."

"Everything is in readiness, sire."

"You will call me when you know my father is en route."

"Of course, Lord Rashid. May I get you something to eat?"

"Not now, thank you. Just have a tray sent to my quarters in an hour or so."

"Certainly, my lord."

Abdul bowed. Nick stepped past him and led Amanda through the hall, past walls of pink-veined marble and closed doors trimmed with gold leaf, to a massive staircase. Halfway to the second floor, she peered over her shoulder.

"Nick?"

"Hmm?"

"He's still bent in half."

"Who?"

"Abdul. Aren't you going to tell him to stand up?"

"No."

"For heaven's sake—"

Nick's arm tightened around her. "Keep walking."

"Yes, but—"

"There is no 'yes, but.' This is Quidar. Things are different here. The customs—"

"Damn your customs! That old man—"

She gasped as Nick swung her into his arms, strode down the hall, elbowed open the door to one of the rooms, stepped inside and kicked it shut.

"Watch what you say to me, woman," he growled, and dumped her on her feet.

"No, you watch what you say to me!" Amanda slapped her hands on her hips. "Who do you think you are, talking to me like that?"

"I'm the Lion of the Desert. And you would do well to remember it."

"My God," she said with a little laugh, "you're serious!"

"Completely serious."

"So much for what you said on the plane. About not being the Lion of the Desert when you're with me."

"My private life isn't the same as my public life," Nick said sharply. "Those customs you think so little of matter a great deal to my people."

"They're antiquated and foolish."

"Perhaps they are, but they're also revered. If I were to tell Abdul not to bow to me, especially on Quidaran soil, he would be humiliated."

"I suppose that's why you left that lineup of slaves standing on their heads outside the palace."

"They're not slaves," Nick said, his voice cold. "They're servants."

"And you like having servants."

"Dammit!" He marched away, turned and marched back. "It's an honor to serve in the royal household."

Amanda gave a derisive snort.

"You might not understand that, but it's true. And yes, that's exactly why I didn't stop them from bowing to me. Only my father, the members of his council and, someday, the woman I take as my wife, will not have to bow to me."

"I'm sure that will thrill her."

Nick grabbed Amanda's arms, yanked her against him and kissed her.

"You can't solve every problem that way," she gasped, twisting her face from his, but he caught hold of her chin, brought her mouth to his and kissed her again and again until her lips softened and clung to his.

"I don't want to talk about Quidar," he said softly, "or its rules and customs. Not right now."

"But we have to—"

"We don't," he murmured, and slipped his tongue between her lips.

She moaned, lifted her hands and curled them into his shirt. "Nick—"

"Amanda." He smiled and kissed her throat.

"Nick, stop that. I'm serious."

"So am I. I'm seriously interested in knowing which you'd rather do—debate the historical and social validity of Quidaran culture or take a bath with Quidar's heir to the throne."

She drew back in his encircling arms and tried to scowl, but Nick's eyes glinted with laughter and, after a few seconds, she couldn't help laughing, too.

"You're impossible, O Lion of the Desert."

"On the contrary, Ms. Benning. I'm just a man who believes in cleanliness."

She laughed again, but her laughter faded as he began unbuttoning her blouse.

"What are you doing?" she said with a catch in her voice.

"I'm doing what I've ached to do for hours," he whispered. Slowly, his eyes never leaving hers, he undressed her. Then he stepped back and looked at her, his gaze as hot as a caress. "My beautiful Amanda." He reached for her, gathered her against him until she could feel the race of his heart against hers. "Tell me what you want," he said as he had done once before, and she moaned and showed him with her mouth, her hands, her heart.

Nick lifted her into his arms and carried her into an enormous bathroom, to a sunken marble tub the size of a small swimming pool. Water spilled into the tub from a winged gold swan; perfume-scented steam drifted into the air like wisps of fog.

Amanda sighed as he stepped down into the tub with her still in his arms. "Mmm. Someone's already run our bath. How nice."

"Uh-huh." Nick lowered her gently to her feet, linked his hands at the base of her spine. "Another little benefit you get when you're known as a lion."

She laughed softly and stroked her hands down his chest. "Lions are pussycats in disguise."

Nick caught his breath as she curled her fingers around him. "I've always liked cats," he said thickly. He drew her against him with one arm, slipped his hand between her thighs. "I like to hear them purr when I stroke their silken fur."

Amanda caught her breath. "Nick. Oh, Nick..."

He stepped back, sat on the edge of the tub, then drew her between his legs. "Your breasts are so beautiful," he whispered, and bent his head to taste them. "I could feast on them forever."

I could love you forever, she thought. I could be yours, Nicholas al Rashid. I could—

He clasped her hips, drew her to him. "Come to me, sweetheart," he said softly.

She put her hands on his shoulders. Then, slowly, she lowered herself on him, impaled herself on him, took him deep into her silken softness until his velvet heat filled her. Nick groaned, lifted her legs, wrapped them around his waist.

"Amanda." He cupped her face in his hand, kissed her deeply. "My beloved."

My beloved. The words had the sweetness, the softness, of a promise. Her heart filled with joy.

"You'll be mine forever," he said quietly. "I'll never let you leave me."

"I'll never want to leave you," she said in a broken whisper, and then he moved, moved again until she was clinging to his shoulders and sobbing his name.

She collapsed in his arms as he drove into her one last time. They stayed that way, she with her face buried against him, he with his arms tightly around her. At last he stirred. He kissed her mouth, her breasts, swung her into his arms, carried her to his bed and held her until she drifted into exhausted sleep.

When she awoke, night held the room in moonlit darkness. She was alone in the bed; Nick was gone and she smiled, imagining him talking with his father, telling him what he had told her, that he loved her, that she would be with him forever.

Tonight, she thought, tonight she would say the words.

"I love you, Nicholas al Rashid," she whispered into the silence. "I love you with all my heart."

A knock sounded at the door.

"Nick?" she said happily. But Nick wouldn't be so formal. Ah. Of course. He'd told Abdul to have a tray sent to his rooms. "Just a minute."

She reached for the lamp on the table beside the bed and switched it on. What was protocol in such a situation? She had no robe. Would it be all right to stay where she was, wrapped in the silk sheet like a mummy? Was that the custom for the woman who was the beloved of the Lion of the Desert? The woman who would spend her life with—

The door swung open. Amanda grabbed the sheet and dragged it up to her chin. "Excuse me. I didn't...Abdul?"

The little man stood in the doorway, but he didn't look quite so little now. He stood straight, arms folded, a look of disdain on his face. Two robed figures flanked him—two tall, muscular figures whose stance mimicked his.

A whisper of fear sighed along Amanda's skin, but she spoke with cool authority. "Is it the custom to enter a bedroom before you're given permission?"

"You are to come with me, Ms. Benning."

"Come where? Has Lord Rashid sent for me?"

"I act on his command."

That wasn't the answer to her question. Amanda licked her lips. "Where is he? Where is the prince?"

The old man jerked his head and the robed figures advanced toward the bed.

"Dammit, Abdul! Did you hear what I said? When I tell Lord Rashid about this—"

"Lord Rashid has given orders that you are to be moved to different quarters. It is your choice if you come willingly or if you do not."

Amanda's heart banged into her throat. "Moved?"

"That is correct."

"But where—where am I to be moved?"

The old man smiled. She had never seen him smile before.

"To the harem, Ms. Benning, where you will be kept in readiness for the pleasure of the Lion of the Desert for so long as he may wish it."

CHAPTER TWELVE

AMANDA shrieked like a wild woman.

She cursed and kicked, and was rewarded by a grunt when her foot connected with a groin, but she was no match for the two burly men.

They subdued her easily, wrapped her in the sheet and carried her through the palace as if she were an oversize package, one man supporting her knees, the other holding her shoulders. Abdul headed the little procession up stairs and down, through endless corridors.

She kept screaming and kicking, but it did no good.

Her captors ignored her, and though they passed other people in the halls, nobody took notice. Nobody cared. As frightened as she'd been when Abdul's henchmen grabbed her, that was the most terrifying realization of all.

Finally, the men came to a stop before a massive door. Abdul snapped out an order, the door groaned open, and Amanda's captors stepped across the threshold and dumped her, unceremoniously, on the floor.

Abdul clapped his hands and the men backed from the room. The door swung shut. Amanda, shaking as much with rage as fear, kicked free of the sheet and sat up. She looked at Abdul, standing over her. He'd traded his shiny black suit for a long, heavily embroidered robe; his face was expressionless.

"You horrible old man!" Panting, weeping, she struggled to her feet, clutching the sheet around her. "You'll rot in hell for this, Abdul, do you hear me? When I tell the sheikh what you've done to me…"

"I have done nothing to you, Ms. Benning. My orders to my men were very clear. They were not to hurt you, and they have not."

"They trussed me up like a—a Christmas gift!"

An evil smile creased Abdul's leathery face. "More like a birthday gift, I think."

"What's that supposed to mean?"

"All will be explained in due time."

"Listen, you miserable son of a—"

"Women do not use obscenities in Quidar," the old man said sharply. "It is against our rules and customs."

"Oh, no. No, that's not the custom. Brutalizing women. Kidnapping them. That's the custom." She hung on to the sheet with one hand and pointed a trembling finger at Abdul. "You're finished. I just hope you know that. When Lord Rashid hears what you've done—"

"There is food and drink in the next room, and clothing, as well."

"I don't care what's in the next room!"

"That is your prerogative," Abdul said calmly. "At any rate, Lord Rashid will be with you shortly."

"You mean Lord Rashid will be with you, you bastard! And when he does, he'll have your head."

Abdul laughed. First a smile, now a laugh? Amanda knew that wasn't good. She was more frightened than ever, but she'd have died rather than let the old bastard know it, so she drew herself up and glared at him.

"What's so funny?"

"You are, Ms. Benning. You see, it was Lord Rashid who instructed me to have you brought here."

"Don't be ridiculous. Nick would never…"

Abdul turned his back to her, walked to the door and opened it. Amanda made a leap for it, but the door swung shut with a thud. She heard the lock click as the bolt slid home, but she grabbed the knob anyway, pulled, tugged...

The door didn't move.

For a moment, for a lifetime, she stood absolutely still, not moving, not blinking, not even breathing.

"No," she finally whispered, "no..."

Her voice rose to a terrified wail. She fell against the door, pounded it with her fists. The sheet she'd wrapped around herself fell, forgotten, to the floor.

"Abdul," she shouted, "old man, you can't do this!"

But he could. The silence on the other side of the door was confirmation of that. Her screams faded to sobs of despair. She gave the door one last jarring blow, then slid to the carpet.

God, what was happening? What was Abdul up to? What had he meant when he said Nick had told him to bring her here? It wasn't true. It couldn't be. And that nonsense about taking her to the harem. Harems didn't exist anymore, except in bad movies.

Okay. She had to calm down instead of panicking. Abdul had done this to frighten her, but she wouldn't let that happen. She'd take deep breaths. Slow and easy. Breathe in, breathe out. Good. She could feel her pulse rate slowing. It was only a matter of time before Nick realized she was missing. He'd come looking for her. He'd find her—

"Ms. Benning?"

Amanda jerked her head up. A dark-haired woman stood over her, holding a pale green caftan over her arm.

"Would you like to put this on, Ms. Benning? Or would you prefer to choose something for yourself?"

"Thank God!" Amanda clutched at the sheet and shot to her feet. "Look, there's been some horrible mistake. You have to get word to Nick—to Lord Rashid—"

"My name is Sara."

Her name was Sara? Who cared about her name?

"Sara. Sara, you must find the sheikh and tell him—"

"Let me help you with this," Sara said pleasantly. "Just let go of that…what is that anyway?" She gave Amanda a little smile. "It looks like a sheet."

"It is a sheet! Two men came into my room—into Lord Rashid's quarters—and—"

"Raise your arms, Ms. Benning. Now let me pull this over your head. That's it. Oh, yes. The pale green is perfect for you." Sara smoothed her hand over Amanda's hair. "Such a lovely color," she said, "but so short. Well, it will grow out, and when it does, I'll plait it with flowers. Or perhaps Lord Rashid would prefer emeralds—"

Amanda slapped the woman's hand away. "I'm not a doll! And I'm not going to be here long enough for you to plait my hair with anything."

"I'm sure you will, Ms. Benning," Sara said soothingly. "A favorite may be kept for months. Years, perhaps."

"Dammit, I've no intention of becoming a 'favorite'. If you know what's good for you, you'll find Lord Rashid and tell him—"

"Tell him what, Amanda?"

Amanda spun around. Nick stood in the doorway.

"Nick! Oh, thank God you've…"

Her words trailed to silence. It was Nick, wasn't it? He looked so different. No jeans, no T-shirt. No carefully tailored suit and tie. Instead, he wore a flowing white robe trimmed in gold. He looked exactly as he'd looked in the Gossip photo. Tall. Proud. Magnificently masculine…

And heart-stoppingly dangerous.

He looked past her to Sara, who had dropped to the floor at the sound of his voice. "Leave us," he said brusquely.

Sara scrambled to her feet and backed quickly from the room.

Nick shut the door and folded his arms. "Well? What did you wish Sara to tell me?"

"Why—why, about this. About what Abdul did to me..."

Amanda fell silent. He was looking at her so strangely. She wanted his arms around her, his heart beating against hers. She wanted him to hold her close and tell her that this was all a terrible mistake or a bad joke gone wrong. She wanted anything but for him to stand as he was, unmoving, a stranger with a stern face and cold eyes.

"Nick?" Her voice was a dry whisper. "Nick, what's going on?"

Nick almost laughed. This woman who had slept with him, who had stolen his heart and sold its contents to the world, wanted to know what was going on. She said it with such innocence, too—but then, why wouldn't she?

She had no way of knowing that Abdul, with his usual efficiency, had managed to get a copy of the lead article in next week's Gossip and that he'd brought it to Nick, trembling as he did, wringing his hands and whispering, "Lord Rashid, the American woman has betrayed you."

"I had you moved to new quarters," Nick said with a tight smile. "Don't you like them? This is the oldest part of the Ivory Palace. I thought it would appeal to you, considering your supposed interest in interior design." He eased away from the door, strolled around the room, pausing at an intricately carved chair, then at a table inlaid with tiny blocks of colored woods. "These things are very old and valuable. There's great interest in them at Christie's, but I've no wish to sell—"

"Dammit!" Amanda strode after him, hands clenched, her terror rapidly giving way to anger. "I'm not interested in tables and chairs."

"No. You most certainly are not."

He'd tossed the words out like a barb, but she decided to ignore them. What she wanted were answers, and she wanted them fast.

"I want to know why you had me brought here. Why you let Abdul and his—his goons wrap me up like laundry, dump me in a heap and lock the door!"

Nick turned toward her. "They brought you here because it is the custom."

"The custom. Well, damn the custom! If I hear that word one more time…" She took a breath and reminded herself to stay calm. "What custom?"

"The Quidaran custom, of course."

God, he was infuriating. That insulting little smile. That I'm-so-clever glint in his eyes. Staying calm wasn't going to be easy.

"Everything is a Quidaran custom," she said coldly. "But if abusing women falls into that category, I'm out of here."

Nick's brows lifted. "No one has abused you, Amanda."

"No? Well, what do you call it, then? Your thugs burst into my room, dragged me out of my bed—"

"It is my room," he said softly. "And my bed."

"I know that. I only meant—"

"And I no longer wanted you in either one."

His words skewered her heart and put a stop to the anger raging through her.

"But you said…" Her voice trembled. She stopped and took a deep breath. "You said you wanted me to be yours forever."

Yes. Oh, yes, he thought, he had. The memory was almost more painful than he could bear. He knew it would be years— a lifetime—before he managed to put it aside.

What a fool he'd been to want her. To call her his beloved. To have told his father he'd found the missing half of his heart, the part of himself each man searches for, without knowing it, from the moment he first draws breath….

"Nick." Her voice was filled with pleading. "Nick, please, tell me this is all some awful joke."

"Did I say I wanted you with me forever?" He smiled

coolly, lifted his shoulders in an expressive shrug. "It was a figure of speech."

Amanda stared at him. "A figure of speech?"

"Of course." Nick forced a smile to his lips. "'Forever' is a poetic concept." He walked slowly toward her, still smiling, and stopped when they were only inches apart. "Don't look so worried," he said softly. "It won't be forever, but it will be a long time before I tire of you."

"Please," she said shakily, "stop this. You're scaring me. I don't—I don't know what you're talking about."

Slowly, he wrapped his hand around the nape of her neck and tugged her to him. She stumbled, put out her hands and laid them against his chest.

"Don't you?"

"No. I don't understand why you had me brought here. I don't even know where I am. The oldest part of the palace, you said."

"Indeed." Nick's eyes dropped to her mouth. Her sweet, beautiful, lying mouth. "I had you brought here because it's where you belong." His gaze lifted, caught hers. "You were my birthday present, darling. Remember?"

She stared at him. "A birthday...? But that was just a joke. You misunderstood what Dawn meant—"

"Nonsense."

"It's not nonsense. I explained everything. That I was a designer. That Dawn only wanted me to do your apartment."

Nick laughed softly. "You're a designer all right. Your 'design' was to worm your way into my life." He reached out a finger, traced the outline of her mouth with its tip. "What you are is a man's dream come true. And now you're right where you belong." His smile was slow and sexy. "Welcome to the harem, Amanda."

She jerked back as if the touch of his hand had scorched her. "What?"

Nick smiled, bent his head, brushed his mouth over hers. She didn't move, didn't respond, didn't so much as breathe.

"Didn't Abdul tell you?"

"He said something about a harem, yes. But I thought…"

His hand cupped her throat, his thumb seeming to measure the fluttering race of her pulse.

"You don't… Harems don't exist," she said quickly. "Not anymore. That's all changed."

"This is the kingdom of Quidar. Nothing changes here unless the king—or his heir—wishes it."

"Do you really expect me to believe you—you have a harem? A bunch of women you keep as—as sexual slaves?" She gave a weak laugh. "Honestly, Nick—"

"Do you recall what I told you about your use of that word, 'slaves'?" Nick cupped her shoulders, drew her stiff body to his. "I assure you, it's an honor to warm my bed."

"This isn't funny, dammit. Surely you can't think I'd—"

She gasped as his mouth covered hers in a long, drugging kiss.

"I must admit, I found you enjoyable," he said calmly, when he finally lifted his head and looked into her eyes. "You have a beautiful body. A lovely face. And you've proven an apt pupil in the ways to pleasure a man."

Her face whitened. She tried to pull free of him, but his hands dug into her flesh.

"So, I've decided to keep you. For a while, at any rate." She cried out as he thrust his hand into her hair and tugged her head back so that her face was raised to his. "Don't look so shocked, darling. You'll enjoy it, I promise. And think of the excellent material you'll have to sell when I finally tire of you and send you home."

"Sell? What 'material'? What are you—"

"Damn you!" Nick's smile vanished. "Don't pull that wide-eyed look on me! You were too impetuous. If only you'd waited…but I suppose you thought you'd be back in New

York, safe and sound, before the next issue of that rag hit the streets."

"What rag? I have no idea what—"

"'My Days and Nights with Nicholas al Rashid'," Nick said coldly. He thrust her from him hard enough so she stumbled. "Such a trite title, Amanda. Or does Gossip write its own headlines?"

Amanda stared at him in disbelief. "What has Gossip to do with this?"

Nick's mouth thinned. He reached inside his robe, took out a sheet of paper and shoved it at her. She gave it a bewildered glance.

"What is this?"

"Take it," he said grimly. "Go on."

She looked down at the paper he'd pushed into her hand. It was a copy of what appeared to be an article bylined, "Special to Gossip, from Amanda Benning."

"'My Days and Nights with…'" she read in a shaky whisper. Her face paled, and she looked up. "Nick, for God's sake, this is a hoax. Surely you don't think I'd write something like this."

"Read it."

His voice flicked over her like a whip. Amanda looked at the paper and moistened her lips. "'My Days and Nights with…'" Color rushed into her face. "'With the sexy sheikh…'" She looked at him again. "Whoever wrote this is talking about—about—"

"About what it's like to make love to…" Nick's jaw tightened. "What was the phrase? Ah, yes. I remember now. "To 'an elegant, exciting savage'." His mouth twisted. "I've been called a lot of things, Ms. Benning, but never that."

"Nick. Listen to me. I'd never do this. Never! How could you even think…? Someone else did it. Wrote this—this thing and used my—"

"Read the final paragraph," he commanded. "Aloud."

She drew a shaky breath. "'As it turns out, the Lion of the Desert is…'" She stopped and lifted imploring eyes to his. "No," she whispered. "Nick, I can't—"

"'As it turns out,'" he said coldly, calling up the ugly words that had been forever burned into his brain, "'the Lion of the Desert is more than a stud. He also has a talent for three-card monte. The sexy sheikh has a souvenir from that time, a two-headed coin that's a reminder of the days when he hustled his school chums…'" Nick looked directly into Amanda's eyes. "I never told that story to anyone," he said softly. "Not to anyone but you."

"And you think…" The paper fell from her hand. She reached out to Nick, her fingers curling into his sleeve. "I swear to you, I didn't write this!"

"Perhaps you didn't hear me. No one knows about that coin except you."

"Someone knows. Someone wrote this, put my name on it. Don't you see? This is a lie. I'd never—"

She cried out as he grabbed the neckline of the silk caftan and tore it from the hollow of her throat to the hem. She tried to tug the edges together, but Nick captured her hands. "Don't play the terrified virgin with me. Not when you've shared the intimate details of my life with millions of strangers."

"Nick. I beg you—"

"Go on. Beg me. I want you to beg me!" He dragged her into his arms, clamped her against him, caught her face in his hands and forced it to his. "So, I'm a savage, am I?" His teeth showed in a quick, feral grin. "That's fine. I think I'm going to enjoy living down to that description."

"Don't. Nick, don't do this. I love you. I love—"

He kissed her, hard, his mouth covering hers with barely suppressed rage, his teeth and tongue savaging her while his fingers dug into her jaw.

"Don't speak to me of love, you bitch!"

He kissed her again and again, deaf to her pleas, unmoved

by her desperate struggles, lifted her into his arms, tumbled her onto a pile of silk cushions and straddled her.

"Speak to me of what you know. Of betrayal. Of mindless sex. Of how it feels to be a whore."

The sound of her hand cracking against his cheek echoed through the room like a gunshot. Nick's head jerked back; he raised his hand in retaliation.

"Go on," Amanda said. Her voice trembled, but her gaze was steady. "Hit me. Dishonor me. Do whatever you came here to do because you couldn't possibly hurt me any more than you already have."

Nick stared down at her while the seconds slipped away. God, he thought, oh, God, how close she'd come to turning him into the savage she'd called him. He cursed, shot to his feet, grabbed Amanda's wrist and dragged her after him.

"Abdul!" he shouted as he flung the door open.

The little man stepped forward. "Yes, my lord?"

"Bring the woman her clothes."

"But, sire..."

Nick shoved Amanda into the corridor. "She will dress and you will take her to the airport. See to it she's flown to Paris and put on the next plane for New York."

Abdul bowed low. "As you wish, Lord Rashid."

"Get her out of my sight!" Nick's voice shook with rage and the pain of betrayal. "Get her out of my sight," he whispered again, once he was back in his own rooms with the door closed and locked.

Then he sank onto the bed, the bed where he'd finally admitted that he'd fallen in love with Amanda Benning, buried his face in his hands and did something no Lion of the Desert had ever done in all the centuries before him.

Nicholas al Rashid, Lord of the Realm and Sublime Heir to the Imperial Throne of Quidar, wept.

An hour later, Abdul knocked on the door. "Lord Rashid?"

Nick stirred. He'd changed back into jeans—the truth was,

he always felt like a fool in that silly white-and-gold robe. He was even feeling a little better.

After all, he'd get over this. Amanda was only a woman, and the world was filled with women....

"Lord Rashid? May I come in?"

It had been his mistake, that he'd opened his heart. He should have known better. Everyone always wanted something from him. The instant celebrity of being seen in his company. The right to mention his name in seemingly casual conversation. The supposed status that came of saying he was a friend or, at least, an acquaintance.

That was just the way things were. He knew it; he'd known it all his adult life. Why should he have expected things to be different with Amanda?

Why should he have let himself think, even for a moment, that she loved him for himself, not for who he was or what he might do for her?

The knock sounded again, more forcefully. "Sire. It is I. Abdul."

Nick sighed, switched on a lamp and went slowly to the door. "Yes?" he said as he pulled it open. "What is it?"

Abdul knelt down and touched his forehead to the floor. "I thought you would wish to know that it is done, my lord. The woman is gone."

"Thank you."

"You need trouble yourself with thoughts of her no longer."

"Did she...?" Nick cleared his throat. "Did she say anything more?"

"Sire?"

"Did she send any message for me?"

"Only more lies, my lord."

"More lies..."

"Yes. That she had not done this thing."

Nick nodded. "Yes. Of course. She'll deny it to the end."

He looked down at the old man, still doubled over with his forehead pressed to the tile. "Abdul. Please, stand up."

"I cannot, sire. It is not the custom."

"The custom," Nick said irritably. "The custom be damned!" He grabbed the old man's arm and hoisted him to his feet. "You're too old for this nonsense, Abdul. Besides, it's time for some changes in this place."

"I think not, my lord. Your father would wish—"

"My father agrees."

"About change?" Abdul laughed politely. "That cannot be, sire. Your father understands the importance of things continuing as they always have. He may not have understood it once, but—"

"What's that supposed to mean?"

Abdul bit his lip. "Nothing, sire. Just—just the meandering thoughts of an old man."

"Well, prepare yourself for some upsets, Abdul." Nick crossed the room and switched on another light. "My father is going to abdicate the throne."

"Already? I assumed he would wait until he was much older, but that is good, sire. Putting the kingdom in your hands while you are still young is—"

"He's not abdicating for me."

The old man paled. "They why would he abdicate?"

"It's time Quidar entered the twenty-first century. There will be elections. The people will choose a council. There'll be no more bowing and scraping, no more—"

"That woman. May her wretched soul burn in hell!"

Nick turned around, his head cocked. "What?"

"Nothing, sire. I, ah, I'll go and arrange for your meal to be served. You must be hungry—"

"Are you referring to Ms. Benning?"

The old man hesitated, then nodded. "I am, my lord. There is no reason not to admit it now. She was not good for you."

"What is good or not good for me is my affair," Nick said sharply.

"Of course. I only meant—"

"Yes. I know." Nick sighed and raked his fingers through his hair. "It doesn't matter. She's gone. And you're right. She wasn't good for me."

"Indeed, she was not. A woman who would pretend illness just to gain access to your study—"

"Access to my…?"

"The night of your birthday party, my lord." Abdul snorted. "Such a lie, that she had a headache."

Nick looked at the old man. "How did you know she had a headache?" he asked softly.

Abdul hesitated. "Well, I—I… You rang for aspirin, sire."

"I rang for coffee."

"Ah, yes. Of course. I meant that. You rang for coffee, and then you told her the story of the two-headed coin." Abdul clamped his lips together.

Nick's eyes narrowed. "You were listening," he said. "At the door."

"No. Certainly not."

"You were listening," Nick repeated grimly. "Otherwise, how would you know I'd told her about the coin?"

"I, ah, I must have…" A fine sheen of sweat moistened Abdul's forehead.

"Must have what?" Nick walked slowly toward his secretary. "How could you know I told her about the coin that night?"

The old man dropped to his knees and grasped the cuff of Nick's jeans in his fingers. "I did it for you," he whispered. "For you, and for Quidar."

"Did what?" Nick reached down, grabbed Abdul by the shoulder and hauled him to his feet. "Damn you, what did you do for me and for Quidar?"

"She was wrong for you, sire. As wrong as your mother had been for your father. Foreign women know nothing of our ways."

"Tell me what you did," Nick said through gritted teeth, "or so help me, Abdul..."

"I did my duty."

"Your duty," Nick said softly.

Abdul nodded.

"How did you 'do your duty', old man?"

"Miss Burgess called while you were in Texas with Ms. Benning. She was angry."

"Go on."

"She said—she said to give you a message, sire. She was writing a piece for Gossip that would teach you that you couldn't make a fool of her."

Nick let go of Abdul. He clenched his fists and jammed his hands into the back pockets of his jeans. He knew that was the only way he could keep from wrapping them around the old man's scrawny throat.

"And?" he said carefully.

"I offered money for her silence. She laughed and said there wasn't enough money in the world to keep her quiet. Oh, I paced the floor for hours, sire, searching for a solution, but I could think of none."

"And you didn't think to call me?"

"I didn't wish to upset you, my lord." Abdul clasped his hands together in supplication. "I wished to help you, sire, and to help Quidar. If I couldn't stop the Burgess woman from writing the Gossip article, I would use it, just as I'd used that picture of you and her on the beach."

Nick stared at Abdul. "Are you telling me that you sold that photo to Gossip?"

"I did not 'sell' it, Lord Rashid. I would never..." Abdul took a quick step back. "Sire, don't you understand? I could see what you could not. These foreign devils, tormenting you—"

"What the hell are you talking about?"

"The Benning woman was the worst. She was a temptress. A succubus. And you were falling under her spell."

"For the love of God!" Nick barked out a laugh and raked his hand through his hair. "This isn't the Dark Ages, man. I wasn't succumbing to a spell. I was falling in love!"

Abdul stood as straight as Nick had ever seen him. "The Lion of the Desert must marry a woman who understands our ways."

"The Lion of the Desert must try damned hard not to slam you against the wall," Nick growled. "Go on. What did you do next?"

"I telephoned Miss Burgess. I suggested we could help each other."

"Meaning?"

"I…" For the first time, the old man hesitated. "I gave her some information. I said she might consider using it, along with a different identity." He made a strangled sound as Nick grabbed him by the neck and hoisted him to his toes. "Lord Rashid." Abdul clawed at the powerful hand around his throat. "Sire, I cannot breathe."

Nick let go. The old man collapsed on the floor like a bundle of dirty clothes.

"You son of a bitch," Nick whispered. "You told Deanna about that coin."

"For the good of Quidar, sire," Abdul gasped. "It hurt no one. Surely you can see that. A simple tale about a coin—"

"A simple tale that I thought proved I'd been betrayed by the woman I love."

Nick swung away from the huddled form at his feet and strode toward the door. Abdul pulled himself up and hurried after him.

"Lord Rashid? Where are you going?"

"To Paris," Nick said. "To New York. To the ends of the earth, until I find Amanda." He looked at Abdul; the old man cowered under that icy gaze and fell to his knees. "And you'd better not be within the borders of this kingdom when I return," he said softly, "or I'll revive one old custom and have your neck on a chopping block."

"Sire. Oh, sire, I beg you. Don't banish me. Please..."

Nick slammed the door. Half an hour later, he was on a jet, hurtling through the night sky toward Paris.

CHAPTER THIRTEEN

WEARY travelers sprawled across the seats in the departure lounge at Paris's Charles de Gaulle Airport.

Their New York–bound plane was still on the ground, its takeoff already delayed by more than three hours. The mechanics had yet to solve a perplexing electrical problem. Until they did, the passengers wouldn't be going anywhere. There was no substitute plane available, so they'd just have to wait it out.

Waiting was the last thing Amanda felt like doing. She knew it was childish but all she wanted was to get home, not just to the States and New York but to her own apartment, where things were familiar and real. Maybe then she could erase the past few days from her head and heart, and start putting things into their proper perspective.

"I just don't understand it!" a querulous voice said.

Amanda turned toward the gray-haired matron who'd dropped into the seat next to hers. "Sorry?"

"The airline," the woman said. "The lie it keeps feeding us. Just look at that airplane out there. Anyone can see there's nothing wrong with it. Why would they expect us to believe an electrical problem is the reason for this awful delay?"

"I'm sure that's what it is," Amanda said politely.

"Nonsense. Electricity is electricity. That's what I told the man at the desk. 'Whom do you think you're fooling?' I said. 'Just put in a new fuse.' And he said…"

The woman's voice droned on. After a while, Amanda closed the magazine she'd been pretending to read and rose to her feet. "Excuse me," she said, and walked to a seat at the far end of the waiting area.

There was no point in trying to change the woman's mind. If there was one thing the past few days had taught her, it was that people would always believe what they wanted to believe, no matter what anyone told them.

Nick had wanted to believe the very worst about her, that she'd tell the entire world about him, about their most intimate secrets—

"Hi."

She blinked, looked up. A man was standing over her. He was good-looking. Handsome, actually. He had a nice smile and a great face—but that was all he had, all he'd ever have, because he wasn't Nick.

"Miserable, huh? This long delay, I mean—"

"Excuse me," Amanda said for the second time.

She stood up, tucked her hands into the pockets of her jacket and walked out of the waiting area toward the end of the terminal where there were lots of empty seats. The lights were turned low. That was fine. She was in the mood for shadows and darkness.

The man she'd cut dead probably thought she was rude or crazy or maybe both. Well, what was she supposed to have said?

Look, this is a waste of time. I'm not interested in men just now. Or maybe she should have explained that she was too busy thinking about another man to manage even small talk with a stranger.

Oh, hell.

There was no point in thinking about Nick. She'd done nothing except think about him and the humiliation he'd heaped on her. That was all he'd done ever since Abdul had marched her out of the Ivory Palace.

Somewhere along the way, self-doubt had taken the place of anger. What would have happened if only she'd said this thing or that; if she'd somehow forced Nick to listen to her. And then, finally, she'd faced the truth.

Torturing herself wouldn't change a thing. Nick would believe what he wanted to believe no matter what she said. It wasn't as if she'd let some chance to make him see the truth slip through her fingers.

The only mistake she'd made was to have gotten involved with him in the first place.

End of story.

Their affair, their relationship, whatever you wanted to call it, was over. Feelings changed, things ended, you moved on. Her mother had done that. She had, too.

I'm so riddled with guilt, she'd told Marta after her divorce. Marriage is supposed to be forever. How will I ever put this behind me?

And Marta had hugged her and said, Sweetie, you just do it, that's all. You move on.

She knew Marta had given her good advice. Excellent advice, really. There was no more logic in agonizing over her failed marriage than there was in wasting time wishing this thing with Nick had never happened or in trying to convince the woman with gray hair that you couldn't fix an airplane's electrical problems by changing a fuse.

You couldn't judge a man's heart by his performance in bed, either.

It was a cold realization but it was honest, and if she'd been fool enough to think Nick's whispered words, his kisses, his caresses, were anything but part of sex, that was her problem.

Amanda sighed, strolled into one of the empty lounges and sank wearily into a chair facing the windows. The jet that would take her home squatted on the tarmac. Mechanics scuttled purposefully around it. Problems were being solved, life was going on, and why wouldn't it?

What had happened with Nick—what she'd been stupid enough to let happen—was nothing but a blip in the overall scheme of things. The planet would go on spinning, the stars would go on shining, everything would be exactly the same.

Certainly they would. She'd be home soon, and Nick would be a distant memory. Thank goodness she'd already figured out that she'd never actually fallen in love with him.

"Mesdames et messieurs..."

The impersonal voice droned from the loudspeaker, first in French, then in English. The flight was still delayed. The airline regretted the inconvenience. Another hour or two, blah, blah, blah.

Amanda stood up and walked closer to the window. The sky was darkening. Was a storm blowing toward them or was night coming on? She couldn't tell anymore. Night and day seemed to have gotten all mixed up, just like her emotions.

Mixed up? That was a laugh. Her emotions had gone crazy. Otherwise, how could she possibly have imagined she loved Nick?

The lengths a woman would go to just to avoid admitting the truth—that she'd succumbed to lust. And lust was what she'd felt for Nicholas al Rashid. Good old garden variety, down-and-dirty lust. Wasn't it pathetic she'd had to tell herself it was love?

This was the twenty-first century. The world had long ago admitted that the female of the species could have the same emotions as her male counterpart. Why should she be any different? One look at the Lion of the Desert and pow, her hormones had gone crazy.

Why wouldn't they? He was gorgeous. It had been as flattering as hell to know he wanted to sleep with her because she'd certainly wanted to sleep with him.

And she had.

Most definitely the end of the story…or it should have been.

The trouble was, no matter how many times she told herself that, the real end of the story intruded.

Amanda leaned back against the wall and closed her eyes. The scene played in her mind over and over like a videotape caught in a loop.

Nick, hatred blazing in his silver eyes.

Nick, calling her a whore.

Nick, believing that she'd written that article, that she would ever hurt him or betray him. How could he think it? Didn't he know how much she loved him? That her heart would always long for him, want him, ache for him?

She drew a shaky breath, then slowly let it out.

Okay. So—so maybe she'd loved him just a little. What did it matter? They'd only spent a handful of days together. Surely that didn't really add up to "love."

Love didn't come on with the speed of a hurricane. It didn't overwhelm you. It grew slowly into something deep and everlasting.

And the foolishness of thinking Nick loved her… Oh, it was laughable! He didn't. He never had. He'd called her beloved, said he wanted her with him forever, but so what? She wasn't naive. Men said lots of things they didn't mean in the throes of passion.

Love—real love—wasn't only about sex. It was about little things. Things like taking walks in the rain. Like laughing, maybe even crying, over a movie you've seen before. It was about trust.

Especially trust.

If Nick had loved her, he'd have taken one look at the Gossip piece and known it was a fake. "It's a lie," he'd have said if he loved her. And then he'd have set out to discover who'd actually written those horrible things, who'd lied and used her name to drive them apart.

But he hadn't done any of that. He'd turned on her in fury, humiliated her, terrified her, believed she'd violated his confidence, talked about the things they'd done together in bed—

"It was a lie," a husky masculine voice whispered.

Amanda's heart skittered into her throat.

"I know it now, beloved. I only hope you can forgive me for not knowing it then."

The world stood still. Please, she thought, oh, please…

She turned slowly, wanting it to be him, afraid it would be him.

Nick stood in the shadows as still as if he'd been carved from stone.

Her knees buckled. He moved quickly and caught her. "Sweetheart. Oh, sweetheart, what have I done to you?"

His face was inches from hers. She longed to touch his stubbled jaw, to trace the outline of his mouth with the tip of her finger, but he had broken her heart once and she wasn't about to let him do it again.

"Let go of me, Nick."

He swung her into his arms.

"No," she said breathlessly. "Put me down."

"Hey. Hey!"

Nick turned, still holding Amanda. The man with the nice smile and the great face came toward them.

"What's going on here?"

Nick looked at him. Whatever the man saw in his eyes made him retreat a couple of steps before he spoke up again.

"Say the word, lady, and I'll send this dude packing."

"You'll try," Nick said softly, "But you won't succeed." His arms tightened around Amanda. "This woman belongs to me."

"I don't belong to you! I don't belong to anybody."

His eyes met hers. "Yes, you do." He bent his head and kissed her gently. "You'll always belong to me, and I to you, sweetheart, because we love each other."

The words he'd spoken stunned her. She wanted to tell him she didn't love him, she'd never loved him. She wanted to tell him he'd never loved her—but he smiled into her eyes and she saw something in those cool silver depths that stole her breath away.

"Lady?"

Nick lifted his head. He was smiling, the way he'd smiled after they made love the very first time. "The lady is fine," he said quietly, his eyes never leaving hers.

The man looked from Amanda to Nick and back again. "Yeah," he said with a little laugh, "yeah, I can see that."

Nick set off through the terminal, Amanda still in his arms. She saw the startled faces all around them, the wide eyes of the women, the smiles on the lips of the men. Her cheeks flushed crimson and she buried her face in his shoulder. Doors opened and shut; she felt the rush of cool air against her hot face, the silence of enclosed space.

When she lifted her head and looked up again, they were in Nick's private plane. He let her down slowly. And when her feet touched the floor, her sanity returned.

"What do you think you're doing, Nick?"

He smiled and linked his hands at the base of her spine. "I love you, Amanda."

"Love?" She laughed. "You don't know the meaning of the—"

Nick lifted her face to his and kissed her. She felt her heart turn over, felt the longing to put her arms around him sweep through her blood, but she would not make a fool of herself ever again.

"If you really think you can—you can just pretend what you did never happened..."

Nick put his arm around her, led her into the cockpit.

"What are you doing?"

"Sit down," he said calmly. "And put on your seat belt."

"Don't be ridiculous. I will not—"

He sighed, pushed her gently into the co-pilot's seat and buckled the belt around her.

"Dammit," she sputtered, "you can get away with kidnapping in Quidar, but this is France. You can't just—"

Nick silenced her with a kiss. She moaned; she didn't mean to, but the feel of his mouth on hers, the soft pressure of it, was almost more than she could bear.

"Neither can you," he said with a little smile. He leaned his forehead against hers. "You can pretend you don't want me, sweetheart, but your kisses speak the truth."

"The truth," she said coolly, "is that I'm as human as the next woman. You're a charming man, Lord Rashid."

Nick grinned as he took the pilot's seat. "A compliment! Who'd have believed it?"

"Charming, and good-looking, but—"

"Very good-looking. That's what women always tell me."

"And clever," Amanda said crisply. "But I'm not going to be taken in again."

"Do you think I flew all the way to Paris to charm you, sweetheart?"

She looked away from him, folded her arms and stared straight out the windshield. "I don't know why you came, and I don't care. I am not going anywhere with you."

"You do care, and you are going with me."

"You're wrong, Lord Rashid."

"I came because I love you, and you love me. And we're never going to be separated again."

"You found me enjoyable." Her voice wobbled a little and she silently cursed herself for even that tiny show of weakness. "Enjoyable, Your Highness. That was your very own word."

Nick sighed. "A bad choice, I admit." He smiled. "True, though. You were wonderful in bed."

Color scalded her cheeks. "Which is why you regret getting rid of me before finding a replacement."

"Amanda. I know I hurt you, sweetheart, but if you'd listen—"

"To what? More lies? More whispers about—about wanting me forever?" Tears rose in her eyes. Angrily, she dashed them away with the back of her hand. "Look, it's over. I slept with you and I don't really have any regrets. It was—it was fun. But now it's time to go back to New York and pick up my life."

"Deanna wrote that article."

"Am I supposed to go saucer-eyed with shock?"

"Hell." Nick sat back and rubbed at the furrow that had appeared between his eyebrows. "Amanda, please. Just give me a chance to explain."

"The same chance you gave me?"

"All right." He swung toward her, eyes glittering, and grabbed her hands. "I was a fool, but now I'm trying to make it right. I'm telling you, Deanna wrote that thing—with Abdul's help."

"Frankly, Lord Rashid, I don't really give a..." Her mouth dropped open. "Abdul? He helped her do such a terrible thing to you?"

"He saw what was happening between us."

"Sex," Amanda said with a toss of her head. "That's what was happening between us."

"He saw," Nick said gently, taking her face in his hands, "that we were falling in love."

"What an ego you have, Your Excellency! I most certainly did not—"

Nick kissed her again. It was a tender kiss, just the whisper of his lips against hers, but it shook her to the depths of her soul. All her defenses crumpled.

"Nick." Her voice trembled. "Nick, I beg you. Don't do this unless you mean it. I couldn't bear it if you—"

"I love you," he said fiercely. "Do you hear me, Amanda? I love you." He lifted her hands to his lips and pressed kisses into each palm. "Abdul listened at the door the night I told you about the double-faced coin."

"He eavesdropped? But why?"

"He must have sensed something even then." Nick stroked a strand of pale blond silk back behind her ear. "The old man knew the truth before I was willing to admit it. I was falling in love with you."

"And he didn't trust me?"

"He wouldn't trust any female unless she was born in Quidar." Nick smiled. "And it would probably help if she had a hairy mole on her chin and weighed only slightly less than a camel."

Amanda laughed, but her laughter faded quickly. "But you believed I'd written that—that piece of filth. How could you have thought that, Nick? If you loved me, if you really loved me—"

"I was wrong, sweetheart. Terribly wrong. And I'll spend the rest of my life making up for it." A muscle flickered in Nick's jaw. "I know it's not an excuse, but—but once I was a man, the only person who loved me for myself was my father. People see me as a—a thing. A commodity. They want what they can get from associating with me. But not you. You wanted what was in here," he said softly, and placed her hand over his heart. "You looked beyond all the titles and saw a man, one who loved you. It's just that I was too stupid to trust my own heart."

"Not stupid," Amanda said, and slipped her arms around his neck. "You were afraid, Nick. And I was, too. That's why it took me so long to admit I loved you." She laughed. "Well, maybe not so long. We've known each other, what, four days?"

"We've known each other since the beginning of time," Nick whispered, and kissed her again.

"I love you," she sighed. "I'll always love you."

"You're damned right you will," he said gruffly. "A man expects his wife to love him forever."

Amanda's eyes glittered. "Yes, my lord," she said, and smiled.

"I have so much to tell you, sweetheart. Things are changing in Quidar. I may not be the Lion of the Desert for much longer."

Her smile softened. She framed his face in her hands and drew his mouth to hers. "You'll always be the Lion of the Desert to me."

Sheikh Nicholas al Rashid, Lion of the Desert, Lord of the Realm and Sublime Heir to the Imperial Throne of Quidar put his arms around the woman who'd stolen his heart and knew that he had finally found what he'd been searching for all of his life.

* * * * *

THE ONE-NIGHT WIFE

CHAPTER ONE

HE CAME into the casino just before midnight, when the action was getting heavier.

Savannah had been watching for him, keeping her eyes on the arched entry that led from the white marble foyer to the high-stakes gaming room. She'd been afraid she might miss him.

What a foolish thought.

O'Connell was impossible to miss. He was, to put it bluntly, gorgeous.

"How will I recognize him?" she'd asked Alain.

He told her that O'Connell was tall, dark-haired and good-looking.

"There's an aura of money to him," he'd added. "You know what I mean, chérie. Sophistication." Smiling, he'd patted her cheek. "Trust me, Savannah. You'll know him right away."

But when she'd arrived an hour ago and stepped through the massive doors that led into the casino, she'd felt her heart sink.

Alain's description was meaningless. It fit half the men in the room.

The casino was situated on an island of pink sand and private estates in the Bahamas. Its membership was restricted to the wealthiest players in Europe, Asia and the Americas.

All the men who frequented its tables were rich and urbane, and lots of them were handsome.

Savannah lifted her champagne flute to her lips and drank. Handsome didn't come close to describing Sean O'Connell.

How many men could raise the temperature just by standing still? This one could. She could almost feel the air begin to sizzle.

His arrival caused a stir. Covert glances directed at him from the men. Assessing ones from the women. Maybe not everybody would pick up signals that subtle, but catching nuances was Savannah's stock in trade.

Her success at card tables depended on it.

Tonight, so did the course of her life.

No. She didn't want to think about that. Years ago, when she was still fleecing tourists in New Orleans, she'd learned that the only way to win was to think of nothing but the cards. Empty her mind of everything but the spiel, the sucker and the speed of her hands.

Concentrate on the knowledge that she was the best.

The philosophy still worked. She'd gone from dealing three-card monte on street corners to playing baccarat and poker in elegant surroundings, but her approach to winning had not changed.

Concentrate. That was the key. Stay calm and be focused.

Tonight, that state of mind was taking longer to achieve.

Her hand trembled as she lifted her champagne flute to her mouth. The movement was nothing but a tic, a tremor of her little finger, but even that was too much. She wouldn't drink once she sat down at the poker table but if that tic should appear when she picked up her cards, O'Connell would notice. Like her, he'd have trained himself to read an opponent's body language.

His skills were legendary.

If you were a gambler, he was the man to beat.

If you were a woman, he was the man to bed.

Every woman in the room knew it. Too bad, Savannah thought, and a little smile curved her mouth. Too bad, because on this hot Caribbean night, Sean O'Connell would belong only to her.

Again, she raised her glass. Her hand was steady this time. She took a little swallow of the chilled Cristal, just enough to cool her lips and throat, and went on watching him. There was little danger he'd see her: she'd chosen her spot carefully. From this alcove, she could observe without being observed.

She wanted the chance to look him over before she made her move.

Evidently, he was doing the same thing before choosing a table. He hadn't stirred; he was still standing in the arch between the foyer and the main room. It was, she thought with grudging admiration, a clever entrance. He'd stirred interest without doing a thing.

All those assessing glances from men stupidly eager to be his next victim. All those feline smiles from women eager for the same thing, though in a very different way.

Savannah the Gambler understood the men. When a player had a reputation like O'Connell's, you wanted to sit across the table from him and test yourself. Even if you lost, you could always drop word of the time you'd played him into casual conversation. Oh, you could say, did I ever tell you about the time Sean O'Connell beat me with a pair of deuces even though I had jacks and sevens?

That would get you attention.

But Savannah the Woman didn't understand those feminine smiles at all. She'd heard about O'Connell's reputation. How he went from one conquest to another. How he lost interest and walked away, leaving a trail of broken hearts behind him. Why set yourself up for that? Emotions were dangerous. They were impractical. Still, she had to admit that Sean O'Connell was eye candy.

He was six foot one, maybe two. He wore a black dinner jacket open over a black silk T-shirt and black trousers that emphasized his lean, muscular body. Dark-haired, as Alain had said. The color of midnight was more accurate.

Alain hadn't mentioned his eyes.

What color were they? Blue, she thought. She was too far away to be sure and, for an instant that passed as swiftly as a heartbeat, she let herself wonder what would happen if she crossed the marble floor, stopped right in front of him, looked into those eyes to see if they were the light blue of a tropical sea or the deeper blue of the mid-Pacific.

Savannah frowned and permitted herself another tiny sip of champagne.

She had a task to accomplish. The color of O'Connell's eyes didn't matter. What counted was what she knew of him, and how she would use that knowledge tonight.

He was considered one of the best gamblers in the world. Cool, unemotional, intelligent. He was also a man who couldn't resist a challenge, whether it was a card game or a beautiful woman.

That was why she was here tonight. Alain had sent her to lure O'Connell into a trap.

She'd never deliberately used her looks to entice a man into wanting to win her more than he wanted to win the game, to so bedazzle him that he'd forget the permutations and combinations, the immutable odds of the hand he held so that he'd lose.

It wasn't cheating. Not really. It was just a variation of the skill she'd developed back when she'd dealt three-card monte. Keep the sucker so fascinated by your patter and your fast-moving hands that he never noticed you'd palmed the queen and slipped in another king.

Tonight was different.

Tonight, she wanted the mark watching her, not her hands or the cards. If the cards came the right way, she would win.

If they didn't and she had to resort to showing a little more cleavage, so be it.

She'd do what she had to do.

The goal was to win. Win, completely. To defeat Sean O'Connell. Humiliate him with people watching. After she did that, she'd be free.

Free, Savannah thought, and felt her heart lift.

She could do it. She had to do it.

And she wanted to get started. All this waiting and watching was making her edgy. Do something, she thought. Come on, O'Connell. Pick your table and let's start the dance.

Well, she could always make the first move... No. Bad idea. He had to make it. She had to wait until he was ready.

He was still standing in the entryway. A waiter brought him a drink in a crystal glass. Bourbon, probably. Tennessee whiskey. It was all he drank, when he drank at all. Alain had given her that information, too. Her target was as American as she was, though he looked as if he'd been born into this sophisticated international setting.

He lifted the glass. Sipped at it as she had sipped at the champagne. He looked relaxed. Nerves? No. Not him. He was nerveless, or so they said, but surely his pulse was climbing as he came alive to the sights and sounds around him.

No one approached him. Alain had told her to expect that. They'd give him his space.

"People know not to push him," Alain had said. "He likes to think of himself as a lone wolf."

Wrong. O'Connell wasn't a wolf at all. He was a panther, dark and dangerous. Very dangerous, Savannah thought, and a frisson of excitement skipped through her blood.

She'd never seduced a panther until tonight. Even thinking about all that would entail, the danger of it, gave her a rush. It would be dangerous; even Alain had admitted that.

"But you can do it, chérie," he'd told her. "Have I ever misled you?"

He hadn't, not since the day they'd met. Lately, though, his attitude toward her had changed. He looked at her differently, touched her hand differently...

No. She wouldn't think about that now. She had a task to perform and she'd do it.

She would play poker with Sean O'Connell and make the game a dance of seduction instead of a game of luck, skill and bluff. She'd see to it he lost every dollar he had. That he lost it publicly, so that his humiliation would be complete.

"I want Sean O'Connell to lose as he never imagined," Alain had said in a whisper that chilled her to the bone. "To lose everything, not just his money but his composure. His pride. His arrogance. You are to leave him with only the clothes on his back." He'd smiled then, a twist of the mouth that had made her throat constrict. "And I'll give you a bonus, darling. You can keep whatever you win. Won't that be nice?"

Yes. Oh, yes, it would, because once she had that money... Once she had it, she'd be free.

Until a little while ago, she hadn't let herself dwell on that for fear Alain would somehow read her mind. Now, it was all she could think about. She'd let Alain believe she was doing this for him, but she was doing it for herself.

Herself and Missy.

When this night ended, she'd have the money she needed to get away and to take care of her sister. They'd be free of Alain, of what she'd finally realized he was... Of what she feared he might want of her next.

If it took Sean O'Connell's humiliation, downfall and destruction to accomplish, so be it. She wouldn't, couldn't, concern herself about it. Why would she? O'Connell was a stranger.

He was also a thief.

He'd stolen a million dollars from Alain in a nonstop, three-day game of poker on Alain's yacht in the Mediterranean one year ago. She hadn't been there—it had been the first of the month and she'd been at the clinic in Geneva, visiting Missy—but Alain had filled her in on the details. How the game had started like any other, how he'd only realized O'Connell had cheated after the yacht docked at Cannes and O'Connell was gone.

Alain had spent an entire year plotting to get even.

The money wasn't the issue. What was a million dollars when you'd been born to billions? It was the principle of the thing, Alain said.

Savannah understood.

There were only three kinds of gamblers. The smart ones, the stupid ones and the cheats. The smart ones made the game exciting. Winning against someone as skilled as you was a dizzying high. The stupid ones could be fun, at first, but after a while there was no kick in taking their money.

The cheats were different. They were scum who made a mockery of talent. Cheat, get found out, and you got locked out of the casinos. Or got your hands broken, if you'd played with the wrong people.

Nobody called in the law.

Alain wanted to do something different. O'Connell had wounded him, but in a private setting. He would return the favor, but as publicly as possible. He'd finally come up with a scheme though he hadn't told her anything about his plan or the incident leading up to it until last week, right after she'd visited her sister.

He'd slipped his arm around her shoulders, told her what had happened a year ago and what he wanted her to do. When she'd objected, he'd smiled that smile she'd never really noticed until a few months ago, the one that made her skin prickle.

"How's Missy?" he'd said softly. "Is she truly happy in that place, chérie? Is she making progress? Perhaps it's time for me to consider making some changes."

What had those words meant? Taken at face value they were benign, but something in his tone, his smile, his eyes gave a very different message. Savannah had stared at him, trying to figure out how to respond. After a few seconds, he'd laughed and pressed a kiss to her temple.

"It'll be fun for you, chérie. The coming-out party for your twenty-first birthday, so to speak."

What he meant was, she'd take O'Connell by surprise. She had yet to play in a casino; thus far, Alain had only let her sit in on private games.

She'd come to him at sixteen, straight off the streets of New Orleans where she'd kept herself and Missy alive scamming the tourists at games like three-card monte. She was good but her winnings were meager. You could only play for so long before the cops moved you on.

Alain had appeared one evening on the edge of the little crowd collected around her. He'd watched while she took some jerks who'd left their brains in their hotel rooms along with their baggage.

During a lull, he'd stepped in close.

"You're good, chérie," he'd said with a little smile. He sounded French, but with a hint of New Orleans patois.

Savannah had looked him straight in the eye.

"The best," she'd said with the assurance of the streets.

Alain had smiled again and reached for her cards.

"Hey," she said, "leave those alone. They're mine."

He ignored her, moved the cards around, then stopped and looked at her. "Where's the queen?"

Savannah rolled her eyes and pointed. Alain grinned and moved the cards again. This time, his hands were a blur.

"Where is she now, chérie?"

Savannah gave him a piteous look and pointed again. Alain turned the card over.

No queen.

"Watch again," he said.

She watched again. And again. Five minutes later, she shook her head in amazement.

"How do you do that?"

He tossed down the cards and jerked his head toward the big black limo that had suddenly appeared at the curb.

"Come with me and I'll show you. You're good, chérie, but I'll teach you to use your mind as well as your hands. We can make a fortune together."

"Looks like you already got a fortune, mister."

That made Alain laugh. "I do, but there's always more. Besides, you intrigue me. You're dirty. Smelly."

"Hey!"

"But it's true, chérie. You look like an urchin and you sound like one, too, but there's a je ne sais quoi to you that intrigues me. You're a challenge. You'll be Eliza to my Professor Higgins."

"I don't know any Eliza or Professor Higgins," Savannah replied sourly.

"All you need to know is that I can change your life."

Did he take her for a fool? Four years in foster homes, one on the streets, and Savannah knew better than to get into a car with a stranger.

She also knew better than to let something good get away.

She'd looked at the limo, at the man, at his suit that undoubtedly cost more than she could hope to make in another five years of hustling. Then she looked at Missy, sitting placidly beside her on the pavement, humming a tune only she could hear.

Alain looked at Missy, too, as if he'd only just noticed her.

"Who is that?"

"My sister," Savannah replied, chin elevated, eyes glinting with defiance.

"What's wrong with her?"

"She's autistic."

"Meaning?"

"Meaning she can't talk."

"Can't or won't?"

It seemed a fine distinction no social worker had ever made.

"I don't know," Savannah admitted. "She just doesn't."

"There are doctors who can help her. I can help her. It's up to you."

Savannah had stared at him. Then she'd thought about the long, thin knife taped to the underside of her arm.

"You try anything funny," she'd said, her voice cold, her heart thumping with terror, "you'll regret it."

Alain had nodded and held out his hand. She'd ignored it, gently urged Missy to her feet and walked them both into a new life. Warm baths, clean clothes, nourishing food, a room all her own and a wonderful residential school for Missy.

And he had kept his word. He'd taught her everything he knew until she knew the odds of winning with any combination of cards in any game of poker, blackjack or chemin de fer.

He hadn't touched her, either.

Until recently.

Until he'd started looking at her through eyes that glittered, that lingered on her body like an unwelcome caress and made the hair rise on the back of her neck. Until he'd taken to pressing moist kisses into the palm of her hand and, worse still, calling her from her room in his chateau or her cabin on his yacht whenever he had visitors, showing her off to men whose eyes glittered as his did, who stroked their fingers over her cheekbones, her shoulders.

Which was why she'd agreed to take Sean O'Connell to the cleaners.

It was the best possible deal. Alain would get what he wanted. So would she. By the night's end, she'd have enough money to leave Alain and take care of Missy without his help. To run, if she had to—though surely she wouldn't have to run from Alain.

He'd let her go.

Of course he would.

Savannah raised the champagne flute to her lips. It was empty. Just as well. She never drank when she played. Tonight, though, she'd asked for the Cristal at the bar, felt the need of its effervescence in her blood.

Not anymore.

She put her empty glass on a table and smoothed down the shockingly short skirt of the red silk slip dress Alain had selected. It wasn't her style, but then the life she was living wasn't her style, either.

Savannah took a deep breath and emptied her mind of everything but the game. She shook back her long golden hair and stepped out of the shadows.

Ready or not, Sean O'Connell, here I come.

CHAPTER TWO

GOLDILOCKS was finally going to make her move.

Sean could sense it. Something in the way she lifted her glass to her mouth, in the way she suddenly seemed to draw herself up, gave her away. He wanted to applaud.

About time, babe, he felt like saying. What took you so long?

Of course, he didn't. Why give the game away now? He'd have bet a thousand bucks she had no idea he'd been watching her, no idea he was even aware of her.

He was.

He'd noticed her as soon as he'd entered the casino. Or not entered it, which, he supposed, was a better way of putting it. He'd learned, long ago, that it was better to take his time, scope a place out, get the feel of things instead of walking right into a situation. So he'd been taking his time, standing in the arched entry between the foyer and the high-stakes gaming room, sipping Jack Daniel's on the rocks as he watched.

Watched the tables. The players. The dealers. In a casino as in life, it paid to watch and wait.

That was when he'd noticed the blonde.

She was tall, with a great body and legs that went on forever. Her face might have inspired Botticelli and just the sight of that lion's mane of sun-streaked, silky-looking hair made him want to run his fingers through it.

Sean sipped his bourbon.

Oh, yeah. He'd noticed her, all right.

She was checking things out, too. At least, that was what he'd thought. After a while, he realized he had it wrong.

What she was checking out was him.

She was careful about it. Nothing clumsy or overt. She'd chosen her spot well. The lighting in the little alcove where she stood was dim, probably in deliberate contrast to the bright lights in the gaming area.

But Sean had long ago learned that the devil was in the details. The success of his game depended on it. He saw everything, and saw it without making people aware he was looking. One seemingly casual glance and he could figure out how Lady Luck was treating players just by taking in the expressions on their faces, or even the way they handled their cards.

Besides, a man would have to be blind not to have seen the blonde. She was spectacular.

And she was gearing up for something. Something that involved him. The only question was, what?

He'd thought about walking up to her, looking into those green eyes and saying, Hello, sugar. Why are you watching me?

It wasn't an opening line to use on a woman if she was about to come on to you, but instinct told him the blonde didn't have girl-meets-boy on her mind. No use pretending that wasn't unusual, Sean thought without a trace of ego. He was as lucky with women as he was with cards. That was just the way it was.

So, what was happening? Goldilocks was getting ready for something and it was making her nervous. He'd seen her hand tremble once or twice when she raised her champagne glass to her lips.

Curiosity had almost gotten the better of him when she began to move.

Sean narrowed his eyes as she stepped from the alcove and started toward him. Yes, the face was beautiful. Definitely Botticelli. But the body reminded him of a classical Greek sculpture. High, firm breasts. Slender waist. Those legs.

And a walk that made the most of all her assets.

Spine straight. Shoulders back. Arms swinging as she strutted toward him, crossing one long leg over the other so that she moved more like a tigress than a woman. It was a model's walk. He'd dated a German supermodel last year; Ursula had done The Walk for him in his living room, wearing nothing but a sultry pout and a lace teddy.

Goldilocks wasn't wearing a smile and her dress covered more than a teddy, though not much more. It was a scrap of crimson silk. He liked the way it clung to her breasts and hips. She had great hips, curved for the fit of a man's hands…

Hell.

He was getting hard just watching her.

Sean downed the last of his bourbon, told himself to concentrate on cold showers and on solving the puzzle of why the blonde had been observing him with such caution.

She was only a few feet away now. She hesitated. Then she lifted her chin, tossed back her hair, took a deep breath and smiled.

He felt the wattage straight down to his toes.

"Hi."

The tip of her tongue crept out, slicked across her bottom lip. Sean almost groaned but he managed a smile of his own.

"Hi yourself," he said. "I'd ask where you've been all my life, but you'd probably slug me for using such a trite line."

She laughed. And blushed. Another nice touch. He couldn't recall the last time he'd seen a woman blush, but her smile still glittered.

"Not at all. Actually, I was wondering how to tell you I was here alone, and that I've been alone for too long."

Her voice was soft. A liquid purr. It reminded him of honey and warm Southern nights. He moved closer.

"Isn't it fortunate that I finally got here?" he said softly. "What's your name, sugar?"

"Savannah."

"Ah."

"Ah?"

"The name suits you. You have moonlight and magnolias in that sexy drawl. You're a Georgia girl."

Another rush of pink to her cheeks. Interesting, that she'd blush and still be so direct in coming on to him.

"Savannah what?"

She touched her tongue to her lips again. Did she know what that was doing to him? The tip of that pink tongue sweeping moistly across her rosebud mouth? He thought she did but when he looked into her eyes, he wasn't so sure. They were a clear green, but there seemed to be a darkness hidden in their depths.

"Just Savannah." She closed the little distance that remained between them. He could smell her scent, a seductively innocent blend of vanilla and woman. "No last names tonight. Is that okay?"

"It's fine." Sean cleared his throat. "I'm a sucker for a good mystery, Just-Savannah."

"Just…?" Her eyebrows rose. Then she smiled. "I like that. 'Just-Savannah.'"

"Good. That gives us two things in common. Honesty and anonymity. That's a fascinating combination, don't you think?"

"Yes. I do. What shall I call you?"

"Sean."

Something flickered in those incredible eyes. Relief? No. It couldn't have been that. Why would a simple exchange of names inspire relief?

"Just-Sean," she said, smiling.

"Just-Sean, and Just-Savannah. Two people without last names who meet and set out to discover what the rest of the night holds in store."

"I like that." She reached out and laid her hand lightly against his chest. "What game will you play tonight, Sean?"

He felt his body clench like a fist. "It depends on who I'm playing it with," he said hoarsely. "What did you have in mind?"

She laughed. Her teeth were small, even, very white against the golden tan of her skin.

"I'm not sure." Her eyes met his, then dropped away. "I'm new at this."

It was a great line, designed to set a man's hormones pumping. All of it was designed for that: the face, the body, the scrap of red silk and the sexy, let's-get-it-on banter…and yet, the only part of it he bought into was her being new at this. Somehow, that rang with truth.

The lady wasn't a pro.

Like moths to the proverbial flame, high-priced working girls were drawn to places where big money and big players congregated, but no matter how elegantly dressed and groomed they were, Sean could spot them at a hundred paces. Besides, a call girl would never get past the door of a private casino like L'Emeraude.

No, Savannah wasn't a pro. She had the looks and the lines, but her delivery was off. It was like listening to an actress who was still learning her part. And there were those moments he'd seen her hand tremble…as the one she'd put against his chest was doing now.

She was working at turning him on and she was succeeding, but she wasn't lying. She was, he was sure, a novice at this game. As flattering as it was to think she'd turned into a lust-crazed creature at the sight of him, he didn't buy it. There was the way she'd been watching him. Besides, he was too much of a realist to believe in bolts of lightning that struck with no warning.

Something else was going on here. He didn't know what, but he was damned well going to find out.

"Sean?"

He focused his gaze on the blonde's upturned face. The smile was still there but the pretty flush in her cheeks was back. Was she flustered? Embarrassed? Or was it part of the act?

"Sean. Have I been too… I mean, I'm sorry if—"

"Savannah." He smiled and covered her hand with his. Her skin was icy. Instinctively, he closed his fingers around hers. "A beautiful woman should never apologize for anything." Sean raised her hand to his mouth and pressed his lips to her knuckles. "Let's make a pact."

"A pact?"

"You won't say you're sorry again, and I'll buy you a glass of champagne. Okay?"

She took a long time before she answered. Then, just when he'd decided she was going to turn him down, she nodded.

"That would be lovely."

"Good." Sean's hand tightened on hers. "You have any thoughts on how to seal our agreement?"

Another rush of color swept into her face. "What do you mean?"

"It's simple. We have a contract." Sean lowered his voice to a husky whisper. "Now we need some way to guarantee it." He looked at her slightly parted lips, then into her eyes. "You know. Sign in blood. Swear before witnesses. Cross your heart and hope to die." He flashed a quick smile. "Something to make it official."

He watched her face, saw the exact second she decided she'd had enough. Or maybe she'd decided to change tack. Try as he might, he couldn't tell which.

"You're making fun of me," she said.

"No, I'm not."

"You are. You think this is funny, and you're teasing me."

"Teasing. Not making fun. There's a world of difference."

"Let go of my hand, please."

"Why? I turn you on. You turn me on. That hasn't changed. Why walk away from it before we've discovered what comes next?"

He didn't know what he'd expected, though he'd gone out of his way to provoke a reaction. Would she blush some more? Lean into him and lift that luscious mouth to his? The combination of brashness and modesty was charming, even exciting, but it only made him more suspicious.

Whatever he might have anticipated, it wasn't the way she suddenly stood straighter, or the way her chin lifted.

"You're right," she said. "Why walk away now?"

Sean nodded. "That's better." It wasn't. She sounded as if she'd decided to go to the dentist after all. What in hell was happening? Acting on impulse, he reached out, put his hand under her chin and tilted her face up. "As for that contract," he said softly, "I know exactly how to seal the deal."

All of her was trembling now, not just the hand pressed to his chest. For a woman who'd tried to convince him of how eager she was to jump his bones, the lady was strangely nervous.

Sean smiled into her eyes, deliberately dropped his gaze to her mouth.

"No," she said quickly, the word a breathless whisper. "Please, don't—"

He hadn't intended to go through with it. The idea was to see how she'd react to the prospect of a kiss but when he saw her lips part, her eyes turn into the fresh green of a meadow after a spring rain, a shudder ran through his body. He wanted to kiss her. Kiss her, take her in his arms, carry her out of the noise and the light to a place where they'd be alone, where he could kiss her again and again until she trembled, yes, but trembled with need for him.

Sean stepped back, his pulse hammering, every muscle in his body tight as steel.

"Don't toast a deal with a bottle of champagne?" he said with forced lightness. "Now, that's definitely something no woman's ever asked of me before."

"Champ…" She caught her bottom lip between her teeth. He tried not to imagine it was his lip those perfect teeth were worrying. "Oh. I didn't… I mean, that would be nice."

"Besides, how could I let you go until I know why you stood in that alcove watching me for so long?"

Her face whitened. "I was not watching you."

"Telling fibs isn't nice, sugar. Sure you were. And now you're as nervous as a cat in a dog pound. Don't get me wrong, sweetheart. I like getting beautiful women flustered—but I like to know the reason for it. Somehow, I don't think your nerves have all that much to do with my masculine charms."

She looked up at him, conflicting emotions warring in her eyes. For a heartbeat, Sean felt as if she were on the verge of telling him something that would set him on a white charger like a knight ready to do battle with a dragon.

But she only smiled and angled her chin so she was gazing up at him through thick, honey-brown lashes.

"You're right about my watching you," she said softly, "but wrong in thinking it had nothing to do with your masculine charms." She smiled again, just enough to give those words the light touch they deserved. "I hoped you wouldn't notice."

"There's not a man in the room wouldn't notice you, if you were looking at him."

She laughed. It was a flirty, delicious sound. "That's very sweet."

"It's the truth."

Her hand was on his chest again, her fingers toying lightly with the lapel of his jacket. Her lips were slightly parted; she tilted her head back and now he could see the swift beat of her pulse in the hollow of her throat.

Sean almost groaned. He'd played games like this before but he'd never felt as if every muscle in his body was on full alert until now.

"I think it's time we got to know each other better, Just-Savannah."

"That sounds nice. What do you have in mind?"

Taking her to bed. That was what he had in mind, but he wasn't going to do that until he knew exactly what was going on here.

"The champagne I promised you, for starters." He linked his fingers through hers. "And some privacy."

"I'd like that."

Warning bells rang in his head. The words were right. So was the come-and-get-me smile, but the look in her eyes was wrong.

Maybe it was time to up the ante.

He turned her hand palm-up and lifted it to his mouth. He felt her stiffen as he pressed his lips to her flesh, felt her start to jerk her hand from his.

"Easy, sugar. I haven't taken a bite out of a woman in years. Not unless she wanted me to."

"I know. I just—I told you, this is all—"

"—new. Yeah, so you said." Sean's smile was deliberately lazy. "Unless, of course, there's more to the story than you're letting on."

"What more could there be, Mr. O'Connell? You're a very attractive man. I'm sure I'm not the first woman to show an interest in you."

The warning bells were going crazy. Mr. O'Connell? How could she know his name? He was Just-Sean. She was Just-Savannah. Definitely, there was more on her agenda. Should he call her on it? Should he play along?

He looked deep into the green eyes fixed to his. Hell. He was a gambler, wasn't he? What did he have to lose?

"Now, sugar," he said softly, "what kind of gentleman would I be if I answered that question?"

A slow, easy smile curved his mouth.

Seeing it, Savannah almost sagged with relief. For one awful minute, she'd been afraid she'd given everything away. She'd come awfully close, saying the wrong things, letting her nerves show, but then she'd turned the situation around by using her mistakes to convince Sean O'Connell she'd never come on to a man before.

That, at least, was the truth.

She couldn't afford any more screw-ups.

She'd thought this would be easy, but it wasn't. Using a deck of cards to scam a dumb mark on a dingy street corner was not the same as using your body, your smile, your words to scam an intelligent man in an elegant casino.

Besides, O'Connell was more than intelligent. He was street-smart. She hadn't expected that. He kept looking at her as if she were a candy bar he wanted to unwrap, but always with a wariness that made her uneasy.

Not that it changed anything.

She was in too far to stop. Either she went forward or she failed. And failure wasn't an option.

He was still smiling, but was there something in his eyes that shouldn't be there? Time to come up with a clever move that would shut down his brain.

A squeeze of her fingers in his might do it. A sexy smile. A flick of her tongue across her bottom lip. He'd reacted to that before.

Yes. It was working. His eyes were darkening, focusing on her mouth.

"If you told me about those other women," she said huskily, "you'd be the kind of man I'd run from. I don't want you thinking about anyone but me tonight."

"There's no way I could," he said softly. Another light brush of his lips against her palm and then he tucked her hand into the crook of his arm. "Have you seen the terrace, Just-Savannah?"

"No." Her voice sounded thready. She cleared her throat. "No," she repeated, and smiled up at him, almost weak with relief. Things were back on track. "No, I haven't. I've never been here before."

"Then you're in for a treat." He began walking slowly through the casino. Because of the way he'd captured her hand, she was pressed close to his side, aware of the warm length of his body, aware of the muscles in his thigh as it shifted against hers. "Let's have a drink on the terrace and I'll show you the most beautiful sight in these islands." He glanced at her, angled his head down to hers and put his lips to her ear. "I take that back, sugar. The second most beautiful sight in these islands."

The warmth of his breath, the promise in his words sent a tingle of anticipation through her. For a moment, Savannah let herself imagine what it would be like if the story she'd spun were true. If she'd come here to gamble, noticed this tall, incredibly good-looking stranger, taken her courage in her hands and gone up to him with seduction, real seduction, in mind.

But she hadn't. She was here for a purpose.

Was O'Connell really as good a poker player as people claimed? Alain said he was.

Maybe. But she was better.

Tonight, that was all that mattered.

CHAPTER THREE

SEAN paused just before they reached the terrace and signaled for a waiter, who hurried to his side.

"Sir?"

Sean drew Savannah a little closer. "What were you drinking, sugar? Cristal?"

She smiled. "Good guess."

"A bottle of Cristal Brut," Sean told the waiter. "Nineteen ninety. Will that be all right, Savannah?"

"It'll be lovely."

The waiter acknowledged the order with a discreet bow, and Sean opened the double glass doors that led onto the terrace.

"Here you are, sweetheart. The most beautiful night sky of the season, for the most beautiful woman in the Bahamas."

He put his hand lightly in the small of her back as they walked to the edge of the terrace. Her dress plunged in a deep vee to the base of her spine and her bare skin was as warm and silky as the tropical breeze drifting in from the sea.

"Oh," she said in a delicate whisper. "Oh, yes. It's perfect!"

"Perfect," he murmured, his eyes not on the softly illuminated pink sand beach or the star-shot black sky, but on her.

"It's so quiet."

"Yeah." A breeze lifted a strand of her golden hair and

blew it across her lips. He caught it in his fingers and tucked it behind her ear, letting his touch linger. "Quiet, dark and private."

Did she stiffen under his caress? No, it was his imagination. He was sure of it when she looked at him, her lips upturned in a Mona Lisa smile.

"Quiet, dark and private," she said softly. "I like that."

He felt his body stir. "Me, too," he whispered, and bent his head to hers.

Her mouth was sweet and soft. One taste, and he knew it wouldn't be enough to satisfy the hunger building inside him. Sean swept his fingers into Savannah's hair and lifted her face to his.

He sensed this could be dangerous. She wanted something from him and he still didn't know what it was, but kissing her was irresistible. Even as he let himself sink into the kiss, he told himself it was okay, that playing along was the only way to find out what she was up to.

It was a great plan…except, he had miscalculated. He couldn't think, couldn't find out anything when deepening the kiss almost drove him to his knees.

God, her mouth! Soft. Honeyed. Hot. And the feel of her hair, sliding like silk over his fingers. The sigh of her breath as it mingled with his.

Sean forgot everything but the woman pressed against him.

"Savannah," he murmured, sliding his hands down her throat, her shoulders, lifting her to him, drawing her tightly into his arms.

She made a little sound. A whisper of surrender. Her lips softened. Parted. She was trembling, as if the world were shifting under her feet just as it was under his, and he gathered her against his body until her softness cradled the swift urgency of his erection.

She stirred in his arms, moved against him, and the blood

pounded through his veins. Groaning, he moved his hand over her thigh, swept it under that sexy excuse of a skirt…

Just that quickly, she went crazy. Gasped against his mouth. Writhed in his arms. Twisted against him.

Sean thought she'd gone over the edge with desire. Thought it, right until she sank her teeth into his bottom lip.

"Goddammit," he yelped, and thrust her from him.

Stunned, tasting his own blood, he grabbed his handkerchief from his pocket and held it to his lip. The snowy-white linen square came away smeared with crimson. He stared at Savannah, his testosterone-fogged brain struggling for sanity. Her eyes were wide and glittering, her face drained of color, and he realized, with dawning amazement, that she hadn't moaned in surrender but in desperation.

She hadn't been struggling to get closer but to get away.

"Oh God," she whispered. She took a step toward him, hands raised in supplication. "I'm sorry."

"What the hell kind of game are you playing, lady?"

"No game. I didn't—I didn't mean to—to—"

Her hair was wild, the golden strands tumbling over her breasts. Her mouth was pink and swollen from his. Even now, knowing she was crazy, he couldn't help thinking how beautiful she was—and how crazy he'd be, if he spent a minute more in her company.

"Sean. I really am terribly sorry."

"Yeah. Me, too." He held the handkerchief to his lip again. The wound was starting to throb. "It's been interesting," he said, brushing past her. "I just hope the next guy you zero in on has better luck."

"Sean!" Her voice rose as she called after him. "Please. If you'd just give me a minute…"

He kept walking, but he was tempted. The bite hadn't been passion but what? Anger? Fear? He didn't know and told himself he didn't care. He wasn't a social worker. Whatever this woman's problem was, he wasn't the solution.

But she'd felt so soft. So vulnerable. When he'd first kissed her, she'd responded. It wasn't until he'd put his hand under her skirt that she'd panicked, if that was what she'd done, and that didn't make a whole lot of sense, not when she'd been damned near asking him to screw her for the past hour.

"Mr. O'Connell! Please!"

He stopped and swung around. She was running toward him. Mr. O'Connell, huh? Sean narrowed his eyes. Two times now, she'd called him that. Pretty surprising, since they hadn't introduced themselves with last names.

So much for walking away.

Why had she pretended not to know who he was? Why act as if she wanted to sleep with him when she'd gone from soft sweetness to what sure as hell seemed to be terror at the touch of his hand?

She stopped a few feet away.

"Please," she said again, her voice a shaky whisper. "I didn't mean to—to—" She swallowed dryly. "Your lip is still bleeding."

"Yeah?" He forced a thin smile. "What a surprise."

She closed the distance between them, that elegant feline walk gone so that she wobbled a little on her sky-high, do-me-baby heels.

"Let me fix it."

"Thanks, but you've done enough already."

She wasn't listening. Instead, she was burrowing inside her ridiculously small evening purse. What'd she expect to find? he thought grimly. A bottle of antiseptic and a cotton swab?

"Here. Just duck your head a little."

A froth of white lace. That was what she pulled from the purse. Sean glowered at her. She stared back. He could see her confidence returning, the glitter of defiance starting to replace the fear in her eyes.

"I'm not going to hurt you, Mr. O'Connell."

A muscle jerked in his jaw. "That's what they all say."

That brought a twitch to her lips. Sean told himself he was an idiot, and did as she'd asked.

Gently, she patted the handkerchief against the wound she'd inflicted, concentrating as if she were performing open-heart surgery. The pink tip of her tongue flicked out and danced along the seam of her mouth, and Sean felt his traitorous body snap to attention.

"There," she said briskly. "That should do—"

He hissed with pain as she pulled the hankie away. A bit of lace had clung to the congealing blood; yanking it free had started a tiny scarlet trickle oozing.

Savannah raised stricken eyes to his.

He'd gotten it right the first time. Her eyes really were as green as a spring meadow. And her mouth was pink. Like cotton candy. Maybe that wasn't very poetic, but he'd always loved the taste of cotton candy.

"I'm sorry," she said on a note of despair. "I know I keep saying that but—"

"You have to moisten it." His voice rumbled and he cleared his throat. "The handkerchief. If it's damp, it won't stick to the cut."

"Oh." She looked around. "You're right. Just give me a minute to find the ladies'—"

"Wet it with your tongue," he said. Hell. Now he sounded as if he'd run his words through a bed of gravel. Her eyes rose to his again. "The hankie. You know. Just—just use your mouth to make it wet."

Her face turned the same color as her dress. Time stretched between them, taut as a wire.

"Sean," she said quietly, "I didn't— When you kissed me, I didn't expect—I didn't know—"

"Know what?" he said roughly, moving closer. He reached out, cupped her face.

"Sir?"

Sean swung around. The waiter stood a few feet away.

"Your champagne, sir. Shall I...?"

"Just—" Sean cleared his throat. "Just put it on that table. No, don't open it. I'll do it myself."

Saved by the proverbial bell, he thought as the waiter did as he'd asked. Kissing this woman again made about as much sense as raising the ante with a pair of threes in your hand.

He waited until they were alone again, taking the time to get himself back under control. Then he looked at Savannah.

"Champagne," he said briskly.

"For what?" She'd pulled herself together, too. Her voice was strong, her color normal.

"It's just what we need. For the cut on my lip."

"Oh. Oh, of course. Will you—"

"Sure."

Sean did the honors, twisting the wire muzzle from the neck of the bottle, then popping the cork. The wine sparkled with bubbles as he poured some on the hankie she held out.

"It'll probably sting," she said, and before he could reply, she moved in and dabbed the cut with the cold, wine-soaked lace.

An understatement, Savannah thought, as Sean O'Connell rocked back on his heels.

"Sorry," she said politely. The hell she was, she thought.

She'd made a damned fool of herself. Worse, she'd probably blown her chance at setting him up for the kill, but it was his fault.

Why did he have to ruin things by kissing her? If he hadn't, everything would still be fine. She hadn't meant for him to kiss her; she was supposed to be the one setting the boundaries for this little escapade, not him.

"Hey! Take it easy with that stuff."

"Sorry," she said again, and went right on cleaning the cut with as little delicacy as she could manage.

Some seductress she was. The mark made a move she hadn't anticipated, gave her one simple kiss, and...

Except, it hadn't been a simple kiss. It had been as complex as the night sky. She'd trembled under it. The texture of his mouth. The whisper of his breath. The silken glide of his tongue against hers.

And then—then, it had all changed. His hand on her thigh. The quick bloom of heat between her legs. The pressure of his hard, aroused male flesh, the message implicit in its power.

All at once, the terrace had become the yacht. She'd remembered the way Alain's friends had taken to looking at her and the way Alain talked to them right in front of her, his voice pitched so low she couldn't hear his words.

She didn't have to.

She had only to see their hot eyes, see the little smiles they exchanged, feel the way a beefy hand would brush against her breast, her thigh, always accidentally…

"Are you trying to fillet my lip or leave it steak tartare?"

Savannah blinked. O'Connell, arms folded over his chest, was eyeing her narrowly, his face expressionless.

"I, uh, I just wanted to make sure I disinfected the cut properly." She dropped her hand to her side, peered at his lip as if she knew what she was doing and flashed what she hoped was a brilliant smile. "It looks fine."

"Does it," he said coldly.

Oh, this wasn't any good! She'd had him right where she wanted him, and now she'd lost him. He was furious and she couldn't blame him.

Well, that would have to change if she was going to get anywhere tonight.

"Yes," she said, with a little smile. "I'm happy to tell you, you won't need stitches. No rabies shots, either."

He didn't smile back. All right. One more try.

"I suppose I owe you an apology," she said, looking at him from under her lashes.

Sean almost laughed. The cute smile. The tease. And, when those failed, the demure look coupled with an apology. All designed to tap into his masculine instincts. He was supposed to say "no, it's okay," because that was what a gentleman would do.

Unfortunately for Just-Savannah, he was no gentleman.

"No."

"No?"

"I don't want an apology."

She almost sighed with relief. He waited a beat.

"I want an explanation."

She blinked. Clearly, she hadn't expected that. Now she was mentally scrambling for a response.

"An explanation," she parroted. "And—and you're entitled to one. I, uh, I think it's just that you—you caught me by surprise."

"You've been coming on to me all evening."

"Well—well, I told you, you're an attractive—"

She gasped as he caught hold of her wrists.

"And yet, the first move I make, you react as if I dragged you into an alley."

"That's not—"

"Game's over, sweetheart."

"I have no idea what you're talking about."

"Nobody plays me for a fool." Sean held her tighter, applying just enough pressure to let her know he was taking charge. "I want answers."

"To what? Honestly, Mr. O'Connell…"

"Let's start with the 'Mr. O'Connell' routine. I was Just-Sean. You were Just-Savannah. How come it turns out you know my last name?"

Savannah swallowed past the lump in her throat. His face was like a thundercloud; his hands were locked around hers like manacles. Missy, she thought, oh, Missy, I'm so sorry.

"I told you," she said in a low voice. "I saw you and I found you very—"

"Forget that crap." His mouth thinned; he tugged on her

wrists and she had no choice but to stumble forward until they were only a breath apart. "I knew something was up, but you were determined to keep trying the same con so I decided to go along. You've been scamming me, sugar, and I've had enough. You tell me what's going on or I'll drag you to the manager's office and see to it you're barred from ever entering this place again."

"You can't do that! I have as much right to be here as you do."

"Maybe you're a working girl."

"A working…" She began to tremble. "That's a lie."

"Is it? Once I describe your behavior, who's going to argue with me?"

"You can't do that!"

His grin was all teeth. "Try me."

Savannah opened her mouth, then shut it. For all she knew, he could do anything. He was known here. She wasn't. Everything was coming apart. She'd have to go back to Alain and tell him she'd failed, that his year of planning had led to nothing.

"Well? I'm waiting for that explanation. And I'll tell you right now, sugar, it damned well better be good."

Desperate, she searched for anything that might get her out of this mess. What could she possibly say that would change things? O'Connell was right. He wasn't about to believe she was interested in him, not after she'd almost bitten his face off when he touched her.

She wouldn't react that way if he did it again.

The realization shocked her. It was true, though. Now that she knew what to expect, if it happened again—which it wouldn't—but if it did, if she ever felt all that heat, saw the hunger in his eyes, she might just—she might just—

"Okay, that's it."

Sean started walking toward the door, dragging her with him. Think, she told herself desperately, think, think!

"All right," she gasped. "I'll tell you the truth."

He swung toward her, towering over her in the moonlight. He said nothing. Clearly, the next move was hers. Savannah took a steadying breath and played for time to work out a story. Something he would buy so she wouldn't have to return to Alain in failure and see that cool smile, hear him say, Ah, chérie, that's too bad. I hate to think of your dear little sister in one of those state institutions.

She took a steadying breath. "I owe you an apology, Mr. O'Connell."

"You already said that."

"Not for biting you. For—what did you call it? For scamming you."

It was a start. At least she'd caught his attention.

"I didn't mean to. Not exactly. I just—"

"You didn't mean to. Not exactly." Sean raised an eyebrow. "That's your explanation?"

"No! There's more."

"Damned right, there's more. Why don't you start by telling me why you pretended not to know who I was?"

How much of the truth could she tell, without giving everything away?

"I'm waiting."

"Yes. I know." She looked down at their hands, still joined, then up at his face. "It's true. I did know who you were. Well, I knew your name but then, everyone knows your name."

She fell silent. Sean let go of her wrists and tucked his hands into his pockets. He'd long ago learned the art of keeping quiet. Do it right and the other person felt compelled to babble.

"Everyone knows you're the world's best poker player."

He wasn't, though he was close to it. Still, he said nothing. She didn't, either, but he knew his silence was getting to her. She was chewing lightly on her lip. If she wasn't careful, she'd leave a little wound to match his.

A wound he could easily soothe with a flick of his tongue. Damn, where had that thought come from?

"And all this is leading where?" he said gruffly.

"To—to the reason I came over and spoke to you."

"Sugar," he said, smiling tightly, "you didn't speak to me, you hit on me. Understand, I've no objection to a beautiful woman showing her interest." His smile faded. "I just don't like being played for a sucker."

"I didn't—"

"Yeah, you did. Or you would have, if you could have gotten away with it." He pulled his hand from his pocket and checked his watch. "I have other things to do tonight. You have two minutes to answer my questions—or we can take that walk to the office."

Savannah knotted her fingers together. She was going to do the very thing Alain had warned her against, but what other choice did she have?

"I play poker, too, Sean."

"How nice." His teeth showed in a chilly smile. "We're back to first names."

"Did you hear what I—"

"You said you play poker. What's that got to do with anything?"

She hesitated. What could she safely tell him? Surely not that the man he'd cheated out of a million dollars had sent her, or that she was going to wipe him out because she was as good a player as he'd ever met.

She certainly couldn't tell him the rest of it, that she'd planned to work him into such a sexual haze that by the time they sat down to play, he'd be so busy drooling over her that he wouldn't be able to concentrate on his cards.

But she could tell him part of it, fancy things up to appeal to his ego. She'd blown her cover as a femme fatale. Could she pass herself off as an overeager tourist?

"I'm American. Like you."

"Congratulations," Sean said dryly. "So what?"

"So, I'm on vacation. You know. Sun, sea, sand. Gambling. I really like to gamble, even though I'm new at it."

A muscle flickered in his jaw. "Go on."

"You're right about my name. I was born in Georgia but I live in Louisiana. That's where I learned to play cards. On a riverboat. You know, on the Mississippi? A date took me, the first time." She grinned, hoped it was disarming and that mixing lies and truth proved the ticket to success. "I picked up the game fast. I'm pretty good, if I must say so myself, but I've never played against serious competition. Against, say, a man like you."

Sean lifted an eyebrow. Was this the whole thing? Had she flirted with him just to convince him to take a seat at the same poker table? Anything was possible. Novices approached him all the time. In his own tight little world, he was a celebrity of sorts.

Except, he didn't buy it.

All this subterfuge, so he could beat her pretty tail off in a game of cards? So she could go home and say she'd played Sean O'Connell?

No way.

"I'd be thrilled if you'd let me sit at a table with you, Sean. I could go home and tell everyone—"

"Anybody can sit at any table. You must know that."

"Well—well, of course I know that. But I'm not that forward. I know you think I am, after all that's happened, but the truth is, I wouldn't have the courage to take a seat at a table you were at unless I cleared it with you first."

He still didn't buy it. She wouldn't have the courage? This woman who'd done everything but jump his bones?

"And that's it?"

Savannah nodded. "That's it."

He moved fast, closed the distance between them before she could even draw a breath. All at once, her back was to the wall and his hands were flattened against it on either side of her.

"You took a big risk, sugar," he said softly. "Coming on to me as hard as you did without knowing a damned thing about me except that I play cards. You got me going a few minutes ago. If your luck had gone bad, you might have gotten hurt."

He saw her throat constrict as she swallowed, but her eyes stayed right on his.

"I told you that I knew you were Sean O'Connell. And Sean O'Connell isn't known for hurting women."

"No." His gaze fell to her mouth. He looked up and smiled. "He's known for liking them, though."

"Sean. About what I've asked..."

"Why did you panic?"

"I didn't. I—"

Sean put one finger gently over her lips. "Yeah, you did. I kissed you, you kissed me back, and then you got scared." His finger slid across the fullness of her mouth. "How come? What frightened you?"

"Nothing frightened me."

She was lying. He could sense it. There was something going on he still didn't understand and, all at once, he wanted to.

"Savannah." Sean cupped her face. "What's the matter? Tell me what it is. Let me help you."

Her eyes glittered. Was it because of the moonlight, or were those tears?

"I don't know what you're talking about."

Sean smoothed back her hair. "Just as long as you're not afraid of me," he said gruffly, and kissed her.

She let it happen, let herself drown in the heat of his kiss. She told herself it was what she had to do but when he drew back, she had to grasp his shoulders for support.

"Tell me what you want," he said softly.

Savannah willed her heart to stop racing. Then she took a deep breath and said the only thing she could.

"I told you. I want to play cards. Then I can go home and tell everybody that I played against the great Sean O'Connell."

"And that's it? That's all you need from me?"

His eyes were steady on hers, his body strong under her hands. For one endless moment, she thought of telling him the truth. That she was here to destroy him. That she was in trouble and had no one to turn to for help but herself.

Then she remembered that he was a thief, and she forced a smile to her lips.

"That's it," she said lightly. "That's all I need."

CHAPTER FOUR

Two hours later, Sean was sitting across from Savannah at a poker table in the high-stakes area of the casino and the warning bells in his head were clamoring like bells inside a firehouse.

The game was draw poker. She was still playing. He'd already folded, just as he'd done half a dozen times since they'd started. His fault, he knew. He'd played with lazy disinterest, underestimated the lady's skill.

And her skill was considerable.

The realization had caught him by surprise. Once it had, he'd played a couple of hands as he should have from the start. She'd folded. He'd won.

That had led to another realization. Goldilocks wasn't a good loser.

Oh, she said all the right things, the clever patter card-players used to defuse tension. She flashed that megawatt smile across the table straight at him. But her eyes didn't smile. They were dark with distress. What she'd said about simply wanting to play him wasn't true.

Just-Savannah needed to win. He decided to let her. There were all kinds of ways to up the ante.

And if she was new to the game, he was Mighty Mouse.

She played with the cool concentration of someone who'd had years to hone her talent. Her instincts were good, her judgment sharp, and by now he'd determined that the cute little things she did when she played, things he'd at first thought were unconscious habits, were deliberate shticks meant to distract him.

A little tug at a curl as it kissed the curve of her cheek. A brush of her tongue across her mouth. A winsome smile accompanied by a look from under the thick sweep of her gold-tipped lashes.

Most effective of all, a sigh that lifted her breasts.

The air-conditioned chill in the casino was cooperating. Each time her breasts rose, the nipples pressed like pearls against the red silk that covered them.

Forget about the odds, she all but purred. Forget about the game. Just think about me. What I have to offer, you'll never get by winning this silly game of cards.

It was hard not to do exactly that. The man in him wanted what she was selling with every beat of his heart. The gambler in him knew it was all a lie. And there it was again. The smile, just oozing with little-girl amazement that she was actually winning.

Bull.

Savannah wasn't a novice, she was an expert. Playing without using any of those distractions, she'd beat every man at the table on ability alone.

Every man but him.

She was good, but he was better. And once he knew what in hell was happening, he'd prove it to her.

Meanwhile, the action was fascinating to watch. Not just her moves but the moves of the rest of the players. Two—a German industrialist and a Texas oil billionaire—were good. The others—a prince from some godforsaken principality, a Spanish banker, a has-been American movie star and an Italian who had something to do with designing shoes—weren't. It didn't matter. The men were all happy to be losing.

Sean didn't think Savannah gave a damn. He'd have bet

everything he owned that she was putting on this little show solely for him.

Why? No way was it so she could go home and boast about having played against him. That story leaked like a sieve, especially because he could see past the smile, the cleavage, the performance art.

Under all that clever artifice, she was playing with a determination so grim it chilled him straight down to the marrow of his bones.

So he'd decided to lay back. Win a couple of hands, lose a couple. Fold early. Look as if he was as taken in as the others while he tried to figure out what was going on.

Right now, he and she were the only ones playing. The rest had all folded. She sighed. Her cleavage rose. She licked her lips. She twirled a curl of golden hair around her index finger. Then she looked at him and fluttered her lashes.

"I'll see your five," she said, "and raise you ten."

Sean smiled back at her. He didn't bother looking at his cards. He knew what he had and he was damned sure it beat what she was holding.

"Too rich for my blood," he said lazily, and dropped his cards on the green baize tabletop.

The German smiled. "The fräulein wins again."

Savannah gathered in the chips. "Beginner's luck," she said demurely, and smiled at him again.

It wasn't luck, beginner's or otherwise. The luck of the draw was a big part of winning but from what he'd observed, it had little to do with her success at this table.

The lady was good.

He watched as she picked up her cards, fanned them just enough to check the upper right-hand corners, then put them down again. It was a pro's trick. When your old man owned one of the biggest hotels and casinos in Vegas, you learned their tricks early.

Not that Sean had spent much time in the casino. State

law prohibited minors from being in the gaming areas. More importantly, so did his mother.

One gambler in the family was enough for Mary Elizabeth O'Connell. She'd never complained about her husband's love of cards, dice, the wheel, whatever a man could lay a wager on, but she also made it clear she didn't want to see her children develop any such interests.

Still, Sean had been drawn to the life as surely as ocean waves are drawn to the shore.

He began gambling when he was in his teens. By his senior year in high school, he bet on anything and everything. Basketball. Football. Baseball. A friend's grades. His pals thought he was lucky. Sean knew better. It was more than luck. He had a feel for mathematics, especially for those parts of it that dealt in probability, combinations and permutations. Show him the grade spread for, say, Mrs. Keany's classes in Trig over the past five years, he could predict how the current grades would play out with startling accuracy.

It was fun.

Then he went away to college, discovered poker and fell in love with it. He loved everything about the game. The cool, smooth feel of a new deck of cards. The numbers that danced in his head as he figured out who was holding what. The kick of playing a hand he knew he couldn't lose or, conversely, playing a hand no sane man would hold on to and winning anyway because he was good and because, in the final analysis, even the risk of losing could give you an adrenaline rush.

By the time he graduated from Harvard with a degree in business, he had a small fortune stashed in the bank.

Sean handed his degree to Mary Elizabeth, kissed her on both cheeks and said he knew he was disappointing her but he wasn't going to need that degree for a while.

"Just don't disappoint yourself," she'd told him, her smile as gentle as her voice.

He never had.

After almost eight years playing in the best casinos and private games all around the world, he was one hell of a player. His bank account reflected that fact. He could risk thousands of dollars on each turn of the cards without blinking.

He didn't win all the time. That would have been impossible, but that was still part of what he loved about the game. The danger. The sense that you were standing on top of the world and only you could keep you there. It was part of the lure. Maybe it was all of it.

Maybe he just liked living on the edge.

He wasn't addicted to cards.

He was addicted to excitement.

And what was happening tonight, at L'Emeraude de Caribe, was as exciting as anything he'd experienced in a very long time.

A blonde with the face of a Madonna and the body of a courtesan was running a scam with him as the prospective patsy, and he was going to find out what she was up to or—

"O'Connell? You in or out?"

Sean looked up. The Texan grinned at him from around the dead cigar stub clamped in his teeth.

"I know the little lady's somethin' of a distraction," the Texan said in a stage whisper, "but you got to make a decision, boy."

"I'm in," Sean said, shoving a stack of chips to the center of the table.

Everyone was in, except for the prince. He dumped his cards, folded his arms and never took his eyes from Savannah. She was, as the Texan had said, something of a distraction.

Soon, only he, Savannah and the German remained. The German folded. He had nothing. Sean had a pair of aces and two jacks. Could Savannah top that? He knew she couldn't. He raised her ten thousand. She saw it, smiled and raised another ten.

Should he meet it? Or should he let her think she'd out-bluffed him, the way he'd done the last few hands?

Savannah began her little act. The tongue slicking across her mouth. The breasts straining against the red silk.

He wondered how she'd look stripped of that silk. Her breasts seemed rounded, small enough to cup in his hands. Were her nipples as pink as her lips? Or were they the color of apricots? They'd taste like honey, he was certain. Wildflower honey, and when he sucked them into his mouth, tugged at them with his teeth, her cry would fill the night...

"Mr. O'Connell?"

He blinked. Savannah was watching him intently, almost as if she knew what he was thinking.

"Are you in or out?"

He looked down at his cards again. The aces and the jacks looked back. What the hell, he thought.

"Out," he said, and dumped his cards on the table. He smiled at her. "You know, you're taking me to the cleaners, sugar."

It was true. He'd lost a lot of money. He wasn't sure how much. Seventy thousand. A hundred. More, maybe.

He waited for her to smile back at him. She didn't.

"You're not going to stop playing, are you? I mean—I mean, it's still early."

She sounded panicked. He'd had no intention of quitting. Now, he decided to pretend that he had.

"I don't know," he said lazily. "Heck, a man's a fool to keep playing when he's losing."

"Oh, come on." She smiled, but her lips barely moved. "One more hand."

Sean pretended to let her talk him into it. He watched her pick up the cards as the dealer skimmed them to her.

Her hands were trembling.

His cards were bad. Evidently, so were those of the others. Some fast mental calculations suggested Savannah's cards were excellent. The others dropped out. Sean raised the ante. Savannah folded before the words were fully out of his mouth.

"You won this time around," she said gaily, but he could hear the edge in her voice. And her hands were still shaking. "Aren't you glad you stayed in?"

Sean nodded and pulled the chips toward him. What she'd done didn't make sense. He was sure she'd had better than even odds on holding a winning hand. Had she folded only to make him want to stay in the game?

It was time to make a move. Change the momentum and see what happened.

"It's getting late," he said. He yawned, stretched, and pushed back his chair. "I think I've had it."

Savannah looked up. He could see her pulse beating in her throat.

"Had it? You mean you want to stop playing?"

"Enough is enough, don't you think?"

When she smiled, her lips damned near stuck to her teeth. "But you just won!"

"And about time, too," he said, and chuckled.

"Come on, O'Connell." The Texan flashed a good ol' boy grin. "You can't quit when the little lady's beatin' the pants off all of us. Pardon me, ma'am, for bein' crude, but that's exactly what you're doin'."

"And we love it," the German said, chortling. "Come, come, Mr. O'Connell. Surely you won't walk away when things are just getting interesting. I don't think I've ever heard of you losing with such consistency."

"True," the prince said, and nudged the man with a sharp elbow, "but then, I doubt if Mr. O'Connell's accustomed to playing with such a charming diversion at the table."

Everyone laughed politely. Not Savannah. The expression on her face was intense.

"Please. I'd be devastated if you left now." Her voice was unsteady, but the smile she gave him was sheer enticement.

Sean decided to let her think it had worked. "Tell you what. How about we take a break? Fifteen minutes. Get some air, whatever. That okay with the rest of you?"

It was okay with everyone except Savannah, who looked as if he'd just announced he was abandoning ship, but she responded with a bright smile.

"That's fine," she said, pushing back her chair, too. "No need to get up," she added, when the men half rose to their feet. "I'll just—I'll just go to the powder room."

Sean watched her walk away. They all did, and it annoyed him. Stupid, he knew. He had no rights to her, nor did he want any. Still, he didn't like the way the others looked at her.

"She is a beautiful woman," the Italian said.

The one-time movie star smiled. "That she is."

"You're a lucky SOB, O'Connell," the Texan said, shifting the unlit cigar in his mouth.

Sean grinned. "Lucky to lose so much money?"

"Lucky to have a woman like that interested in you." The prince leaned forward. "I'd be happy to lose twice what I have, if she'd do that little tongue trick with me in mind."

Sean's smile vanished. "I'll be back," he growled, and headed for the terrace.

The terrace was as empty as when he'd been out there with Savannah. Empty, quiet, and a good place to get some fresh air and reconsider the point of letting a woman he didn't know think she was getting the best of him.

He walked to the rail, leaned against it and stared blindly out over the sea. Maybe he was dead wrong about Savannah. He could be reading things into the way she was behaving. Wasn't it possible she'd told him the truth? That all she wanted was to play cards? Those feminine tricks could just be part of the action. She might have used them to advantage back on the riverboat, where she said she'd learned to gamble.

And even if she was lying about being new to gambling, about wanting to play him…what did that change? Not a thing, he thought, answering his own question. He was making a mystery out of something that was probably, at best, simply an interesting situation.

If she was up to anything at all, it might just be scamming him so she could take him, big-time.

So what if he could still remember the sweet taste of her mouth? If her eyes were deep enough to get lost in?

If her hands trembled, and sometimes he saw a fleeting expression on her lovely face that made him want to gather her into his arms and kiss her, hold her, tell her he'd protect her from whatever it was she feared—

"Lovely night, Mr. O'Connell, isn't it?"

Sean started. The prince, who'd come up alongside him, inclined his head in apology.

"Sorry. I didn't mean to take you by surprise."

"That's okay. I was just—just listening to the sound of the sea. I didn't hear you coming."

The prince leaned back against the rail as he reached into the pocket of his tuxedo jacket and took out a slim gold cigarette case. He opened it and held it out to Sean, who shook his head.

"No, thanks."

"You don't smoke?" Sighing, the prince put the cigarette in his mouth, flicked the wheel of a small gold lighter and put a flame to the tip. "I've been trying to quit for years." He exhaled a plume of smoke and smiled. "My wife assures me it's a worse affliction than gambling."

Sean nodded. He wasn't in the mood for conversation.

"And I assure her that a man must have some vices, or there isn't much point in living." The prince inhaled again. "She's a stunning young woman."

"I'm sure she is." Sean made a show of checking the luminous dial on his watch. "Would you excuse me, Prince Artois? I want to make a stop in—"

"I wasn't referring to my wife—though she is, of course, a beautiful woman." The prince blew out a perfect smoke ring. "I was talking about our poker player. Savannah."

Something in the man's tone made the hair rise on the back of Sean's neck.

"Yes," he said carefully, "she is."

"You're fortunate she has such an interest in you."

"She's interested in winning," Sean said, just as carefully. "We all are."

"And yet, you are losing. I doubt if anyone has ever seen you lose this way before."

"It happens."

"Indeed." The prince turned to stare out over the sea, the burning tip of his cigarette a tiny beacon in the night. "What I find most amusing is that she's so good that the rest of us would surely lose against her even if she weren't such a distraction, but you—you shouldn't be losing at all. You're not easily diverted, or so I've heard."

"Diverted?"

"Come on, O'Connell. You and I both know the lady is doing her best to keep your attention off the game."

"Perhaps she's succeeding," Sean said, his eyes fixed to the prince's autocratic profile.

"Perhaps. Or perhaps you're letting her win, for your own reasons."

Sean straightened up. "I'll see you inside."

He began walking toward the lighted door, but the prince called after him.

"You know who she is, of course?"

A muscle knotted in Sean's jaw. He stopped, but didn't turn around.

"A woman named Savannah," he said, "from the American South."

"Savannah McRae," Artois said. "That's her full name."

Slowly, Sean turned and looked at him. "You know her?"

"We've never been introduced until tonight." He gave Sean a thin smile. "But I know who she is. And what."

Sean went toward him, his steps deliberate, his eyes never leaving Artois's face.

"Would you like to explain that?"

"She plays cards." Artois flicked the glowing cigarette butt over the railing. It flickered like a tiny shooting star as it arced toward the beach. "It's how she earns her keep."

Her keep. Not her living, which would no longer have surprised Sean, but her keep.

"Her keep?" he asked softly.

"Is this really unknown to you, Mr. O'Connell?"

The muscle in Sean's jaw leaped. "Get to it, Artois," he growled, "and stop screwing around."

The prince smiled. "She's Alain Beaumont's mistress."

He didn't believe it.

Savannah, Beaumont's mistress? No. It was impossible.

Sean paced the terrace on the other side of the casino, far from the sound of the surf, the lights, the all-too-vividly remembered taunting smile Artois had shown him.

Beaumont was slime. His little cruelties to the maids who worked in the elegant houses on these islands and in Europe were whispered about; his perversions were the topic of quiet speculation among those who found him either fascinating or revolting.

Sean had met him at a casino in Monte Carlo. Just watching him fondle the backside of a waitress whose face blazed with shame, hearing his lewd jokes, listening to his boasts about his sexual prowess, had been enough to make him despise Beaumont.

Somehow, they'd ended up playing at the same baccarat

table, the same roulette wheel, the same poker table, where Beaumont lost to Sean. Lost badly.

Beaumont's eyes had burned with fury but his voice had been unctuous as he invited Sean to give him the chance to win back his money. Sean had wanted only to see the last of him, but honor meant accepting the challenge.

"Deal the cards," Sean had snapped.

But Beaumont refused. He wanted Sean to play on his yacht, anchored in the harbor. And because Sean wanted nothing more than to see the man lose again, he'd agreed.

They'd taken Beaumont's tender to the yacht, just the two of them, and played through the night and the morning, Beaumont's line of oily chatter gradually giving way to tight-lipped rage as the pile of chips in front of Sean grew.

By noon the next day, he'd won a million dollars. Beaumont slammed his hand on the table, called Sean a cheat. Sean grabbed him by his lapels, hauled him to his feet, demanded an apology or he'd beat him to a pulp.

He'd almost hoped Beaumont wouldn't oblige. Beating him insensible held enormous appeal.

But Beaumont conceded, making up for not giving Sean the chance to beat him by wetting his trousers. Sean had laughed in scorn, scooped up his money and left. Once on shore, he walked into the first charity office he found and gave his winnings to a shocked and delighted little old lady seated behind a battered desk.

He had not seen Beaumont since.

Sean reached the end of the terrace and came to a dead stop.

Savannah, Beaumont's mistress? That greasy pig, taking her into his bed? His thick lips sucking at hers? His hands on her breasts, his thigh parting hers, his...

Sean balled his hands into fists, threw his head back and glared up at the stars as if they were to blame for what had happened. God knew, the fault was his own. He'd been fooled by Alain Beaumont. Now, he'd been fooled by Beaumont's mistress.

Obviously, Savannah was supposed to win back the million Beaumont had lost.

Sean narrowed his eyes.

Beaumont wanted to play? Sean would oblige him, only this time, he'd lose more than his money.

He took a steadying breath, thrust his hands into his hair and smoothed it down. Then he strolled back into the casino.

Savannah was in her alcove again. Her back was to him; she had one hand to her ear. She was talking to someone on a cell phone.

Another deep breath, this time to keep himself from giving the game away. He approached her quietly, from behind.

"I understand," she was saying, her voice low-pitched. "Alain, yes, you've told me that already…"

Alain. Alain. Sean felt his stomach roil, again saw Savannah in the pig's arms.

"I will. Of course, I will. I just wanted you to know that it might not go as we'd— Because he's clever, that's why. There are moments I think he's on to me, and…" Her shoulders bowed. Her head drooped. "No," she whispered. "Alain, please, just give me a little more time."

Sean stared at Savannah's dejected posture. Heard the desperation in her voice. For one wild minute, he saw that white horse again, saw himself in silver armor, galloping toward her.

"Yes, Alain. You know I do. Do you need me to say it? You mean—you mean everything to me."

Sean's gut knotted. He thought about going to her, spinning her around, slapping her face even though he'd never laid a finger on a woman in his life.

Instead, he swallowed past the bitter taste in his throat.

"Savannah?" he said casually.

She spun around, her face turning white when she saw him.

"There you are," he said, and forced his lips to curve in a smile. "Where've you been, sugar? We said fifteen minutes, remember?"

She stared at him blankly. "Sean?"

He mounted the two steps that led into the alcove. "Who are you talking to, sugar?" Still smiling, he held out his hand. "The folks back home, I bet. Are you telling them how you're playing and winning?"

Slowly, she took the tiny phone from her ear and looked at it as if she'd never seen it before. Then she hit the button to end the call, opened her evening purse and dropped the phone inside.

"Yes," she said. Her smile was shaky but he had to give her credit for managing to smile at all. "That's exactly what I was doing. They're all green with envy."

"I bet." Sean waggled his hand. She took it, and he drew her into the curve of his body. "Well, come on, sweetheart. Let's see how well you do now that I've had some time to get myself together."

"Yes," she said. "Let's."

She laughed up into his face but he could feel a tremor run through her.

Hours later, he could actually see her shaking. He wasn't surprised. He'd played without mercy. The others had long ago folded. They were watching what was happening with the fascination of rabbits watching a weasel in their hutch.

Sean had won or intimidated them all. There were half a million dollars worth of chips piled in the middle of the table. He'd just added the hundred thousand that had brought the chips to that amount.

His cards were good. Savannah's were, too. He could tell by the way she ran her fingers over them.

Now she had two choices. Meet his bet and call, or fold.

He knew, with every instinct he possessed, she couldn't afford to fold. He also knew she didn't have any more money.

She had something else, though. And he was going to force her to risk it.

"Well?" He smiled at her. "What's it going to be, sugar?"

She looked at the chips, then at him. They'd gathered a crowd by now. Even high-stakes players had never seen a game quite like this.

"I don't—" She cleared her throat. "I don't have…" She looked around her, as if money might drop from the sky. "I'll give the casino a chit."

Sean's teeth showed in a hungry smile. "No chits here. Check, if you like, but those are the house rules."

"Then—then surely you'll take my personal note, Mr. O'Connell."

"My, oh my, just listen to that. We're back to the 'Mr. O'Connell' thing again." Sean leaned forward. "Sorry, Just-Savannah. I don't take personal notes."

"I told you, I don't have—"

"But you do," he said softly.

"I do?" Her gaze flickered to her wrist and the diamond watch linked around it. "My watch," she said breathlessly. "It's worth—"

"It's worth zero. What would I do with that watch?" Sean let his eyes slip over her, doing it slowly, from her face to her breasts and then back. She was pale and for one second, he felt sorry for her.

Then he remembered why she was here and who had sent her, who owned her, and his heart turned to ice.

"Make it something worth my while."

"I told you, I don't have—"

"Yeah," he said, and he could hear the anger, the hunger, damn it, in his voice. "One night."

"What?"

"I said, if you can't come up with the money, I'll take a night with you in its place."

The crowd stirred, a whisper of shock and delight rushing through it like the wind through a stand of trees.

"You mean—you mean—"

"I mean," Sean said coldly, "you win, the money's yours." He paused, drawing it out for all it was worth, trying not to listen to the blood thundering in his ears. "You lose, you come with me." She didn't answer. Anger and his hot, unwanted desire for her drove him on. "You sleep with me, babe. You got that, or you want me to be more direct?"

He could tell that she was holding her breath. Hell, the whole world was holding its breath.

He didn't know what he'd expected from her in response. Fury? Disbelief? She didn't show either. Nothing changed in her expression and when she spoke, it was slowly, with dignity.

"I understand."

It was Sean's turn to hold his breath. "And?"

"And," she said, "I'll see your cards."

She fanned her cards out. Some of the pink had come back to her face; when he didn't say anything, she even smiled. She had reason to smile. She'd been holding a straight flush. The three, four, five, six and seven of hearts were spots of bright color against the green baize.

"Your turn, Mr. O'Connell."

Sean pursed his lips. "You've got one fine hand there, sugar. An excellent hand. No wonder you were willing to make that bet."

The crowd sighed. So did Savannah. Her smile became real as she leaned across the table and began reaching for the chips.

Sean put his hand over hers. "Not so fast," he said softly.

Her eyes met his. Smiling, never looking away from her, he turned over his cards.

The crowd gasped. So did Savannah. Not Sean. He'd known how this would end. He had the ace, king, queen, jack and ten of spades. A royal flush.

Emotion flashed through him, so swift and fierce he knew he'd never felt anything even remotely like it before. He kicked back his chair, ignored the stack of chips and the crowd. He went around the table to Savannah and held out his hand.

An eternity passed. Then she stood up, ignored his outstretched hand and began walking. He moved alongside her, wrapped his arm tightly around her waist and led her into the night.

CHAPTER FIVE

SAVANNAH wanted to die.

People were staring, whispering behind their hands. Every eye was on her as Sean laced a hard, proprietorial arm around her waist and led her through the casino. The whispers that had started back at the poker table must have spread like wildfire.

Even in this place, where money and excess were as common as grains of sand on the beach, winning a woman on the turn of a card was big news.

She couldn't blame anyone but herself. What a fool she'd been! Sean had toyed with her, letting her win hand after hand. Had she ever been in control of the game, or had he only let her think she was?

She'd gambled for the highest stakes and lost. Lost her sister's future, her future...

Lost to a man in whose bed she would spend the night.

The realization sent a ribbon of terror whipping through her blood. Savannah stumbled and would have fallen if Sean hadn't had his arm around her. His grasp tightened, his hand spread even more possessively over her hip.

"What's the matter, sugar? You having trouble keeping up with me?"

His words were soft; he dipped his head toward hers and she knew those watching would think he was whispering something low and sexy into her ear. But she heard the hard edge in his voice and when she tilted her face up, she saw his eyes glittering like sea-ice.

"No," he said, his smile slow and cruel, "we both know that's not the problem. You can more than keep up. Fact is, you've been ahead of me from the start."

He'd gone from lust to rage in a heartbeat. Why? Did he know something? He couldn't. Alain had planned things so carefully.

Alain.

Her throat constricted as she imagined his reaction when he heard what had happened. Losing to Sean O'Connell hadn't been an option. Alain had made that clear. Right before the tender took her to shore, he'd cupped her chin and lifted her face until their eyes met. He'd smiled, almost the way he used to when he'd first taken her from New Orleans. For the first time in months, the light kiss he dropped on her mouth had not made her shudder.

"A kiss for good luck, chérie."

"I'll do my best, Alain."

"Oui. I am certain you will." Another smile, but this one so cold it chilled her to the bone. "And if you need more than a good-luck kiss for a talisman, think of your dear sister as you play. That should cheer you on."

The warning had not been subtle. Remembering it, knowing how she'd failed, Savannah stumbled again.

Sean hauled her against his side. "You want me to pick you up and carry you out of here?"

He'd do it, too. It would add to her humiliation and he'd like that, though she didn't know why. And wasn't that funny? It was supposed to have gone the other way around. She was to have humiliated him.

Savannah reached deep inside herself and summoned up what remained of her pride. She'd be damned if she'd let him know the true depth of her despair.

"Don't push your luck, O'Connell," she snapped. "You won the bet. You didn't win the right to parade me around like a trophy."

"But that's what you are, sugar." A tight smile flashed across his face. "It's what you were meant to be. A prize I'd want so badly I'd think with my hormones instead of my head."

A cold hand seemed to close around her heart. Was that the explanation for his change in attitude? Was what she'd done so obvious?

"Surprised I figured it out?"

"I don't know what you're talking about."

"No. Of course you don't. You need an explanation, I'll give it to you when we get to my hotel room. For now, just keep moving."

That was all right with her. The sooner they left this place, the better. Anything to get away from the stares and smirks, the soft trills of laughter. The tragic part was that there was nothing funny in what was happening.

Alain's plan had failed. O'Connell hadn't been fooled by her brazen display of sexuality. It hadn't been her fault but Alain wouldn't see it that way. He'd lay the blame on her.

Yes, she'd changed things by telling Sean she wanted to play against him, but she hadn't had much choice. It hadn't bothered him. If anything, he'd seemed amused by her admission.

It had all gone so smoothly at first. She'd played as well as she ever had, better, really, because she knew how high the stakes were. And Alain's predictions had been correct. O'Connell was too busy watching her to pay attention to the game. She'd won and won and won—well, except for that time his interest seemed to be waning. She'd folded early and let him win.

Things had been going just fine… Until that break.

All the others at the table had wanted to take a breather.

She had to give in. What else could she have done? The last thing she'd wanted was to call attention to herself.

But she hadn't wanted to give O'Connell time to think, either. She'd thought of an easy solution. All she had to do was ask him to go with her. Step out on the terrace for some air. There, in the warm, sea-scented darkness, she could have smiled up at him from under her lashes. Tossed back her head when she laughed. Men liked looking at her when she did that. She won because of her skill at poker when she played for Alain, but that didn't mean she'd never noticed the hot male eyes that took in her every motion.

And yet, she hadn't done it. Something about the idea of being alone in the night with him again had made her feel... What? Uncomfortable? Uneasy? Maybe it was because she didn't like knowing she was cheating him, even though he deserved it. Maybe it was because she wanted to win as much on ability as she could.

Maybe it was because the thought of being alone in the dark with Sean made her pulse quicken. Things could happen between a man and a woman on a warm tropical night. He might reach for her. Draw her into his arms. Take her mouth in a slow, drugging kiss.

It was hard enough, playing at seduction, promising something she had no intention of delivering. She'd fled to the ladies' lounge, let cold water run over her wrists, then called Alain on her cell phone to tell him how well things were going.

And jinxed herself.

She'd sensed a change in Sean as soon as he led her back to the table. The Texan had started to say something but Sean's sharp voice silenced him.

"Let's not waste time," he'd said. "Just play the game."

A couple of minutes later, she'd known it was all over. Her adversary was playing with a single-minded intensity that was frightening, and exhibiting a level of skill and daring that made it clear he was out for blood.

He showed no mercy. A desire for something more than winning was fueling him.

Each time he looked at her, she saw rage in his eyes.

Smart players knew when to call it quits. Under normal circumstances she'd have bowed out but nothing about this night was normal. She had to win. So she'd kept playing. She won a couple of small pots, but she lost big each time it came down to only O'Connell and her until the others were simply spectators at what had become a blood sport.

Eventually, she'd stared disaster in the face. She was out of money. Every dollar Alain had given her was gone. No options left except going back to Alain and admitting failure. Then that terrible moment, Sean looking at her and in an impassive voice offering her a final, desperate chance...

"Get in the car."

Savannah looked up, startled. Somehow, they were out of the casino. A low-slung black sports car stood purring at the curb. A valet held the passenger door open.

The full reality of what awaited her was a dagger of ice straight to the heart. She was going to bed with a stranger. With a man who'd taken to looking at her as if she were something that had crawled out of a sewer.

Her steps faltered. "Wait a minute."

"Are you going to welsh on the bet, McRae?"

He'd called her by her name, but she'd never given it to him. God, oh God, oh God!

"Get in the car. If you walk away, I'll make sure there's not a casino in the world that will let you in the door."

She stared at him. His face was a mask of contained rage. Why? What did he know? Better still, what choice did she have? She could go with him or go to Alain.

Either way, she was lost.

Numb, Savannah did as he'd commanded. The valet shut the door. Sean got behind the wheel. "Fasten your seat belt."

She almost laughed. Who gave a damn what happened to her now? If the car went off a cliff and into the sea, what would it matter?

He muttered something, leaned over and reached for the ends of the belt. His hand brushed across her breasts. To her horror, she felt them lift, felt her nipples harden. He knew it, too. He stopped what he was doing and looked into her eyes and then, with slow insolence, at her breasts. He smiled when their eyes met again but this time, the smile didn't chill her to the bone.

It made her think.

Whatever O'Connell knew or thought he knew, he had no right to sit in judgment on her. He was a cheat and a thief. She wasn't either one.

As for losing… Yes. She had. But Alain wasn't an animal. She'd explain things to him. He wouldn't make good on his threats about Missy. No. He wouldn't do that to her. They'd sit down together, come up with a better plan to defeat Sean O'Connell.

In the meantime, she wouldn't let O'Connell see her fear. She'd do what she had to do, the way she used to on the New Orleans streets long ago.

She'd learned to block out the real world with a better world inside her head. Think of a million other things so she didn't have to think about her empty belly or her sister's soft weeping or the brush of a rat's tail as it ran across her legs while she and Missy slept huddled together in a doorway.

All those hard-earned skills would save her tonight. Sean O'Connell would claim his prize. He'd do what men did to women in bed. And she—she wouldn't be there. Not really. She'd be inside her own thoughts where there was no fear, no panic, no pain.

He'd won her body, but she'd never let him take her soul.

Sean's hotel was on the southern coast of Emeraude, far from the casinos and the glitter that drew the rich and famous of the world.

The hotel was a former plantation house restored to glory by the whim and wealth of a deposed European prince. One look at the elegant suites, the quiet beaches and coves, and Sean had known he'd never stay anywhere else when he was on this island. The place was a half-hour drive from the busy casinos and that had always seemed a fine thing. It gave him time to unwind as he headed home.

Tonight, he was sorry for the delay.

Damn it, he was angry. Angry? He choked back a laugh as he took his Porsche through the hairpin curves that wound along the coast. Hell, no. He wasn't angry. He was enraged. It had been all he could do to play out the game. To keep from reaching across the table, dragging Savannah from her chair, shaking her until her teeth rattled...

Kissing her until she begged him to stop.

He wouldn't have stopped. No way. She'd been set out as bait, and bait was expendable.

What kind of woman would use herself to break a man's bank account? What kind of woman would be Alain Beaumont's mistress? Sleep in his bed, turn her naked body into his arms, let him run his slimy hands over her soft flesh?

Sean gritted his teeth.

A woman who'd bet one night with a stranger against the stakes in a card game.

Headlights appeared in the darkness. The road was narrow, narrower still along this last stretch that led to his hotel. Normally, he'd slow his speed, pull the car over toward the scrub palmetto and wild beach grasses that lined the verge. Not tonight. Instead, he stepped down harder on the gas. The horn of the oncoming vehicle blasted as Sean roared by. He mouthed an oath and drove faster.

Who gave a damn about safety tonight?

Not him. Jesus, not him! He'd been taken in by a woman with hair of gold and eyes of jade, a woman whose soft, pink mouth he'd imagined savoring the minute he'd first seen her. Her kiss had shaken him as no other woman's ever had.

And she was a pawn owned by a piece of scum like Beaumont.

But he'd come out the winner. He'd taken Beaumont's money once again. Now he'd take his woman as well. He'd use her every way a man could, until those big eyes glittered with tears of shame, until that sweet-looking mouth was swollen and her thighs trembled because he'd spread them so many times.

No way she'd be thinking about her pig of a lover by then.

The tires clawed for control as he made a sharp turn into the hotel's circular drive. The parking valet trotted up and opened Sean's door as he shut off the engine. The boy smiled and greeted him but Sean wasn't in the mood for pleasantries. He brushed by the kid and flung open Savannah's door before the doorman could get there.

"Get out."

The soft glow of the interior lights illuminated her face. She was as pale as death except for two red streaks along her cheeks. The valet threw him a surprised look. Sean didn't give a damn. All that mattered was getting his pound of flesh.

"Out," he said again, and bent toward her. She pulled back, her face becoming even whiter as he reached toward her seat belt. She wasn't stupid, he thought grimly. She'd learned the limits of his patience and she didn't want him to touch her again.

Had the instant of awareness when he'd brushed his hand over her breast been part of the game, or had she actually responded to his touch? Sean narrowed his eyes. It had been an act, the same as everything else. Savannah McRae was Alain Beaumont's toy.

Tonight, she would be his.

He tossed the valet a bill, clasped Savannah's arm and hurried her up the wide marble steps to the lobby. Only one clerk was at the reception desk at this time of night. He smiled politely when he saw Sean but his eyebrows rose at the sight of Savannah. Women in too-short red dresses, wearing heels that made the most of their up-to-their-ears legs, weren't the standard here.

"Mr. O'Connell," the clerk said politely, his composure regained. "Good evening, sir."

"Edward." Sean looked at the man. "I'd ask you to have room service send up some champagne, but we won't need it. Will we, sugar?" He shot Savannah a smile he knew was all teeth. "Why waste a bottle of good wine when it's not necessary?"

Savannah paled. The clerk turned crimson. Good, Sean thought savagely. Two birds with one stone.

He tugged her toward the elevator. Once inside, he put his key in the lock that would take them up to the penthouse. She tried to pull away but he had a grip of steel.

"What's the matter, sugar? Not in the mood? I can't believe that. Not after the big come-on earlier."

She didn't answer. Damn it, why not? He wanted her to say something. To plead with him to forget their bet, or at least to ask him to treat her with courtesy.

The elevator doors opened; he hurried her straight through the sitting room and into a bedroom overlooking the sea.

Sean kicked the door closed and turned the lock. And that—the sound of the bolt clicking home—finally changed the expression on Savannah's beautiful face.

What he saw there was fear.

For a heartbeat, the fury inside him subsided. He wanted to go to her, take her in his arms, tell her he wouldn't hurt her, that he'd be gentle, make slow love to her until she was sobbing with pleasure...

"Unlock the door."

The words, almost whispered, brought him back to sanity. He'd almost forgotten how good she was at acting.

"Relax, sugar. I'm just seeing to it we aren't disturbed."

"We made a bet. I'm prepared to go through with it but—"

"But?" he said, cocking his head as if he really gave a damn what she said next.

"But..." She swallowed, caught her lip between her teeth. "But I won't—I won't do anything—anything—"

"Kinky?" He grinned, shrugged off his jacket and tossed it aside. "Oh, I think you will, Just-Savannah. In fact, I'm willing to bet on it."

He watched her breasts rise and fall as she took a deep breath, then exhaled. Color was returning to her face. If he hadn't known better, he'd have sworn she was willing herself to be strong, but that was crazy.

A woman who slept with Alain Beaumont would sleep with anybody, even a man who won her at a poker table.

"You'd lose that bet, O'Connell."

Sean shrugged his shoulders. "No problem, babe. You give me whatever you give your lover and we'll call it even."

"My lover?"

Oh, she was good! That look, the total innocence in her eyes, even the surprise in her voice... She was better than good. She was great.

Would she be that great in bed? Yes. Oh, yes, she would be. Sean could almost taste her mouth. Her nipples would be honey on his tongue, her belly would have the scent of vanilla when he kissed it. Her golden thighs would carry the clean, erotic scent of a woman aroused as he parted them to reveal the hidden essence of her.

God, he was hard as stone.

"Yeah," he said gruffly as he started toward her. "Your lover. Beaumont. Remember him?"

"I didn't—he isn't—"

Sean reached her. He looped one hand around her throat. She flinched but stood her ground. He could feel the hammer of her pulse beneath his fingers. Slowly, he ran his hand over her, lightly cupping her breast, then curving it over her hip.

"Stop lying. You didn't learn to play cards on a riverboat. Alain Beaumont taught you."

"I don't know what you're talking ab—"

She gasped as he put both arms around her and drew her up against him. He knew she could feel his erection. Hell, he'd never been this hard in his life.

"What else did Beaumont teach you, sugar?"

The idea of lying flashed through her mind. Sean could almost see her thought process.

"Come on," he growled. "Be honest just once tonight. Admit he's your lover, that he put you up to this, that you were supposed to take me down and walk away laughing."

She didn't answer. Sean cursed, pulled her to her toes and crushed her mouth beneath his. She gave a sob that pierced his heart before he remembered this was all a game. She was playing a part. Nothing more, nothing less.

"Admit it," he said roughly. "Beaumont put you on to me."

Tears glittered in her eyes. "You stole from him."

"I what?"

"Stole. Cheated him out of a million dollars. In a card game on his yacht."

"That's one terrific story, sugar."

"It's the truth!"

"Let me get this straight. I stole a million bucks from your lover and you decided to steal it back to get even?"

"I wasn't trying to steal your money. I was winning it in a poker game."

"You were winning only because you kept me so busy looking at you that I couldn't think straight."

"That's not true! I'm a good poker player."

"Right. You're so good that you lost your lover's stake and ended with nothing to put on the table but yourself." Sean took a step back. "And now it's time to deliver."

"Sean. Mr. O'Connell..." Savannah heard the sudden desperation in her voice. No. She'd promised she wouldn't let him see her fear or hear her beg... but Lord, how could she do this? Give herself to a man who despised her? Let him touch her, explore her, take the last of her innocence, the only innocence she'd been able to hang on to in her life?

He was leaning against the dresser, arms folded over his chest, feet crossed at the ankles, watching her with no expression at all on his face. He was a thief, yes, but he wasn't unkind. Another man might have laughed and dismissed her when she'd told him that lie about why she wanted to play against him.

He hadn't. He'd listened.

Maybe he'd listen now.

"Mr. O'Connell." Savannah moistened her lips. "There's—there's been a misunderstanding. I—I wasn't thinking straight when I agreed to—"

"Strip."

She blanched. "Please. If you'd just hear me out—"

"Are you going to pay me the money that you lost to me tonight?"

"I can't. But—but—"

But what? She owed him a small fortune. She didn't have the money to pay it. She never would. And Alain would never give it to her, either. It was bad enough she'd return to him in defeat. She couldn't return and ask him for money, too.

"Either pay me the money or start getting undressed. Take your time about it. I want to enjoy the show."

Sean waited, hardly breathing. What would she do next?

Run for her life, probably. Make a dash for the door, fumble with the lock and, damn it, he'd let her get away. He wanted her, yes. Why lie to himself? He wanted her badly, but not this way.

He couldn't go through with this. Even if she was willing, he'd—he'd—

The slow movement of her arms as she reached behind her stopped his thinking. His heart hammered as she slid down the zipper of the sexy red dress. One strap drooped against her shoulder, then the other. Her head was down but she must have felt his eyes on her because she lifted her chin and looked at him.

What he saw on her face almost killed him.

Here I am, she was saying. Do what you will. Take what you want. It doesn't matter. I won't feel anything you do to me.

But she would. He'd make her feel. He'd make her know it was his hands on her, not Beaumont, that she was in his bed, not anyone else's.

Eyes still on his, she began to ease off one of those incredible shoes. Sean cleared his throat.

"Leave them on," he said hoarsely. "Take off the dress and leave the rest."

She took a deep breath and the red silk slithered to the carpet. She was wearing a black lace bra that cupped her breasts as lovingly as a man's hands, a black lace thong that covered that part of her that was all female, thigh-high, sheer-as-a-whisper black stockings and those shoes.

She was the most beautiful woman he'd ever seen and, for tonight, she belonged to him. He'd make her forget everything else.

He walked toward her slowly. The tears trembling on her lashes might have gotten to him if he hadn't reminded himself that they were about as real as the rest of her act.

"Beaumont is a lucky man," he said. She didn't answer.

Sean trailed a finger down her throat, skimmed the curve of her breasts. "You're a feast for the eyes, Savannah. Do you taste as good as you look?"

She was shaking. Hell, he thought coldly, she was incredibly good at this. He clasped her face, lifted it to him, intending to brand her with his kiss. Instead, he found himself brushing his lips over hers, gently, softly, groaning at the sweetness of her mouth.

Everything he'd been thinking fled his mind. He drew her close and kissed her, again and again, until she made a sound deep in her throat. Her hands came up, touched his chest, slid up to his shoulders. She was weeping silently now, her tears leaving glittering streaks down her silken cheeks.

It was the tears that did it.

The ice around Sean's heart melted. Savannah was afraid of him. How could this be an act? She was terrified, but she didn't have anything to fear. He wouldn't hurt her. He'd be gentle, stroke her with slow hands, kiss her until she clung to him with desire.

"Savannah," he whispered. "Don't cry. I won't hurt you. Let me show you. Let me."

He kissed her again, still with tenderness even though he wanted more, wanted her with a ferocity that shocked him. He held back with a strength he'd never known he possessed. When her mouth began to soften and cling to his, he nipped lightly at her bottom lip until she sighed. Then, slowly, he eased the tip of his tongue into her mouth. She made that little sound, the one she'd made before, and tried to twist her face away but he wouldn't let her. He held her, kissed her, whispered to her until she began to melt in his arms.

She wanted him.

The knowledge hit him like a thunderbolt. She wanted him.

Sean murmured her name and bent her back over his arm. He buried his lips in the sweet softness of her throat, cupped the high curve of her breast and caught her lace-covered nipple between his teeth.

Savannah moaned his name.

And then sanity returned.

What in hell was he doing? Of course this was an act. The woman in his arms was giving an Oscar-winning performance and he was letting himself get sucker-punched all over again.

He let go of her, shoved her away. She stumbled; her eyes flew open, and for one impossible second he let himself believe that what he saw in their depths was confusion. But she could make him see whatever she wanted. She had, from the minute he'd laid eyes on her.

Sean snarled an oath as he snatched up her dress and flung it at her. She caught it and clutched it to her breasts.

"Get out!"

"But—but I thought—"

"Yeah. I know what you thought." His mouth twisted. "You thought wrong, sugar. I don't take another man's leavings." He took a step toward her, dug a handful of bills from his pocket and flung them at her feet. "Here's cab fare. Go back to Beaumont and tell him you still owe me. Tell him I'll come around one of these days to teach him a lesson he should have learned the last time we met."

He strode into the bathroom and slammed the door. When he opened it again, the bills still lay scattered on the carpet.

Savannah was gone.

CHAPTER SIX

WHAT did a man do to work off his anger when he couldn't get the woman who was the cause of it out of his head?

Sean paced like a caged lion. He took a shower so long and cold he risked frostbite. He grabbed the prior day's newspaper and flipped the pages without reading a word.

And yet, all he could do was think about Savannah and how she'd scammed him. He was a gambler, for God's sake. He'd seen people pull a thousand cons. Making it seem you were doing one thing while you were really planning another was at the heart of the game he played best.

But he'd never come up against a woman like this before.

What an ass he'd been. He'd known a lot of beautiful women in his life—too many, probably. He'd always been able to see past the lovely faces, the toned bodies, and figure out what they really wanted.

Not tonight. Savannah had pushed his buttons and gotten what she wanted.

And what had he been thinking, that he hadn't collected on their wager? Forget her tears. They'd been as phony as everything else about her. A bet was a bet. If he'd taken her to bed, he wouldn't be so damned angry now. The whole nasty episode would be behind him. He'd be done with that soft mouth. The silken skin. Those rounded breasts and endless legs. Done with her.

He flung the newspaper aside.

The hell he would.

If he'd had her once, he'd have wanted her again. All through the night, through the first flush of dawn. Once wouldn't have been enough, not for him, not for her.

Yes, the weeping, the trembling, had been part of the act. But maybe that little sob of passion, the way she'd melted against him, had been real. Maybe she'd really felt something when he touched her. Maybe…

Sean cursed in disgust. What pure, unadulterated bull. The lady hadn't felt a thing, except when she was winning. When he was letting her win. That was another reason he was so furious, not just at her but at himself. She'd played him for the worst kind of jerk, he'd let it happen, and she'd done it for Beaumont, the lying, cheating son of a bitch!

Okay. It was too late to change what had happened, but not too late to get even. Alain Beaumont would pay. So would Savannah. What was that old saying about revenge being a dish best served cold? Sean smiled with grim amusement. The time would come. He'd find a way. Until then, all he had to do was be patient.

Too bad patience wasn't in his nature.

He pulled on a pair of trunks, went down to the dark beach and plunged into the surf. He swam out beyond the breakers, swam out farther than any intelligent man would, but then he had no claim on intelligence, not after tonight. Under the cool gaze of the setting moon, he floated on his back in the warm sea until, finally, he felt the tension drain away.

When he returned to his suite, he fell into a deep, exhausted sleep.

The ring of his cell phone jolted him awake.

Sean sat up and peered at his watch. It was four-fifteen. Nobody phoned with good news at this hour. Dozens of possibilities ran through his mind but when he heard his older brother say, "Kid, it's me," he knew that the news was the worst it could be.

"Is it Ma?" he asked hoarsely. "Another heart attack?"

"No," Keir said, but Sean's relief was short-lived. "A stroke."

The bed seemed to tilt. Sean swung his feet to the floor. "Is she—is she—"

"She's still with us, but I won't mince words. The doctors don't know how things are going to go."

The heart attack had almost killed their mother. If Keir was saying this was worse...

No. Sean wasn't going there. If Mary Elizabeth was alive, there was still hope.

"Where is she? Vegas? Same place as last time?"

"She's in New York. Mount Sinai Hospital, cardiac care ICU. She and Dan were on vacation when it happened."

"I'm on my way. I'll see you in..." Sean checked the time again and did some quick calculations. "Four hours."

"Right. Cull's here, and the girls, and— "

"Keir?"

"Yeah, kid?"

"Tell her I'm coming, okay? And that I love her."

"She doesn't..." Keir cleared his throat. "Sure. Sure, I'll tell her."

"Will she—do the doctors think—" Sean's voice broke.

"Just hurry," Keir said, and hung up the phone.

Sean sat still for a long moment. Then he punched in the number of a company that leased private jets. Forty minutes later, he was on his way to the States.

Hospitals all smelled the same. Not that Sean had been in many, but you remembered from one time to the next. Antiseptic. Disinfectant. Lots of both, as if they could cover up the stench of pain, despair and death.

Mary Elizabeth O'Connell-Coyle lay motionless on a

bed in the cardiac care ICU. Sean's heart lurched when he saw her. His mother was a beautiful woman. Not now. Her normally ruddy face was white, her eyes were shut and her once-firm mouth was slack. Tubes ran from under the white cotton blanket that covered her to a stand holding bottles that dripped fluids into them. A tangle of thin wires led to a panel of blinking lights on a monitor.

He couldn't stop watching those lights. They marked his mother's continuing struggle to hang on to life.

He sat beside her, clutching her hand, talking to her in a soft voice, telling her how much he loved her, how he needed her, how they all needed her. Then he waited, hoped, prayed for a response. Anything. It didn't have to be much. A squeeze of her fingers. A flicker of the eyelid. He'd have settled for that.

The only things that changed were the nurses who came and went. They checked the tubes, straightened the linen, did things that didn't really mean a damn when what he wanted was someone to come in and announce they'd found a cure for her ailing heart, a magic potion that would make her young and whole again.

"Sean?"

He blinked back his tears and looked up at his brother, Cullen, who put a comforting hand on his shoulder.

"I know you just got here," Cull said, "but—"

"But everyone else wants to be with her, too." Sean nodded and got to his feet. "Sure. I understand."

Of course he understood. They were allowed into the cubicle for fifteen minutes each. Multiply those scant quarter hours by a husband and six children. Add two sons-in-law and the same number of daughters-in-law, and you could see that there just wasn't enough time.

There'd never be enough time.

His throat constricted as he leaned down and kissed his mother's pallid cheek. He and Cullen exchanged quick embraces. Then he went into the ICU waiting room and hugged the rest of the O'Connell clan before settling into an imitation leather armchair that looked as worn and weary as the room's occupants.

All they could do now was wait.

In late afternoon, his sisters went to the cafeteria and brought back sandwiches that might or might not have been edible. Nobody knew because nobody could manage more than a bite. Keir bought out all the candy bars in the vending machine; Cullen fed dollar bills into the maw of a contraption that promised coffee but oozed sludge. They all gulped it down, mostly because it gave them something to do. Nobody needed the caffeine. Though they hovered on the brink of exhaustion, sleep remained as elusive as good news.

Their stepfather told them he'd rented a large suite in a nearby hotel. "Get some rest," Dan urged. "What good will any of us be to Mary if we're out on our feet when she awakens?"

When, not if. They clung to the subtle message, nodded in agreement, but nobody left. After a while, Dan went back into the ICU to be with his wife. Sean watched his sisters, Megan and Fallon, lean against their husbands. He saw Keir put his arm around his wife and smile wearily when she laid her hand against his cheek, saw Cullen press a kiss to his wife's forehead as she whispered to him.

Only Sean and his kid sister, Briana, were alone.

Bree must have read his thoughts. She rose from her chair, crossed the room and sat next to him.

"Only you and me left," she said, with a little smile. "Everyone else got hitched."

Sean managed a smile in return. "Who'd a thunk it?"

Bree gave a deep sigh. "Guess it must be nice to have somebody at a time like this, though, don't you think?"

A face flashed through Sean's mind. A woman with

cascading hair the colors of gold and caramel, and eyes as green as the sea. The image shook him and he pushed it away.

"We do have somebody," he said gruffly. "We have each other."

His sister took his hand and squeezed it. "Sean? You think Ma will be all right?"

"She'll be fine," he said with more conviction than he felt, and he put his arm around Briana and hugged her tight.

Hours passed. Daylight faded and it was night again.

The men gathered in the hall for a whispered consultation. When they stepped into the waiting room, they all had the same determined look.

Sean nodded toward his two brothers-in-law. "Stefano and Qasim are going to the hotel," he told his sisters. "They're taking you ladies with them."

There was a blur of protest. The men held fast.

"No arguments," Cullen said firmly.

The women rose reluctantly. Sean turned to Dan.

"Come on," he said to his stepfather, and used Dan's own earlier words. "Ma's going to need you when she regains consciousness. You'll have to be here, one hundred percent."

Again, it was when, not if. They were all taking strength from that. Dan gave a reluctant nod. "I'll do it, but only so I can give your mother my opinion of the hotel. She always likes to know what the competition's doing."

It was a forlorn attempt at humor but they grabbed it like a lifeline, especially since it was a reminder of Mary Elizabeth's vitality as head of the Desert Song Hotel in Las Vegas. Keir, Cullen and Sean promised to phone if there was the slightest change and yes, of course, they'd take a breather themselves in a few hours.

When the others had gone, the brothers sat in silence for a while. Then Sean cleared his throat.

"How did it happen?"

Cullen and Keir shook their heads. "It just did," Cull said. "Dan and Ma were in Central Park. He says they were walking along, talking…"

"About what? Was she upset over something?"

"No, she wasn't upset. She was talking about you and Bree."

"About Briana and me?"

"Yeah. The usual thing. You know, how she'd be happy if Bree would find a guy to love, and if you'd get married and settle down."

"What do you mean, 'the usual thing'?" Sean frowned. "Ma never said—"

"Well," Cullen said uncomfortably, "she wouldn't. Not to you, but to us, you know, she says she worries about you guys, that you're alone."

"No," Sean said tightly. "I don't know. And if you're trying to tell me that's why she had—that I'm the reason for—"

"Settle down, little brother," Keir said quickly. "Nobody's even suggesting that. You asked what she was talking about. We're telling you."

Sean glared at his brothers. Then his face crumpled. "Right. I know that's not why this happened. It's only that—that it's hard to—to—"

"Yeah," Cullen said, "it is."

"What about the doctors?"

"They're doing everything they can."

"Did you call in a consultant? I know this guy's supposed to be top-notch, but—"

"He is top-notch," Cullen said quietly.

"We flew in Ma's own doctor," Keir added. "He agreed on her treatment."

Sean sprang to his feet. "Treatment? What treatment? She's lying in that bed. I don't call that treatment, I call that—"

"They gave her a drug. It's supposed to dissolve the clot that's causing the problem."

Problem? Sean almost laughed. That was a hell of a way to describe something that might kill their mother.

"Sean." Keir stood up and put an arm around his younger brother. "We're all going nuts here, but we have to wait. It's all we can do."

Sean's shoulders sagged. "You're right. It's just—"

He sat down. So did Keir. The three O'Connells were silent for a long time. Then Cullen mouthed an oath.

"I hate this place," he growled.

"Take a walk," Keir told him. "Get some air. Go around the block."

"No. No, I want to be here if—when…" Cullen fell silent, struggling for self-control. "Hey," he said, his tone as artificial as the flowers on a corner table, "did I tell you guys that Marissa and I drove down from Boston and took Ma and Dan to dinner the other night?"

He was, Sean knew, trying to change the subject, which was probably a damned fine idea. Okay. He'd do his part.

"Smart woman, our mother," he said briskly. "Won't catch her risking ptomaine by having a meal at Big Brother's la-ti-da restaurant in Connecticut."

Keir forced out a laugh. "Hey, kid. Just because you wouldn't know haute cuisine from hamburger doesn't mean the rest of the family has no taste. Ma and Dan came up for supper with us and stayed the night as soon as they hit the city."

"Only because Marissa and I didn't get into town until the next day," Cullen said.

"Yeah," Sean added, "and what's with that crack about my taste buds?"

"It wasn't a crack," Keir said. "It was the truth. There we were, growing up with room service ready to provide anything from beef Wellington to lobster thermidor, and what did you ask for, night after night? A cheeseburger and fries."

"Oh, not every night," Cullen said. "Our little brother used to cleanse his palate with an occasional hot dog."

"They were chili dogs," Sean said, "and did you really just say 'cleanse his palate'?"

"What can I tell you? I've got a wife who decided she loves to cook. She gets these magazines, you know? And sometimes I leaf through them."

Sean looked at Keir. "Cullen's learned to read," he said solemnly.

"Miracles happen," Keir replied.

Miracles. Would one happen in this hospital tonight? The same thought hit them all and ended their forced attempt at levity. Sean tried to think of something to talk about but came up empty. Keir was the one who made the next try at conversation.

"So," he said, "where were you when I phoned?"

Sean looked up. "Emeraude Island. In the Bahamas."

"Nice?"

"Yeah."

More silence. Cullen cleared his throat. "Marissa and I've been thinking of getting away for a long weekend. What's Emeraude like?"

"You know. Pink sand beaches. Blue water. Lush mountains."

"And casinos."

"A couple."

"How'd you do?"

Sean stretched out his legs and crossed them at the ankles. "Okay."

"Okay, he says." Cullen raised his eyebrows. "What'd you win this time? A trillion bucks?"

"No."

"My God," Keir said, "don't tell me. You lost!"

"I didn't say that."

"Well, that's how you made it sound." He smiled. "How much did you win, then?"

Sean gave a shrug. "A few hundred thousand."

"And that wasn't enough to make you happy?"

No, Sean thought in mild surprise, it wasn't.

"Kid? What's the matter?"

A muscle knotted in Sean's jaw. "I won something else."

"Ah. No, don't tell us. Let me guess. A car? A yacht?" Keir grinned at Cullen. "A French chateau?"

"A woman," Sean said flatly.

His brothers' jaws dropped. "A what?"

"You heard me. I won a—"

"Mr. O'Connell?"

The O'Connells sprang to their feet. Sean could feel his heart trying to pound its way out of his chest until he saw the smile on the face of the nurse who'd come into the room. They all let out a breath in one big whoosh.

"Your mother's regained consciousness, gentlemen." Her smile broadened. "And because she won't have it any other way, the doctor's agreed to let her visit with all of you at once."

Mary Elizabeth was back.

Maybe not completely. After a week, she was still paler than anyone liked, still looking fragile. Her speech was a little slurred and there were times she had to search for words.

But her smile was the same as it had always been. Her sense of humor was intact. So was her determination to take charge, even from a hospital bed.

She insisted Dan had to fly home and oversee things at the Desert Song. She told Cullen and Marissa it was more important they be at home with their baby than here with her, and tried to shoo Keir and Cassie away with the same message. She gave marching orders to Fallon and Stefano, then to Megan and Qasim.

Yes, they all said, yes, of course, absolutely, they'd leave. Nobody did.

In the end, the only people she didn't try to boss around were Briana and Sean. It was, she said, lovely having her youngest daughter nearby. And when she and Sean were alone, she told him it was better to know he was here than to imagine him wasting his time at a card table.

Sean knew his mother had never really approved of the way he lived but she'd never come out and said so before. He was surprised by her candor and she knew it.

"It's what a little glimpse of your own mortality does to you," she told him as he sat with her in the hospital's rooftop conservatory one afternoon. "A mother should speak bluntly to her favorite son."

Sean smiled. "I'll bet you say the same thing to Keir and Cullen."

"Of course," Mary said, smiling back at him. "You're all my favorites." Her smile dimmed. "But I worry about you the most. After all, you're my baby."

Sean raised his mother's hand to his mouth and kissed her knuckles. "I'm thirty years old," he said gently.

"Exactly."

"I'm almost disgustingly healthy."

"Good."

"And I'm happy."

"That's what you think."

"It's what I know, Ma. Trust me. I'm happy."

Mary shook her head. "You're a gambler."

"I like gambling. I'm not addicted to it," he said, smiling at his mother, "if that's what you mean. I can stop whenever I want."

"But you don't."

"Because I enjoy it. You should understand that. Pa was a gambler."

Mary nodded. "He was, indeed," she said quietly. "It was the one thing about him that broke my heart."

Sean stared at her. "I thought—"

"Oh, I loved your father, Sean. Loved him deeply." She sighed. "But I wish he'd loved me more than the cards."

"Ma, for heaven's sake, he worshiped you!"

"He did, yes, in his own way, but if I'd been enough for him, he'd have settled down. Made a real home for us. You remember how bad it was, the years before we stumbled onto the Desert Song." Mary clasped her youngest son's hand and looked deep into his eyes. "A man should find his happiness in a woman, not in the turn of a card."

"We're not all the same, Ma. What's good for Cull and Keir isn't necessarily right for me."

His mother sighed. After a minute, she squeezed his hand. "My birthday's the week after next."

"Your..."

"My birthday, yes. And don't look at me as if I've slipped 'round the bend, Sean O'Connell. I can change the subject without being daft, though I'm not really changing the subject. I'm just thinking how quickly life slips by."

"Ma—"

"Let me talk, Sean. Why shouldn't we admit the truth? I almost died."

"Yes." A hand seemed to close around his heart. "But you didn't," he said fiercely. "That's what counts."

"Lying in that bed, drifting in that place halfway between this world and the next, I kept thinking, 'It's too soon.'"

"Much too soon," Sean said gruffly.

"I don't want to leave this earth until all my children are happy."

"I am happy, Ma. You don't need to worry about it."

"You're alone, Sean."

"Times have changed. A person doesn't need to be married to be happy."

"A person needs to love and be loved. That hasn't changed. You have your father's itchy foot and his gift for the cards, but that can't make up for the love of a good woman."

Unbidden, a face swam into Sean's mind. Green eyes. A mane of golden hair. A soft mouth tasting like berries warmed by the sun. It was the face of a woman a man would burn to possess, but love? Never. Thinking of Savannah McRae and the word "good" at the same time was absurd.

Besides, his mother was wrong. A man didn't need love. He needed freedom. His father had loved his wife and children but Sean suspected he'd have been happier without them. In his heart, he was the same. It was the one bond he and his old man had shared.

"I know you think you're right, Ma," he said gently, "but I like my life as it is." He smiled. "You want to be a match-maker, why not take on Briana?"

"Bree will find somebody," Mary said with conviction. "She just needs a little more time. But you…"

"I'll give it some serious thought," Sean said, trying to sound sincere even if he was lying through his teeth, but it was a white lie, and white lies didn't count. "Maybe, someday, when I meet the right woman."

Mary sighed. "I just hope I live long enough to see it happen."

"You'll be here for years and years."

"Nobody can see the future," his mother said softly.

What could he say to that? Sean swallowed hard, searched for a change of subject and finally found one.

"That birthday—"

"Ah, yes. Dan and I want to have a big party."

"Not too much, though. You need peace and quiet."

"What I need is to get back into life."

Sean smiled. "You sound as if you're back into it already. And what would you like as a special gift?"

"Just all my children and grandchildren gathered around me."

"Nothing more?" Sean grinned. "Come on, Ma. Tell me your heart's desire and I'll get it for you."

Mary's eyes met his. "You will?"

"Yes. Absolutely. What do you want, hmm? Emeralds from Colombia? Pearls from the South Seas?" He bent forward and kissed her temple. "Name it, Mrs. Coyle, and it'll be yours."

His mother gave him a long look. "Do you mean it?"

"Have I ever made a promise to you and broken it?"

"No. No, you haven't."

"Well, then, tell me what you want for your birthday and you'll have it. Cross my heart and hope to die."

Sean said the words as solemnly as if he were seven years old instead of thirty, and he smiled. But his mother didn't smile. Instead, she looked so deep into his eyes that he felt the hair rise on the nape of his neck.

"I want to see you married, Sean O'Connell," she said. And from the expression on her face, he knew she meant every word.

CHAPTER SEVEN

AMAZING, what a combination of medical science and determination could accomplish. Ten days after Mary O'Connell-Coyle's stroke, her doctors pronounced her well and sent her home.

Keir, Cullen and Sean accompanied Dan and their mother to the airport. They sat with her in the first-class lounge and asked if she wanted anything so many times that Mary finally threw up her hands and said if they didn't stop fussing over her, she was going to go and find a seat in the terminal.

"One seat," she warned, "with no empties nearby." She looked at her husband, who smiled, and smiled back at him. "All right. Two seats, then, but not another within miles."

The brothers looked at each other sheepishly. Then they hugged her and kissed her, waited until the plane that would take her to Vegas had safely lifted off, and headed, by unspoken consent, for a taxi and a quiet, very untrendy bar Keir knew in lower Manhattan.

"My arms hurt," Sean said solemnly. His brothers raised inquisitive eyebrows. "From doing all that lifting to get the plane in the air."

He grinned. His brothers laughed, and Keir raised his glass of ale. "To Ma."

The men touched glasses. They drank, then leaned back in the time-worn leather booth.

"So," Keir said, "I guess we can all head home. Me to Connecticut, Cull to Boston." He looked at Sean. "You going back to that island?"

Sean felt a muscle knot in his jaw. "Yes."

"Can't get enough of the sea and sand?"

"I have unfinished business there."

"Must be important."

Getting even was always important, Sean thought coldly. "Yeah. It is."

Cullen grinned and nudged Keir with his elbow. "Something to do with that woman, I bet."

"What woman?" Sean said, much too quickly.

"Come on, bro. The babe you won in a game of cards." Keir reached for the bowl of peanuts. "You never did explain that."

"There's nothing to explain."

"There's nothing to explain, he says." Cullen dug out a handful of nuts, too, and started munching. "A man wins a night with a hooker, and he says—"

"Did I say she was a hooker?"

Sean's voice was glacial. Cullen and Keir exchanged glances. He could hardly blame them. What was he doing? Defending Savannah's honor? It would be easier to defend a Judas goat.

"Well, no. But I figured—"

"Forget it."

"Look, I didn't mean to imply you'd sleep with a call girl, but who else would—"

"Leave it alone."

"All I meant was, what kind of woman would—"

"I said, leave it alone, Cull."

Keir and Cullen looked at each other again. Sean sat stiff and silent, trying to figure out why he'd almost made an ass of himself defending a woman who was not much better than Cull's description of her.

He was returning to Emeraude to deal with Alain Beaumont. It had nothing to do with Savannah. With the way she came to him in his dreams so that he'd lived that same moment a thousand times, her suddenly trembling in his arms, returning his kiss, sighing against his mouth...

"So," he said briskly, "Ma really does seem fine."

His brothers nodded, both of them grateful for the change in conversation.

"Absolutely." Cullen grinned. "Did you hear her chew out the nurse who insisted she had to leave the hospital in a wheelchair?"

The brothers chuckled, then took long pulls at their mugs of ale. Keir circled the wet rim of his glass with the tip of his index finger.

"That birthday party is gonna be some kind of event."

"Nice of the girls to offer to plan it," Sean said.

Cullen gave a dramatic shudder. "Whatever you do, don't let 'em catch you calling them 'girls.' Besides, 'nice' has nothing to do with it. They just don't trust Dan or us to get it right." He motioned to the waitress for another round. "Either of you have any idea what you're going to give Ma as a gift?"

"Cassie thought maybe a cruise to Hawaii."

"Marissa's thinking along the same lines. She suggested a week in Paris."

"Not bad. Hawaii this winter, Paris come summer... Sean? Want to toss in a spring vacation?"

Sean shifted uneasily in his seat. "I've got a problem with that."

"What? With giving her a trip?"

"With what to give Ma. She won't want a trip. Not from me."

"How do you know that?"

Sean took a few peanuts from the bowl and rolled them in his hand. "Idiot that I am, I asked her what she wanted."

"And?"

"And she told me."

Cullen and Keir looked at each other. "Well?" Cullen said. "You gonna keep us in suspense?"

"She wants…" Sean hesitated. Even now, it sounded impossible. "She said she wants me to get married."

There were a few seconds of silence. Then Keir laughed. "Trust Mary Elizabeth to get straight to the point."

"It's what she wants."

"Sure it is, but she'll settle for a trip to… What?"

Sean took a deep breath, then let it out. "I promised."

His brothers stared at him. "You what?"

"Don't look at me that way! How was I to know she'd ask for something so crazy?"

"Right. And Ma won't expect you to keep a crazy promise. She'll understand."

"Exactly. It's like when you're joking around and somebody says, you know what I'd really like? And you say tell me what it is and I'll do it, but both of you know it's just…" Cullen's words drifted to silence. "You really promised?"

"I really promised." Sean looked up. "I'd do anything for Ma. But this…"

"Do you even know a woman you'd want to marry?" Keir asked, and sighed with resignation when Sean laughed. "Well, you could always hire an actress."

"Yeah," Sean said glumly. "Too bad Greta Garbo's dead."

The brothers all chuckled. After a while, the topic turned to the latest baseball trade and everybody but Sean forgot all about it.

Ma won't expect you to keep a crazy promise. She'll understand.

Sean turned off the reading lamp above his seat in Trans Carib's first-class cabin. That was the trouble. His mother would understand. She'd look at him and sigh, and give that little smile that meant he'd failed her again.

He'd always failed her.

Cullen won every athletic award in high school. Keir won every academic honor. They'd both finished college, gone to grad school and made places for themselves in the world.

What had he ever done besides cause trouble?

He'd been suspended more times than he wanted to remember in high school, mostly because he hated sitting in a classroom. He'd loved hockey and he'd been good at it. Great, maybe, until the day a puck damned near took his eye out because he'd been a smart-ass who wouldn't wear a helmet with a visor. Yeah, he'd finished college but he'd floated through, all the time just yearning for graduation so he could bum around the world with a backpack.

Sean frowned at his reflection in the window.

That was then. This was now. He'd made a fortune. The backpack had turned into handmade leather luggage, he stayed in five-star hotels instead of hostels, and if he didn't have a permanent base, it was because he preferred it that way. He'd changed. He'd found success. He was the luckiest O'Connell brother. The one with nothing holding him down, nobody holding him back...

He was the brother who had nobody.

The universe seemed to hold its breath. A chasm, dark and deep, yawned at Sean's feet.

"Mr. O'Connell?" The flight attendant smiled. "Your dinner, sir."

"I'm not..." Sean hesitated, forced a smile. "Great. Thank you."

The girl set down his tray, poured his wine. Alone again, Sean ignored the filet mignon and reached for the burgundy. His mother's brush with death must have affected him more than he'd realized. Funny, how easily a man's perspective could get skewed.

He had everything. He was living a life he loved. Sean raised his glass and saw his reflection. Not everybody could say that, he thought, and suddenly, the face he saw in the glass wasn't his.

Savannah looked back at him.

Was scamming strangers a life she loved? Coming on to men to ensure a win? Did having Alain Beaumont put his hands on her make her happy?

What was with him tonight? What did he care what made Savannah McRae happy? How come he couldn't get it through his head that the tears she'd shed, the way she'd melted in his arms, had all been part of the act?

Sean tilted the glass to his lips and drank. He was going to stop thinking about Savannah. She didn't mean a thing to him. And he was going to take his brothers' advice and tell his mother the truth.

Ma, he'd say, I never should have made you a promise I can't possibly keep.

But before he did that, he'd confront Beaumont and his mistress. They owed him, and he was damned well going to collect.

Ivory moonlight dappled the dark waters of the Caribbean where the Lorelei lay at anchor. The night was warm and still. Savannah, alone in her stateroom, was counting the minutes until Alain left to go ashore.

Only then would she feel safe.

A tremor raced through her. Despite the heat, she felt chilled. She reached for a sweatshirt and pulled it on over her thin cotton T-shirt.

Ten days had passed since the night she'd ruined everything. Ten days, but it felt like an eternity. Alain alternated between rage and deadly silence. Of the two, she'd begun to think his silence was the worst.

He was planning something. She knew it. He had been, ever since...

She had to stop thinking about that terrible night, but how could she? Alain was going to do something to punish her for what had happened. Wondering what and when was killing her.

It had taken her a very long time to get back to the harbor that night. She'd left the hotel by a back door, walked down the hill, then along the road. At dawn, an old man with a donkey cart gave her a lift. He hadn't asked her any questions. Maybe women with tear-stained faces, limping along in evening wear, were standard issue here.

The tender had been waiting at the dock; for one wild minute, she'd imagined turning around and running away. Then she'd thought of Missy, and she'd stepped into the boat and let the crewman take her to the Lorelei.

Alain was waiting in the yacht's salon, his face white, his mouth twisted into a narrow line. One look, and she knew he'd already heard the story.

Not all of it, of course. Not what had happened in O'Connell's bedroom, how the realization of what came next had suddenly become real.

All Alain knew was that she'd lost. It was enough.

"Alain," she'd said quickly, "I'm sorry. I did everything I could and it almost worked, but—"

He grabbed her so hard that she'd borne the marks of his fingers on her arms for days. Grabbed her and shaken her like a rag doll.

"You stupid putain!"

Even now, she shuddered, remembering the venom in his voice.

"How could you do this to me?" he'd roared.

"I told you," she whispered, "I don't know what happened. He was losing. And then—and then—"

Alain slapped her, hard enough to whip her head back. "Do you know what you cost me tonight?"

"Yes. Yes, I know. Almost five hundred thou—"

"Almost half a million dollars. How will you pay it back?"

"I'll win it at cards. I promise."

"How? By playing with my money? Does that sound reasonable to you?"

"It's—it's the best I can—"

"Shut up!" His spittle flew into her face as he leaned toward her. "Did you think I was joking? About wanting you to make O'Connell look like a fool?"

"No. No, of course not. But—"

"You didn't make a fool of him. He made a fool of you!"

"Alain, you must believe me. I was winning. I don't know what happened, only that suddenly—"

"When did you tell him you know me?"

"I never—"

"Don't lie to me! You told him. And that's who you made a fool of, you brainless creature. Me. Me! O'Connell's probably still laughing."

"No. He didn't laugh. Not at you!"

"I told you not to lie to me." Alain flung her from him. "And I told you the price you'd pay," he snarled and reached for the phone.

Missy. He was going to take Missy out of her safe haven in Switzerland. Savannah threw herself between him and the desk.

"I beg you, don't take this out on my sister."

"You failed me, Savannah. Apparently, your sister's welfare doesn't mean as much to you as I thought."

"Alain." Her voice trembled. She'd swallowed hard, fought for composure. "I'll win back the money. Every cent. I swear it."

His smile was the epitome of cruelty. "And will you win

back your virginity? That's all you ever had, you know. Your skill at cards and your hymen." He thrust his face inches from hers. "And now they're both gone."

She started to tell him he was wrong, that she hadn't slept with Sean, but she caught herself just in time. That might make him only more furious, knowing she'd reneged on her wager. In the small world in which they lived, it meant she and anyone closely associated with her would be known as welshers.

Alain cursed, grabbed her arm, hustled her out of the salon and into her stateroom, slamming the door after her. Savannah had stood in the darkened cabin, shaking and shaken.

What he'd said, the way he'd said it… He'd made her virginity sound like a prize in a lottery. She wasn't surprised he knew she was innocent; when he'd first taken her from New Orleans, he'd demanded she undergo a complete physical examination.

"I'm entitled to know if there's any danger you carry disease," he'd said, and she'd burned with embarrassment even though the doctor had been brisk and professional.

But what did he mean, that all she'd ever had was her skill at cards and her virginity?

You know, a sly voice had seemed to whisper. It had to do with the way he'd taken to looking at her lately. The way he'd started talking about her with his friends. The way they'd turn their eyes on her, smile, all but lick their lips.

Savannah had shuddered. No. She wasn't going to think like that. Alain was just angry. He'd get over it.

But he hadn't. For ten days now, she'd been waiting for something to happen. Thus far, Alain had done nothing. He hadn't arranged any card games on his yacht, or sent her to play on shore. And he'd made a point of assuring her that Missy was still in her school.

The cabin door suddenly swung open, cutting short Savannah's musings. She swung around, saw Alain—and, for a moment, felt a weight lift from her shoulders. He didn't look angry. He didn't look threatening at all. He was dressed in a tux and, most surprising, he was smiling.

Then she realized it was the kind of smile that made the cabin seem suddenly airless. Savannah forced herself not to react. Whatever happened next, she wasn't going to give him the pleasure of hearing her beg.

"Good evening, chérie."

"Alain."

"You have half an hour to dress."

"Excuse me?"

"Is there a problem with your hearing, Savannah? I said you have half an hour to dress. Wear something long. Slinky. No, on second thought, put on something elegant." A smile lifted the corners of his lips. "It always amazes me that people think they know what's in a book by the look of the cover."

She almost sagged with relief. She'd read him wrong. Everything was okay. Alain was going to take her to the casino, or perhaps to one of the island's mansions. She didn't care where he took her. What counted was that he was going to let her play for him again and win back the money she'd lost.

"Thank you, Alain. You won't regret it. Where are we going? I'll win a lot of money, more than I lost, and—"

"We're not going ashore." He shot back his cuff and checked his watch. "I'm expecting guests in a little while. Forty minutes, to be exact, but, of course, I want to see how you look before they arrive."

"Alain," she called as he swung away from her. "Wait." He looked at her, eyebrows raised, and she forced a smile. "Who am I going to play?"

"Play?" He chuckled. "I can't see that it will matter to you."

"You know that it does. You can tell me the weaknesses of the other players."

"Ah." He nodded solemnly and tucked his hands into his trouser pockets. "I'm afraid you misunderstood, chérie. You see, I've a plan that will enable you to repay me the money you lost."

"Yes. I realize that. And I promise, I'll play well. It shouldn't take too long."

"To win back the money?" He smiled, rocked back on his heels. "No, it probably won't. Now that I've had time to think things over, I'm willing to admit you're still worth something to me."

She nodded. Her mouth was dry with relief. She'd be playing again. Winning again. With all this time on her hands, she'd thought of a couple of ways she might be able to skim a little money. It would be dangerous, and it would take a very long time, but if she were careful, if she were lucky, she might be able to put together enough to see her through a few months of Missy's care while she found a job to support them both.

Just thinking about the future made it easy to smile.

"Thank you, Alain. You won't regret this. I lost to Sean O'Connell, but I'm still one of the best card—"

"I told you, that's not at issue. In fact, I don't want you to win."

She stared at him. "You don't? But if I don't win, how can I pay back what I owe you?"

"Darling girl, I'd expect more creativity from a street hustler! Why would you think there's only one way to repay your debt? You have other talents besides playing cards, Savannah. Many of my friends have noticed. And I've noticed that many of them lead dull lives. I've come up with a way to combine their appreciation of you with their desire to lead more interesting existences, chérie. Isn't that clever of me?"

A chill speared through her blood.

"Well," she said, forcing a little smile, "your friends always seem to enjoy playing poker here. The Lorelei is—"

"Most of them own yachts of their own," he said with a

dismissive gesture. "Charming as Lorelei may be, she's nothing new to them."

"I don't—I don't—"

The sound of the tender's engine interrupted her words. Alain tut-tutted and checked his watch again.

"Our first guests. They're early but it's understandable. Who wouldn't be eager to play our new game?"

Savannah felt her legs giving out. She couldn't show weakness. Not now.

"I don't understand what you're suggesting, Alain."

"It's quite simple, chérie. I've devised an entertainment, something a bit unusual. It will be far more profitable than if you were simply to play against them and win."

Slowly, he reached out and ran his hand down her cheek. Savannah flinched. That won her an oily grin.

"Come on, darling, don't play dumb. The streets of New Orleans schooled you well, non? I'll provide the players. You'll provide the incentive. Why do you still look puzzled, Savannah? It's a simple plan. We're going to hold a poker elimination tournament. Several, to be precise, until the novelty fades. A timed game each weekday night, with the biggest winners to play against each other on Saturdays." He flashed another smile, bigger than the last. "The stakes will be very, very high, chérie. High enough to be worthy of you."

"Worthy of me?" Savannah said in a small voice.

"Certainly." Alain grinned. "Don't you see? The final winner wins you!"

Savannah felt the blood drain from her head. "Are you crazy?"

"I admit, your value might be a bit greater if you were still, as we say, intact, but look at the amount O'Connell was willing to wager without even realizing you were a virgin." He chuckled. "I suppose I should thank him, should I ever have the misfortune to see him again. After all, this is his idea, when you come down to it, and it's brilliant."

She stared at him, struggling for words that wouldn't come. Her heart, her breath, seemed to have stopped.

"Alain," she said, trying to sound calm, "this isn't funny."

"It isn't meant to be." Alain tucked his hands in the pockets of his trousers and rocked back on his heels. "Life can get so dull, chérie. I should think you'd applaud my efforts to brighten it."

"I'm not a whore!"

His false smile vanished. "You'll be whatever I tell you to be."

"No. No!"

"After all I've done for you and that pathetic sister of yours, I finally asked one thing in return. 'Humiliate Sean O'Connell,' I said. And you didn't do it."

"I tried. I'm sorry it went wrong, but—"

"There are no 'buts,' Savannah. Failure is failure. All things considered, I think I'm going out of my way to be generous. After I deduct the money you owe me and expenses, there'll be a tidy sum left. It will be yours."

Bile rose in her throat. "I won't do it!"

Alain's false good humor vanished. He caught hold of Savannah's wrist. "Yes, you will."

"You're insane!"

"The lady's right, Beaumont," a deep, lazy voice said, "You always were a crazy son of a bitch."

Alain let go of Savannah and spun toward the door. Savannah caught her breath.

"Sean?" she whispered. "Oh God, Sean!"

Sean dragged his eyes from Beaumont long enough to look at Savannah. Her face was white; her eyes were enormous, but when she saw him they began to shine. Her mouth trembled, then lifted in a smile.

She made him feel as if he were mounted on that prancing white horse.

For one heart-stopping minute, he wanted to go to her, sweep her into his arms and tell her he'd protect her. Then he remembered what he'd overheard. It looked as if he'd walked in on a lovers' quarrel about money.

His gut knotted. He'd been a fool to let Savannah haunt his dreams and not to have taken her when he could. She wasn't even a call girl, as Cullen had implied. That was too high-class a term.

"O'Connell?" Alain's voice was strained. "How did you get on this boat?"

Sean turned his attention to Beaumont. "Why, you were kind enough to send your tender for me," he said softly. "I thought that was a mighty decent gesture."

"You lied your way onto this vessel!" Beaumont grabbed the intercom. "I'll have you thrown overboard. I'll have you—"

The words became a cry of pain as Sean caught his hand and bent it back. The intercom slid from Beaumont's grasp and he sank slowly to his knees.

"You're hurting me," he gasped.

"I want my money."

"What money? I don't know what—"

"Your lady friend played against me ten days ago. She lost."

"You just said, she played you. What has that to do with me?"

"Give me a break, Beaumont. She played for you."

Beads of sweat popped on Beaumont's forehead. "So what? She paid her debt."

"She didn't."

"What do you mean, she didn't? You won her for the night."

"Yeah, and I didn't collect."

Beaumont shot a look at Savannah. "What does he mean?"

"Nothing. Of course he collected, Alain. It's just—it's just that he wants more. Isn't that right, Mr. O'Connell?"

She turned away from Beaumont and stared at Sean. Her eyes, even her body language, implored him to go along with her lie. But why would he? He owed this woman nothing.

"Please," she mouthed silently.

"Yeah," Sean growled, mentally cursing himself for being a fool, "that's right. So I'm going to let you make up for it, Beaumont. I want a million bucks."

Beaumont turned whiter than he already was. "Why would I give you a million dollars?"

"Lots of reasons, starting with the fact that you wouldn't want me to spread the word that you're not only a liar, you're a man who sends a woman to seek a revenge he's too cowardly to attempt himself." Sean's smile had a savage edge. "Then there's the little matter of the lies you've spread about me. I've heard the rumors. You said I cheated you last summer when the truth is that you couldn't admit you'd lost."

"Alain?" Savannah whispered. "Is that true?"

"Your lover boy wouldn't know the truth if it bit him in the butt." Sean tightened his grip on Beaumont. "A million bucks, and I'm out of here."

"Even if I wanted to give you that much, I couldn't. Ahh! You're breaking my wrist, O'Connell. Let go!"

"Let him go. Please."

Sean flashed a look at Savannah. She looked desperate. Was there a heart somewhere inside her, and if so, did she really feel something for this pig?

The possibility made Sean's jaw clench. What in hell did it matter to him? Savannah McRae could have the hots for King Kong for all he gave a damn. Still, he was tired of listening to Beaumont whimper. Abruptly, he let go of the man's pudgy hand.

"Get up."

Beaumont dragged himself to his feet as if he were dying and cupped his hand against his chest.

"You're almost as good an actor as your lady friend."

"I think you broke a bone."

"No such luck. Come on, Beaumont. I know your safe is in the salon. Take me to it, get me what you owe me and I'm gone."

"I don't have that much money here. If you wait until Monday…"

Sean laughed. Beaumont swallowed hard.

"My marker is good everywhere."

"Maybe, but not with me. I want cash."

Braver now that Sean had let him get to his feet, Beaumont's mouth thinned. "I could charge you with theft."

"No, you couldn't." Sean jerked his chin at Savannah. "I have a witness who'll say otherwise."

"She'll say what I tell her to say. Won't you, chérie?" Savannah didn't answer. Beaumont narrowed his eyes. "Won't you?" he said in a menacing whisper.

He raised his hand. Sean moved quickly, grabbed him and threw him against the wall.

"Don't touch her," he growled.

"She's mine. I created her and I'll do whatever I like to her."

A soft cry burst from Savannah's throat. Sean watched as she buried her face in her hands. Her hair, loose as it had been that night, tumbled around her face…but it wasn't as it had been that night. Not really. Then, it had been combed into artful disorder. Now, it hung in curls that were wild and real.

Everything about her was different from the last time. She wore no makeup, no jewels. No do-me heels and sexy dress. Instead, she had on a baggy sweatshirt, faded, loose jeans and sneakers.

She looked vulnerable. Beautiful. Sweet and innocent, the kind of woman a man would give his soul to possess.

The kind a man could take home to his mother.

Sean blinked. Beaumont chuckled. "Ahhh," he breathed.

Sean's eyes flashed to his face. Beaumont had gone from looking as if the world were about to end to smiling, if you wanted to call the smirk on his fleshy lips a smile.

"Ah, what? Did you just remember that you have enough money in your safe?"

"No, Mr. O'Connell. I just thought of what I can offer you to satisfy your demand."

"I'm not in the market for a yacht, Beaumont."

"How about a woman? Are you in the market for that?"

"No!" Savannah shook her head wildly. "Alain. You can't. I won't. I swear, if you try to do this, I'll—"

"This woman owes me five hundred thousand dollars. And you just said you came here because you want more of her. Well, you can have her," Beaumont said, jerking his chin at Savannah. "For... Let's see. A week?"

"Alain. Please, Alain..."

"Not enough? How about two weeks?" A smile crawled across his mouth. "Surely you can think of something to do with a woman like Savannah for fourteen days and nights."

Sean saw a blur of motion out of the corner of his eye, and then Savannah was on Beaumont, clawing at him while he staggered and tried to protect his face.

"I'll kill you," she panted. "I swear, I'll—"

Sean grabbed her, pulled her back against him and pinned her in place with an arm wrapped tightly around her waist. His hand lay just under her breast; he could feel her heart beating against his palm.

Once, decades before, he'd felt a heart beating that same way.

He'd been eight, maybe nine; he'd been in big trouble at home for playing hooky and had gone to a hidey-hole he knew in a lot behind the Desert Song. That day, his hiding place already had an occupant. A tiny songbird lay on its back, beak open as it panted for breath.

He knew something terrible had happened to the bird and he wanted to help it, but he couldn't. All he could do was cradle it in his hand and feel the terrified gallop of its heart.

"Well, O'Connell? Yes or no?"

To hell with that long-ago wounded bird. He had an opportunity here that could solve his problem.

"The woman," Sean said. "For two weeks."

"No," Savannah moaned, but Beaumont nodded his head and the deal was done.

CHAPTER EIGHT

SAVANNAH didn't go quietly.

She shrieked, raged, yelled that she wasn't property, but Sean encircled her wrist with a hand that felt like a manacle and propelled her up the ladder to the deck.

"Move," he said through clenched teeth, "or I'll toss you over my shoulder and carry you off this damned boat."

Had she really felt her heart lift with hope when she first saw O'Connell in the doorway? She was a fool to have expected anything good from a man with his morals. So what if he'd won her that night and not taken her to bed? That wasn't enough to mark him as her savior. Whatever the reason he hadn't demanded full payment, he was going to demand it now.

He could demand what he liked, but she'd be damned if he'd get it without a fight.

Savannah slammed her elbow into his belly. He grunted at the force of the blow.

"You stupid son of a bitch," she panted. "Do you really think you can get away with this? Let go or I'll report you to the police."

"You'd have to get past your boyfriend first." Sean dragged her to where a ladder led down to the tender. "Somehow, I don't think he'd let that happen. Besides, what would you tell the cops?" She balked when they reached the ladder and he pushed her forward. "I can get fifty witnesses to tell them how you handed yourself over to me a couple of weeks ago at the casino."

"That has nothing to do with what you're doing now."

"Sure it does. We're just picking up where we left off. Get down that ladder."

"I won't!"

Savannah jammed her feet against the teak deck coaming. Sean cursed and slung her over his shoulder, just as he'd threatened. She roared with frustration and pounded her fists against his back. The ladder swayed precariously under his feet.

"You want to go for a swim, babe? Keep that up and, so help me, I'll dump you in the drink."

She believed him. He was a man of zero principles. Maybe Alain had lied about him cheating in that card game. Maybe he hadn't. A man who'd accept a woman in payment and carry her off was capable of anything.

"Alain lied," she said desperately, as he dropped her into a seat in the tender. "He keeps a lot of money in his safe."

Sean folded his arms and spread his feet apart.

"And you'd know all about his money."

"A million, at least," she said, refusing to be drawn away from the topic. "You could tell him you changed your mind. That you want money, not—not—"

Sean smiled coldly. "But I haven't changed my mind. I have exactly what I came for."

Her face flooded with color. "Is that the kind of man you are, O'Connell? Do you buy your women?"

"You're the one who put yourself up for sale, sugar."

"That's not true! You were the one who suggested I make that wager that night."

"And you leaped at it like a dog at a bone. Besides, what would Beaumont say if I told him I was bringing you back because you were uncooperative? According to you, I came back for more of what I already got." He smiled thinly. "I don't think he'd be very happy but hey, what do I know? Maybe I don't understand the complexity of the relationship."

The threat seemed to work. He could almost see the fight going out of her. Her head drooped forward; her hair tumbled around her face. Seeing her like this, her posture one of defeat, put a hollow feeling in Sean's belly. She was a liar. A cheat. A better con artist than any he'd ever met, and that was saying a lot.

But he could make things easier. All he had to do was tell her the truth, that Beaumont had triggered an idea and it had nothing to do with sex.

"What's wrong, sugar? It's just another slice off the loaf."

Savannah's head came up. She opened her mouth, on the verge of telling him she had never slept with Alain or anyone else, but why bother? He wouldn't believe her. More to the point, why defend herself to a man like this?

He was right. She really didn't have any choice. She'd cost Alain a fortune. Worse, she'd cost him his pride. He was demanding payback and he held her sister's well-being in the palm of his hand. If she refused to do his bidding, Missy would pay for it.

"You're right," she said wearily. "What does it matter which of you I'm with? You're both snakes in the same pit."

Her words jolted Sean. It wasn't true. Beaumont had used this woman in a scheme of revenge, but he...he—

Her head was down again, her face made invisible by her hair. When she raised a hand and brushed at her eyes, he knew she was crying.

Hell. The truth was, he was going to use her, too, and he suspected that even an ethicist would have a tough time making it sound as if his using her to live a lie was better than Beaumont using her in a petty game of get-even.

But he wasn't Beaumont, damn it. Not that it mattered what she thought of him, but he wanted her to know that.

"Maybe it's true," he said gruffly. "Maybe there isn't a lot of difference between him and me—except for one thing."

Savannah looked up. He'd judged correctly. Tears glittered on her lashes and he fought the desire to take her in his arms and brush them away, until he recalled how she'd pulled that same stunt the last time.

"I don't believe in owning people, Savannah."

She gave a watery laugh. Sean stood straighter.

"You behave yourself, do as you're told, give the kind of performance I expect, and I'll pay you."

Her face turned white at the word "performance." He was about to explain what he'd meant but before he could, she drew a deep breath and expelled it. When she looked at him again, her eyes were flat.

"How much?"

Her voice was low. So low that he had to lean forward to make sure he'd heard the question. It staggered him. Was it that simple? Mention money, and she turned docile as a lamb?

It shouldn't have come as a surprise. He knew exactly what she was. The tears, tonight's sweetly girlish looks didn't mean a thing. They were window dressing laid over the skeleton of what Savannah McRae really was.

"How much?" she said again, her voice a little stronger.

Sean clenched his jaw. "Don't you want to know what you're going to be required to do first?"

Color swept into her cheeks. "I'm not stupid, O'Connell. You don't have to spell it out."

He thought of telling her she was wrong, but he'd be damned if he was going to tell her anything more than he had to. What she did didn't matter to her. Only money was important.

Besides, she'd never believe him. What would he say? I

want you to pretend to be my fiancée? He was having a bad enough time believing it himself. What had ever possessed him to come up with such an impossible scheme? Why hadn't he taken the time to think it over?

Then again, why would he? Life on the edge had always been his thing.

He swung away, snapped "Shove off" to the crewman. The engine started and the tender leaped forward. The roar of the motor and the slap of the sea against the hull provided enough of a sound block so the guy driving the boat wouldn't hear what he said next.

"What's the most you've ever won in a poker game?"

She gave him a chilly smile. "Women and cards. Yours is a simple world, O'Connell."

"Sleeping with Beaumont and scamming strangers," Sean said coldly. "Anybody can see that your world is far more intricate than mine."

Her eyes filled with heat. She wanted to fly at him as she had earlier; he saw it in her face. Hell, he wanted her to. Wanted to hold her against him, subdue her, kiss her until she moaned...

"Answer the question," he snapped, his anger at himself almost as great as his anger at her.

"Four hundred thousand," she said, lifting her chin in defiance. "That was my record. I'd have topped it by a hundred thou if I'd won the night I played you."

"But you didn't."

"I came close."

"Only because I let you."

"Am I supposed to apologize for that? Poker's as much a game of tactics as it is chance."

The lady gave as good as she got. That was probably her only redeeming quality.

"What you mean is, it helps to be a good actor." The wind

ruffled Sean's hair. He pushed it back from his forehead. "It's why I wanted you."

Color filled her face again. Sean almost laughed.

"Forget that. I don't want you for anything kinky."

Nothing kinky, but he wanted her to act when he made love to her? She hated him. Despised him almost as much as she despised Alain.

"Five hundred thousand, Savannah. Exactly the amount I won from you." Sean smiled with his teeth. "That's what I'll pay you, if I'm satisfied with the job you do."

Her mouth fell open. For a second, she looked as if she were going to leap up and dance him in wild circles. His gut knotted with distaste. Half a million bucks could go a long way toward making a woman like this happy.

Then she seemed to get herself under control. "Those terms are acceptable."

She spoke without emotion. For the second time in minutes, he wanted to take her in his arms, not to comfort her but to shake her.

I just bought you, he wanted to snarl. I can use you any way I want. Doesn't that bother you?

Evidently not.

"Done," he said, and held out his hand as the tender bumped against the dock.

O'Connell herded her into his car. Then he took out his cell phone. She didn't pay much attention to his conversation, which seemed to consist mostly of commands.

He had a command for her, too. "Buckle up."

She'd already done that. The memory of his hand slipping across her breasts was still vivid. He'd touch her soon enough, but she wasn't going to offer up an opportunity.

Savannah shuddered. Think about something else, she told herself. Fortunately, O'Connell made it easy to do.

The man drove like a maniac.

He was in a hurry to get to his hotel. Things had not gone as he'd hoped the last time he'd brought her to his bedroom. This time would be different.

She'd given her promise.

It was too late for regrets. Agreeing to O'Connell's offer had been her only choice. Now, all she could do was hope. That he wouldn't hurt her. That he wouldn't force things on her.

She knew some of what could happen when a rich, powerful man thought he owned a woman. The men who played cards on the yacht sometimes brought women with then. She'd overhead things.

Savannah shuddered again. Two weeks, that was all. Surely, she could endure whatever he did to her for that long. He was handsome. Not that it mattered but at least she wouldn't have to gag whenever he came near her.

She knew that there were women who'd envy her.

A woman wouldn't have to act if this man took her to bed. She'd go willingly. Eagerly. She'd sigh when he put his hands on her, moan when he teased her lips apart with his.

She shut her eyes and thought back to that first time he'd taken her to his hotel. He could have done anything he wanted. And he'd wanted, all right. There'd been no mistaking the hardness of his arousal when he'd gathered her into his arms, but she'd wept and he'd sent her away. Yes, he'd been furious and, yes, he'd humiliated her by tossing money at her feet, but he hadn't done what he'd been entitled to do.

He'd done enough, though. Touched her. Kissed her. Sometimes, in the deepest part of the night, she thought she could still feel his hands on her, his mouth…

Savannah sat up straight.

What did any of that matter? She'd made a deal with Sean O'Connell and if she kept her part of it and he kept his, she'd have the money it would take to fly to Switzerland and take Missy to a new place where she'd get the same excellent treatment. She'd cover their trail carefully so Alain could never find them.

She had to keep all that in mind. It would make what came next bearable.

The car purred as Sean downshifted. Savannah blinked and focused on the blur of palms, white sand and blue water outside the window. Had they sped past the turnoff to his hotel? Yes. Yes, they had. A town called Bijou lay ahead of them. It was reputed to live up to its name by being a jewel box of designer and couturier boutiques, all in keeping with Emeraude's profile as an unspoiled playground for the incredibly rich.

Why was O'Connell taking her there?

"We're going to do some shopping," he said, as if she'd spoken the question aloud.

Shopping? In Bijou?

"If you'd given me time to pack, you wouldn't have to buy me a toothbrush."

She tried to sound flippant. It didn't work. Her voice was scratchy and it shook. Damn it, she wasn't going to let him see her sweat. What kind of shopping did he have in mind? Leather? Teenybopper minis? A froth of lace that would turn her into an obscene version of an upstairs maid? Maybe the shops here carried such things. From what she'd observed of Alain's friends, the very rich could also be very decadent.

O'Connell slowed the car as they entered the town. Under other circumstances, she'd have been enthralled. Cobblestone streets radiated from a central fountain surrounded by lush beds of bougainvillea. Mercedes, Ferraris, Maseratis and Lamborghinis were neatly parked along the curbs.

How did they get all those cars to this dot in the ocean? Savannah thought, and almost laughed aloud at the absurdity of the question. The rich and powerful could arrange for anything. Wasn't her presence at O'Connell's side proof of that?

He pulled into a parking space, got out of the car, came around to her side. "Out," he said, pulling open the door.

She got out. It was late—almost nine—and the shops were shuttered. So much for O'Connell's shopping trip, she thought, but he took her arm and tugged her toward the nearest door.

No leather in the windows. No cheesy minis or endless yards of lace, either. There was nothing in the windows except discreet gold script that spelled out a name so well-known it seemed to ooze money.

"They're closed," she said, and came to a halt.

"They're open. I phoned when we left the harbor."

So that was what the commands had been all about. O'Connell could get a place like this to stay open for him?

"How'd you pull that off?" she said pleasantly. "Is the manager into you for a gambling debt?"

"You've got a smart mouth, McRae." Sean's hand tightened on her elbow. "Let's go."

"I don't know what you're thinking," Savannah said quickly, "but I promise you, I am not spending a penny of what you're going to pay me on anything this place sells."

He turned toward her. She saw a muscle knot in his jaw.

"Is that your deal with Beaumont? Does he give you money, then make you pay for your clothing out of it?"

Alain bought her clothes. Not jeans or shorts or the cotton tops she lived in. She ordered those online, paid for them with the small amount of money he permitted her to keep from her gambling winnings. He bought her gowns and the accessories to go with them. His taste had never been hers but lately, it made her stomach turn. He'd begun buying her things that made her feel cheap.

"You're a beautiful woman, chérie," he said when she protested a dress cut too low, a gown with too high a slit. "Why hide it from the world?"

But there wasn't a reason in hell to tell any of that to this man.

"My arrangements with Alain have nothing to do with you," she said coolly. "I'm talking about our deal, O'Connell."

"Relax, sugar. I have no intention of making you pay. In our little drama, wardrobe's the director's responsibility."

"Just what is our little drama? I think I'm entitled to know."

He bent his head to hers. "You're my fiancée."

"Excuse me?"

"You heard me," he said with impatience. "For the next two weeks, you're my fiancée. We're here to buy you whatever you'll need to return to the States with me and meet my family."

Savannah stared at him. So much for leather and upstairs maids. "That's your fantasy?"

His laugh was quick and harsh. "Believe me," he said, "it's damned near as much a surprise to me as it is to you."

He put his hand into the small of her back and opened the door. A bell tinkled discreetly somewhere in the distance as they stepped into a hushed world of ivory silk, mirrored walls and low couches. The elusive scent of expensive perfume drifted on the air.

A salesclerk, dressed in the same ivory silk that paneled the walls and covered the couches, glided toward them.

"Wait," Savannah said frantically. "What assurance do I have that you'll keep your end of our bargain?"

The cold look O'Connell gave her almost stopped her heart. He held up his hand. The clerk smiled and stayed where she was.

"The same assurance I have that you'll keep yours," he said in a low voice. "My word."

She thought about telling him his word didn't mean much, but that would have been a lie. A gambler's word was everything.

"You don't want to accept it, we can call the whole thing

off. I'll take you back to the Lorelei. You can explain your return to Beaumont."

Savannah shook her head. "Your word is good enough."

"And yours?"

Their eyes met. He'd slipped his arm around her waist; he was holding her against him, a little smile playing on his mouth. She knew it was in preparation for the charade they were about to perform for the clerk but for a moment, oh, just for a moment, she imagined what it would be like if he were taking her to this place because she mattered to him, because he wanted to see her in silks and cashmeres, wanted to enjoy the sight of her in them in public, the excitement of stripping them from her when they were alone.

A tremor went through her, and she blanked the ridiculous images from her mind.

"My word's as good as yours, O'Connell."

"Sean."

"Does it matter?"

"Yes. My fiancée would call me by my first name."

"You want to explain what this is all about?"

His lips twisted. "In due time." His gaze dropped to her mouth. "But first—first, I think we need to formalize our arrangement."

"Formalize it?"

"Uh-huh." He looked into her eyes. What she saw in his— the heat, the hunger—made her breath catch. "Something in lieu of signing a contract in front of a notary public."

Slowly, he lowered his mouth to hers. From the corner of her eye, she saw the clerk turn discreetly away. There was no question what he was going to do. And there was time, plenty of time, to draw back or at least to turn her head to the side. Savannah did neither. She would let him kiss her. Wasn't the kiss part of what she'd agreed to?

She'd let it happen solely for that.

Still, when his mouth touched hers, she felt her knees

buckle. He drew her closer, kissed her again. The blood roared in her ears and she moaned softly against his lips. Her heart began to pound. She knew that his was, too. She could feel it galloping against hers.

Sean drew back, his hands cupping her shoulders, holding her away from him. Savannah opened her eyes. His expression was shuttered and cold.

"My fiancée is ready now," he said.

The words were directed to the clerk, but they might as well have been for her. His message was clear. He could turn her on anytime he wanted. He knew it. Now, she knew it, too.

The realization made her feel cheaper than she already did.

Really, she hadn't thought that was possible.

CHAPTER NINE

THEY were still choosing clothes and accessories as midnight approached.

At least, Sean was. Savannah was simply a mannequin standing before him on a little platform in front of a wall of mirrors.

At first, he didn't even bother asking her opinion. The clerk would bring out an armful of clothing and display it.

Yes, he'd say, no, yes, maybe.

Then the clerk would take Savannah to the fitting room where she'd put on the dress or suit or whatever Sean had chosen, slip into matching shoes the clerk seemed to whisk out of the air, and go out to the platform to await a nod of approval.

After a while, Sean began asking what she thought.

"Do you like this?" he'd say, and she'd look into the glass, at the stranger looking back, a woman with her eyes, her face, her body.

Where was the girl who'd worn clothes salvaged from thrift shop donation bins? The supposed sophisticate whose clothes were chosen by Alain? What had become of the con artist dressed in red silk?

Sean was turning her into someone she'd never been. Or maybe someone she'd always wanted to be.

Yes, she wanted to say, oh, yes, I like it. I like it a lot.

But she didn't because this wasn't real and he didn't actually care if she liked something or not. He was just getting tired or maybe bored. Maybe both. So she shrugged her shoulders and said yes, sure, the outfit was okay.

"We'll take it," Sean would say.

By then, the clerk had lost her laid-back façade. She looked like someone who'd won the lottery. Even her French accent started slipping, and when Sean approved a long column of white silk that had to cost the earth, moon and stars, the accent disappeared altogether in a rush of pure New York.

"Doesn't the lady look gawjiss?" the clerk babbled. A rush of bright pink flooded her face. "I mean—I mean, madame is so chic!"

Savannah laughed. It was an unlikely thing to do, considering the circumstances and her state of mind, and she buried the burst of laughter in a cough. She fooled the clerk but one look in the mirror and she knew she hadn't fooled Sean. He was grinning like the Cheshire cat. Without thinking, she grinned back.

What a great smile he had. Lazy. Open. And yes, sexy enough to make her breath catch. Had he done this before? Taken a woman on a shopping spree? Bought her things that made her feel beautiful. Looked at her as if—as if—

Savannah tore her gaze from his. What did it matter? Sean was a smart, hard-as-nails gambler. His charm, when he chose to use it, was as much a lie as the easy smile.

How could she have come so close to forgetting that?

This wasn't a shopping spree, it was a step in some complex game he'd devised. He was remaking her. Did he have a thing about only bedding women whose appearance was genteel? Maybe that was why he'd sent her packing the night he'd won her. Maybe the red dress, the heels, had backfired, turning him off as much as they'd turned him on.

A wave of exhaustion shot through her, so intense and unexpected it rocked her back on her heels. She swayed and would have fallen if Sean hadn't already been at her side, enfolding her in his arms.

"Savannah?"

He turned her to him, said her name again. She wanted to tell him to let her go but she didn't. Just for this moment, she let herself lean against him and take strength from the feel of his body.

"What's wrong?"

She licked her dry lips. "Nothing."

"Try another answer." He cupped her chin in one hand and raised her face to his. "Are you ill?"

She shook her head. "I told you, I'm okay."

"Savannah." He bent his knees and peered into her face. "Hell," he said roughly, "you're white as a sheet."

His eyes were the palest blue she'd ever seen, and they weren't cold with anger or mockery as they had been that first time in his hotel room. He had a small scar on the bridge of his nose, another that feathered out delicately from his eyebrow, and she wondered how he'd gotten them, if they'd hurt, if anyone had soothed them with a touch.

"Savannah? What's the matter?"

She shook her head. His voice was soft. For some reason, the sound of it made her throat tighten. He was right, something was the matter, but how could she give him an answer when she didn't know it herself?

"I'm just—I'm tired," she said, "that's all."

His eyes narrowed. She expected them to flash with those familiar angry sparks but before she could read anything in their depths, he swept her up into his arms.

"Pack up everything and send it to me at the hotel Petite Fleur first thing in the morning," he told the astonished clerk.

"Everything, monsieur?"

"You heard me. Toss in whatever else my—my fiancée might need. Lingerie, purses, shoes… You figure it out."

Sean let the woman dance ahead of him to open the door. He stepped out into the dark night, bon soirs and mercis flying after him like a flock of nightingales.

"Really, O'Connell," Savannah said. "I can walk."

Her breath was warm against his throat. Her hair tickled his cheek. Holding her like this, he became aware of her scent, something that reminded him of summer flowers and misting rain.

"O'Connell…"

"I'll put you down as soon as we get to the… Here we are." He let her down gently, held her close against him while he opened the door to his car. Her hair brushed lightly against his face again as he eased her inside. He shut his eyes and concentrated on the silky glide of it against his skin. She turned her face; for an instant, their lips were a sigh apart and then she jerked back and he straightened so quickly he slammed his head on the roof. "Damn," he said, hissing with pain.

Savannah made a little move, as if she were going to touch him. Obviously, he was mistaken because when she spoke, her voice was cool.

"Sorry," she said, without sounding sorry at all. "You should have let me walk."

He'd tried to do something decent and what did he get for it? A contemptuous retort and a rap on the skull. So much for being a nice guy. Still, part of him knew he was overreacting. Not that it stopped him.

"You're right," he said as he went around the car and slipped behind the wheel, "but for a couple of minutes there, you looked as if you were going to collapse." He checked for traffic, found none, and shot away from the curb. "I can't afford to let my investment get damaged."

"No. Certainly not." There was a beat of silence. "Do you think you could let me know what's going on anytime soon?"

"When I'm good and ready."

"No problem. Have it your way."

Sean glanced at her. Her hands were locked together in her lap, her profile was stony and her words had been tossed off with a lack of care, but she didn't fool him. She was nervous. Well, why wouldn't she be? Whatever he thought of her morals or her lack of them, not knowing what she was getting into had to be disturbing.

He checked the mirror and stepped down on the gas pedal. The car gave a throaty roar and sped up the narrow coast road.

"I need you to put on a performance."

"I'm not stupid, O'Connell."

"Sean," he said through his teeth.

"All those clothes… The question is, who am I performing for? What role am I expected to play? And why? Unless you're one of those men who needs a fantasy to get it on."

Her voice quavered on the last few words, but the disdain was still there. He thought about jamming on the brakes, pulling her into his arms and showing her how little he needed fantasy or anything else as a turn on, but he wasn't stupid, either.

The unvarnished truth was, she excited him.

It was one of the reasons he'd forgotten the lateness of the hour or that he hadn't so much as bought either of them a cup of coffee. At first, he'd told himself he just wanted to get this whole thing going before he came to his senses and asked himself what, exactly, he thought he was doing.

Halfway into the fashion parade, he'd known it was because he was too busy looking at Savannah to want to do anything else.

It wasn't the clothes. She looked beautiful in everything the clerk brought out, but he'd seen a lot of beautiful women in a lot of beautiful stuff over the years. He was beyond that as a turn-on.

What he'd gotten caught up in was watching her face in

the mirror, how she'd gone from wariness to acceptance to surprised joy. It made him remember the time he'd sat in on a fashion shoot of his sister, Fallon. Her expression had gone through similar changes and she'd explained that it was part of the feature they were shooting.

I'm supposed to be a plain Jane, she'd told him, transformed into a ravishing beauty by this designer's things.

His sister was one fine model and the camera had captured her pleasure at the transformation but then, the magazine had been paying her something like ten thousand bucks for the morning's work.

He wasn't naive. Savannah was getting paid, too. Fifty times his sister's fee, but she hadn't looked half as happy when he'd offered her the money as she had the last couple of hours, just staring into the mirror. Something was happening within her. She was coming out of her chrysalis, watching herself change, and she liked what she saw.

So did he.

Then, minutes ago, she'd giggled. Giggled, as if she and the world were both innocent. And when he smiled at her in the mirror, she'd smiled back. Really smiled, the way a woman would smile at a man who was making her happy.

Sean's mouth turned down.

Damned right, he was making her happy. He'd promised her a half-million dollar payoff and now he was buying her more clothes than she'd ever need for what would ultimately be a couple of days' charade. What she'd been looking at, in that mirror, was one extremely fortunate female.

"Well?"

He looked across the console. Savannah was looking at him, her chin up, her arms folded over her seat belt. She was waiting for an answer and no matter what he thought of her, he figured it was time she got one.

"I come from a very close-knit family."

Her lips turned up at the corners. "How nice for you."

Sean gritted his teeth. Her tone made it clear she didn't give a damn if he came from a close family or from a den of serpents, but he couldn't see any sense in giving her less of an answer than she'd need to understand the part he expected her to play.

"I have two brothers and three sisters."

She yawned. "I'm thrilled."

"Two of my sisters are married. So are my two brothers."

"Listen, O'Conn… Listen, Sean, this is all very interesting if you're into family, but I'm not. How about getting to the bottom line?"

"My mother had a stroke a couple of weeks ago."

"Oh." Savannah swung toward him. "Did she…? I'm sorry."

Maybe she was. She sounded it. Not that he gave a damn. An actress didn't have to believe in a role, she just had to play it.

"She came though it with flying colors." He grinned; he couldn't help it. Just thinking about his mother's feistiness made him smile. Mary Elizabeth would like Savannah, he thought suddenly. She'd admire her toughness. Her resiliency…and what in hell did that have to do with anything?

He frowned and cleared his throat. "But for a while there, we thought she wasn't going to make it. And afterward—afterward, I asked her what she wanted for her birthday." He gave a little laugh. "I said I'd give it to her, no matter what it was."

"That was nice."

Savannah's voice was low. He glanced at her. She sounded as if she might be smiling, but it was too dark to see her face.

"Yeah. I mean, it was supposed to be, but she caught me by surprise when she told me what it was."

She laughed, the same way she had in the dress shop. The sound was so sweet that it made him smile, too.

"Let me guess. She wanted an elephant."

"If only." Sean let out a sigh. "An elephant would have been a snap, compared to what she asked me for."

"A snap? Just a snap?"

Oh, yes. There was definitely a smile in her voice. He liked it.

"No question about it."

"I give up. What does she want for her birthday?"

Sean took a deep breath. "She wants me to get married."

"She wants you to..." She shifted toward him. "To get married?"

"I told you, an elephant would have been a snap."

Savannah stared at him. No. It couldn't be. But everything was starting to make sense. Telling her he was going to call her his fiancée in the clothing shop. All those expensive clothes. All the talk about her playing a role.

"Wait just a minute, O'Connell. Are you saying you want me to pretend that I'm—that you and I are—"

"Engaged. You got it."

She couldn't seem to take her eyes from the crazy man sitting next to her. He wanted to pass her off as his fiancée?

"Engaged?" she repeated, in a voice that seemed to climb the scale from alto to lyric soprano.

"Uh-huh. A perfect young couple, head over heels in love."

His tone mocked the words. Why did that make her feel sad?

"Come on, McRae, don't look at me as if I asked you to stand on your head while playing the piano. This isn't rocket science. People get engaged all the time. All you have to do is—"

"No."

"You've already proved what a great actress you are. The way you came on to me that night..." His voice roughened. "All an act, right?"

"Right," she said without hesitating.

"So, what's the problem? You don't have to sleep with me, if that's what's worrying you. All I require is—"

"I said, no." Savannah sat straight in her seat and stared out the windshield. Sean had just turned onto the road that led to his hotel; the entrance was not far ahead. "As in, En Oh. There's not a way in the world I'm going to do this."

"I don't want to upset you, sugar," he said in a voice that made a lie of the promise, "but you don't have a say in the matter."

She looked at him. His profile, seen in the lights of the hotel as they approached it, was stony. And, of course, he was right. She didn't have a say, not unless she could come up with half a million dollars to repay Alain...and another half million to secure Missy's future.

How could he expect such a thing of her? To pretend to be his fiancée? Pretend she loved him, wanted him, wanted to be in his arms as she had been just a little while ago?

Pain pierced her like a forsaken dream. She swung away from him as they pulled up in front of the hotel. The parking attendant and the doorman were both hurrying toward them, just as they had last time. Everything was the same, except what Sean wanted.

"People don't do things like this," she said in a low voice.

"Thanks for that bit of insight, McRae. I don't know what I'd have done without—"

The car doors swung open simultaneously. "Good evening," the attendant said. The doorman smiled at Savannah. "Ma'am," he said pleasantly, "it's nice to see you again."

Nice? She was back at the scene of the crime. What could possibly be nice about that?

She stormed past the man but she didn't get very far. Sean grabbed her arm and led her toward the steps.

"Let go," she hissed.

"So you can run? No way, sugar. You already did that once. It's old."

"I didn't run. You threw me out. Damn it, will you let go?"

"Well, I'm not throwing you out this time," he said, hustling her inside the lobby.

"Listen, you—you egocentric fraud—"

The desk clerk looked around in surprise. So did a couple who'd been talking with him. All six eyebrows reached for their hairlines.

Why not? Sean thought grimly. They probably made an interesting sight, he damned near towing Savannah toward the elevator, she trying her best to dig in her heels and halt his progress.

"Madame? Sir? May I be of service?"

It was the desk clerk, scurrying toward them, trying to smile while looking terrified.

"No," Sean snarled.

"Yes," Savannah snapped. "Find a shrink and have this man committed."

"She has an unusual sense of humor," Sean said as he banged on the elevator call button. When the ornate glass and silver doors opened, he pulled Savannah inside the car.

"Ma'am?" the desk clerk said uneasily, and Savannah rolled her eyes.

"Oh, for God's sake," she said, "just go away!"

The doors slid shut. Sean slid his key card into the penthouse slot and the car rose. Savannah wrenched free and glared at him. "You're good at this. Kidnapping women and shoving them around."

The doors opened again. Sean caught her by the elbow, hurried her through the entry hall and into the sitting room.

"Let me be sure I've got this right," he said. "You were willing to sleep with me but when I tell you there's no sex involved, that all you have to do is pretend to be my fiancée, you go crazy."

Crazy was exactly how it sounded, but she wasn't about to admit that.

"You want me to lie."

"Oh, I see." His lips curved in a smirk. "The McRae Morality Code frowns on lies."

"Obviously, yours doesn't."

That seemed to hit the target. Sean's shoulders fell.

"You think I'm thrilled about it, you're wrong. I just don't have a choice." He went to the minibar and opened it. "Besides, what do you care? She's my mother, not yours."

"It's not right."

"You never lied to your mother?"

"I never had to. She didn't know what I did or didn't do, and..." Savannah frowned. Why tell him that? She never talked about her life, her family. It was nobody's business, certainly not O'Connell's. "Besides, you couldn't pull it off."

Sean tossed two cans of Diet Coke, a bag of chips and a couple of candy bars on a low table.

"Eat something," he commanded.

"I'm not hungry."

"Of course you're hungry. So am I, and ordering up dried-out chicken sandwiches and coffee from the bottom of the pot doesn't appeal to me."

He opened the bag of chips and held it out. The wonderful aroma of salt and fat rose to her nostrils. To her horror, her stomach did a low, long rumble.

"Not hungry, huh?" He pushed the bag at her. "Eat."

Reluctantly, she reached in and took a handful of chips. They tasted as good as they smelled, and she took another handful.

"Why can't you just tell her you shouldn't have promised such a thing in the first place?"

He sighed, sat down on the sofa and laced his hands behind

his head. The movement brought his biceps into sharp delineation. It did the same for the long muscles in his thighs and when he stretched out his legs, his black T-shirt rode up an inch, revealing a hard, flat belly.

"Because I've disappointed her too many times already."

Savannah blinked. "What?"

"You asked me why I didn't just tell her that—"

"I got that." She hesitated. "But you'd disappoint her with this anyway. Eventually, you'd have to tell her the truth."

That got him to his feet. He ran his hands through his hair until it stood up in little spikes and paced from the living room to the bedroom. Savannah followed.

"Engagements fall apart all the time. She'll accept that."

"I thought you said you'd promised her you'd get married."

"Right. I did. But…" He paused, then let out a long sigh. "You're right, I did. Okay. I'll introduce you as my wife. I'll say—I'll say we met, went crazy for each other, eloped… Now what?"

"I told you, I don't want to do it."

His smile was quick and unpleasant. "Remember what I said about not having a choice? Well, neither do you… unless you're not interested in earning that money."

"It's an impossible plan."

In his heart, he was starting to think so, too. The last thing he needed was to hear those words from her lips.

"It'll be a cinch. We'll buy a ring. Rings. Engagement, wedding bands—one for you, one for me."

"Only a man would think that's all there is to marriage!" Savannah threw out her hands. "Has it occurred to you that we don't know the first thing about each other?"

"I thought of that. It's why I need you for two weeks. It'll give us time to get acquainted, so to speak, before my mother's birthday, and…Savannah?"

She shook her head, turned her back to him, but not before

he'd seen the tears in her eyes. He went to her quickly, stepped in front of her and clasped her shoulders.

"Savannah," he said softly, "what is it?"

What, indeed? He wanted her to play a game. It was a lot better than the games she'd expected he wanted, or Alain's obscene plans. Two weeks of acting and a half-million dollar payoff. How come her heart felt as if it might break?

"Listen to me," she said desperately. "What you want us to do is a mistake."

"Then you'll do it?"

Her chin came up. "You said it yourself. I don't have much choice, do I?"

Sean looked at her. Her eyes were smudged with exhaustion; the night breeze had turned her hair into a tangle of curls and her sweatshirt bore a smattering of potato chip crumbs.

She was, in other words, even more beautiful. How could a woman be a mess and still be beautiful? No way could he figure it out.

"Why don't you have a choice?" he said, after a minute.

"That's a dumb question."

"It's the first intelligent question I've asked you." His hands cupped her shoulders. "I'm not talking about our arrangement, I'm talking about your—your relationship with Beaumont." She tried to pull away; he held her fast before him. "Why do you let him run your life? Why are you with him?"

She stared at him. Could she tell him? About herself, and her childhood. About Missy. About everything?

God, was she losing her mind? This man had all but bought her. He'd bought her. What could she possibly tell him that would mean a damn?

"I can't—I can't explain."

"Maybe I can help. If he has something on you—"

"Has something?"

"Yeah. You know. If you've ever done something you don't

want anyone to know about. Been arrested. Been charged with—"

"You think I'm a criminal?"

"No. I don't think that. I just think there must be a reason you're with a man like that."

"I'm with him," she said flatly. "That's all."

"You despise him. And he treats you as if—as if—"

"O'Connell, I'm tired. We made a deal and I'm prepared to go through with it. You want a fiancée? You'll have one."

Her voice had turned hard. So had her eyes. Who was the real Savannah? Was she someone who didn't think it was nice to lie, or someone who'd do anything for money?

"I want a fiancée for two weeks," he said. "Then a wife for a one-time, show-stopping performance."

"A one-night wife," she said, with a bitter smile.

"Yes. Can you manage that?"

"I can manage anything for five hundred thousand dollars," Savannah pulled away from him. "Where do I sleep?"

He looked at her for a long minute. Then he smiled, though the smile never reached his eyes.

"What if I said you sleep in my bed?"

She felt her pulse quicken, but she kept her eyes locked to his. "I thought you said—"

"Maybe I changed my mind."

Again, the seconds ticked by. She couldn't read his face at all. Did he mean it? Would he demand she sleep with him? She wouldn't do it, not for all the money in the world. She wouldn't let him undress her, caress her, take her on that journey she'd never experienced. It would be terrible. It would be...

It would be ecstasy. She'd dreamed of his hands on her breasts. His mouth on her thighs. His body, pressing her down into the softness of the bed.

Savannah raised her chin. "Maybe you want too much for the money, O'Connell."

He laughed softly. "Maybe," he said, and before she could

do anything to stop him, he pulled her into his arms and kissed her. It was a kiss given without mercy, hard and demanding and, heaven help her, it was everything she wanted.

She stopped thinking, stopped wondering, stopped doing anything but feeling. She wound her arms around Sean's neck and met his explosive passion, matched it, opened her mouth to the sharp nip of his teeth. He groaned, lifted her into his erection, slid his hand under her sweatshirt, under her T-shirt and cupped her breast.

"Yes," she sobbed as he bent his head and took her nipple into his mouth. A flame seemed to shoot from her breasts straight down into her belly. She dug her hands into his hair, needing his kisses against her breast, needing them on her mouth, needing him as she had never permitted herself to need anyone.

"Sean," she whispered. "Sean, please…"

"What?" His voice was thick. "Please, what? Tell me."

"I want—I want—"

All at once, he stopped. He raised his head and looked at her through cold eyes.

"I know exactly what you want," he said. "That's good, sugar. It's very good. Thanks for letting me see you'll be as terrific in this role as you were the night we met."

"No. Sean—"

"Relax." He spoke calmly, as if they hadn't just been in each other's arms. "You won't have to take your act on the road. Hell, if you can be this convincing after a couple of kisses, why would I want you to do anything more?"

Savannah's heart seemed to stop beating. She wanted to die. She wanted him to die. What he'd done…

"You can have the bedroom." He looked her up and down, a satisfied little smile tugging at the corners of his mouth. "Hell, McRae, nothing's too good for a performer like you."

The smile, the cutting words, brought her back to life.

"You," she sputtered, "you—you—you—"

She grabbed a vase, flung it, watched it shatter into a million pieces as it hit the door that swung shut behind him.

"I hate you," she screamed. "I hate you, Sean O'Connell!"

Savannah buried her face in her hands and sank to the floor. What a lie! She hated him, yes, but the person she hated most was herself.

CHAPTER TEN

SEAN was up well before six o'clock the next morning.

He tried phoning down for coffee. Room service, it seemed, wouldn't be able to accommodate him for another half hour.

"We do have coffee at the reception desk for our early-rising guests," the clerk told him.

Grumbling, Sean headed to the lobby, poured himself a cup of the stuff from a silver pot and glugged it down.

On the way back to the elevator, he made a pit stop in the men's room. Bad idea. The face that greeted him in the mirror wasn't pretty. He needed a shave, a shower and a way to stop scowling, but everything connected to those necessities was behind his closed bedroom door.

He went back to the desk, took the silver pot and a cup, offered a terse "You don't mind, do you?" to a clerk who looked as if he'd sooner argue with one of the crocs that inhabited the island's swampy north shore, and headed back to his suite.

Half an hour later, he was going crazy. He paced, he drank coffee, he paced some more. The coffee was his second bad idea of the morning. He could damn near feel the caffeine hightailing it through his system.

As if his nerves weren't jangling enough already.

He'd had a miserable night. The living-room sofa was too short, too soft, too everything but comfortable. He'd slept in his jeans and T-shirt, and he normally slept in his skin. Not that he'd actually slept.

How could he, considering the mess he'd created? Man, he wanted out! First the stupid pledge to Mary Elizabeth, then the even stupider determination to make good on it, and now this—this thing with Savannah...

"Hell," he muttered, running his hands through his hair.

Why had he ever imagined that he could take a stranger and pass her off as his wife? That he could make a woman like Savannah seem sweet, soft and innocent?

Except, there were moments she really did seem sweet, soft and innocent. Moments like the ones last night, when he'd taken her into his arms to prove a point, when she'd trembled at his touch before losing herself in his kisses.

Sean's jaw tightened.

An act. All of it. How come he kept forgetting that her talent for make-believe was the reason he'd thought of using her in the first place? The lady was good. Really good. Anybody seeing what had happened would have thought she meant it, that she'd really wanted him.

That he'd really wanted her.

Okay. He had. Damned right, he had. Kissing her, caressing her, had nothing to do with proving things. He kept telling himself that because it made him feel like less of a sleaze.

What kind of man lusted after a woman who made her living doing God knew what for a creep like Alain Beaumont?

Sean downed the last of the coffee. It was bitter and cold, but maybe the last jolt of caffeine would kick-start his brain. He needed to begin thinking straight. Make sense of things, starting with who and what Savannah McRae really was.

That conversation he'd walked in on when he'd boarded Beaumont's yacht. The key might be there. Beaumont had been talking about some sort of deal. She'd turned it down. No. "Turned it down" was the wrong way to phrase it. She'd been frantic. Hysterical.

Terrified.

In his anger, he'd thought she and Beaumont were just arguing over money. Truth was, they'd been fighting over more than that. Beaumont wanted her to do something. She didn't want to do it. Why hadn't she just walked out on the man? Told him what he could do with his plans, whatever they were, his yacht, his wealth?

Why was she willing to stay with such a pig?

A simple question, with a simple answer. She stayed for the life and the money. What else could it be?

Sean reached for the coffee, shuddered and pushed it aside. He'd lived among the rich and famous a good part of his life, first growing up in Vegas, then as a gambler. Some were okay people. Some weren't.

And some—only a few and almost always male—were downright monsters, certain that their wealth entitled them to live by codes of their own devising. They surrounded themselves with people who accepted that conviction. He'd seen servants who might as well have been slaves, business associates who turned a blind eye to stuff that was immoral if not downright illegal, wives willing to pretend they didn't see infidelities that were right under their noses.

He'd seen the mistresses of such men tolerate treatment that made his stomach turn.

Did that explain Savannah? He'd been sure it did, except the more he saw of her, the more he had this funny feeling that he was only seeing the surface.

And how come she was in his head all the time? How come—be honest now, O'Connell—he'd sought her out for this bit of subterfuge?

Forget the stuff about her acting talent. She was good, yeah, but how tough would this performance be? One night, pretending she was his wife? With a little effort, he could come up with half a dozen women who could have carried it off and who'd have found it a lark. No metaphorical arm-twisting needed.

The truth was, he wanted her playing the part, not some other woman. There was something about her that got to him and not just sexually, although yeah, she got to him that way, too.

It was why he hadn't slept last night. The intensity of the kiss had stunned him. Those things he'd said about kissing her just to see if they'd be able to make the relationship look real was bull. The truth was, he'd let go of her because the need he'd felt to take her shocked him.

He'd never felt such hunger before.

Not that he'd solved the problem by saying something he regretted and walking away. Hell, those moments he'd had her in his arms had played in his head all night, like a loop of tape. He'd tossed and turned for hours, sweaty as a schoolboy, imagining what would have happened if he hadn't come to his senses. He thought about how it would have been to undress her. Bare her to his hands and mouth. See if all of her tasted as sweet as her high, perfect breasts.

Finally, he'd leaped from the damned sofa and stalked out to the terrace. He had a bad case of ZTS, was all. Zipper Think Syndrome, the name he and his brothers had jokingly given to the way men were led around by their anatomy.

It hadn't helped.

What he needed was either a shrink or a cold shower, but both were out of the question. You didn't go to a shrink just because you wanted a woman you shouldn't want. To get to the shower, he'd have to go through his bedroom, assuming she hadn't turned the lock. Not that it mattered. He wouldn't do it.

Even the thought of it—his bedroom, his bed, Savannah lying in it asleep, warm and sweet-smelling—was a mistake.

Or maybe the mistake had been not taking what he'd wanted, what they'd both wanted, last night...

"If you want to get into your bedroom, it's all yours."

Savannah stood in the bedroom doorway wearing her jeans and sweatshirt. Idly, he wondered if she'd slept in her clothes, same as him.

From the look on her face, Sean knew they were still at war. Maybe it was time to declare a truce. How else were they going to get through the next two weeks?

"Thanks," he said, trying for a neutral tone.

"There's nothing to thank me for." She strode past him. "I'll see you around."

She'd see him around? Anger shot through him and he moved past her and blocked the door.

"What the hell does that mean?"

"It means I'm leaving. It's what I should have done last night."

"You can't leave. We have an arrangement."

"Not anymore. I thought things through, O'Connell. I can't do this."

"Maybe you didn't understand me. I said, we have a deal."

Savannah's eyes flashed. "Get out of my way."

"You owe me money. Is this how you repay your debts?"

"I don't owe you anything."

"Sure you do. Two weeks ago you laid it on the line... and lost."

Her face colored. "I tried to keep my end of that wager, O'Connell. You sent me away."

She was right, but what did being right have to do with anything? They had a deal.

"How about Beaumont?"

"What about him?" she said, but the color began draining from her cheeks.

"Give me a break, okay? I don't know exactly what I walked

in on the other night, but I suspect he's not gonna be happy to see you."

Not happy to see her? The depth of Sean's understatement almost made her laugh. She still wasn't sure how she'd handle Alain; all she could hope was that he'd calmed down. Surely, he didn't really want to use her as a—a prize in a tournament.

He'd be past such craziness by now. He'd agree to let her play cards to win back the money, to let Missy stay in Switzerland, to remember that once he'd treated her with courtesy and kindness.

Right. And polar ice caps floated in the Caribbean.

"Well?" Sean folded his arms. "I don't hear you telling me Beaumont will greet you with open arms."

"That's not your problem." She jerked her chin at the door. "Please step aside."

Sean hesitated. Stop her, a voice inside him said. What for? another voice replied. So what if she left? The entire plan was a bad idea.

He shrugged and did as she'd asked. "Go on. Just be sure and tell your boyfriend he still owes me."

Savannah swung toward him, her face livid. "He's not my boyfriend."

"Whatever you say, sugar."

"He's not!"

"Yeah, whatever. Just tell him I expect my money within 24 hours, now that you've reneged on the deal he and I made."

"Damn you," she said, her voice so low he had to strain to hear it. "Damn you to hell, Sean O'Connell! Do you hear yourself? Do you hear what you're saying?" Sean jerked back in surprise as she jabbed her finger into the center of his chest. "The deal you and he made. The deal you and Alain made!" Another jab, followed by a flat hand slamming against him. "How dare you, you—you no-good son of a bitch? How dare you think you can treat me like—like a streetwalker?"

"Hey. Wait just a minute. I didn't—"

"Yeah, you did." She slammed him with her fist this time, and she wasn't gentle about it. "Buying me!"

"Whoa," Sean said, holding up a hand. "I did not buy you."

"You want to get technical about it? No. You didn't. You—you made a deal with Alain."

"No way," he said, with all the self-righteous indignation of a man who knows he's wrong. "Your boyfriend—"

Without warning, her fist slammed into his belly with enough force to make the air whoosh from his lungs.

"He—is—not—my—boyfriend! He's a monster. How can you even suggest such a thing? I loathe him. Loathe him, loathe...."

Tears poured down her cheeks. Sean cursed and pulled her into his arms. She was crying as if the world were about to end and it damn neared killed him. He'd been fooling himself, trying to pretend all he wanted was to make love to her when the truth was, he wanted to protect her from whatever demons stalked her.

Gently, he lifted her face to his and kissed her. She shook her head wildly but he ignored it and kissed her again, holding her as if she were precious because she was, and he was done with trying to figure out why he should feel that way about her.

He kept kissing her, stroking his hand down her spine. When she sighed and leaned into him, he felt as if he'd beat back those demons, at least for the moment.

The kiss deepened. Her mouth clung to his. Her hands slipped up his chest; her fingers curled in the soft cotton of his shirt and Sean knew there was no sense in kidding himself.

He'd started this to comfort Savannah but comfort was the last thought in his head right now. She tasted like honey, smelled as sweet as summer, and they fit one against the other like matching pieces of a jigsaw puzzle just begun.

His need for her was almost overpowering.

But he couldn't, wouldn't let her know that. She wasn't herself. She was in pain. In despair. She was weeping. He'd done so many wrong things since they'd met, he wasn't going to add taking advantage of her to the list.

"Sweetheart." His voice was so rough he was amazed he could talk at all. Carefully, he held her by the shoulders and took a single step back. "Savannah. Let me just…let me just—"

"Sean," she whispered and rose to him, clasping his face, bringing his mouth to hers, and he was lost.

A torrent of desire flooded his senses. He groaned and swung her into his arms, never taking his mouth from hers as he carried her into the bedroom and laid her down on the bed that was still warm from her body.

When he drew back, she gave a little cry of distress and he took her hands and pressed kisses into the palms.

"Are you sure?" he whispered.

"I've never been surer of anything in my life." Tears still glittered on her lashes, but her lips curved in a smile. "Make love to me, Sean. Please."

He undressed her slowly, kissing each bit of skin as he bared it to his mouth. Her sighs, her moans, the beat of his heart became the only sounds in the universe.

When she was naked, he spent a long moment just looking at her, the delicacy of her breasts, the gentle rounding of her belly, the gold of her skin, but she stirred uneasily and when his gaze moved to her face, he saw a shadow in her eyes. Wariness. Trepidation.

Fear.

Was she afraid of what he might do to her? Had Beaumont…? No. He wasn't going to think about that son of a bitch. Not now. Now, all that mattered was Savannah.

"Savannah," he whispered urgently, "don't be afraid. I'll never hurt you."

She shook her head. "I'm not afraid of you. But—but there's something I should tell you—"

"No," he said, silencing her with a kiss. What she was going to say, that she'd been with a lot of other men, that some of them had done things… He didn't want to hear it. Didn't need to hear it. All he needed was this. Her mouth. Her breasts. The way he could make her breath catch when he licked her nipples. The way she moaned when he slid his hands under her, lifted her to him, kissed her belly, her thighs.

"Sean. Oh God, Sean…"

She was trembling again, but not with fear. With passion. The intensity of her need for him filled him with joy. This was how he wanted her. Open to him. Wanting him.

Him. Only him.

He kept his eyes on hers as he parted her thighs. She moaned; her eyes went wide as he stroked a finger over her labia. She cried out, jolted like a filly who'd never before carried a rider.

"Sweet," he whispered. "So sweet…"

Slowly, carefully, he opened her to him. Breathed lightly against the waiting bud that had bloomed for him. Kissed it. Caressed it, and suddenly she arched like a bow. Her cry soared into the heavens and she sobbed his name.

Sean pulled off his clothes and came down to her. Caught her hands, entwined his fingers with hers, watched her face, her beautiful face, as he moved between her thighs and entered her…

And discovered that his lover was a virgin.

The realization shocked him into immobility. "Savannah?"

A world of questions were in that one word. Savannah understood them all and knew she'd have to provide answers but for now, only one mattered.

"Sean." She sighed his name, lifted her head and bit lightly into his shoulder. The taste of man and musk quickened the race of her already-galloping heart. "Please. Make love to me."

Groaning with pleasure, Sean slid into her warmth and took her with him to the stars.

They lay tangled together, breathing raggedly, a fine film of sweat drying on their skin.

"You're a virgin," he said in wonderment.

"Not anymore," she said softly, her lips curving at the awe in his voice, at the joy in her heart, and felt his lips curve, too, against her throat.

"You should have told me."

"Oh, sure. There's always an easy way to bring something like that into the conversation."

"I'd have gone slower."

"Mmm. Slower sounds nice."

Her words were a teasing purr. Sean smiled again and bit lightly into her flesh.

"Are you all right?"

"Yes." She moved beneath him, stretching like a cat. "I'm very all right."

He lifted his head. Her face was inches from his. Her eyes glowed and her smile would definitely have tempted Da Vinci. She looked sated and happy, and his heart did a little two-step of absolute male satisfaction.

"I'm glad. Still, if I'd known…"

"Would you have believed me?"

A muscle knotted in his jaw. After a couple of seconds, he turned on his side but kept his arm tightly around her.

"No."

Savannah nodded. His honesty was one of the things she liked about Sean O'Connell. It was a rare quality.

"I'm sorry, Savannah. I know you wanted me to say I would have, but—"

She rolled toward him and put her finger across his

mouth. "Don't apologize for speaking the truth. Of course you wouldn't have believed me." She traced the outline of his lips. "Why on earth would you?"

Sean sucked her finger between his teeth and bit down gently. Then he took her hand from his mouth and kissed it.

"So, he isn't—"

"No." Savannah shuddered. "God, no. He's not."

"Then, what is he to you? Your business partner?"

"Alain is…Alain was—" she said, hastily correcting the error "—he was my friend."

"Beaumont?"

She could hear the incredulity in his voice. She couldn't blame him. The man Alain had recently revealed himself to be couldn't be anyone's friend, but the Alain she knew—the one she thought she knew—was different.

"I met him a long time ago," she said, propping herself on her elbows so she could see Sean's face. "He was—he was good to me."

"Oh, yeah. He sounded like he was being good to you the other night, all right. Almost as good as the night he sent you to seduce me."

"He didn't tell me to—to go to bed with you that night," Savannah said quickly.

"No," Sean said coldly. "He just told you to keep me so busy thinking about taking you to bed that I wouldn't concentrate on the game."

"He's changed. The Alain I knew… That Alain isn't there anymore."

The Alain she'd thought she knew, Sean told himself, and what did she mean, he'd been good to her? From the little he'd seen, Beaumont treated her like dirt.

"How was he good to you?"

"What?"

"You said he was good to you. I'm trying to figure out how."

There was an edge to his voice. He wanted explanations but how could she give them? She wasn't ready to talk to him about Missy or the way she and her sister had lived. Lying naked in the arms of a man she hardly knew seemed less intimate than telling him the ugly details of her life.

"He just was," she said stiffly, and started to pull away. Sean drew her close again.

"I'm sorry."

"Let me up, please."

"No." Gently, he pushed her onto her back. "I'm a fool," he said gruffly, "talking about Beaumont when we have so many other things to discuss."

He kissed her. She tried not to respond but he kissed her again and she felt her resolve slipping.

"What things?" she said softly, brushing his hair back from his forehead.

"Important things." His voice grew husky. "The way you taste." He kissed her again, gently parting her lips with his. "I love the way you taste."

She smiled. "Do you?"

"Uh-huh. Your mouth." He dipped his head, touched the tip of his tongue to the hollow in her throat. "Your throat." He dipped his head again and licked one nipple, then the other. "And your breasts. You have beautiful breasts, Savannah."

Her breath caught as his teeth closed lightly on one pink bud. "When you do that…when you do that…"

"I love the feel of your nipples on my tongue."

"Oh God. Sean…"

"What?"

He looked up. Her eyes were becoming dark; the color in her face was rising. Her skin was turning warm and fragrant and his heart was doing flip-flops in his chest. He brought his mouth to hers, whispered his desire.

"Savannah. I want to make love to you again."

She cupped his face, kissed him, openmouthed, sighed his name against his lips.

"Is it too soon? I don't want to hurt you."

"You won't. Not by making love to me. I want you to. I want—"

She cried out as he slipped his hand between her thighs.

"This?" he said thickly. "Is this what you want?"

"Yes. That. Oh, and that. And—and—"

He entered her on one long, deep thrust. She sobbed his name and wrapped her legs around his waist. He moved and the world shattered, shattered again as she took him deeper inside her. And when he threw back his head, cried out and exploded inside her, Savannah wept, not with sorrow but with joy.

Why had she thought this man was a stranger? How could he be, when she had waited a lifetime to find him?

CHAPTER ELEVEN

SAVANNAH came awake slowly, her muscles filled with a delicious lassitude. Eyes still closed, she reached for Sean...

And found the space beside her empty. Sean was gone, and from the feel of the linens, he'd been gone for quite a while.

She sat up against the headboard, clutching the duvet to her breasts. In the air-conditioned silence of the room, she felt the sudden chill of being alone...and the foolishness of what she'd done last night.

What time was it? Ten o'clock, at least. The sun slanting in through the blinds had the feel of midmorning. Was that the reason she felt so disoriented? Or was it because she'd spent the night in bed with a man she barely knew?

Savannah closed her eyes. What on earth had she been thinking?

Quickly, she swung her feet to the floor.

Sleeping with Sean had only made things more confused. He already had a low opinion of her. What had happened surely wouldn't have made it better. Plus, he'd hired her to do a job. There was nothing personal in the make-believe story they were going to create.

By now, he was sure to have as many regrets as she did. Or—or maybe she was wrong. Maybe making love hadn't been a mistake.

"You're awake."

One look at Sean and she knew she'd had it right the first time.

He stood in the doorway, beautiful enough to make her skin prickle and removed enough to make his thoughts apparent. Arms folded, feet crossed at the ankles, his smile polite and remote, she knew immediately that he regretted what had happened.

So be it.

"Yes." She forced an answering smile as she drew the covers nearer her chin. "Sorry to have slept so late."

He shrugged. "No problem."

"You probably have a million things to do and here I am, keeping you from them."

Another shrug. "We have all day."

"Right." She hesitated. How long could you hold a smile until the muscles in your face froze? "Well, if you give me a few minutes—"

"Sure."

But he didn't move. Did he expect her to get up in front of him? Head for the bathroom, naked? It wasn't going to happen.

Enough. Savannah narrowed her eyes.

"I'd appreciate some privacy."

"Oh." He stood away from the door jamb and nodded. "I'll be in the sitting room."

"Fine. Ten minutes, I'll be out of your way."

"You're not in—"

"Oh, give me a break," she snapped, her patience gone. "Yes, I'm in your way. Yes, we're wasting time. The sooner you leave, the sooner I can get moving."

Something flickered across his face. Discomfort? Embarrassment? Whatever it was, she didn't give a damn. All she wanted was to see his back as he closed the door behind him.

"Uh, the stuff we bought... It got here a while ago."

"What? Oh. The clothes." Somehow, the thought of that stack of boxes, all of them holding things he'd purchased to turn her into someone she wasn't, made her feel angrier. "Fine. You pick out something you'd like me to wear and leave it on the chair, okay?"

"The clothes are yours, Savannah. You make the choice."

"They're not mine."

"Damn it, what is this? I come in to say good morning and next thing I know, I'm involved in an argument." His jaw shot forward. "They're yours," he said coldly. "Is that clear?"

"A lot of things are clear," she said, just as coldly. "Funny how daylight can make that happen."

"What the hell are you talking about?"

"Oh, for God's sake! Will you just get out of here?"

His mouth thinned. "Yeah. I'll do that."

The door closed with a bang. She grabbed a pillow and flung it across the room. She hadn't expected roses and champagne this morning but O'Connell could have been a little nicer. Couldn't he have pretended that last night—that last night—

Savannah shot to her feet. "To hell with you, Sean O'Connell," she muttered, hating herself for sounding as if she were going to burst into tears.

The duvet tangled around her legs as she stomped toward the bathroom and she tugged at it without mercy, which only made things worse. Words she'd learned years ago on the New Orleans streets hissed from her lips just as the door flew open.

"Damn you, Savannah McRae," Sean said, and pulled her roughly into his arms.

"Let me go. O'Connell, I swear, if you don't let me go—"

"Shut up," he commanded, tunneling his hands into her hair, holding her face to his so he could kiss her. His mouth was hot, his kisses deep and dangerous and with a little cry, she gave up fighting and kissed him back.

"I'm sorry," he whispered, his lips a breath from hers.

"So am I. I thought you regretted last night."

Sean kissed her again. "I did," he said bluntly, framing her face with his hands. "I told myself making love was a mistake. That we should have stuck to business." His eyes dropped to her parted lips, then met hers again. "It took a while before I was ready to admit the only mistake I've made since the minute I saw you was trying to pretend I didn't want you."

Savannah gave a watery smile. "Me, too," she said, and rose on her toes to press her mouth to his.

Long moments later, Sean clasped her hands, kissed them and brought them to his chest.

"I took your virginity."

"No," she said, shaking her head. "I gave it to you."

His smile was soft and sweet. "I almost went crazy sitting out there, telling myself what a bastard I was." His voice roughened. "Truth is, I'm glad you did. It means everything to me, sugar, knowing you gave me such a gift."

"Sometimes— sometimes I used to think it was the only part of me that was still worth anything, you know? That I'd done so many things over the years—"

He silenced her with another tender kiss. "I haven't been an angel, either. Besides, the one thing I'm certain of is that whatever you've done, you did because you had to."

Sighing, she let him draw her close against him, closed her eyes under the restful stroke of his hand down her spine.

"You're a good man, Sean O'Connell."

A deep laugh rumbled through his chest. "I've been called a lot of things, sweetheart, but that's a first." Gently, he pressed a kiss into her hair. "You know what else I thought about while you were sleeping?" She leaned back in his embrace and shook her head. "I thought how I could stop wasting time regretting something so wonderful, wake you with my kisses and make love to you again."

"Mmm. Sounds lovely."

"But—"

"But?"

Sean tipped her face up to his. "But," he said, smiling into her eyes, "if we don't eat some real food soon, all my get-up-and-go will have gotten-up-and-gone."

She laughed. It was, he thought, one of the loveliest sounds he'd ever heard. He touched the tip of his finger to her mouth.

"Plus, we have an appointment at noon."

"We do?"

"Uh-huh. And that means you have little more than an hour to get ready."

"I'll be quick."

His smile turned devastatingly sexy. "We can save time by showering together."

"I don't think that would work."

"No. Probably not." He stepped back. "Okay. I'll get those boxes. You take your shower."

Savannah kissed him, then started for the bathroom, but she turned back when Sean spoke.

"The thing is," he said gruffly. "The thing is, Savannah, I've been a loner all my life. It's tough, letting somebody in."

She knew it wasn't a line that would rank high in the annals of romantic declarations but it made the last of her reserve slip away. She knew what it took for him to say such a thing because it was true of her, too. It was the reason she'd panicked when she woke and he wasn't there, why she'd done everything she could to make herself believe the night had been an error.

Somehow, she kept her tears from flowing. "Yes," she whispered. "I know."

Sean's face took on a taut, hungry look. "To hell with getting things done quickly," he said, and scooped her into his arms. And, as he carried her to the bed, Savannah knew that what they'd just admitted to each other had the power to heal them both...

Or to destroy them.

They had breakfast on the terrace. Afterward, Sean made a phone call. He was changing the time of their appointment, he said, but he wouldn't tell her more until they were in his car, speeding down a narrow dirt road toward the sea.

"We're meeting with a Realtor," he said casually.

Savannah stared at him. "You're buying a house?"

"Sure," he said, as if people decided to buy homes on islands in the Bahamas all the time. He flashed her a quick smile and added that he'd been thinking, on and off, about buying a place here for a while.

"Ah. So you set up this appointment a while back."

"Weeks ago."

It was a lie, though he didn't know why he was lying. He'd made the appointment this morning, even while he paced the living room and tried to figure out what in hell he was getting himself into.

But, he'd told himself, it made sense, didn't it, to own property here? He'd been investing in expensive real estate for a long time. Nobody in his family knew it—why spoil their conviction that he was as impractical as he was footloose?— but the fact was, he could give up gambling at the drop of a hat and still live as comfortably as any of the rest of the O'Connells.

There just wasn't any reason to give up gambling. He loved the risk, the emotional highs, had never found anything to give him that same thrill.

Until now.

That thought, unbidden, unwanted and terrifying, had

almost sent him into the bedroom to wake Savannah, pay her the half-mil and tell her sorry, sweets, the deal is off.

But it was too late for that. He'd come this far; he'd see his scheme through. And yes, buying a place made sense considering one of the reasons he'd given himself two weeks with Savannah before his mother's birthday party was so they could get to know each other well enough to be convincing as lovers.

Sorry. As husband and wife.

How could they manage that in the sterile environment of a hotel? You weren't really yourself in a hotel, no matter how elegant. Maybe because it was so elegant. They'd get acquainted better if they were alone.

So he'd phoned the Realtor, told her exactly the kind of property he wanted and set up the appointment.

He'd felt good after that call. He'd buy a place on the beach. Hire someone to come in and pick up the place, maybe cook, but that was it. There'd be nothing to intrude on the private little world he and Savannah were about to create.

Whoa, he'd thought. What was that all about? He didn't need a private world with anybody, he only needed the right setting to make this stunt work.

He'd reached for the phone to cancel the appointment. He could buy a house anytime, and really, how much of a bother would it be to have maids or clerks or other guests around? He and Savannah could still set the groundwork for their make-believe marriage.

That was when he'd heard her stirring. He'd gone into the bedroom to be sure she understood that what had happened the previous night wouldn't happen again.

Instead, his heart had turned over at the sight of her, looking early-morning beautiful and vulnerable as she did her best, like him, to pretend the night hadn't meant a thing.

For the first time in his life, Sean had known he was tired of taking risks that put nothing but money on the line. He'd wanted to take Savannah in his arms, and he had. He'd even told her part of what he was feeling, how he'd always been a loner, but there was more. He knew that. He just didn't know, exactly, what else he wanted to say...

"Is that the house?"

Sean dragged his attention back to the road. A handsome wrought-iron fence rose ahead, a discreet For Sale sign on a stake beside it. A small TV camera, high in a tree just beyond the gate, angled toward them as he slowed the car. The gates swung open, revealing a crushed oyster-shell drive shaded by thickets of sea grape, bougainvillea and prickly-pear cactus.

The Realtor was waiting for them on the wide marble steps of an enormous, elegant house.

Sean bent his head toward Savannah's as he helped her from the car. "Do you like it?" he said softly.

She hesitated, then smiled. "It's beautiful."

Yes, he thought, it was, but it reminded him of a hotel. A hotel for two, perhaps, but a hotel just the same. He put his arm around her and when they reached the steps, he shook the Realtor's hand.

"Mr. O'Connell," the woman said pleasantly. "I'm delighted to meet you."

Sean nodded. "My pleasure." His arm tightened around Savannah. "This is Miss McRae. My fiancée."

He felt Savannah's muscles jerk, felt the sudden tension radiate through her body at his use of the word. The Realtor's smile broadened.

"How nice! And where are you folks staying right now?"

"At the Petite Fleur," Sean said pleasantly, "but we're hoping to move as soon as we find a house to buy." Savannah damn near jumped. He drew her closer. "Right, Savannah?"

She looked stunned but she managed a quick "yes." It troubled him that she didn't really seem all that thrilled. Should he have told her his plans ahead of time instead of keeping them as a surprise? Why had he wanted to surprise her, anyway?

Could it have been because he was still surprising himself?

"The people who built this house were very well-known on the international scene." The Realtor leaned closer. "I'm sure you'll recognize the name. They were very happy here. They did lots of entertaining. Well, you can see it's a perfect place for that. The former owners had a staff of six—"

"Six?"

"But you'd need extra help for big parties, of course."

So much for privacy but then, if Savannah liked it… "Yeah," Sean said, "of course."

"Let me show you through the house. I'm sure you'll both love it."

Savannah didn't. Sean could tell, even though she said all the right things. He was coming to know his pretend-fiancée's expressions. Right now, she wore a smile like a mask.

What didn't she like? He had no opinion, one way or the other. Okay, maybe he did. Truth was, growing up in overblown Las Vegas, he might have preferred something smaller. Simpler. A place where he could be himself, and she could be…

His gut tightened. Savannah would only spend the next couple of weeks here. She didn't have to love the place. It just made him wonder, was all, why she didn't.

Was it because she was accustomed to the Lorelei? Did she want gold cupids, dark wainscoting and crimson velvet? No. He'd watched her reaction to the things the clerk showed her at the shop in Bijou. The simpler, the more classic, the better.

What was it, then? Was it the prospect of the two of them rattling around alone here? The house was isolated on acres of property with nothing but shore and seabirds for company. There'd be servants—that cast of six—but well-trained servants would know how to be unobtrusive.

The more he thought about it, the more likely that seemed.

Why kid himself? Alone, what would they do? What would they talk about? It wasn't as if he couldn't clue her in on things that would make them seem a real couple in the comfort of the hotel.

As good as last night had been, it was only sex. Being in bed would only get them so far. There were two weeks ahead of mornings, afternoons and evenings. Two weeks of empty hours to fill.

Why had he figured they'd be better off living alone than in the hotel?

Sean interrupted the Realtor midway through a spiel about the joys of the restaurant-size kitchen range.

"Thanks," he said. "I'll be in touch."

The look on her face mirrored Savannah's. He was lying and all of them knew it.

"Of course," the woman said, sounding disappointed. Hey, he thought coolly, she would be, losing a six-figure commission.

Savannah looked relieved.

It made him angry as hell. She should have told him she didn't want to be alone with him right away, he thought grimly as he hustled her to the car.

"If you didn't want to move out of the hotel," he growled, "you should have said so."

She shot him a surprised look. "How could I? You said you were buying a house. You never mentioned you expected us to live in it."

"Well, you can stop worrying. We won't."

"Good." Savannah folded her arms and glared straight ahead. Why was he so ticked off? She was the one who had the right to be angry. He'd decided to buy a house. Well, that was his affair. That he'd decided to move her into it was hers. Why hadn't he told her? To spring something like that, to let the Realtor think they were a pair of starstruck lovers... "Living together here wasn't part of our deal."

"You're right. It wasn't." The tires squealed as Sean turned onto the main road at a speed that made trees blur as they sped past them. "I had an idea we'd find it easier to get to know each other away from the hotel. It was dumb."

"You should have asked me."

"I said, it was a dumb plan."

Seconds passed. Savannah shifted in her seat. "I can see where you'd think it made sense."

He looked at her. She was sitting as stiff as a ramrod, her profile as stern as that of the sixth-grade teacher who'd sent him to the principal's office when she'd discovered him teaching a couple of his buddies how to play craps.

"Yeah?"

"Uh-huh. I mean, if we were actually engaged, we'd want to spend time alone."

Sean nodded. "That was my thinking but, like I said, it was—"

"Did you really like that house?"

Sean looked at her again. She'd turned toward him, eyes filled with defiance.

"Why?"

"For heaven's sake, O'Connell, just answer the question. Did you like it?"

"No," he said bluntly. "It was—"

"Too big."

"Well, yes."

"Too formal."

"Right again."

"If we were a couple, if we really—if we really were lovers, would we want to live in a place so huge we'd need to leave trails of bread crumbs to find each other?"

Sean grinned. "My sentiments exactly."

She nodded and looked straight ahead again. "See? If you hadn't sprung this on me, if you'd said, 'Savannah, I think we should live someplace away from the artificial climate of a hotel so we can get to know each other better, and how would you feel living in a house the size of the Taj Mahal,' we wouldn't be having this quarrel now."

She was trying her best to sound pragmatic but what she sounded was quintessentially female. Sean's grin widened.

"Is that what we're doing? Having a quarrel?"

Something in his voice made her look at him. "Aren't we?"

"Our first."

"You're kidding. We've done nothing but quarrel since we met."

"Our first as lovers," he said, pulling under a tall palm tree on the side of the road and shutting off the engine. He undid his seat belt, leaned over and gently undid hers. "Because that's what we are," he said softly. "We're lovers, Savannah."

"You know what I meant. I meant if we were—"

Sean gathered Savannah into his arms and kissed her. She tried not to respond but his mouth was sweet and his body was warm, and it took less than a heartbeat for her to sigh and kiss him back.

"We're lovers," he said, stroking the curls back from her cheek and tucking them behind her ear. "Even the Realtor could see that."

"It was a logical conclusion, O'Connell. You introduced me as your fiancée."

"Yeah." Sean took her hand and lifted it to his lips. "Which reminds me...we have to make the trip to Bijou again."

"No way. As it is, you bought enough clothes for ten of me!"

He chuckled. "If my sisters heard you say that, they'd hustle you off to a psychiatrist."

"Oh, right. You mentioned them before. Two sisters?"

"Three, and every last one of them would—well, maybe that's an overstatement. Two of 'em, for sure, would tell you a beautiful woman can never have too many things in her closet."

That won him a little smile. "Honestly. I don't need anything. You bought me so much—"

"A ring."

Her eyes widened. "A what?"

"A ring." Sean kissed her hand again, then gently sucked the tip of her ring finger into his mouth. "Men who are engaged to be married give their fiancées engagement rings."

"Don't be silly. They don't. Not always."

"Always," he said firmly, deliberating ignoring the fact that one of his brothers hadn't married conventionally enough to have time to put a ring on his fiancée's finger. It was a reasonable demand, wasn't it? He had a mother, an entire family, to fool.

A ring. His ring, on her finger. It would only be part of the game, but...

Savannah leaned her forehead against his. "Sean. This—this is getting complicated."

"I'm just trying to make sure we seem believable."

She looked up. "Is that the reason you made love to me last night? So we'd seem—"

His kiss left her dizzy.

"You know it wasn't," he said gruffly. "I made love to you for the same reason you made love to me, because we need to be together as much as we need to breathe."

Need, Savannah thought. He'd said need. As if what they'd shared would go on. As if they had a future that stretched further ahead than two short weeks.

She sighed, closed her eyes and buried her face against his throat.

"Complicated," she whispered, with a little catch in her voice.

This time, he didn't argue. She was right but he didn't want to talk about that now or even think about it. Instead, he held her close, reveled in the feel of her in his arms, and wondered if he'd ever, in all his life, felt so complete.

"Savannah?"

"Hmm?"

"You said I should have asked you what kind of house you preferred. Well, I'm asking."

"I didn't say that. Not exactly. What I said was—"

"There's a place up the road a couple of miles. I saw the For Sale sign and drove in for a quick look the last time I was here. I haven't seen the inside but from the outside…" He took a breath. Why did he feel so nervous? All he was doing was describing a house. "It's small. Well, compared to the monster we just saw, it is. Three bedrooms, maybe four."

Savannah's smile was as bright as the sky. "Darn," she said softly. "You mean, we wouldn't need six strangers underfoot to keep things going?"

"Just you and me," Sean murmured, stroking the back of his hand down her cheek. "Truth is, the house is beautiful. And it's on the beach, comes with maybe five, six acres of land you'd need a machete to get through."

"We'd have privacy."

Sean nodded. "Yes. All we could ask for. There's a pool, a small garden, a conservatory like the one Cullen has at his place on Nantucket."

"Who?"

God, there was so much she didn't know about him, so much he didn't know about her…but there was time to learn. There was plenty of time, and he was looking forward to every second.

"One of my brothers. Cull lives in Boston with his wife and baby, but he has a house on the Atlantic and this room I've always liked. Glass walls, a big telescope. He can watch the ocean, see whales and dolphins and—"

He fell silent, suddenly feeling foolish. Maybe Savannah

thought whales and dolphins were kid stuff. But she smiled, and the way she smiled set his concerns to rest.

"I love to watch whales and dolphins! Whales, especially. The way they seem to dance in the sea, you know? I never get tired of seeing them, even if Alain always says I'm foolish to—to…"

Her words trailed away. For a moment, Beaumont seemed to be in the car with them, his presence a stain on the bright afternoon. The questions in Sean's head fought to surface, but what mattered right now was the sudden darkness in Savannah's eyes.

He gathered her close and kissed her until the darkness was gone and they were alone again in their make-believe universe.

"Beaumont's out of your life forever, sweetheart," he said. "I promise."

Because she had already learned that Sean would never lie to her, because the sun was shining down from a cloudless sky, but mostly because she was safe in her lover's arms, Savannah did a foolish thing.

She let herself believe it.

CHAPTER TWELVE

SEAN called the Realtor on his cell phone. Yes, she said happily, she knew the property he meant and it was still on the market.

She met them at the foot of a long, winding driveway. A couple of hours later, the deal was done.

The house was his.

Though he already owned other properties, this was the first time he'd bought one to live in, the first time he'd wanted to do that…and, most definitely, the first time he'd wanted to share his space with a woman.

The realization shook him. He reminded himself that this was all simply a logical part of a plan. Still, he felt almost unbearably happy when he saw the excitement and pleasure that glowed in Savannah's eyes as they walked through the house together the next day.

"It's beautiful," she said.

Beautiful, indeed. Sean couldn't get enough of looking at her.

The house came furnished. A good thing, because they moved in right away. Standing on the porch, Sean wondered what it would be like if this weren't make-believe. If they were really moving in together.

If the diamond ring he'd bought and slipped on her finger, and the matching wedding band he intended to surprise her with once they headed for Vegas, weren't part of a plan but marked a turning point in his life.

The thought shocked him. Horrified him. What kind of craziness was this? He wanted this woman, yes, but he'd wanted other women. This relationship only seemed special because of the circumstances.

That was all it was, he told himself, and he swung Savannah into his arms and headed for the bedroom. Laughing, she clung to his shoulders.

"What are you doing, O'Connell?"

"It's an old Irish custom," he said with a lightness he didn't feel. "We have to inaugurate the bed for good luck."

Long moments later, they lay spent in each other's arms, Sean staring up at the ceiling and knowing that it was time to stop lying to himself.

What he felt for Savannah was special. Two truths revealed in one day. What in hell was happening to him?

Maybe it was safer not to find out.

The house was perfect, eight big rooms with walls of glass. Anywhere you stood, you could look at the pink sand and deep blue sea, or at the rich tangle of green that shielded the estate from the world.

The shower room in the master bath had glass walls, too. Standing inside it, warm water cascading down your body, you could turn your face up to the hot yellow sun by day, the cold white stars by night.

It was as perfect a place, Sean said huskily, to love each other as the bed.

That first night, standing in the shower, her lover's moon-washed eyes looking into hers, his hands molding her to him as he caressed her breasts, then laved them with his tongue, Savannah trembled.

"What is it, sweetheart?" Sean murmured.

She shook her head. She was happy. So happy that admitting it might be dangerous.

Sean could have told her he understood. He read what she was thinking, what she was feeling, in her eyes and knew those emotions were inside his own heart.

"Savannah," he said huskily. "Savannah, I—I—"

The words he needed were there. So close. So very close. He just couldn't find them. He only knew that whatever was happening to her was happening to him, too.

It was magic, and only a fool would try putting a name to magic.

Savannah had never lived with a man before.

Her years with Alain didn't count. She'd been a guest on his yacht and in his chateau, always with a room and bath of her own and no greater connection to him than to the servants who attended him.

Now, she knew she hadn't been a guest at all. She'd been a servant, a different kind of servant, but that was what she'd been. His cook prepared meals, his maid cleaned, his chauffeur drove his big black limousine...

And she was a source of amusement.

All this time she'd let herself think she was valuable to him because she played cards so well. The truth, which she'd only just started admitting to herself, was that she was good but Alain was better. Aside from that, she'd been his clever pet. A puppy taken from the streets, cleaned up, taught manners and little tricks.

He'd liked teaching her which fork to use, which wine to drink because it made him feel superior. But most of all, he'd liked watching her sit at a table filled with important men and beat them at cards because the men all thought he was the reason she was so skilled.

Now, it would give him a bigger kick to sell her to them.

Horrid as the thought was, she knew it was the truth. That

was what he'd intended all along. Alain had simply used what had happened with Sean as an excuse to move up the calendar.

Was he sick? Evil? She didn't care. Fate had given her the chance to escape and she was going to take it.

It was the same fate that had given her Sean O'Connell— and would, she was certain, eventually take him from her.

Winning streaks never lasted.

The longer they lived together in the house on the beach, the more terrible that truth became.

Savannah told herself not to think about it. To enjoy these days. These nights. To be happy.

Oh, and she was happy! It didn't matter what they did. Dance in one of the island's beautiful clubs, walk the beach barefoot, dine in an elegant restaurant, have conch burgers at a little shack Sean knew near the harbor, or grill lobsters when the sun sank into the sea, whatever they did was wonderful. Her lover was wonderful. And she—she—

Savannah's thoughts skittered in panic. She what? Feelings were dangerous things. Life had taught her that early on. What she felt for Sean was affection. Gratitude. Respect. There was no sense in trying to make more of it than it was.

She did love being with him. It was safe to use the word that way. He seemed to enjoy being with her, too. True to his promise, they spent their days learning about each other. He was a meat-and-potatoes guy. She preferred salads. He liked watching documentaries on TV. She liked watching old movies. He liked chess. She'd never played the game. He taught her and after a slow start, their games often ended in stalemates.

He also adored rough-and-tumble sports. She learned that the hard way, when he swore up and down one rainy night that there was nothing on their satellite TV but football, rugby and soccer.

"Liar," she said huffily, snatching the remote from him

and clicking through the channels until she found a pair of women earnestly discussing how to get in touch with your inner self. She suffered through five minutes of it until Sean groaned and held his hands over his ears. Then she giggled, flung herself on him and said there were really better ways to get in touch with your inner self.

And he obliged. They loved and played and avoided anything serious…until one morning. They were having breakfast on the patio—mangoes from a roadside stand, croissants from a bakery in Bijou—when Sean suddenly asked her a question.

"Tell me about yourself," he said.

The question took her by surprise. She looked up from her plate and flashed a quick smile.

"There's not much left to tell. I mean, you already know I can't cook worth a hill of beans. Remember those conch fritters?"

She grinned but he wasn't going to let her off. She knew it as soon as he took her hand, lifted it to his lips and kissed it.

"Come on, Savannah. Think of all I've told you about me these past days."

It was true. He'd regaled her with stories about his family, about growing up in a big, glitzy hotel.

"Compared to yours, my life story's dull."

"Nothing about you could be dull." Sean kissed her fingers, one by one. "I want to know everything."

She looked at him. "Do you think your family will ask you detailed questions about me?"

"My fam…" Of course. She thought he was asking because the answers would help him maintain the fiction that they were getting married. Truth was, he'd damned near forgotten that was the reason they were here. "You never know," he said, hoping he sounded sincere. "What am I gonna do when Keir asks if you got straight A's in school, or Cull wants to know if you were a Girl Scout?" He tapped the tip of her nose with his finger. "Some things are very important to the O'Connell clan."

For a second, she thought he was serious. Then he grinned, reached for her and hauled her into his lap.

"I'll bet you did get straight A's."

She had, for a while. When her mother was still alive, and even the two years in that first foster home, before the man she was supposed to call Daddy started noticing her budding breasts, and the woman she'd never been able to call Mom realized he was noticing.

"Savannah?" Sean kissed her mouth. "Hey," he said softly, "I'm only teasing. You don't have to tell me anything you don't want to tell me."

"No. You're right. You need to know more about me."

The look in her eyes made him sorry he'd raised the subject. "I don't," he said fiercely. "I'm going to be introducing you as the woman I love. Nobody's going to have the right to question either of us."

Savannah's heart skipped a beat. "As the woman you'll be pretending to love," she said carefully.

Their eyes met. "Yeah," he said, after a minute. "That's what I meant."

An honest answer from an honest man. She couldn't ask for anything more, could she? At the very least, he deserved honesty in return.

"Well," she said slowly, "I was never a Girl Scout…"

She told him everything. About her father, who'd left when she was so small she couldn't remember him. About her mother, a drug addict, and how she'd died.

She told him about her sister, cruelly disabled by an illness no one really understood, and how Missy had screamed and screamed when the authorities separated them and put Savannah in the first of a series of foster homes and Missy in an institution.

She told him how she'd hated those homes, though she left

out the uglier details, and how she'd run away from the last and worst one, how she'd found a way to snatch Missy, how they'd hitchhiked from Savannah—the city her mother had named her for—to New Orleans. How they'd survived with her earning money using skills she'd picked up and honed in one of the endless series of foster homes.

She told him all the things she'd never told anyone, and by the time she talked of Alain, how he'd rescued her and Missy, how she'd thought he was her savior, she was weeping, the sound so raw and heartbreaking, Sean cursed the fates that had kept him from finding her sooner.

"Hush," he said, as he lifted her tearstained face to his and kissed her and kissed her until the world was reduced to only the two of them. Only the two of them, because only the two of them mattered.

That was the minute when he knew that he loved her.

He told her that night.

It was their last on the island. The next afternoon, they would fly to Las Vegas. He'd thought he'd tell her there. Or maybe on the plane. He'd wait a little while, until the time was right.

But walking hand in hand along the beach, under the benevolent gaze of a fat, ivory moon, he suddenly knew it would never be more right than this. He'd never felt more vulnerable in his life as he turned her toward him.

"Savannah," he said. "Savannah…"

She raised her face to his, and when he looked into her eyes, he saw something that told him everything would be all right.

"Savannah," he said softly, smiling with wonder, "you're in love with me."

She jerked under his hands. "My God, O'Connell, you have the most monumental ego—"

Sean lifted her to her toes and kissed her. "You'd better be in love with me," he whispered against her mouth, "because I love you. I adore you. You hear me, Just-Savannah? I love you with all my heart."

Time seemed to stop. Nothing moved, not the sea or the air or Savannah. Sean felt a chill in his blood. Maybe he was wrong. Maybe she didn't feel what he did. Maybe—

And then she gave a little cry and threw her arms around him.

They made love there, on the still-warm sand, and then he carried her to the house and they made love in the shower. They went to bed and slept curled together, and when they awoke before dawn, they made love again.

"I love you," Savannah whispered, looking up at him, her eyes wide with wonder as he slipped deep, deep inside her. "I love you, love you, love—"

He kissed her and they flew, together, into the blinding white heat of the universe.

CHAPTER THIRTEEN

SAVANNAH didn't want to leave their house or their island.

That was how she'd come to think of this place where she and Sean had forged their love. They were safe here. They belonged here.

Heaven only knew what the real world had in store.

Boarding the jet for their flight to Las Vegas, her teeth were all but chattering. Sean kept his arm tightly around her and hugged her to his side.

"There's nothing to worry about. My family's going to love you."

She nodded, as if she believed him, but she didn't. Those brothers he always talked about sounded just like him. Big. Strong. Smart. They'd see right through her, know in an instant she didn't measure up to their wives who were undoubtedly women from good, solid backgrounds—backgrounds that were nothing like hers.

And his sisters... She could almost see them. Bright. Beautiful. Proper. One single, two married to men who were so powerful it made her head spin. Fallon's husband was head of an international conglomerate. Megan's was a sheikh.

A sheikh! she thought, and bit back hysterical laughter.

And then there was Sean's mother. Mary Elizabeth O'Connell-Coyle. The matriarch of the clan. Sean adored her—that was obvious. What son wouldn't adore a woman who sounded like a cross between a queen and a saint?

You couldn't leave his stepfather out of the equation. His name, Sean told her, was Daniel. He'd been a cop. Cops always made her nervous, ever since her days on the streets. They saw right through a person. It would take Dan Coyle five seconds to know what she really was, just a dirty-faced street kid who was about to pull the biggest scam of her life on some very nice people who deserved better.

She told herself it wasn't a complete scam. She wasn't Sean's wife but they were in love. They'd only be stretching the truth a little.

Who was she kidding? They'd be stretching it a lot.

The money. She had to concentrate on the money, though thinking about it was agony. She had to take it. With it, she could save her sister's life—but Sean didn't know that. She hadn't told him about Alain's threats, not just to Missy but to her. That he'd intended to use her as a prize.

She couldn't risk telling Sean. He despised Alain already. She was afraid of what he might do if he knew the true extent of Alain's villainy. Not that she gave a damn about Alain. It was Sean she was worried about.

If he went after Alain because of her, if he hurt him, got in trouble, she'd never forgive herself.

The plane was airborne. Savannah shut her eyes and told herself she had no choice. She had to do this. Had to take the money. The money. The money…

Oh God!

How could she accept money from her lover? How could she lie to his family? She couldn't, that was all. End of story. She'd find another way.

"Sean," she whispered frantically, as their plane leveled off. "I can't do this!"

Sean took her hand. "Sure you can."

"Lying to all those people...? I don't know why we ever thought it would work."

He didn't answer, not for what seemed a long time. Then he nodded. "You're right," he said calmly. "It wouldn't."

She stared at him. "Then, what are we doing? Why are we going to this party?"

"We're going because it's my mother's birthday."

"But you just said—"

"And because I made her a promise."

"O'Connell, are you crazy? Two seconds ago, you and I agreed that—"

"That lying to my family would be a mistake." Sean undid his seat belt. Slowly and deliberately, he undid hers and drew her to him. In the hushed darkness of the first-class cabin, they might as well have been alone. "So we're not going to lie." He took a deep, deep breath. "You're wearing my ring." He reached into his pocket and took out the matching wedding band. "I want you to wear this, too."

Savannah looked at the band glittering in his palm. It was beautiful but it was as meaningless as the diamond winking on her left hand. Seeing it made her want to weep.

"I won't put it on. This is wrong, Sean. Don't you feel guilty? This is your family! You love them. How could I—how could we—"

"I do love them." He put his hand under her chin and tilted her face to his. "But I love you in a way I never imagined I could love anyone." Another deep breath. Hell, it was a good thing he was sitting. He'd spent the whole day thinking about this. He knew what he wanted. Nothing would change that. Then, how come his knees were knocking together? "Savannah McRae, will you be my wife?"

She stared at him in shock. "What?"

"Marry me as soon as we get to Vegas. I don't want to wait. We've waited too long as it is." His hands tightened on her shoulders. "I adore you, Savannah. I want to spend my life with you. I'll make you happy, I swear it. Are you worried about what this will do to your sister? Don't, sweetheart. We'll bring her to live with us. Or move her where she can get the best treatment." His voice grew rough. "Damn it, Just-Savannah, say something!"

Savannah's eyes filled with tears, but they were the kind he'd prayed he'd see.

"Yes," she said, "oh, yes, yes—"

He didn't let her say anything more. His mouth was already on hers.

The wedding ceremony didn't take very long, but it was perfect.

Sean bought her a dozen pink roses, held her hand tightly in his while they took their vows.

"I love you with all my heart," he said once they were man and wife, and Savannah smiled into his eyes and kissed him.

His family had already gathered by the time they arrived at the Desert Song Hotel. The party wasn't until the next night, but they wanted some time alone together.

They were just what Savannah had expected they'd be.

They were nothing like she'd expected they'd be.

But they definitely were stunned when Sean drew her forward and introduced her as his wife. Nobody moved, nobody said a word. Then Mary Elizabeth laughed and kissed her on both cheeks.

"My son made me a promise," she said, and shot a sly look at Sean. "And he's a man who keeps his promises. Welcome, Savannah. It's lovely meeting a new O'Connell."

They all surrounded her then. His sisters, who weren't proper or stuffy at all. His sisters-in-law, who were as down to earth as they could be. His brothers-in-law, who could have been two nice men from anywhere instead of the billionaires they were. Dan, his stepfather, hugged her and said it was remarkable how he kept gaining new daughters.

Only his brothers seemed a little reserved.

They were polite and welcomed her to the fold. But all that evening, all the next day, she caught them checking her out with quick glances. Looking at each other in a way that was disconcerting.

"Is this for real?" she heard the one named Keir mutter to the one named Cullen.

Was what for real? What did they know?

Savannah told herself it didn't matter. She had Sean. He loved her. She loved him. What could possibly hurt her now?

The answer came in a phone call an hour before the big party. The family, all but Mary Elizabeth, was gathered in the living room.

"We told her she has to make an entrance," Megan said. "Actually, we arranged for a big surprise."

Fallon nodded. "One of the guests is a singer Ma adores. The second she steps into the room, he's going to launch into Happy Birth—"

"Savannah?" Bree was coming toward them with the phone in her hand. "Sorry to interrupt, guys, but there's a call for Savannah."

"For me? Are you sure? Nobody knows I'm here."

Bree smiled and handed her the phone. "Somebody does."

Savannah put the phone to her ear. "Hello, chérie," Alain said softly.

She felt the blood drain from her head. She looked around her, half-afraid he might be in the room. Sean caught her eye. Something? he mouthed. She forced a smile and shook her head. "Just a last minute—a last minute gift I ordered for your mother," she said, and went out on the terrace. She slid the door shut and took a deep breath. "What do you want, Alain?"

"Only what you were supposed to do a month ago, chérie. The public humiliation of Sean O'Connell."

She closed her eyes. "That's not going to happen."

"Ah, but it will, Savannah. And I'm indebted to you for setting things up so nicely." He chuckled. "A big family gathering, lots of important guests arriving from all parts of the globe…"

"How do you know all this?"

"I know everything, chérie, including the fact that you will do as you're told."

"No." Savannah clutched the terrace railing with her free hand. "Whatever you want, I won't do it. Do you understand, Alain? Everything has changed."

"Not everything," he said with a soft laugh she knew she'd never forget. There was a brief silence and then she heard a sound that almost drove her to her knees.

Her sister's incoherent weeping.

In the end, it was easy. When your life hung by a thread, you could do anything.

Alain told her what to do, and she did it. And don't disconnect, he said. I want to hear every word.

Savannah went back into the O'Connell apartment. It was crowding up; the first early guests had arrived. A quick look showed her that Mary Elizabeth had obeyed her daughters and hadn't yet appeared.

Savannah offered a silent prayer of thanks. Mary Elizabeth's absence was the only kindness fate would show tonight.

There was a microphone at the front of the room. For the singer, for those who wanted to offer toasts…

For what Savannah had to do next.

She went straight to it. "Everyone?" she said, and when

her voice quavered, she cleared her throat and said it again. "Everyone?"

Faces turned toward her. People smiled. Surely, she was going to be the first to offer good wishes. Sean looked surprised but happy as he came through the crowd toward her.

"My wife," he said, slipping his arm around her waist. "I was going to introduce her to you all, but I guess she couldn't wait."

People laughed. Savannah swayed. "Savannah?" Sean murmured.

She stepped away from him. "My name," she said in a clear voice, "is Savannah McRae."

"It's Savannah O'Connell," Sean said, with a little smile that told her he didn't know what was happening but he'd play along.

"It's Savannah O'Connell," she said into the suddenly hushed room, "only because—because Sean O'Connell thinks that the best way to keep a promise is to lie to the people he supposedly loves."

A murmur swept the room. Jaws fell. Eyes widened. "Savannah," Sean said urgently, "don't." He reached for her but she slapped his hand away.

"A year ago, Sean O'Connell cheated at cards and walked off with a million dollars that wasn't his."

The murmur grew louder. She had to raise her voice to continue.

"I know this because—because my lover is the man he cheated. And now—and now, he's cheated again. Sean hired me to play the part of his fiancée. Of his wife. He paid me five hundred thousand dollars to—to make his mother, to make all of you think that—that he's a good and dutiful son. He isn't. He's a liar. A cheat. He's a—a—"

Sean went crazy. He caught Savannah around the waist, threw her over his shoulder and carried her from the room. It was like the night he'd carried her from the Lorelei.

He'd been angry at her then.

Now, he wanted to kill her.

It took all his self-control to get her out the door and drop her on her feet next to an elevator.

"Sean," she whispered, but he didn't even look at her.

"One question," he growled. "Just tell me one thing, sugar…"

Was it all a lie? That was what he wanted to ask her, but what for? He already knew the answer.

"Get the hell out of my sight," he said, "before I put my hands around your throat."

His brothers were waiting at the door. Without a word, they flanked him and headed for the fire stairs. Nobody spoke through the long descent. Nobody spoke as they headed for a corridor behind the reception desk and the office that had been Keir's when he ran the hotel.

Cullen shut the door. Keir opened a cupboard, dug around inside and took out a bottle of whiskey and some glasses. He poured; the brothers picked up the glasses and tossed down the whiskey. Sean held his glass out again and Keir refilled it.

"Well?" he finally said. "Aren't you going to tell me what a stupid son of a bitch I am?"

"You're a stupid son of a bitch," Cullen said, but without any heat.

"Yeah," Sean said roughly, and tried to swallow past the lump in his throat.

"Was she the same one?" Keir said. "The hooker you told us about?"

"Watch your mou…" Sean's shoulders drooped. He'd told enough lies, especially to himself. "Yeah. The same one."

"And you hired her for tonight?"

"Yes. At first."

His brothers looked at each other. "What's that supposed to mean?"

"I hired her." Sean hesitated. "Then I fell in love with her. And married her. And if either of you tells me again that I'm a stupid son of a bitch—" His voice broke. He saw his brothers' horrified looks and he turned away. "Listen, I'm going to go for a walk, okay? No, you guys stay here. I want to be alone for a while."

"Sean—"

"Kid—"

The door swung open. Their stepfather looked from one brother to the other, then set his gaze on Sean.

"I got a trace on that phone call your, uh, Savannah got just before she—I got a trace."

"Pays to have an ex-cop in the family," Cullen said with a tight smile.

"It came from—"

"A yacht off an island in the Bahamas." Sean nodded. "Thanks, Dan, but I could have saved you the trouble."

"It came from the Shalimar Hotel."

Sean stared at the older man. "The Shalimar two blocks from here?"

"That's right. So I called the head of security over there, asked some questions…" Dan pulled a notepad from his pocket. "Call was placed from a suite. Number 937. Occupants are one Alain Beaumont and a young girl." He glanced at the pad again. "A Melisande McRae."

It took a second to register. "Missy?" Sean said, staring at Dan.

"Also…maybe you don't want to hear this, son, but the front desk called me, said there was a young woman sobbing her heart out as she ran through the lobby. One of our people went out after her, got to her just before she jumped into a taxi. 'Can I do anything for you?' our guy said, and this girl—blond and blue, five-seven, maybe 110—the girl looked at him and said nobody could do anything for her, that her—this is a quote, son—that her world had just ended and—Sean? Sean, you want us to come with you?"

"Let him go alone," Keir said softly, putting a hand on Dan's arm. He waited until Sean raced from the room. Then he flashed a tight smile at his brother and his stepfather. "But I'll be damned if I can see any harm in us following him."

Vegas was where he'd grown up.

It was easy to get to the Shalimar, easy to go straight through the lobby to the elevators as if he were just another guest. It was even easier to find the door to suite 937, knock and say "Room Service" in a way that sounded authentic.

What wasn't easy was to keep from pounding his fist into Beaumont's face when the man opened the door.

"I didn't order room ser—" he said, but the words turned into a terrified squeal as Sean kicked the door shut, grabbed him by the throat and shoved him back inside.

"Where is she?"

Beaumont clawed at his throat. "You're choking me!"

Sean slammed him against the wall. "Where is she, you slimy son of a bitch? Tell me or so help me, I'll—"

"Sean?"

He swung around. Savannah stood in the doorway to a bedroom. Her eyes were red, her nose was running, and he knew she had never been more beautiful to him than she was at this moment. He could see a girl on the bed behind her, sleeping peacefully.

"Sean?" Savannah said again, and he flung Beaumont to the floor like the vermin he was and went to her.

"Savannah. Are you all right?"

"Yes. I'm— How did you find me?"

"Your sister. Missy. Is she all right, too?"

"She's fine. She cried when she saw me..." Savannah's voice broke. "I thought I'd lost you forever."

Sean opened his arms and she flew into them. He held her tightly against his heart.

"It's okay," he crooned. "Sweetheart, it's okay, I promise. Everything's going to be fine."

"He took Missy. He said—he said he was going to leave her at a place. A—a horrible place…"

"Hush, baby. I'm here now. I'll take care of everything."

Savannah buried her face against Sean's throat, her tears hot on his skin. From the corner of his eye, he saw Beaumont rising to his knees.

"Don't," he said softly, "not unless you want your face rearranged."

"Sean." Savannah looked up. "Sean, I love you with all my heart. I had to say those things. Beaumont—"

Sean kissed her until he felt some of the tension begin to ease from her body.

"I know you do. I should never have believed any of that stuff you said."

She gave a watery laugh. "I'm a good actress, remember? You told me that yourself."

"Please," Beaumont whimpered. "Sean. Mr. O'Connell. This is all a terrible misunderstanding."

There was a knock at the door. "Sean? Sean, you in there?"

Sean grinned, reached back and opened the door. Keir, Cullen and Dan stepped into the room. They looked at Beaumont, cowering on the floor, then at Sean and Savannah, wrapped in each other's arms.

"Looks like you need somebody to take out the trash," Keir said.

"Please," Beaumont whispered, "gentlemen, I beg you…"

"Dan?" Sean shot Beaumont one last cold look. "Dan, your pals in law enforcement might be interested in knowing how this man took a minor from a sanitarium without the consent of her legal guardian, and what plans he had for her next."

Dan grinned. "How charming. Mr. Beaumont, I think we have several things to discuss."

Cullen looked at Sean. "You gonna be okay?"

Sean nodded. "I'll be fine."

He looked at Savannah, too. "Anything we can do to help?"

"My sister... I'd like a doctor to see her, just to make sure she's all right. And—and if you would be kind enough to find a room for her for tonight—"

"A room?" Keir snorted. "We have an entire hotel. Come to think of it, Cassie and I have a room adjoining ours that would be perfect, especially if we arrange for a nurse to keep her company. That sound okay?"

"It sounds wonderful." Savannah laughed and wiped the back of her hand across her eyes. "You're wonderful. All of you. How can I ever make up for tonight?"

"Just keep making the kid happy," Cullen said, smiling. "That's all we ask. Right, BB?"

Keir rolled his eyes. "You call me Big Brother again, pal, you're in trouble."

The brothers grinned, grabbed Beaumont by the arms and hauled him from the room. Dan was already on his cell phone, making arrangements with the district attorney.

"We'll send a car for you," Cullen called over his shoulder.

Once they were alone, Sean did his best to look serious. "Here's the thing," he said sternly. "You always have to tell me the truth, even if it's bad. That's what you should have done the minute that bastard phoned."

Savannah sighed. "I know. But I was afraid. I didn't know what he'd do to Missy. That was why I'd agreed to play you in the first place. Alain made threats..."

"Yeah," Sean said tightly, "well, those days are over."

"And I couldn't tell you. I was afraid you'd do something crazy and get hurt."

Sean kissed her. "The only thing that could ever hurt me," he said gruffly, "would be losing you."

Smiling, she looped her arms around his neck. "I'll never leave you, Sean O'Connell. You're stuck with me. We're married, remember?"

"Damned right we are," he said gruffly, and drew her closer. "And I've been thinking… A married man needs to settle down. Get a job—"

"A job?"

"Well, maybe not a job, exactly. Start a business. Hotels. Casinos. I'm not sure." He kissed her. "You'll have to work out the details with me."

Savannah laughed softly. "My pleasure, O'Connell."

"And I've been thinking about that ceremony we had this afternoon…"

"It was lovely," she said dreamily. "Despite Elvis."

Sean grinned. "It was, but, I don't know, maybe a once in a lifetime event should be a little more dignified."

"Dignified? You?" she said, but she smiled.

His arms tightened around her. "How would you feel if we did it all over again? The works. You in a white gown, me in a tux, my whole impossible family doing their best to drive us nuts. What do you think, Just-Savannah?"

"I think you're going to make me cry," she whispered.

"I'll never make you cry," he promised, "except with happiness."

Savannah raised her mouth to his and Sean kissed her until they were alone again in a world of their own making.

A world that would always and forever be real.

* * * * *

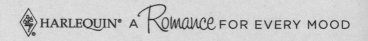
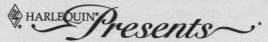

Sandra Marton

**brings you an all-new story
from the popular miniseries**

*Darkly handsome—proud and arrogant
The perfect Sicilian husbands!*

FALCO:
THE DARK GUARDIAN

Falco Orsini agrees to protect a young model
because of the vulnerability in her eyes.
But to Elle Bissette, Falco is danger incarnate,
because his kisses leave her breathless....

Available November 2010
from Harlequin Presents.

If you enjoyed this story from Sandra Marton,
here is an exclusive excerpt from her upcoming book
FALCO: THE DARK GUARDIAN
Available November 2010 from Harlequin Presents®

ELLE STARED at this stranger with eyes so dark they resembled obsidian. "What would you do," she asked slowly, "if I hired you?"

"You can't hire me," he replied bluntly. "I'm here as a favor. As for what I'll do... Leave that to me."

"So how would we do this? How could you watch over me and do whatever you need to do without people knowing?"

Falco had considered that dilemma during the six-hour flight from New York. There were lots of ways to move into someone's life to provide protection and search out information without raising questions. He could pass himself off as her personal trainer—it would give him access to her no matter where she went.

"Mr. Orsini?"

"Falco," he said, looking down into her eyes. He saw the rise and fall of her breasts and knew he wasn't going to pretend to be her trainer after all.

"Simple," he said calmly. "We'll make people think I'm your lover."

She stared at him. Then gave a little laugh.

"That's crazy," she said. "No one will believe—"

"Yeah," he said, his voice low and rough, "yeah, they will."

Falco reached out, gathered Elle into his arms and kissed her.

The feel of her mouth under his was incredible. Warm. Silken.

And soft. Wonderfully soft.

He was kissing her to wipe that smug little smile from her face. To show her, in no uncertain terms, that they could play the part of lovers.

"No," she gasped against his mouth, but Falco speared his fingers into her hair, tilted her face to his and kept on kissing her.

She tasted of honey and cream, and felt warm and soft against him. He nipped lightly at her bottom lip, touched the tip of his tongue to the seam of her mouth. With heart-stopping suddenness she stopped fighting and leaned into him, sighing, and parted her lips. His tongue plunged deep.

The taste of her made his mind blur.

Desire pulsed hot and urgent in his blood. He slid his hands to her shoulders and drew her so close he could feel her heart racing against his.

This was what he had wanted since he'd seen her in that first, unaltered ad. The eyes and mouth that promised passion, the made-for-sex body—

The knife that pressed against his belly caught him fully unaware.

Falco went absolutely still.

How will Falco persuade Elle that he's the best man to protect her? And will they ever give in to their electrifying attraction? Duty wars with pleasure in this powerfully passionate Harlequin Presents story by bestselling author Sandra Marton!
FALCO: THE DARK GUARDIAN
Available November 2010 from Harlequin Presents

HARLEQUIN *Presents*

Michelle Reid

MIA AND THE POWERFUL GREEK

Glamorous international settings…unforgettable men… passionate romances— Harlequin Presents promises you the world!

Save $0.50 on
the purchase of 1 or more
Harlequin Presents® books.

SAVE $0.50

on the purchase of 1 or more
Harlequin Presents® books.

Coupon expires January 30, 2011. Redeemable at participating retail outlets.
Limit one coupon per customer. Valid in the U.S.A. and Canada only.

5 2 6 0 9 3 0 5

Canadian Retailers: Harlequin Enterprises Limited will pay the face value of this coupon plus 10.25¢ if submitted by customer for this product only. Any other use constitutes fraud. Coupon is nonassignable. Void if taxed, prohibited or restricted by law. Consumer must pay any government taxes. Void if copied. Nielsen Clearing House ("NCH") customers submit coupons and proof of sales to Harlequin Enterprises Limited, P.O. Box 3000, Saint John, NB E2L 4L3, Canada. Non-NCH retailer—for reimbursement submit coupons and proof of sales directly to Harlequin Enterprises Limited, Retail Marketing Department, 225 Duncan Mill Rd., Don Mills, ON M3B 3K9, Canada.

5   65373 00050   2   (8100)0 11682

U.S. Retailers: Harlequin Enterprises Limited will pay the face value of this coupon plus 8¢ if submitted by customer for this product only. Any other use constitutes fraud. Coupon is nonassignable. Void if taxed, prohibited or restricted by law. Consumer must pay any government taxes. Void if copied. For reimbursement submit coupons and proof of sales directly to Harlequin Enterprises Limited, P.O. Box 880478, El Paso, TX 88588-0478, U.S.A. Cash value 1/100 cents.

HSCHPCPN0710